Growing up near the beach, **Annie West** spent lots of time observing tall, burnished lifeguards—early research! Now she spends her days fantasising about gorgeous men and their love-lives. Annie has been a reader all her life. She also loves travel, long walks, good company and great food. You can contact her at annie@annie-west.com or via PO Box 1041, Warners Bay, NSW 2282, Australia.

Joss Wood loves books and travelling—especially to the wild places of Southern Africa and, well… anywhere! She's a wife, mum to two teenagers, and slave to two cats. After a career in local economic development she now writes full-time. Joss is a member of Romance Writers of America and Romance Writers of South Africa.

Also by Annie West

A Consequence Made in Greece
The Innocent's Protector in Paradise
One Night with Her Forgotten Husband

Royal Scandals miniseries

Pregnant with His Majesty's Heir
Claiming His Virgin Princess

Also by Joss Wood

The Rules of Their Red-Hot Reunion

South Africa's Scandalous Billionaires miniseries

How to Undo the Proud Billionaire
How to Win the Wild Billionaire
How to Tempt the Off-Limits Billionaire

Scandals of the Le Roux Wedding miniseries

The Billionaire's One-Night Baby

THE DESERT KING MEETS HIS MATCH

ANNIE WEST

THE POWERFUL BOSS SHE CRAVES

JOSS WOOD

MILLS & BOON

First published in Great Britain 2022
by Mills & Boon, an imprint of HarperCollins*Publishers* Ltd,
1 London Bridge Street, London, SE1 9GF

www.harpercollins.co.uk

HarperCollins*Publishers*
1st Floor, Watermarque Building,
Ringsend Road, Dublin 4, Ireland

ISBN: 978-0-263-30096-3

08/22

This book is produced from independently certified FSC™ paper
to ensure responsible forest management.
For more information visit www.harpercollins.co.uk/green.

Printed and Bound in Spain using 100% Renewable Electricity
at CPI Black Print, Barcelona

THE DESERT KING MEETS HIS MATCH

ANNIE WEST

MILLS & BOON

This is for all those who like a book to
sweep them away to another world.

It's especially for those of you who read
The Sheikh's Marriage Proclamation and
wondered what happened to Tara's cousin Salim.
I always intended to write his story,
but your many queries about him spurred me on!

I hope you love this book as much as I do.

PROLOGUE

'SOMEONE SHOULD OUTLAW the playing of bagpipes indoors.'

The woman on the terrace swung around at his words, the dark waves of her hair swirling invitingly about her shoulders.

Their eyes met and Salim's pulse gave a thud of satisfaction as he felt again that spark of heat.

Indoors the sensation had been muted, for he'd seen her only at a distance. Yet whenever their gazes collided, or he felt her watching him, awareness had prickled between his shoulder blades.

Her lips curved into a wry half-smile that appealed far more than the beaming grins of the socialites he'd fended off inside. 'You're not a fan?'

Salim moved nearer to where she stood, illuminated by flambeaux set on the edge of the lawn. Behind her stretched a silvery loch and beyond that a dark mountain then the vastness of a Scottish summer evening.

Unlike the other female guests, she didn't wear an evening dress but a tuxedo, tailored to fit her curves and long legs. Enticingly long legs. Yet even in basic black she stood out. And not just because of the glittering silver top visible between her satin lapels.

'I wouldn't say that,' he murmured. 'Bagpipes can be quite stirring in the right circumstances.'

He was fascinated to discover a stirring of his own. A physical response to her closeness, low in his body.

It intrigued him. This woman wasn't precisely beautiful, yet she was…alluring.

More, something about her made his inner self whisper a word that sounded remarkably like *Mine.*

That was unusual enough to secure his attention.

Salim was a modern man who dealt in concrete reality, proven facts and double-checked figures. Yet he had a healthy respect for his instincts. They'd saved him more than once in the past. He listened to them now.

Her smile widened and Salim felt it like the slow spread of dawn heat warming the earth after a chill desert night. 'Perhaps you can put in a request for the piper to wake you at dawn. But I doubt it will make you popular with the other guests at the castle.'

The sound of her throaty chuckle sent a ripple of arousal skidding down his spine and straight to his groin.

Salim's brows twitched together. It was one thing to recognise his body's reaction to an attractive woman. It was another to feel arousal like an unbroken horse, stampeding straight through him, galloping out of control.

Perhaps on reflection this wasn't such a good idea.

As he thought it, she half turned away, as if to admire the glen in the fading light. Giving him a reason to end the conversation and return to the party.

As if she weren't interested in him, despite the looks she'd sent his way.

Suddenly, retreating wasn't an option.

Because what else could it be, other than retreat?

As if on cue, Salim heard the French doors open behind him, and the measured steps of the waiter to whom he'd given his order.

'Madam? Sir?' He proffered a silver tray with two champagne flutes.

Salim lifted both glasses and nodded his thanks. As the waiter disappeared he offered one to his companion.

She'd turned towards him again, frowning up under dark eyebrows. Now he was near enough he discovered her eyes were a clear, dark grey. Like the pewter of the loch behind her, or the silvery curve of his ceremonial scimitar.

'You ordered these?'

Her words were sharp like a blade too. Yet Salim read not temper in her eyes but a shadow of something unexpected in this elegant, self-contained woman. Nerves.

Was she, too, wary of this attraction?

'I did. I saw you leave and the idea of quiet conversation seemed infinitely more appealing than the crush inside.' He paused. 'But if you'd prefer solitude…'

'No!' The swift denial reassured. As did the self-aware twitch of her mobile mouth, as if she couldn't find it in herself to pretend. 'Thank you. A drink would be lovely.'

Rosanna didn't do casual flings.

She didn't kiss total strangers.

So how did she come to be plastered against this handsome stranger, her heart thundering in her chest, trying to get still closer to all that luxurious masculine heat?

Even with one strong arm lashed around her waist, his other hand supporting the back of her head as he delved deep into her mouth, she didn't feel close enough.

Even with their tongues tangling, their breathing laboured, heat searing everywhere they touched, she wanted more. So much more.

Rosanna clutched his shoulders with needy hands. She arched, pressing her breasts up against that hard chest, and heard a soft sound, like a growl of approval in the back of his throat, that sent excitement skating through her.

She'd never, in all her twenty-six years, been kissed like

this. Or responded so. Such desperate hunger was new and exhilarating.

Fleetingly Phil came to mind. But her brain instantly shied away.

Instead came flashes from tonight.

This man's casual good humour.

The teasing dark gleam of his eyes as they chatted about everything and nothing while inside the other guests partied. The sound of his cut-glass consonants melded with a lilting undercurrent that turned his voice into flagrant temptation.

The way he *listened* to her, even as his eyes dared her to live in the moment.

When had a man ever seduced her with his humour and insight? With wit and charm and that dark, sizzling *something* that reached out and curled around her insides, tugging, tugging, tugging at her until she'd given in and moved closer.

That first touch, hand to hand, that had sent electricity arcing to her breasts and lower, to the place between her legs that pulsed with blatant hunger.

She would have drawn back then, scared by the sudden conflagration inside her. Except she'd seen him frown as if he hadn't expected this full-on slam of need either.

Her hand had somehow drifted to his chest and he'd lifted it from there to his mouth. Her knees had loosened at the sight and feel of his lips on her skin and he'd gathered her close.

Rosanna tilted her head, eagerly shifting against him until he slid his hand down through her hair, past her shoulder and under the lapel of her jacket. Long fingers brushed the spangled fabric of her top, so incredibly slowly she couldn't tell if he gave her time to object or wanted to torture her with longing.

Finally, in desperation, she covered his hand with hers and slid it down to cover her breast.

Lights spun behind her closed eyelids as he cupped her there. His thumb brushed her peaking nipple and she shuddered, clutching at him. Then he squeezed gently and everything inside melted as darts of fire rayed out from his touch. Her desperate gasp tasted of him, champagne, exotic spice and sensuality.

Rosanna gave thanks to the overzealous maid who had offered to launder her blouse and accidentally scooped up her bra while Rosanna showered. The feel of his hard, gentle, capable hand massaging her braless breast through a thin layer of fabric was bliss.

He gathered her closer. She felt the rigidity in his tall frame and the hard shaft of arousal now pressed against her belly.

Heat poured through her. Her flesh prickled. She wanted to be skin to skin against him. A tiny part of her brain registered surprise but she didn't care.

Rosanna's hand went to the soft silk of his formal bow tie and—

'Excuse me, sir.'

They froze. She felt her companion's fingers tighten reflexively and even that felt good. So good her inner muscles clenched needily.

For one heartbeat, two, neither moved. Then he raised his head. For a moment she felt his breath as a caress across her face. Dark eyes glittered down at her with a promise that weakened something fundamental inside her.

How eagerly Rosanna wanted to accept that promise.

Then he straightened and tucked her in against his shoulder, as if to protect her from the view of the man behind him.

'Yes? What is it?'

'I'm sorry, but there's a call. It's important or I wouldn't have—'

Her companion breathed out, a long exhale that pushed his wide chest against her.

'It's okay, Taqi. I understand.' Another slow breath. 'I'll be there in a moment.'

Rosanna didn't hear the man's footsteps as he left because her pulse was thrumming in her ears.

But he must have gone because suddenly cool air wafted around her. Her companion's hand slid from her breast and she had to stifle a cry of protest as he stepped back, holding her upper arms as if he realised how weak-kneed she felt.

'My apologies,' he murmured and this time that indefinable accent was much stronger.

Rosanna looked into ebony eyes and silently nodded. Was he apologising for the interruption or for getting so carried away in such a public place? They were lucky it was someone he knew, someone apparently discreet, who'd found them.

Yet as she stood there, trying to catch her breath, it wasn't regret she felt, except at the interruption. She'd fallen headlong into a tsunami of desire and it had been the single most exciting event of her life.

Which said an awful lot about her life up until now!

She watched his Adam's apple move jerkily in his throat and felt a burst of relief seeing proof that he too struggled to come back to reality.

'I have to go. It must be important for Taqi to search me out.'

She nodded. 'I understand.'

Still he didn't move, just stood, looking down at her from dark, unreadable eyes. Then he inclined his head. 'Thank you.'

A second later she stood alone as he strode with loose-limbed grace back towards the party.

Rosanna watched him go, hand to her throat as if to keep in her fast-beating heart that had risen there.

She moved away to the dark corner at the end of the

terrace, waiting till her breathing returned to normal and the fireworks he'd set off in her body stopped detonating.

Rosanna couldn't quite believe what had happened. She'd never felt such a visceral response to any man, even Phil, whom she'd once planned to marry! Such combustible passion was outside her experience. The realisation should shock her. Yet all Rosanna felt was a sense of inevitability, as if it were utterly natural for a woman who never did one-night stands and had learned to think twice about trusting men to respond this way to a stranger.

And to feel bereft at his departure.

She smoothed down her hair and straightened her jacket, doing up the buttons that had come undone during their embrace. Then she settled on a nearby stone seat, waiting for his return.

He didn't come.

Not long afterwards the doors opened and guests spilled out. For half an hour everyone stood on the terrace, watching an impressive firework display in honour of the laird and his new bride. Tonight was part of a series of celebrations to mark their recent marriage.

But to Rosanna the pyrotechnics were a distraction. In their lurid light she moved through the crowd looking for a particular dark head and broad shoulders. Her fingertips tingled at the memory of his sculpted head and soft, short hair beneath her touch.

But he'd gone.

And she didn't even know his name.

CHAPTER ONE

'BUT, MARIAN, I'M not ready for this!'

'Of course you are. You're a recruitment expert, aren't you? This is just another recruitment job.'

'*Just* another job?' Rosanna's eyebrows rose as she stared, unseeing, through the huge window that gave out over her aunt's lovely Chelsea garden. 'Surely even by your standards, this isn't just any other job.'

There was a pause on the line and Rosanna imagined her diminutive aunt leaning back in her hospital bed and setting her mouth in a firm line.

'All right. It's not average, even by my standards.'

Which was saying something as Marian Best was known as exactly that, the best in the business. That was how she commanded such high commissions and could afford this gracious house in one of London's most expensive suburbs.

Rosanna breathed a sigh of relief at the acknowledgement that she wasn't stressing over nothing. She was used to working in a high-pressure environment with tight deadlines and sometimes unreasonable demands, but this was way out of the ordinary.

'I can't imagine anyone describing this contract as average. Not when the client is so incredibly high profile—'

'Which is something we don't discuss in public,' her aunt said crisply, as if fearing a hospital orderly or a nurse passing her room might overhear.

Rosanna drew herself up straighter. 'It's okay, Marian. You can count on me to be completely discreet.'

That at least was something she *could* promise. Absolute confidentiality was second nature to her given her previous work as a corporate headhunter. She'd found the right people for jobs that were often sensitive or high profile and absolute discretion was essential.

It was the rest of this task she wondered about.

'I know, Rose. And I can't tell you how grateful I am to have you on board for this.'

Rosanna heard her aunt's voice soften and realised it was concern that had sharpened it earlier.

She was probably as worried as Rosanna about her new-to-the-business niece handling such an extraordinary job. But there was no other choice. Marian's business was very, very exclusive and discreet. So exclusive and discreet it consisted of her and her part-time secretary. And now Rosanna, still learning the ropes. But this was a commission that couldn't be passed up.

And if it didn't work out…

Rosanna shivered and clutched the phone tighter. It wasn't just her reputation and career that would be at risk if she failed, but her aunt's business.

If she failed and their powerful client was displeased, a few dismissive words from him to other, potential clients could wreak destruction.

She drew a careful breath, working to slow her pulse.

'I'll do whatever you want, Marian, but I'll need guidance.'

Was that a sigh of relief from the other end of the line?

Rosanna wished she could sit with her aunt while she waited for surgery but Marian had insisted there was no time to waste. She'd vetoed a hospital visit and ordered her straight to Chelsea and her home office.

'Of course, and I'll be here, on the other end of the line.'

There was a pause. 'Remember everything I've taught you, and that I wouldn't have brought you in to join me if I didn't have faith in you.'

Before Rosanna could thank her for that vote of confidence, Marian went on. 'The stakes may be higher in this case, given the remarkably high profile of our client, but the principles are the same. Now, make a note. These are the files I want you to load to your laptop…'

Twenty minutes later the list of instructions had grown but that was good. Because having specific tasks to do meant there was no time to fret. Until Marian mentioned one last thing.

'The car will collect you at ten o'clock this morning from my front door.'

'Ten?' Rosanna stared at the time, calculating how long it would take her to race to her tiny flat and pack.

'Precisely. So don't dawdle. And good luck.'

Rosanna would need all the luck she could get. For the first time she'd take the lead role in her aunt's phenomenally successful matchmaking business.

If that wasn't tough enough, her first solo job was to find the perfect bride for a sheikh.

A royal sheikh!

It was a long, long way from working in corporate Sydney. Or even helping Marian with her discreet research.

After Phil's duplicity Rosanna's world had fallen apart. Marian's offer of work in Britain had been a lifeline, one she'd grabbed with both hands to escape the gossip and sidelong looks at home. Even her family's sympathy and outrage had felt like a burden.

But she'd only worked in her aunt's firm a little over six months and corporate recruitment wasn't the same as helping a king choose a bride.

Rosanna had left Australia under a cloud, albeit not of her making, and that weighed heavily. She couldn't squash the self-doubt that had plagued her since she'd been taken in by her ex. She should have seen through Phil. So much for her vaunted skills in assessing people! It was no excuse to admit she'd been more focused on her career than their wedding. That maybe she hadn't been as much in love as she'd first thought.

Rosanna breathed deep and focused on the positive, refusing to undermine herself this way. With her professional skills and her aunt's advice and connections, she was perfectly capable of playing fairy godmother to an aspiring Cinderella.

She just hoped the royal prince wasn't some warty toad.

That was how, in the early evening, Rosanna found herself in the back of a limousine, purring along a well-made road that skirted the capital of Dhalkur.

The sun sank over distant purple hills, gilding the ancient city and turning its shadows from amber to dark ochre and violet. Fascinated, she saw a massive crenellated city wall and beyond it a skyline of spires, domes and towers.

Rosanna looked forward to telling her parents about this place when they spoke next. They still worried about her after the scandal and her move to the UK. It would be good to divert them with something so exciting.

She swallowed hard, her throat dry despite the fruit juice and water that had been supplied for her.

This was a whole new world. Not just because she found herself in a kingdom that had, until today, been only an exotic name on a map. Even the air was different, dry, warm and faintly scented with something that made her want to take her time and fill her lungs.

From the moment she'd been collected from her aunt's house, Rosanna had entered a world of ease and luxury that she'd occasionally glimpsed courtesy of her aunt's moneyed clients but to which she didn't belong.

Never had international travel been so easy. Even the formalities of passport and customs control had been finessed by the sheikh's staff and Rosanna had spent the flight in the comfort of a private luxury jet.

Not that she'd been able to relax.

She was plagued with the disquieting feeling she'd forgotten something. But it was too late to worry whether she'd packed the right clothes to visit a royal palace.

Rosanna bit back a nervous laugh. Fortunately she wasn't important enough to stay there. She'd be in a nearby hotel, which suited her perfectly.

No, what really niggled were doubts over her preparation. She didn't feel ready, despite the hours she'd spent on the plane, reading the files on prospective matches for the sheikh from Marian's copious records. She would put in a few more hours of reading once she got to her accommodation.

Plus do more detailed research on her client.

His Majesty Sheikh Salim of Dhalkur.

Her heart dipped then rose again, pattering faster. She smiled, recognising that, despite her nerves, she was thrilled to have this opportunity. To take responsibility once more for a major project, even if one outside her previous expertise. It felt good.

As for His Majesty, she'd followed Marian's advice and concentrated so far on potential brides rather than him. Apparently the sheikh would provide information on his specific likes and dislikes after she arrived.

Nevertheless she'd feel better when she had more background on him than his name, age—thirty one—marital status—single but actively looking—and occupation—newly minted king.

She'd read about his programme of civic development and modernisation plus speculation that he'd need to be both visionary and determined to make change succeed in his staunchly traditional country. But there'd been nothing about him personally. No insights into him as a man.

The sheikh was the ultimate authority in Dhalkur. Did he also have a stranglehold on press reporting in the country?

A shiver tickled her spine. She'd dealt with powerful people, but never someone who ran his own country. Did he expect instant and total obedience?

Even the photo she'd found of him at his coronation was unsatisfactory. He'd been at a distance, a tall, proud figure standing before a crowd of jubilant citizens.

Rosanna reached for her phone, intending to do a thorough trawl for a royal photo, when the car turned into an enormous gateway and she caught her breath.

They passed through incredibly thick walls, complete with not one but two high-tech guard posts. Then they entered a long, sprawling garden.

Palms towered overhead and Rosanna caught the glint of ornamental pools beyond a screen of flowering shrubs as the car turned up to the most imposing entrance she'd ever seen.

Wide steps, tiled in azure blue, ascended to a lofty, ornamented arch, embellished with intricate carvings in shades of emerald and gold. A few metres beyond that was a slightly smaller arch, even more beautifully decorated in tones of turquoise and silver. Beyond that was a third, smaller archway, stunningly embellished with cobalt and gold, which housed a pair of studded metal doors, glowing bright bronze in the dying sunlight.

Rosanna gasped as a thrill ran through her, drawing her skin tight.

'It's amazing,' she whispered. 'I've never seen anything like it.'

The entrance was grand and architecturally magnificent with the arch within an arch, within an arch, drawing you inside before you even reached the doors. It was also simply beautiful.

'It is one of our treasures,' the chauffeur said, pride in his voice. 'It's said it took thirty artisans thirty years to complete the western entrance.'

'I feel privileged to see it,' she murmured, watching as one of the tall doors opened and a man in a long white robe emerged.

Rosanna realised the car had stopped. She met the driver's eyes in the rear-view mirror. 'Aren't we going to my hotel?'

She'd assumed he'd brought her here on the way to show her this special highlight.

'My instructions were to bring you to the palace.'

Of course it was the palace. She should have realised when they passed the security checks. Perhaps this man approaching from the grand entrance was going to provide details of her accommodation.

Her door opened and her driver invited her to get out. Beyond him was an older man with proud features and a slight smile who introduced himself as the palace chamberlain.

'Ms MacIain, welcome to Dhalkur. I hope you had a pleasant journey?'

'I did, thank you very much.'

Rosanna stepped forward only to see him turn and head back towards the imposing entrance.

'Excellent. Now, if you'll please come with me?'

'But I…' She moved quickly to keep pace. 'I thought I was going to my accommodation first.'

He paused, sweeping her with a quick, assessing look. 'So you are. You'll be a guest at the palace. It was thought more discreet and convenient.'

'Of course.'

Rosanna was pleased to find her voice sounded calm,

as if she took visits to royal palaces in her stride. Not just a meeting to speak to the sheikh or one of his trusted staff, but a *stay* in a palace.

It will be the experience of a lifetime.

And she'd never been more daunted in her life.

She slid her damp palms down her lightweight trousers. It was one thing attending lavish social events organised by Marian's clients. But as she stepped under the portico of magnificent arches and saw that the workmanship and materials were even more lavish than she'd imagined, a flicker of fear flared alongside exhilaration.

Were they *jewels*, studded between the tiles? What sort of world had she entered?

Her steps faltered and the chamberlain turned, nodding when he saw her gaping up at entrance.

'Forgive me,' he said. 'I forget the impact Her Majesty's gate has on first viewing.'

Rosanna stared up at the thousands of exquisite tiles, finding images of flowers and birds picked out in iridescent colour. 'Her Majesty?'

'She lived several centuries ago. Story has it that the sheikh asked for her hand in marriage twice and each time she refused. It was only the third time that she agreed to marry, after he offered his heart along with his wealth and position. To celebrate he had this entrance made with three arches for each proposal, the last, and most beautiful, representing the joy of their eventual union. This was the entrance they used daily as they went out riding together.' He paused and pointed. 'He had her favourite stones, emeralds and lapis lazuli, set within the design.'

Not one or two but a king's ransom in gemstones. No wonder the place was well guarded!

'That's very...romantic.' And the last thing she'd expected in a country where, she'd thought, the sheikh had ultimate power. 'She must have been a remarkable woman to say no to a king.'

The chamberlain spread his hands and lifted his shoulders. 'As you say. But the sheikhs of Dhalkur have a reputation for strength and determination. Why would such a man want a weak wife?'

Which immediately made Rosanna think of her cache of files on prospective brides. Were any of them weak? She hadn't thought so but she'd better do more homework. And on her client. Was he also a strong man who wanted a feisty wife, or did he seek someone who'd defer to him?

The chamberlain shot a look at his watch and ushered her forward. 'I'm sorry to rush you, Ms Maclain, but you're expected. We cannot keep His Majesty waiting.'

Rosanna hurried forward into a mosaic-floored hallway as wide as her whole flat. 'His Majesty?'

'Yes. When he heard you'd landed he requested you attend him straight away.' Another look at his watch. 'But I fear it will be a short audience. He has another appointment soon.'

Rosanna nodded and waited till he'd turned away to surreptitiously smooth her hair back and straighten her jacket as she walked. She wished she'd had time to change into something fresh before meeting her client. More to the point, she wished she'd finished her preparation.

This wasn't what she'd expected but she'd cope. She was capable and experienced.

But not, yet, as a fully fledged matchmaker.

She pushed that thought aside.

Her head spun with a host of questions. About Dhalkuri sheikhs and the surprisingly romantic story she'd just heard. And about the man she was about to meet who worked late into the evening.

Unless his next appointment wasn't work but pleasure.

If that were the case it suggested he separated pleasure and his upcoming marriage. Maybe the current sheikh wasn't as much of a romantic as his ancestor.

Rosanna's curiosity burgeoned as they turned into yet another corridor. That stupendous entrance should have warned her that the palace was on a lavish scale. They seemed to walk kilometres before the chamberlain paused before a tall door of gleaming wood. He turned and caught her eye as if checking she was ready, then rapped once.

'Enter.'

The chamberlain pushed the door open and took a step inside before bowing. 'Ms MacIain is here, Your Majesty.'

'Thank you. That will be all.'

That deep voice pulled a thread of heat along Rosanna's spine and right down into her core. She told herself it was from excitement, not nerves. And definitely *not* from something familiar in the resonating timbre of that voice.

The chamberlain stepped back and gestured for her to enter, closing the door behind her.

Rosanna knew the barest amount about Dhalkuri etiquette but this she *had* checked. She stepped through the door with downcast eyes and sank into a curtsey, thankful for childhood ballet lessons that made the movement easy despite the fatigue that began to drag at her after her eventful day.

'You may approach.'

Rosanna rose on legs that suddenly felt wobbly. Something about that voice…

No time to worry about it now. She lifted her head as she stepped forward then slammed to an immediate halt.

Her eyes rounded and she had to snap her jaw shut as her mouth sagged. Because there, on the other side of a massive desk, sat not the Sheikh of Dhalkur but a man she knew.

A man she'd last seen six months earlier at a party in Scotland.

A man who'd charmed and seduced her into the most

passionate kiss of her life. A man she'd been about to give herself to in her first ever sexual encounter with a stranger.

Until he'd walked away and never returned.

'You!' she croaked. 'What are *you* doing here?'

CHAPTER TWO

SALIM WATCHED THE woman before him rise and felt the slam of recognition as a physical blow to his chest.

Heat ignited in his groin.

Those eyes. That mouth. The way she stood. Even the husky quality of her voice dragged him instantly back to that memorable night half a year ago.

So much had happened in six months yet he recognised her instantly. Despite her changed appearance.

Once more she wore trousers and a jacket, but there the similarity ended. There was no soft cloud of hair caressing her shoulders. No metallic silvery top catching the light like liquid mercury and drawing attention to the sweet curve of her breasts. No spike heels to complement her look of elegance melded with pure sexy siren.

She appeared all business in light grey trousers and jacket, unremarkable mid-heeled shoes and dark hair yanked back in a bun. The only hint of softness was the dark russet colour of her high-necked blouse, vivid against the dull grey.

And that moment of recognition when her mouth had softened and her eyes ate him up.

Salim's body went rigid, every muscle tensing at the sight of her and the remarkable coincidence that brought her here.

Was it a coincidence?

For a second he pondered the possibility she'd inveigled her way here under false pretences, then dismissed it. She'd never have got past his eagle-eyed staff.

'Good evening, Ms MacIain.' He took his time over her name, letting his tongue linger over the syllables as he watched her reaction.

There. He'd been right. Behind the shock, a blast of heat in those bright pewter eyes.

Intriguing how much he liked having that effect on her. Perhaps because his reaction to her that first night had been unprecedented. He'd attended Alistair's party to finalise a commercial deal. Not to be seduced by a temptress with silvery eyes and an allure he felt like a runnel of molten metal pouring through his veins.

Salim sat back and gestured her forward. 'You intrigue me. Who were you expecting to find in the sheikh's private study, if not me?'

She stepped closer, not with the easy poise he recalled from the party, nor the grace of her curtsey, but with short, staccato steps as if she didn't trust her balance.

'You're the Sheikh of Dhalkur? Really?'

Salim frowned. She had to ask? It didn't say much for her professionalism.

'You *are* Ms Rosanna MacIain, representing Ms Marian Best of London?'

He'd had his doubts about this project since it was mooted by his advisors. But in the circumstances it seemed the easiest way of dealing with at least one pressing obligation, giving him time to concentrate on the others.

'Yes. Yes, I am.' She stopped before his desk and straightened her shoulders, her hands disappearing behind her back as she stood to attention.

'Then I'd expect you to know who your client is.' Salim shoved his chair back and rose. 'Is this a joke?'

Hiring a matchmaker was incredibly old-fashioned, even

for Dhalkur. How did he know she hadn't come here under false pretences? He'd had experience of women finding innovative ways to invade his personal space.

Yet from the horrified look on her face, that wasn't likely. Besides, Alastair had given the company a glowing reference and so had the staff who had checked its suitability.

The firm was renowned for its phenomenal success rate and discretion. If word spread that he was actively seeking a wife, half of Dhalkur's aristocratic families would push forward their daughters and the other half would argue their merits—a sure recipe for dissension.

'I apologise… Your Majesty.'

Salim felt that breathy catch in her voice as she said his title. It was like the brush of phantom fingertips across bare skin. Like the glide of her fingers tracing his cheek and jaw, then sliding down his neck to the place where his throat tightened. He frowned, surprised to find his imagination so wayward, his response to *her* so strong.

'It's entirely my fault,' she said, shuffling her feet wider and lifting her chin. 'The circumstances that prevented Ms Best coming in person meant I was briefed at the very last moment. I spent the flight reviewing potential candidates and not—'

'Researching your employer.'

She inclined her head.

Salim frowned. 'It's not an auspicious start.' He raised a hand when she opened her mouth to interrupt. 'I expect the best service. Discreet. Professional. Exceptional.'

'And you'll have it. Believe me, Your Majesty, we are committed one hundred percent to meeting your requirements, whatever you desire.'

A tingle of static sparked at his nape and raced down his backbone.

Whatever you desire.

It reminded him forcefully of what he'd desired the night they met. A desire that was unsatisfied because of the urgent news that had come out of Dhalkur, making an immediate return home necessary.

Why had Rosanna MacIain chosen that particular word?

Was it a Freudian slip? Proof that she too still felt the attraction between them?

But a king didn't dally with the hired help.

He could imagine his stern father rolling over in his grave at the thought. Those old-fashioned elders who bayed at Salim to take a bride and secure the succession would be horrified. Not at their sheikh feeling lust. But at him prioritising a foreign mistress over finding a suitable queen as soon as possible.

Salim reined in his racing thoughts.

'So you say, but your expertise remains to be proven.'

She swallowed, the movement drawing attention to the slenderness of her neck and the determined cast of her jaw.

If anyone could deliver what she promised, he had a feeling it was Rosanna MacIain, despite her lack of preparation.

It was a pity circumstances meant she'd never deliver on the unspoken promise she'd given him six months earlier. For unbridled passion. For her soft, eager body and, he was sure, pure bliss. Because their business was more important than satisfying lust. Even a lust that burned so fiercely.

He unclasped his hands and placed them palm down on the desk, annoyed more with his wandering thoughts than with her unpreparedness. After all, he'd been the one to insist she come here *immediately*.

To give himself no time to change his mind?

Being railroaded into a marriage he didn't want nettled him.

But Salim would accept the push for him to marry and provide an heir. His country needed stability.

As absolute ruler he made his own decisions but he

knew the importance of following tradition where he could. Showing respect for some of the old ways would make his reform program easier, especially among traditionalists.

His elder brother, Fuad, had done untold damage with his erratic ways while their father was dying and Salim was abroad. The Royal Council had made Salim sheikh instead of Fuad because of Salim's reputation for hard work and integrity. But some were still wary. He'd spent the last few years overseas, pursuing investment opportunities and diplomatic goals for Dhalkur. Some even looked for signs that he, like Fuad, might develop signs of instability.

Which is why he would conform to expectation and take a bride.

Not just any bride. She had to be the *perfect* bride with no hint of scandal or poor behaviour in her past. Dhalkur had had enough of that with Fuad and wouldn't tolerate any more. He wanted a woman who'd be acceptable to the conservative elements who feared change, yet a woman who'd help him implement his reforms, charming foreign investors and winning the hearts of his people. Above all, a woman with whom he could spend his life.

'I have yet to sign the contract to employ you. In the circumstances I'll need to consider that carefully.'

Surprisingly, instead of bursting into hurried reassurances, Rosanna MacIain stood calmly, returning his stare confidently.

Salim's life had changed immeasurably. Returning home to his father's death, he'd been acclaimed as sheikh and lost his brother the same day. Livid at being passed over for the crown, Fuad had taken out his anger with furious speed in his favourite sports car and paid with his life.

Within a couple of days Salim had lost his family and become absolute ruler. All eyes were on him, always, seeking answers to everything his country needed. His occasional days as an almost private citizen were over.

Now few people met his gaze. Most bowed their heads in deference, whether he wanted it or not.

Maybe that's why this woman's direct stare felt unusual. Her expression was serious, as befitted doing business with a monarch. Yet Salim felt the scratch of something else beneath the surface.

Challenge?

It was an intriguing thought.

'Of course, Your Majesty. Finding a life partner is a major undertaking. When that partner will also become queen, it's even more important to choose well. Take all the time you need to consider engaging us. Naturally I'm happy to provide any further information you need about our work.'

Salim's eyebrows rose. She made it sound as if she were graciously granting him time to dither over his decision.

Or was that sour grapes because she hadn't recognised him instantly?

It wasn't as if he preferred the idea that Rosanna MacIain had schemed her way here to pursue what they'd begun in Scotland.

He wasn't interested in an affair. Not with his work commitments.

And yet… His gaze drifted from her eyes to her mouth and that molten sensation in his belly flared hotter.

'May I ask…?'

'Yes?' He was intrigued to know what made her look suddenly uncertain, her gaze dipping to his collar.

'When you contacted Marian, Ms Best, did you know I worked with her?'

Salim took a moment to digest that. He'd never had to work hard to attract a woman who interested him. He tried to imagine concocting such an elaborate plot when instead it was women who schemed to be near him.

His brother had enjoyed manipulating people. Salim

preferred to be direct. If he wanted a woman he'd tell her, not lie about needing her expertise, or use his power to his advantage.

His nostrils flared in distaste. 'You think this is a hoax? That there's no job and I contacted Ms Best as an excuse to see you again?'

She flinched and colour streaked her cheekbones. Salim was intrigued to feel his ribs tighten around his lungs as their gazes meshed.

'No, I… No. But it's an amazing coincidence that we should meet again this way.'

She was right. But he couldn't let her believe he'd engineered this meeting to pursue an affair. The last thing he needed was a woman haunting his every move, getting in the way while he had so many important matters to juggle.

'Let me assure you that I had no idea the woman I met at Alistair's party was linked to Ms Best. Did you even work for her at the time?'

She nodded. 'I was just starting. Marian was supposed to be at the party but was held up in the States so I went in her stead.'

Now it began to make sense. 'As a representative of the company that brought Alistair and Leonie together.'

It had been Alistair's mention of the successful and utterly discreet matchmaking service which had prompted Salim to try the company himself.

Rosanna MacIain opened her mouth then paused. 'I couldn't possibly say. Marian simply asked me to attend to wish the happy couple well, and to make the acquaintance of some of the guests.' Her eyes widened and she hurried on. 'But not you. Neither of us knew you'd be there.'

Salim nodded. His visit to Scotland had been brief and low-key, out of the public eye. He'd been finalising some crucial and sensitive business deals in Europe and North America before flying home to Dhalkur.

He eyed the woman before him, admiring the way she hadn't taken the easy option to admit Alistair had been one of her company's clients, though he knew it to be so. Such reticence spoke of true discretion, the one absolute Salim insisted on in this whole archaic process.

'You're saying you had no idea who I was when we met in Scotland?' he murmured.

Salim worked to keep his private life out of the limelight but he wasn't naïve enough to believe women weren't interested in his royal status. Even when he'd been a mere prince, there was a definite cachet attached to the title. Not to mention wealth and power.

He watched something ripple across her features. What was it this contained, oh-so-professional woman fought to hide?

'Absolutely not.'

Her tone indicated that if she'd known she wouldn't have come near him. Why did that rankle?

'You're in the habit of giving yourself to a total stranger, Ms MacIain?'

Even as he said it he berated himself for stirring trouble. But there was something about her cool dismissal that he didn't like. As if what they'd shared had been easily forgotten.

He hadn't forgotten. Possibly because in the last six months there'd been no time to relax with a woman. His life revolved around an overfilled schedule of royal duty. That had to be the reason why the memory of their brief interlude seemed so fresh and appealing.

'I didn't *give* myself to you!'

'It felt like it.' His gaze shifted to the tight set of her mouth, remembering her fiery, luscious kisses. 'You didn't hold anything back. If we hadn't been interrupted—'

'Your recollection of the evening is rather different to mine.' Her gaze pierced him and he was reminded of the acres of burnished steel weapons in the armoury downstairs, swords, knives and lances all honed to lethal sharpness. 'I remember it being fun and—' she shrugged '—pleasant.'

'Pleasant.' Salim tested the word on his tongue and found it wanting. He shook his head. 'You underestimate yourself, Ms Maclain.'

That brought a rush of bright heat to her throat and a flare of something in her expression that might have been arousal. Or temper.

Either way, Salim discovered he liked it a lot better than her crisply businesslike attitude.

What was it about this woman that made him want to tip her off balance? He'd never been one to tease a woman, except to heighten her pleasure while making love.

He drew himself up, disturbed by the direction of his thoughts.

'Someone at that party, someone I trust, recommended your company. As I now find myself in want of a wife, I approached Ms Best. I had no idea of your connection to her.'

In want of a wife.

He *didn't* want a wife at all. He needed one to allay the fears of his people. Anxiety had risen when Fuad had taken control of the country during their father's terminal illness, nearly bringing the nation to ruin.

Two generations previously, the country had teetered on the brink of instability when the then sheikh had no male heir and the country faced the prospect of noble families vying to rule. His solution had been to marry his best friend's widow and adopt her son, Salim's father, as his own.

Salim's father had been a powerful and benevolent ruler, if wary of embracing change.

Dhalkur was a country which prized strong, stable government, and the government was, in effect, its sheikh.

Salim would do his duty and marry, hoping to provide heirs and the promise of stability as soon as possible, while he got on with saving the country from the effects of his brother's depredations.

Salim looked at his watch. It was time for his video conference with the American investment consortium.

'We'll meet tomorrow, Ms MacIain, and I'll give you my decision.'

Her lips parted, as if to offer some persuasive argument, but instead she moistened her lips with the tip of her tongue and nodded. 'Thank you, Your Majesty.'

Salim dragged his attention away from her glistening lips, telling himself he couldn't seriously be intrigued by such an obvious ploy, if ploy it was. But now, as he surveyed her, he noted the hint of tiredness in her eyes and the strain around her mouth. If there was any ploy here it was simply the attempt of an exhausted woman to appear on top of an unexpected, taxing situation.

He pressed a buzzer on his desk and instantly the door opened, a footman appearing. 'You'll be escorted to your room. I hope you sleep well.'

'Thank you, Your Majesty.'

Then, with another deep curtsey, she was gone.

Yet it took Salim a long time, too long a time, to turn his mind to mining leases and investment options.

And long into the night he found himself wondering how well Rosanna MacIain slept in her bed under his roof.

CHAPTER THREE

ROSANNA WAS GRATEFUL that her next meeting with Sheikh Salim of Dhalkur wasn't scheduled until late the next morning. It gave her time to gather her scattered wits.

The shock of finding her client was her almost-lover from months ago had kept her awake long into the night. In an effort to relax she'd ended up taking a long soak in the sunken marble tub, using one of the scented bath oils provided. But the warm water and delicate hyacinth fragrance hadn't worked.

When she'd finally slept it had been a restless, fitful slumber. She'd spent the night rolling from side to side in a tangle of dreams that she preferred not to remember.

Because for six months he hadn't just been her almost-lover. He'd been the man she'd dreamed about constantly.

And in her dreams they did far more than kiss.

Only pride had stopped her from questioning her Scottish hosts that night about their disappearing guest. If he'd wanted to see her again he would have given her his number and name.

Yet that night Rosanna MacIain, cautious, measured, sensible Rosanna, had been swept up in something so glorious, so visceral, she'd forgotten everything else.

It had put what she'd once felt for Phil in perspective. Surely, if she could feel such an unstoppable need for any man, it should have been for the man she'd once planned to marry. The man who'd so deceived her.

Rosanna shuddered and tightened her grip on her laptop as she followed the footman down a long, marble-floored corridor.

Part of her discomfort was from these opulent surroundings. Everything about it reinforced the difference between her life and the rarefied world inhabited by a royal sheikh. Everything spoke of refinement and privilege. From the antique rugs to the exquisite detailing on every item, from the silver pitcher that had contained her morning juice to the heavy, embossed stationery on her desk. Even her view, of a courtyard dripping with blowsy, richly scented roses framing decorative pools and shaded seats, took her breath away.

As they walked, they passed another beautiful courtyard garden, this one filled with citrus trees in bloom. The air was heavy with the hum of bees and redolent with the scent of orange blossom.

Which reminded her of brides.

Her heart slammed her ribs.

That was the only reason she was here. To find a bride for a sheikh.

Not to spend the night imagining herself held tight in his arms. Warmth flushed Rosanna's cheeks and she stiffened her spine.

Everything depended on him signing the contract. If he turned her away before giving her a chance, she'd never forgive herself.

Despite what he thought, Rosanna *was* professional.

More to the point, she had to make this work for Marian, who'd supported her since she'd arrived in England, heartsore and distressed. Marian was relying on her now and Rosanna couldn't let her down.

Even if there was still a tiny part of Rosanna that recoiled from the idea of Salim being with another woman.

How crazy was that? It was her *job* to match him with the perfect wife.

She didn't know him, not really. Didn't even have the right to call him anything other than Your Majesty.

He didn't want her. He'd made that clear.

She told herself she felt unsettled only because of the peculiar circumstances. She was still adjusting to the reality of who he was. And to the self-knowledge he had forced on her in Scotland. That there was a side to herself she hadn't known. A live-for-the-moment hedonist willing to find bliss with a total stranger.

Rosanna firmed her lips and forced her mind back to her research this morning. She'd gleaned all she could about Salim and Dhalkur.

But while there was a lot written about the country and the previous sheikh, Salim had managed for the most part to keep under the radar of the world's press. Even though he'd spent a good part of the last couple of years overseas, she found no photos of him socialising. No paparazzi shots of him partying. Just the occasional mention in financial circles of him pursuing business interests in a number of quarters.

As if his behaviour in Scotland wasn't the norm for him either.

Wishful thinking, she chided herself. Just because he wasn't seen flaunting a series of lovers didn't mean he was into sexual abstinence.

He doesn't kiss like a man who's celibate.

Rosanna frowned. She shouldn't be thinking of her client like that. Not when it made her feel hot and bothered.

The trouble was, she found it difficult to think of Salim as her client.

Even last night when he'd made it clear this wasn't some outlandish scheme to spend time with her, she'd found it hard to get beyond remembering the pair of them together.

The magnificent, hard heat of his tall frame, the softness of his lips, the knowing, coaxing, breath-stealing rightness of his kiss.

The footman knocked on a door, opened it and suddenly here she was again, entering the gracious, book-lined study.

Once more Salim sat at his desk. This time he didn't wear a western suit but a long robe and head scarf that she knew was called a *keffiyah.* It was a reminder that he was a sheikh who ruled a realm that was totally foreign to her.

The man she'd thought she'd known didn't exist. He'd been an illusion.

The story of her life, twice now drawn to men who weren't at all what she'd thought.

Yet her gaze lingered on the hard, beautiful lines of his face. His olive skin seemed darker against the stark white clothes, his spare features so compelling she found it impossible not to stare.

Abruptly he looked up from the papers before him. His eyes pinioned hers and heat fizzed in her blood.

Just like that.

With no more than a look.

Despite her stern lectures not to fantasise about him any more. Despite her determination to cut free of the madness she'd felt on that one, solitary night.

Feeling that stirring in her blood, knowing it for weakness, evoked a deep-seated anger. At herself. And at this man who, however unwittingly, still dazzled her into unwary, unwanted thoughts.

Setting her jaw, still holding his gaze, Rosanna sank into a deep curtsey.

The door closed on the footman as Rosanna MacIain caught his gaze and a frisson of awareness feathered his nape. And backbone. And belly.

Salim set his jaw as she dipped into a curtsey so low it

spoke of utter obeisance. Except her bright eyes belied that, glittering and steely as they held his.

It was provocation of the purest kind and something in him—the part that wasn't a sensible, busy ruler trying to focus on the wellbeing of his people—leapt in response.

He wanted to stride around the desk and haul her to her feet and straight into his arms. Kiss her till she turned soft and melting against him as she had that first night, purring her delight at what he did to her.

But Salim was a king. He didn't indulge in scandalous behaviour.

No matter how much he wanted to. His training and his early years in Fuad's shadow had taught him self-reliance. Acting rashly was an indulgence he couldn't permit.

'You may rise, Ms MacIain, and take a seat.'

For an instant longer he met her eyes, then forced himself to look down at the petition he'd received. The text wavered and, instead of seeing words, his brain conjured an image of bright eyes.

It wouldn't do. He wasn't like his brother, easily diverted from duty. Salim was stronger than that. He had to be, for Dhalkur's sake.

He needed a bride to quell the unease of his subjects about the lack of a royal heir. But it would be madness to employ this woman if they couldn't work together.

Firming his mouth, he closed the petition and set it aside.

But when he looked up Rosanna MacIain was the picture of professionalism. She sat with her hands loosely clasped and her back straight. She met his stare with a slight smile of acknowledgement and an air of attentiveness. No challenge. No heat in those grey eyes.

Had he imagined it?

The thought sideswiped him. Had he been *looking* for, hoping for, a personal response from her?

Surely not.

Yet he remembered how his thoughts had strayed to her again and again through last night's video conference and diplomatic reception. And later, as he lay in bed.

'I've decided to employ you.' He watched her shoulders lower on a deep exhale. Relief? Naturally. Her company's fee for a successful match was hefty. 'I've signed the contract and it's been sent to your principal.'

'Thank you, Your Majesty. I'm sure you'll be pleased with our service.'

Pleased? He'd be relieved if they found someone appropriate, someone he wouldn't mind marrying, though he couldn't get enthusiastic at the prospect of tying himself to anyone for life.

Salim pushed a document across the desk. 'All that remains is for you to sign this.'

She took it, scanning the print, her brow furrowing in concentration as she caught her bottom lip with her teeth.

He felt a flicker of something deep inside but told himself it had nothing to do with the fact that she looked…cute. More likely it was satisfaction that she was concentrating on business. That soon he'd have a bride lined up and that would be one major task sorted.

'Surely all this is covered in our standard contract.' She looked up, frowning. 'Absolute discretion is vital to our business success.'

'Nevertheless, I insist. I need to be completely sure that nothing you learn while working on my behalf finds its way beyond these walls. It's not just a matter of protecting my personal privacy. You'll learn a lot, not just about me but other people within the palace, our processes and customs. I want that protected.'

He sat back, watching as she read, wondering if she'd refuse. She took her time and Salim felt respect rise. Many people in the presence of royalty were too eager to agree to whatever was proposed. He liked that this woman chose to inform herself about what she'd be agreeing to.

Salim saw her eyebrows rise. 'The penalties for disclosure are incredibly harsh.'

He shrugged. 'You're in my world now, Ms MacIain, and I value my privacy.'

She nodded. 'Very well.' Seconds later she'd pulled out a pen, placed the document on the desk and signed it. 'There you are.'

He reached out and drew the agreement to him, noting her neat signature. Strange the sense of deep satisfaction he felt. Almost as if she'd signed away something other than her guarantee of discretion.

Shaking off the odd sensation, he nodded. 'Excellent. Now we can begin. What do you want to proceed?'

'First it's important to know what you're looking for in a wife. Your likes and dislikes. Any dealbreakers, things that mean you wouldn't consider a particular woman no matter what else she brings to the table.'

'Such as?'

'That's up to you.' When he didn't add anything she continued. 'For instance, some men prefer a woman who hasn't publicly been in a committed relationship.'

'You mean, they want a virgin?'

She shrugged.

He watched the hint of colour appear in her cheeks as she met his gaze, though her narrowed stare looked disapproving. Did she think him one of those? Perhaps she thought his country so traditional that no one other than a virgin would be considered.

Either way, Salim felt a niggle of distaste at the assumption. She hadn't called him hidebound, she was too adroit for that. But otherwise, why raise it?

Then he swallowed a huff of wry amusement at the idea

of setting Ms MacIain to ask potential wives if they were virgins. It would serve her right if he did.

'We'll leave the issue of sexual experience aside for now. What else?'

After a pause she began to reel off a list. Did he have a time frame? Advisors to help him make his decision? Would he travel or meet women in Dhalkur? Would he meet them together or separately?

'You plan to parade them before me?' He'd thought himself prepared for this process. Now he wasn't sure.

'Certainly not. This isn't a beauty pageant,' she snapped, and Salim felt a flicker of relief.

'Good. I want to get to know them, spend time with them, before I make any decisions.'

How he'd find time to do that with his current schedule remained to be seen. But this was important so he'd find a way. He had no intention of saddling himself with a woman who was a total stranger.

'Once I have your answers to those, and a few other questions, I can proceed. I'll need a contact in your office to ensure anything I arrange fits with your schedule.'

'Taqi, my assistant, will meet you to discuss options. He'll be the one making arrangements, not you.'

'But I—'

'That's not negotiable, Ms MacIain. You can pursue your contacts but arrangements to meet these women will be made via my office.' When she made to respond, Salim raised his hand. 'Unless you fancy yourself an expert on royal protocol as well as matchmaking?'

Again that spark in her gaze, turning dark grey irises to startling silver. Salim had always thought grey a cool colour but he now associated it with fire and restrained temper. Fascinating.

It would be petty to enjoy having the last word. Instead he moved to business.

'The time frame is as soon as possible. You'll report directly to me. No one else will be involved.' He imagined marrying a woman chosen by committee and shuddered. 'I don't want this to become a matter of speculation in Dhalkur.'

Especially if the search failed.

'I won't travel beyond my borders for the next few months though I'm not averse in principle to seeing someone in their own environment.'

'I see.' She surveyed him carefully. 'That will make the task more difficult.'

'Just tell me if you're not up to it, Ms Maclain.'

There it was again, that flash of temper, quickly hidden. Salim shouldn't enjoy provoking it, yet he preferred it to that coolly assessing stare of hers, as if her only interest in him was as a business client.

That's all you are now, remember?

You walked away from her the night you got the news your father was dying. Whatever you thought you shared is long over.

It didn't feel over. It felt real, that simmering stew of desire in his groin, that hyper-awareness.

Salim drew a deep breath, steepling his hands under his chin, forcing his thoughts back to the task in hand.

'You mistake me—'

'Then you *do* feel up to managing this task? Good. As for it being difficult, yes, I agree. That's why I was persuaded to hire in your particular expertise.'

He paused to let her digest that.

'There are ways we can bring the candidates to Dhalkur without gossip or unnecessarily raised expectations. There will be a festival here in the capital soon. Traditionally it's a celebration for the Dhalkuri people but this year we're expanding it to showcase business, investment and research opportunities to the wider world.'

It was a new direction for Dhalkur and there were still sceptics but Salim was determined to make it work.

'In association with that we're hosting a range of cultural, scientific and leisure events that we hope will attract foreign interest.'

He watched her expression change. Her pursed mouth softened into a slow smile and her eyes lit, not with impatience but approval.

Salim told himself it was interesting to observe the turnaround in her. It wasn't that he liked the quick way she grasped the potential opportunities, or the fact he could easily read her changing mood.

No, this wasn't personal. It was simply important they were on the same wavelength.

'So,' she mused, 'there will be a range of events that might bring all sorts of women to Dhalkur.'

Salim inclined his head. 'Either by specific invitation, or at the suggestion of business or cultural contacts.'

'Which your assistant can arrange?'

Salim smiled. 'He's a man with many contacts.'

She sat back in her seat, nodding, her eyes fixed on a distant point as if visualising something he couldn't see. 'I like your thinking. Lots of people. Lots of events. A chance to socialise and even, perhaps, see some of the women working among their peers.'

Salim's mouth hooked up in wry amusement. In six months no one had treated him like this, as an equal rather than a ruler. No one except his cousin, Tara, now queen of the neighbouring country of Nahrat.

What would Tara make of Rosanna MacIain? He had an inkling the pair had a lot in common, both straight-talking, neither easily intimidated, even by a king. In Tara's case her determination had led her to escape the clutches of his appalling brother but then put her in conflict with the powerful Sheikh of Nahrat, whom she'd eventually fallen in love with and married.

Maybe after all, she and Ms MacIain didn't have so much in common.

'I'm glad to win your approval, Ms MacIain.'

That made her start and turn her focus on him.

Did he imagine a fizz of warmth beneath his skin in response to that bright stare?

'It's a great idea. But if this festival starts soon there's no time to waste.' She began making notes. 'Let's start with what sort of woman you want. We need to narrow the options.'

Salim didn't have a coy bone in his body but it felt plain *wrong* to have this woman questioning him on that particular topic.

Because the woman who came instantly to mind when he thought of attraction was *her*.

'What about physical preferences?'

'I don't have a favourite type. Some women are just more appealing than others. It's not necessarily a matter of appearance.'

Often it was as much about personality. An intellectual equal, not afraid to voice an opinion. Or a great sense of humour, that appealed too.

She looked unconvinced. 'I'm sorry if this feels too intimate. Especially as we're strangers.'

She paused and Salim silently corrected her. That was the problem, he realised. They *weren't* strangers. They *had* been intimate. He remembered the feel of her body against his, her taste—

'But we need to specify these things.' Her lips turned up in a brief smile. 'Surely it's better to be a little uncomfortable now than waste your time later if I introduce you to women who just don't light a spark with you?'

Inevitably Salim's thoughts veered to that night in Scotland. To the sparks he'd felt as they flirted. Then the conflagration of desire as they melded in each other's arms. Even leaving the estate, his thoughts turning to Dhalkur and his ailing father, he'd watched fireworks explode against the dark sky and known that if he'd stayed with his fascinating, sultry stranger, he'd be experiencing another sort of fireworks in her bed.

His fascinating, sultry stranger now looked as if she bit back annoyance. Who could blame her? She'd been hired to introduce him to suitable women and he couldn't even articulate a definition of suitable.

'Blonde,' he blurted out. 'I like blondes.'

His last lover had been blonde.

Rosanna's eyebrows rose. 'Anything else?'

She looked like a long-suffering teacher, barely restraining impatience with a slow pupil.

'Some height. I don't want a permanent kink in my neck from bending down to kiss her.'

Though at the moment, he seriously doubted this scheme would produce a woman he'd want to kiss at every opportunity. This would be a marriage of convenience. He didn't expect romance, or set-the-world-alight passion. Yet Rosanna was right, for his own sake he needed to find someone he could live with, permanently. He wanted mutual respect, affection and, yes, attraction.

She raised her eyebrows. 'That's it? Blonde and not short? It's not much to work with.'

Salim bit back the urge to tell her the truth. That at the moment what he wanted was a woman with dark, cloud-soft hair and eyes that glittered first dark pewter then silver as her mood changed. A woman whose kisses were fiery and demanding, but who felt almost vulnerable in his arms.

Arms that ached, not, he assured himself, with emptiness, but with tension at being put through this undignified trial.

'I'm not used to choosing women like they're items on a menu.'

That startled her. Salim watched her eyes darken and her mouth soften as if he'd surprised and pleased her. Was that understanding he read on her face?

For a moment he felt again the sense of communion that he'd experienced in Scotland. It eased the edginess in his belly.

'Fair enough. Are you sure there are no negatives you want to specify?'

'A high-pitched giggle,' he found himself saying. 'It grates. I once spent an evening at an official dinner next to a woman who kept tittering at me.'

He'd ended up with a sore jaw from grinding his teeth.

'Maybe she was nervous. You can be rather daunting.' At his stare she hurried on. 'Being royal and so on.'

Except he'd been incognito and the girlish giggle had been an unsuccessful attempt to appear cute and helpless. Personally he preferred a woman who didn't feel the need for a protector. He liked a woman with spirit.

Rosanna sat straighter, rolling her shoulders as if they'd grown tight. 'Okay, Your Majesty. Can you tell me anything you *do* want, if you can't specify physical attributes?'

'Ideally?' Salim muffled a laugh. 'The aim is to find someone acceptable to me and suitable as my queen. That's a long list.'

Anticipation sparkled in her eyes. 'Try me.'

He shrugged. 'She must be someone who won't be overwhelmed by life as a royal. Someone either born to such a position or who already lives a high-profile life. She must cope with the stresses of life at court and being in the public eye.'

Rosanna's eyes narrowed. 'So she must be royal or aristocratic.'

Her tone gave nothing away but Salim suspected she

thought him elitist. He felt a tiny burr of discomfort under his skin.

'Yes. Or from a humble background, as long as she's now used to moving in privileged circles. Not someone who's going to be overawed by the pomp and ceremony of life as my queen.'

He didn't care about her pedigree, but he didn't have time to hold his wife's hand if she felt overwhelmed. This would be no love match. He didn't believe in love, not for himself. He *needed* someone who could adapt effortlessly and hit the ground running.

'Not someone self-absorbed,' he continued. 'I need someone who thinks about what others want and need.'

Did he imagine her mouth pinched at the corners as she typed? 'Someone attentive to your needs then.'

'I'm not looking for a servant, Ms MacIain.' Her head jerked up as if pulled on a string and he saw that's precisely what she'd thought. 'I have a palace full of people to cater to my needs. I was thinking of someone interested in my people's needs.'

'Of course. I understand.'

Rosanna ducked her head again, making another note, but not before Salim caught a flush of colour on her cheeks.

'But yes, since you mention it,' he relented. 'Someone interested and willing to listen to my needs, as I hope to take an interest in hers. I want a partner, Ms MacIain, as far as that's possible.'

Salim hadn't thought about it in those terms before, but that was exactly what he needed. He'd spent his life training to serve his country but he was no fool. Things would be easier with someone to share his burdens.

Burdens that were so much heavier thanks to his brother's instability and excesses. Instead of inheriting a stable kingdom, Salim had to deal with a level of fear and volatility that were legacies of Fuad's period in control.

Yet Salim wasn't searching for a soul mate. He didn't believe in them.

Life had made him a loner. The early death of his mother. A decent but distant father, preoccupied with governing. A spiteful elder brother who'd resented him and found endless opportunities to torment and torture him. Salim had survived by drawing in on himself, becoming self-reliant, guarding himself by expelling obvious signs of weakness that could be exploited.

That meant he never opened up his deepest self to others. Survival had meant maintaining a level of reserve even with friends.

'I want someone attractive, interesting, willing to listen but also to contribute to conversation as a hostess. By that I don't just mean wearing fancy clothes and attending royal events. But someone who can put people at ease when, as you say, they might be daunted by royalty.'

Salim fixed Rosanna with a stare. Her earlier reference to him being daunting had been a thinly veiled personal jab.

'Someone who can hold their own and keep an even temper in difficult social situations. But not a pushover. She must be strong enough to demand respect and receive it graciously.'

He paused, listening to the light click of computer keys. Really, there was too much to list.

'I need a woman with an unblemished background. It's absolutely vital she has no past scandals or gossip dogging her.'

Did he imagine that Rosanna stiffened? Surely that went almost without saying.

'Someone who likes people. Who is patient with strangers wanting to see her or tell her their stories, even if she's tired. There will be times, when we are touring the provinces, in particular, when the days will be long and the demands of the public high. I need someone who can be gracious and caring.'

'She must speak your language, then?'

'Ideally yes, or able to learn it.'

He watched her add a note. 'Someone from this region then, or with linguistic skills to help her fit in.'

Salim shrugged. 'That would be easiest, but if they fit the other criteria, I'm happy as long as they're willing to learn and respect our ways.'

He wasn't hung up on nationality. In fact, he'd always had more affinity with women he'd met outside his country, perhaps because they weren't so obsessed with his royal position.

Personally he wanted a woman who wasn't afraid to express herself, including when it came to seeking pleasure. But there were more important criteria to be satisfied first.

He looked up to find Rosanna waiting for a response. 'Sorry?'

'I asked if there was anything else. It's quite a long list for someone initially unwilling to give specifics.'

Salim felt his mouth tug up in a smile. That was exactly what he meant. No Dhalkuri woman would talk to him like that. Rosanna MacIain made a refreshing change.

Not, of course, that she was on his list of potential brides.

'In the interests of making sure you earn your salary, let me add a few more. Kindness.' He ticked off his thumb. 'I'd like to marry someone with a good heart. Reasonable intelligence and education.' He ticked a second finger. 'I don't want someone who will flounder trying to understand the political, diplomatic and social issues around them.'

'A very well-rounded woman, then,' she said under her breath.

Did he detect a sour note? No matter. She'd asked what he needed and he was obliging. He raised a third finger.

'Stylish, or with potential to be so with some assistance.

As my queen she will be in the spotlight a lot. So, confident too.' He raised a fourth finger. 'A wilting violet won't do at all.'

'Anything else, Your Majesty?'

Yes, there was a definite crispness in her voice. Strange how much he enjoyed hearing it.

Everything he said was completely true. But he rather enjoyed setting the bar high and seeing her reaction. Would she rise to the challenge?

'Now you mention it, yes. The most important of all.'

She looked up from her typing and, as her gaze met his, Salim felt a tightening deep in his body that took him straight back to Scotland and her total abandon in his arms. It made his next words emerge with a gravel edge.

'She must be willing and able to have children.'

CHAPTER FOUR

WILLING AND ABLE to have children.

His words echoed in Rosanna's ears for the hundredth time, making her insides roll over.

It wasn't the memory of the gruff ultra-masculine timbre of his voice that made the fine hairs at her nape rise. Of course not. It was the sheer sense of arrogant entitlement embodied in his requirement. Willing and able to have children.

Would he insist on a medical examination?

It seemed outlandish and outdated. Yet, now she'd been here a couple of days and learned about the importance of the monarchy in Dhalkur, she understood the sheikh's desire to have heirs soon.

Male heirs, of course.

What if his poor spouse only provided females?

On the upside, Rosanna suspected that his wife would find a good deal of enjoyment trying for those heirs. She could attest that Sheikh Salim of Dhalkur was a man who knew women and how to please them. His bride would probably consider intimacy with him one of the major pluses of marriage.

Rosanna flattened her lips, ignoring the shimmy of female reaction deep inside. It wasn't her concern. Her concern was arranging for His Majesty to meet the woman of his dreams.

If that were possible!

Any woman who actually met all his requirements would be a paragon. Rosanna seriously doubted she'd find anyone who could meet every item on his wish list. For a man who initially demurred at stating his qualifications for a bride, he'd sure warmed to the task.

Her already difficult job seemed to grow tougher by the day. Especially as, after two days, Salim hadn't been available for a follow-up meeting. Yet, until he gave approval, she wouldn't make arrangements to invite any of the women she had in mind to Dhalkur.

'His Majesty will see you now, Rosanna.'

She looked up to see the sheikh's personal assistant in the doorway. Instantly she got to her feet. 'Wonderful. Thanks, Taqi.'

He'd been an enormous help, clarifying details about the upcoming festival, Dhalkuri customs and royal protocol. As a result, Rosanna had been able not only to put together a list of potential brides, but a plan that would allow Salim to meet them without it being obvious he was looking for a wife.

Taqi inclined his head gravely and something about his assessing expression made her pause.

Did he finally recognise her as the woman his boss had been kissing that night in Scotland?

She'd recognised him because Salim had called him by name that night and it had stuck in her mind. Now she wondered if, despite the darkness and Salim's attempt to shelter her with his body, his assistant knew about those moments of madness.

Heat flushed her throat.

'Is everything okay?' she asked.

'Yes, of course. It's just…' He shook his head. 'It's been a busy few days for His Majesty. Try to keep it short.'

Reluctantly Rosanna nodded. There was a lot to discuss and she'd hoped to get sign-off on it all tonight. But she was aware Taqi had squeezed her in after the sheikh's final official event.

'I'll do my best.'

He nodded, his face breaking into an approving smile. She realised he wasn't just an efficient assistant. He genuinely cared about the sheikh's wellbeing. Nor was he the only one. The other people she'd dealt with in the last two days admired and respected their sovereign.

As she followed Taqi down an unfamiliar corridor, she realised it made her feel good, knowing others approved of Salim. That had been her first reaction too. Not just that dazzle of sexual attraction, but *liking*. She'd enjoyed their banter, his insightful comments, wry humour and easy charm.

After he left she'd decided she must have been wrong about him. Just as she'd been wrong about Phil. Familiar doubts had surfaced about her flawed judgement in both cases, eating away at the fragile self-confidence she'd worked hard to rebuild since leaving Sydney for the UK.

That was one good thing to come out of this bizarre situation. Learning Salim's identity and realising his sudden departure in Scotland was linked to his father's death. He must have been called back that night to a deathbed. Her indignation and hurt at being so easily brushed aside vanished in face of that knowledge.

Taqi knocked on a door, opened it and gestured for her to enter.

Thanking him, Rosanna stepped through, then stopped, eyes widening as the door clicked closed behind her.

She'd expected an office. Instead it was a lounge room. Large by normal standards, it felt pleasingly intimate with a grouping of comfortable-looking sofas, glowing lamps, a scatter of papers across a side table and plates of food on a low table at the centre of the sofas.

But what made her chest contract was Salim. He wore black, tailored trousers and a formal shirt undone just enough to reveal a tantalising V of dark golden flesh. A silk bow tie dangled loose at the collar and his dark hair was rumpled as if he'd run his hands through it.

Or as if some woman had.

Rosanna's gaze skimmed the room but there was no one else here. A door on the other side of the room caught her attention. Did it lead to a bedroom? Had his lover slipped through there?

Why that mattered, she refused to consider.

He looked up and she saw he was chewing. Golden lamplight highlighted the movement of his strong throat and Rosanna felt a strange trembling inside.

She'd had two days to push her unresolved feelings for this man into a locked box. She'd done it well enough during the day. It was only her dreams she hadn't been able to control. But now, entering what looked like his personal domain late in the evening, discovering that he looked every bit as delectable as he had that night six months ago, jarred her confidence.

'Your Majesty.'

The words sounded strident, too abrupt, and Rosanna hid a wince as she sank into a curtsey.

'Please, Ms MacIain—' he rose and gestured for her to take the sofa side-on to his '—have a seat.' He smiled and her body responded as a galloping heat raced through her. 'I hope you'll excuse me snacking as we talk. I missed my evening meal when a crisis cropped up.'

Rosanna sank onto the lounge. Shame rose at her earlier suspicion that he'd avoided her because he hadn't relished their earlier discussion, addressing personal issues. And at her imagining him busy with a lover.

Now she looked beyond his flagrant sex appeal and she

noticed lines of weariness around his mouth and a hint of shadows beneath his eyes.

'It must be tough, taking on responsibility for a whole country,' she blurted, then snapped her mouth closed, horrified at how her thoughts had slipped out.

Salim's eyes widened and he paused with a piece of flatbread in his hand. Belatedly she wondered if anyone was ever so frank with him. She was sure the answer was *no.*

Then his shoulders lifted in the tiniest of shrugs. 'It has its moments. This has been a particularly demanding week.'

'I'm sorry… I—'

'Don't apologise. It's refreshing to have someone say what's on their mind. Most people are cautious expressing themselves around royalty.'

Rosanna winced. Usually she was more circumspect. What was it about this man that made her respond without thinking? She was struggling to convince him she could do this job. She didn't need to plant more seeds of doubt in his head. 'Nevertheless, Your Majesty, it's none of my business and—'

'Please. It's late and it's been a long day. Shall we dispense with the formality, Rosanna?' He paused. 'If you don't mind me calling you Rosanna?'

Mind? How could she mind when the sound of her name in that dark, velvety voice sent a wash of eagerness through her? When the way he spoke her name made her sound like a glamorous, seductive stranger, not the ordinary woman she was. She felt her skin tighten and something deep within her clench.

She *should* mind. She should do everything she could to keep distance between them. Not that she feared him, more that she didn't trust her reactions to him.

'If you prefer, Your Majesty.'

She looked down at the laptop on the cushion beside her and pulled it close, determined to focus on business.

'I *do* prefer.' Rosanna felt his gaze touch her face but didn't look up, pretending to be busy with her computer. 'When we're alone, you needn't bother to curtsey and I prefer that you call me Salim.'

That jerked her head up. She met eyes the colour of a midnight sky. Rosanna had the disturbing sensation that if she looked long enough she'd fall into those inky depths and not want to come back to reality.

'Your Majesty seems far too formal after what we shared.'

And there it was, out in the open.

Everything she had tried to forget.

Or if not forget, then at least pretend hadn't happened.

The air rushed from her lungs, as if in relief. Yet her pulse hammered too fast. Surely the only way they could work together was if they forgot what had passed between them in Scotland? Surely mentioning that kiss, and the embrace that was far more than a kiss, opened a Pandora's box that was better left closed?

Because, while it might have meant little to him, Rosanna struggled not to be distracted by the memory of passion more urgent than she'd ever known. Even when she'd been engaged to marry the man she'd thought she loved…

She swallowed and moistened her bottom lip with her tongue. 'Do you really think it's wise to drop those barriers?'

The sheikh's eyebrows shot up and the hint of a smile on his mouth flattened.

'Don't overcomplicate things, Rosanna.' He paused on her name as if daring her to disagree. 'I'm simply aiming to make our working relationship easier. Let me assure you I don't expect anything from you except your matchmaking skills.'

That was her told.

Whatever had drawn them together before clearly no longer existed for him. Maybe what had seemed to Rosanna a once in a lifetime experience was for him nothing out of the ordinary. A little flirting to pass the time.

'Is that clear?'

His voice was crisp, so different to the sultry voice of seduction at their first meeting.

'Perfectly, Your Majesty.'

His eyebrows rose in an imperious slant. Clearly he'd heard the huffiness in her tone. Just as clearly he was used to instant, unquestioning obedience.

A chill raced down Rosanna's backbone. This man truly was ruler of all he surveyed, the absolute authority in his country. If she didn't satisfy him, if he judged her work to be below par, it would be her aunt as well as she who paid the price.

'I understand, Salim.'

She swallowed, ignoring the thickness in her throat and the burr of excitement at the taste of his name on her tongue. She had to end this now, stop remembering what had been and concentrate on business.

'I have a preliminary shortlist for you to consider.'

'Already? Excellent.'

Did she detect surprise? As if he hadn't expected her to produce any options so soon?

Rosanna didn't know whether to be annoyed at his apparently low expectations or pleased to surprise him.

'Do you have time to go through it now?' Rosanna remembered his assistant warning her to keep this meeting short. 'Or would you prefer to look at the material in your own time? I can email you the profiles.'

He shook his head. 'Let's get this started.'

Yet he didn't sound eager, she mused as she opened her laptop. Not like a man excited to find his perfect match.

But this was a business arrangement. Finding a bride to

fulfil a set of requirements. She'd heard no sentimentality as he talked of finding a wife.

Salim wasn't seeking a love match.

Yet, a voice whispered in her mind, it wouldn't be entirely business.

She looked up as Salim plucked a bunch of grapes from a bowl and lounged back, picking one grape at a time and popping them into his mouth.

The lamplight accentuated the hard angle of his jaw as he chewed. His powerful body sprawled in an attitude of utter relaxation. His bow tie dangled like a sexy invitation against the V of enticing skin at his open collar and her fingers twitched.

He looked flagrantly male and provocatively sensual.

Change the clothes and he could model for a pampered pasha in some erotic story, waiting for a concubine to please him through the night.

'Rosanna? Are you ready?'

Heat rushed up her throat and into her cheeks as glittering dark eyes snared hers. A thump of something smacked her chest and she ducked her head.

What a shame she'd pulled her hair back off her face. If it had been down it might have masked her reaction.

Like a virgin who's never seen a sexy man.

At least he had no way of knowing what had produced her furious blush.

'Yes, absolutely ready.' She put the laptop on the corner of the table between them, turned to face him. 'Here's our first candidate.'

Any hope she'd had that this might be easy faded as Salim rejected the first three women before she'd even finished reciting all their details.

He wasn't unreasonable, but nor was he as easygoing as his casual sprawl suggested. The man had a mind like a steel trap and an unerring eye for detail. Details that had him dismissing contenders quickly.

Rosanna busied herself, making notes on his observations and preferences. She was getting a better feel for his likes and dislikes now they were talking specifics. That would help inform her search.

'You think I'm being unduly difficult?'

She looked up to find him watching her, the intensity of his dark gaze at odds with his indolent sprawl. He reminded her of a large, predatory cat, ostensibly at rest, until you noticed his laser-sharp focus.

Rosanna had always been a sucker for an intelligent, quick-thinking man. In her experience they were competent and resourceful, both qualities she found hugely sexy.

But not in an employer.

Not when she was being paid to find him a woman.

Rosanna cleared her throat. 'Not at all. You're making an important choice and I appreciate your decisiveness.' Memories of recruitment processes where decision makers had dithered were vivid in her mind. 'This is very helpful.'

Besides, she hadn't been foolish enough to present her best candidates first. She knew enough to give him time to settle and begin to think clearly about his wants and needs.

'So, who have you next?'

Rosanna leaned forward and brought up the profile of the next candidate, one who hadn't been on her original list but who was a natural contender for Salim's queen. Her portrait filled the screen. It was an informal shot, showing a warm smile, pretty face and dark eyes sparkling with humour.

'I took a chance with this one. She's not blonde or particularly tall, but she ticks so many other boxes.'

On paper she seemed perfect. Yet Salim didn't look impressed.

'Princess Amina? You're telling me she's on your matchmaking books? She's a client of yours?'

'No. But this isn't a dating service. I'm not here to find a husband for someone on our books, though it's a possibility. My sole focus is to find you the right wife, whether it's someone previously known to us or not.'

His look of surprise made Rosanna wonder again if he had low expectations of their service. If so, why engage them?

She was determined to do the best job possible. It wasn't just her aunt's business that rode on a successful outcome. Rosanna's personal competence was on trial. This was her first major test after the cataclysmic blow to her ego and reputation in Australia. Her confidence was shaky, and she needed this success to shore up her sense of self-worth.

Rosanna took a deep breath and looked Salim straight in the eye. He might be all-powerful and prefer to ask questions instead of answer them. But he was a client and she needed to understand his requirements and his doubts.

'Your Majesty. Salim. Am I missing something? Is there some reason you think us incapable of doing this job properly?'

The slight rise of those straight dark eyebrows told Rosanna he wasn't used to being questioned. Was he offended? Or surprised that she'd read his response?

Rosanna took a calming breath, marshalling the patience she had perfected in dealing with difficult men in the corporate world. 'If there's a problem I would rather you were frank about it so I can deal with the issue. Then we can focus on achieving the outcome you want.'

'You're right,' he said. 'I apologise. The process of hiring a matchmaking service seems outmoded. Though your company was recommended, in my mind there's still a disconnect between the idea of serious business and something as nebulous as matchmaking.'

Before she could respond, he went on. 'Plus, I'm not comfortable talking about my personal life and preferences.

Blame my upbringing or my family circumstances. And, as you'll appreciate, in the past, choosing a woman has always been intensely private.'

Rosanna blinked. 'Thank you for being so frank.'

Despite her hopes she hadn't expected it.

Her mind buzzed with questions about his family circumstances which she would *not* be asking. No matter how much she wanted to know. As for him choosing a woman, she'd been on the receiving end and could vouch for the fact it was indeed very private. Despite telling herself not to, she still hoarded that particular memory to herself as if it were precious.

'I totally understand your discomfort at discussing such personal matters. Though I work in the field I'm not sure how easy I'd find it to use a matchmaking service.'

She'd always assumed she'd simply meet the right man, they'd fall in love and everything would be straightforward. That had happened, except Phil hadn't been the right man and it had been anything but straightforward.

Rosanna's flesh crawled at the memory and she forced her thoughts to Salim, watching her steadily. She liked his direct stare, she realised, even when it made her self-conscious. Better a man who looked you in the eye than...

'I assure you my questions are solely so I can get the right outcome for you.' Rosanna spread her hands. 'As for this being an outmoded industry, you'd be surprised.'

She had been, when she'd started working for her aunt.

'Matchmaking has been around for thousands of years and probably will be in the future. It offers cool logic and careful assessment. As well as introducing people who might not otherwise meet, it's a safety mechanism when so many people rush into marriage because of lust or blind hope.'

Salim sat forward. 'That sounds almost...disenchanted.

Don't you believe in love? Or attraction as a starting point for a relationship?'

Do you? she wondered. But she already had her answer. Love wasn't on Salim's agenda.

His dark stare captured hers and Rosanna felt that familiar fire ignite in her body. It took all her discipline not to squirm in her seat and reveal her discomfort. Because even now he made her feel things, urges and wants, no other man made her feel.

'Not disenchanted.' More disappointed, but she wasn't going there. Rosanna refused to relive the fiasco of her private life with Salim. 'Just sensible and careful. Our aim is to do our best so our clients are happy in the long-term, not just in the beginning.'

He looked like he wanted to ask more. Could he sense she avoided a direct answer? But to her relief he eventually nodded and turned his attention to the screen.

'So, tell me about the princess. Why you think she's such a good match?'

Rosanna dragged in a relieved breath. Being in the spotlight of that searing scrutiny made her simultaneously nervous and thrilled. Would she ever be able to meet him and *not* react like a smitten woman?

'Princess Amina is a strong contender. She's well educated. She's from a neighbouring kingdom so knows the region and the politics, has diplomatic skills and is used to being in the public eye. She meets your requirement of looking good in public and from what I've been able to find she's kind and has a sense of humour, both pluses in a partner.'

Salim inclined his head. 'You *have* done your homework. I wouldn't have thought of her.'

Rosanna frowned. That seemed odd. Had he assumed she would only put forward western women? Could it be that was why she'd been hired? Maybe all his years abroad had given him a preference for foreign women.

And maybe that's wishful thinking.

'Anything else?'

Rosanna looked at her notes, not that she needed to. 'She also seems to be in good health.'

That was as far as Rosanna would go towards speculating on her ability to bear children.

'Unfortunately you've missed one major consideration.'

'I have?'

She frowned. She'd spent hours not just looking up the princess's CV but trawling for references to her character and interests.

Salim nodded. 'Her older sister.'

Rosanna shook her head. 'Well,' she said slowly, 'you *could* consider her. However, from what I gather she wouldn't make an attractive spouse.' By all accounts the elder sister was selfish, overindulged and petulant. 'I'm not sure she has the qualities you're after.'

Salim's mouth curled into a smile that was as devastating as it was sudden. It was so full of amusement that Rosanna felt her lips twitch in response. Those ebony eyes beckoned with humour, banishing any last trace of formality between them.

A tiny inner voice cried out *danger*. Yet her body listed closer, drawn by the crackling current of energy between them.

'That's the understatement of the decade.' His eyes danced in a way that did strange things to Rosanna's internal organs. 'She's moody, self-important and very pushy. She's also convinced she'd make a perfect queen for Dhalkur, despite my views on the matter.'

Rosanna felt her eyes widen. 'She tried…?'

He shrugged, his humour fading abruptly. 'Let's not go

into details. I'll just say that the idea of being closely connected to that family doesn't appeal.'

Rosanna wondered what the older princess had done. *Pushy* made it sound like she'd made an effort to ingratiate herself with Salim.

Had she set out to snare him? Maybe seduce him?

Rosanna's teeth ground at the thought. Until she realised what she was doing. Yet the feeling of outrage persisted. Why? Not out of protectiveness. Salim was a powerful man who could look out for himself.

It couldn't be…jealousy, could it? That was impossible.

Yet the ache in her jaw, the hot flush in her belly and the tension from her nape to her shoulder blades signalled something unprecedented. Something she'd never experienced before.

Horrified, she jerked back, one arm flying out in an instinctive gesture of protest, and the laptop slid off the table.

Rosanna crouched down, reaching for it, and collided with Salim, doing the same thing. Their shoulders bumped, their hands meeting on the metal surface.

Rosanna froze as his hand covered hers.

Suddenly she couldn't hear anything over the harsh sound of her breathing and the pound of her pulse. Her fingers twitched as long fingers circled her wrist.

The air caught in her lungs as she forced herself to look up. Those midnight eyes were on her, bright but enigmatic. He was so close she felt the warm waft of his breath on her cheek. Could see the tiny individual dark hairs of his night-time stubble just beginning.

Her palms itched to reach out and touch him there, run her hand over his jaw and feel the raspy friction against her flesh.

The thought of it sent a luxurious shiver tumbling down her spine and rolling through her belly.

All the feelings she'd tried to suppress around this man

burst back into roaring life. Breathless anticipation. Desire so profound she felt it as an ache in her womb and a dampness between her thighs.

She needed to break this stasis. She told herself mere seconds had elapsed, that all she had to do was move. But it felt like she was in a bubble, encased in a space where nothing existed but her and him, not even time.

Salim swallowed and Rosanna followed the movement of his throat muscles as if mesmerised. How could such a simple thing be so deeply arousing?

Desperately she moistened her lips, trying to find sensible words. Instead she heard, 'Rosanna,' in a deep, hoarse voice that drew her nipples tight.

Her rush of yearning jarred her free.

She stumbled to her feet, grabbing the lounge to pull herself up then wobbling on her heels as if her ankles were made of jelly and these weren't her most comfortable, familiar work shoes.

By the time she straightened Salim was standing, holding out her laptop. His face was unreadable as she took it, careful not to touch his hands.

'It's late.' His voice was firm and easy. She must have imagined that rough edge to it. 'Send me the profiles and I'll look at them in my own time and get back to you.'

'Of course.' She fought a cringe and instead pulled her mouth up in what she hoped looked like a smile. She nodded, her gaze on a point near his ear. 'Yes, that's good,' she gabbled. 'I'll...wait to hear from you.'

Sheer willpower helped her walk from the room, head up and back straight. All she could do was hope that Salim had no idea how close she'd come to ignoring pride and her job and the fact he wasn't interested in her.

That she'd almost thrown herself into his arms and begged him to make love to her.

CHAPTER FIVE

'I MUST CONGRATULATE YOU, Your Majesty, on your plans for the upgraded medical facility.'

Salim met a pair of blue eyes in a smiling face. 'Thank you, Doctor. I have hopes it will make a difference to Dhalkur.'

The doctor shook her head, her golden hair slipping around her shoulders. 'Please, call me Ingrid.'

'Thank you, Ingrid.'

In her elegant, red dress and high heels she looked more like a model than a paediatric specialist. And, he was pleased to see, she'd been at ease at this evening's reception to welcome visitors to the first of the capital's festivities.

He wanted a woman who could function in formal settings and not be intimidated. From what he saw, it would take more than a mere monarch to intimidate the good doctor.

'The facility won't just help your country,' she continued, 'but the whole region. The medical research centre, with the funding you've announced, has potential to become a world leader.' She paused. 'And to have maternal and infant health as a priority area…' She shrugged. 'I could say it's far-sighted but I believe it's long overdue.'

She began to compare regional statistics for infant illness and life outcomes.

The doctor was outspoken but in this case for good reason. The need was great, especially as Salim's brother had removed money from the health budget to fund a pet project to design and manufacture luxury cars in Dhalkur. As the project had been inspired by enthusiasm rather than careful planning, it had died a swift, expensive death. Leaving Salim to make up the shortfall in medical services.

He admired Ingrid's focus. He needed a wife who could stand up for herself. The doctor, one of the women on Rosanna's list, combined brains, beauty and an air of competence that ticked several boxes.

Yet, as he listened, his gaze flicked across the room again to Rosanna.

She looked slender and understated in a dress of darkest green overlaid with a sheer layer of smoky grey that reminded him of the mists he'd seen rising off Norwegian fjords. There was an air of subtle enticement about her.

All night he'd been aware of her, as if some internal radar kept signalling her presence.

He'd barely seen her since that night in his rooms. When he made the mistake of touching her and she'd shied away.

As if she felt the same inexplicable connection and rejected it.

His mouth flattened.

Salim had been sensible and circumspect these last ten days. He'd kept their meetings to a minimum and always in his office rather than his private suite. But that didn't stop the buzz of awareness under his skin whenever he saw her or thought about her, which was far too often.

He'd only meant to pick up her laptop. Yet when his hand touched hers something changed. He hadn't consciously reached for her, but when his hand encircled her wrist and he felt that wildly fluttering pulse, it called to something just as wild in himself. Something untamed and primitive that didn't sit well with the self-contained man he'd trained all his life to become.

With his mother's early death, a busy father who had little time for his sons and a strict upbringing designed to make him a man who might one day rule the nation, self-denial was second nature.

That had been reinforced by life with a cruel older brother always ready to exploit signs of weakness or tenderness. Since returning to Dhalkur Salim had slipped back into ingrained behaviours, re-erecting personal barriers as easily as putting on clothes.

Salim never let emotions rule him. Not when his country needed his full attention. He was ever conscious of the need to prove himself more reliable, more serious and stable than Fuad, whose passions had weakened him and Dhalkur. The country needed him strong and focused.

Salim *couldn't* indulge himself with Rosanna. He'd hired her. The imbalance of power meant any approach by him would be sexual harassment. Besides, she was finding him a wife! What sort of man started an affair in those circumstances?

Yet he hadn't been able to banish that idea from his mind, no matter how he tried.

When he read reports he fancied he saw her sultry grey eyes on the pages. During long meetings he thought he heard her soft voice coaxing him to kiss her again. And at night…

'Ah, the intriguing Ms MacIain. It's good to meet you.'

Rosanna smiled even as a warning grazed the bare skin under the long, translucent sleeves of her dress. This man was trouble. His steely stare belied his greeting.

Dhalkur's Minister for Finance was powerful and reputedly eager for even more power, if the hints she'd heard in the palace's administration wing were to be believed. Taqi, Salim's assistant, was careful what he said but Rosanna suspected he wasn't a fan of the politician.

'I'm pleased to meet you too, sir. Though I fear I might disappoint. I've never thought of myself as intriguing.'

He nodded briskly before she'd finished even speaking. He definitely had an agenda.

'So what brings you here? Someone just pointed you out, saying you're working closely with our sheikh. But they didn't know what you're advising him on. Something personal, perhaps?'

His curiosity had an unpleasant edge as he leaned over her. Reflexively Rosanna stood taller, refusing to shuffle back when he tried to dominate her.

Was he jealous that someone else might have the king's ear? Or did he suspect the sheikh was seeking a bride?

Salim was adamant that their project be secret. He wanted no rivalry between powerful families. If they discovered he was choosing a bride, each would put forward their own candidate.

Fortunately Marian's company had a discreet online presence with no staff names included. No one searching would connect Rosanna to a matchmaking business.

'As to that—'

A deep, smooth voice interrupted from just over her shoulder. 'Ms MacIain is a recruitment expert.'

The rich timbre of Salim's voice had an instant effect. Muscles clenched, heat swirled and the fitted bodice of her dress felt suddenly too snug. As if her breasts swelled. Now the brush of her dress against her skin felt like the caress of deft fingers.

Rosanna's thoughts fixed on that night when he'd touched her. He'd captured her wrist and she'd wanted, so badly, for him to tug her close and kiss her.

'Ms MacIain is assisting me with some personnel issues. But don't worry, I'm paying her myself, not taking funds from your budget.'

'Of course, Your Majesty. I didn't for a moment want to imply—'

'Of course you didn't.' Salim's voice held a note she couldn't identify. She wanted to turn and see his expression but it felt imperative to face this man and not risk showing her feelings for Salim. 'Ms MacIain has a degree in psychology and considerable experience in corporate management. Perhaps she might advise your department when she finishes assisting me. I hear there were irregularities...'

Rosanna bit her lip to stop a smile as the minister flinched then fixed on a wary smile, so different from his earlier, superior stare.

'I'm afraid circumstances were misreported. It was a trifling matter, soon dealt with.'

Minutes later, after a conversation about the sights Rosanna should see during her stay, the older man excused himself, claiming to see someone he'd promised to speak with.

'What was the problem in his department?' she asked softly when he left. 'He didn't like that one bit.'

Salim stepped forward and turned to face her. He looked tall, commanding and haughty. Every inch the powerful ruler. Yet humour lurked in his eyes and his mouth twitched in the hint of a smile that bathed her in the warmth of shared understanding.

How could that hint of expression, the tiniest indication of pleasure, affect her so profoundly?

Salim angled his head closer. 'Nepotism. My brother preferred important jobs went to those he favoured rather than those who merited it. Some in the government took their lead from him.' He shot a look to where the minister was talking gravely with a small group. 'I made it clear on my accession that favouritism wouldn't be tolerated. But some took a while to change their ways.'

'No wonder he didn't look happy.'

To a man who obviously valued his dignity and authority, the hint of a personal reprimand from his sheikh would be hard to swallow.

'He's rarely happy. I should have known he'd question you.'

'How so?'

Rosanna had kept in the background, working behind the scenes. Tonight was the first time she'd attended an official event and that was only because some of the women she'd suggested be invited to Dhalkur were here.

Salim's gaze moved past her as if checking if they could be overheard. 'He likes to know what's going on. Plus his niece is one of the women on your list.'

'She is? I wasn't aware of any family connection. How could he know? Only you and I—'

'Of course he doesn't know. But he's one of the senior government members pushing for a royal marriage so he understands the pressure on me to marry.'

'You think he suspects why I'm here?'

Salim's eyes met hers again and it was like colliding with a force of nature. That direct gaze seemed to penetrate deep inside, pinioning her to the spot and making her worry how much he saw of what she tried to hide. Her lungs squeezed tight. Deep in her pelvis heat blossomed.

Now his expression wasn't amused. 'I doubt it. He suspects you're here for completely different reasons.'

Rosanna tilted her head, trying to read Salim's expression. His chiselled features looked more pronounced, as if the flesh pulled tight across his face.

'You'll have to explain. I don't have a clue what you're talking about.'

One ebony eyebrow rose. 'Why might a man invite a beautiful woman to stay as a private guest in his home?'

It took a moment for Rosanna to digest his meaning. She'd been distracted by the fact he'd called her beautiful. She wasn't and never had been that. She would have written off the comment as casual flattery, yet there was nothing casual about Salim now. She was close enough to feel tension emanate from him, a tension that tightened her own muscles and sinews till she felt at breaking point as his meaning sank in.

The minister suspected she was the king's lover.

She didn't know whether to be flattered or horrified.

'But that's—'

'Predictable? I admit I should have foreseen it.'

Stunned, Rosanna scanned the vast reception room. But no one in the glamorous crowd was watching her in that superior, judgemental way the Minister for Finance had.

'He can't really think I'm an obstacle to his niece…' She paused, conscious that while they stood alone, it was better to be discreet. 'That I'm in the way.'

'You underestimate yourself. You're intelligent and engaging. And you look charming tonight.'

Charming. That deflated her illicit exhilaration at being thought the sheikh's lover. *Charming* was a word her grandma used when she couldn't find something more positive.

'In fact—' his voice dropped to a deep, mesmerising whisper '—I'm surprised you don't have a coterie of admirers swarming around. That dress was designed for seduction.'

'Seduction!' she yelped, then jammed her lips together.

'Don't act surprised. You must know you look ravishing.'

Rosanna opened her mouth then closed it again. Ravishing! The idea knocked her off balance. She'd never thought of herself in that way. Phil had never called her anything like that.

The cocktail-length dress had been a rare indulgence, purchased at a bargain price from an up-and-coming British designer grateful to Marian and Rosanna for their introduction to the suave Brazilian who was now her husband.

Rosanna loved the swish of satin as she moved and the deeply feminine style. She'd thought it elegant but demure, perfect for a formal occasion in Dhalkur. The dark green satin might have tiny shoulder straps and cling at the bodice and waist, but it fell in discreet folds from her hips and a sheer overdress of cobweb grey covered her bare arms and shoulders as well as the satin underdress.

'You think the dress seductive?'

'You have to ask?' Salim's eyes gleamed but not, this time, with amusement. 'The see-through cover just makes a man want to explore what's beneath, and the way it shapes to your body…' He shook his head. 'You're not naïve, Ms MacIain. You know exactly what effect you have on a man.'

You. Not the dress.

Salim was calling her seductive.

She shouldn't be thrilled but she was.

It had been a long time since Phil had made her feel desirable. Since then she'd been too busy trying to reshape her life and put the past behind her to think about being sexy or desirable.

Except with Salim.

'I'm not going to apologise.' It wasn't as if she was showing excess cleavage. 'It's a lovely dress and I like wearing it.'

'I don't expect you to.' Yet he didn't smile and his voice sounded almost grim. 'It's time I circulated. I still have guests to greet.'

Rosanna followed his gaze to the other side of the room. The Scandinavian doctor she'd recommended as a potential wife stood among a cluster of attentive men. Clearly, despite what he just said, Salim wanted to return to her.

That was good news. So far he hadn't shown much interest in the other candidates, whereas the lovely doctor had obviously caught his attention.

Why did his interest niggle at Rosanna? It was positive, knowing she made progress, introducing him to a woman he found appealing.

Because you don't want him attracted to the lovely blonde.

You want him attracted to you.

Rosanna gasped and put a hand to her ribs as if that would still her knocking heart.

'Is something wrong?'

That acute gaze raked her and she felt abruptly vulnerable.

'No.' Rosanna scrambled for something to distract him. 'I just wondered how you knew about my psychology qualification.'

'You don't think I'd hire you without due diligence?' Reading her expression, he went on. 'No, I didn't have you investigated. Just the usual check of references. I don't do business with someone without ensuring they're able to deliver.'

Was that a reference to her lack of preparation when she came to Dhalkur? Or a simple statement of fact?

Either way it was a timely reminder that she was here to work, not fantasise about a relationship that could never be.

'Of course.' Rosanna stepped back. 'I'd better leave you before people think I'm monopolising you.'

Rosanna MacIain mightn't be monopolising his company but she'd taken over his thoughts. He spent the rest of the evening watching her from the corner of his eye. Even as he spoke to the women invited here for him to meet.

She'd chosen well. They all had qualities to recommend them and were all bright, self-possessed and attractive.

They were all blonde too, and at least topped his shoulder. Rosanna had taken those comments to heart.

He thought of her devoting her time to finding the perfect woman to meet his needs and the idea sent a forbidden thrill through him.

Since she'd come into his life he had needs that it seemed only she could satisfy.

He'd told himself his celibacy since taking the crown was to blame. But that was only part of the problem. The main part was Rosanna MacIain. Serious and conscientious. Intelligent and obstinate. Tenacious and effortlessly sexy. She even made a trouser suit look enticing. As for those soft lips and her give-everything brand of passion…

No wonder he craved her, waking nightly in a hot sweat, body throbbing with unassuaged need.

Dragging his mind back to the conversation around him, he congratulated one of Rosanna's candidates on her grasp of his language. She was a French diplomat who spoke five languages, had a throaty, attractive laugh and a love of the outdoors. She was also chic, sexy and engaging.

Theoretically they were an excellent match.

Yet, even as he leaned closer, telling her about four-wheel driving in the desert, his attention strayed to a dark head and a sensuous body in smoky green on the other side of the room.

Anger coiled in his gut.

Anger at Rosanna and at his wayward inclinations.

This wouldn't do.

He didn't have the time or inclination to drag out his search for a wife. The sooner it was sorted the better. But Rosanna MacIain was proving as much a hindrance as a help, distracting him at every turn.

She was surprisingly good at her job. Surprising because at heart he'd never quite believed a matchmaker could find a woman he'd consider marrying. She'd proved him wrong, producing several candidates who might fit the bill.

If only he could concentrate on them and not her.

Either she had to go or he had to find a way to neutralise her hold over his libido.

CHAPTER SIX

'YOUR MAJESTY.'

Rosanna kept her voice even despite rising frustration. Despite his delay acknowledging her amongst the throng waiting to speak to him at the museum opening. He only deigned to recognise her because she refused to move away.

His congenial smile solidified as the other guests melted away.

He inclined his head briefly, his tone as cool as hers. 'Ms MacIain.'

What had happened to the man who, at last week's royal reception, had called her beautiful and seductive? Whose dark gaze had made her feel more feminine and alluring, more *alive* than she'd ever felt in her life. He'd even come to her aid when the Minister for Finance had grilled her.

But Salim had only intervened because he didn't want the secret of her work getting out. It had been nothing to do with Rosanna herself.

Strange how his indifference hurt. She felt it as a crushing weight in her chest and a ridiculous prickling behind her eyes. That made her angrier still.

Rosanna tilted her jaw, her gaze locking with his. This wasn't about her. It was about her work, and *nothing*, she vowed, would stand in the way of her delivering what she'd promised.

Not even a client who refused to see her.

Every meeting she'd tried to organise had been cancelled except for a brief quarter of an hour with his assistant present. It was as if Salim didn't want to deal with her.

'We need to talk.'

'Indeed?'

His expression didn't change, yet the look in his eyes reminded her that she spoke to an absolute ruler. A man used to instant and complete acquiescence.

'If you please, Your Majesty.' Rosanna made her voice soft and coaxing but she was damned if she'd bow her head or break eye contact now she finally had his attention. 'I need to update you and I can't proceed without your guidance.'

Because, despite producing a selection of gorgeous, talented women, Salim didn't seem interested in any of them. Not even Ingrid, the Scandinavian medico with the grace of a queen and the looks of a film star.

At this rate Rosanna would be here for months.

She shuddered. She had to pin him down and get him to spend more time with the ones he liked best.

Was he deliberately sabotaging her work?

But that made no sense. Salim had made it clear he needed a wife quickly, even if he acted like a man who would prefer not to marry.

'I'm sure my assistant will be able to—'

'With all due respect, Your Majesty, it's you I need to speak with, not your assistant.'

If Salim had looked proud before, now he was positively imperious, staring down that aristocratic nose as if she were the first person who had ever interrupted him.

Perhaps she was. Anxiety curdled her stomach as she thought of the consequences of displeasing this powerful client.

'I was about to say—' he paused as if challenging her

to interrupt again '—that my assistant will make an appointment.'

He looked up and instantly Taqi hurried towards them.

'Thank you, Your Majesty. I'll look forward to it.'

Rosanna suspected her smile was more like a baring of teeth, but her patience was fraying, especially with Marian calling regularly from London asking for progress and Salim refusing to give enough useful feedback.

'Excellent.' He was already turning away with Taqi in tow, leaving Rosanna to wonder what she'd done to earn his displeasure.

But she'd had difficult clients before. She vowed that not even the Sheikh of Dhalkur at his most regal and uppity would get the better of her.

'Ms MacIain, Your Majesty.'

Late that same afternoon Salim watched Taqi usher Rosanna into his sitting room then leave, closing the door behind him.

Salim rose from the sofa where he'd been reviewing a report, silently cursing his earlier distraction.

He'd come to his private apartments to search for notes he'd made last night on a new project and become absorbed comparing them with the progress report he'd received. When he hadn't returned to the office, Taqi must have assumed he was happy to meet Rosanna here.

Not what Salim had intended. It felt safer meeting her in the administrative wing, with his staff nearby.

But surely such a precaution wasn't necessary. He could hear her out and send her on her way.

'Please, come in.'

His voice was half an octave lower than usual and seemed to rumble from somewhere far deeper than his larynx.

Her voice, by comparison, was crisply uninflected. 'Thank you.'

She still wore the dress of cobalt blue from the museum event. Less severe than her work clothes, it skimmed her body in a way that made Salim's throat dry. Even the sight of her slender legs felt like too much temptation to a man battling for control. Like a teenager instead of an experienced man of the world.

A mighty shudder rippled down Salim's spine.

A portent of trouble? Or anticipation?

Her chin was up and her gaze direct, as if ready for a confrontation.

Was that the real reason he'd come to his rooms and stayed here?

Because he knew their relationship teetered on the brink of something perilous.

Perhaps, subconsciously, he courted that danger.

Salim's pulse slowed to a heavy thud as he battled the urge to reach for her and see those gunmetal eyes glitter silver with desire.

That would be a monumental error. He wasn't a man to be undone by physical urges, no matter how compelling. Even if he knew that he wasn't the only one feeling this way. Rosanna might pretend to be untouchable but she hadn't been able to hide completely her response to him.

Salim's life had been a lesson in self-mastery and strategic focus. Spur of the moment impulses, giving in to selfish desires, weren't encouraged in royal princes. That had been his brother's style, which was one of the reasons he'd been passed over as sheikh and Salim, the dependable, hardworking brother, had been chosen.

He didn't feel dependable now. He felt…

'Please, take a seat.'

He gestured to the long sofa opposite before sinking back onto his own.

As soon as she sat, in a sinuous movement that notched his temperature higher, he realised his mistake. They should be at a desk, a very wide desk where Rosanna would be safely on the far side out of reach and those shapely legs out of his line of vision.

Although she sat with her knees together and ankles demurely crossed, her dress rode distractingly higher and Salim had to concentrate on not staring.

He cleared his throat. 'You had matters to discuss.'

She did. Lots.

Rosanna had been busy, which is what he'd come to expect. She had a slew of new candidates for him to consider. A proposed schedule which would allow him to meet them at upcoming events. Plus her observations on the women to whom he'd already been introduced. All detailed, all insightful, all logical.

Yet Salim couldn't focus on the meeting's desired outcome. Moving closer to choosing a bride.

Finally she paused, looking at him in expectant silence.

'You've done well. I can see why your aunt's enterprise is so successful.'

'But?' She looked at him, eyebrows raised and lips pursed. 'I hear a *but* in there.' She drew a slow breath as if searching for calm. 'We don't seem to be making progress. You need to be open with me about your responses to these women. Then we can move forward and find the right one for you.'

I've already found her.

The thought jammed his tongue and stopped his breath for a second.

Not as a wife. Rosanna MacIain didn't fit those criteria.

Fuad's unstable, selfish temperament and his excesses while ruling for their ailing father proved how the wrong person in a royal role could damage the nation. Even a well-meaning but unprepared person would flounder. Salim needed an absolute paragon as a wife. A woman with an unblemished past who wouldn't undermine the royal family's prestige but help him rebuild it. A woman with the unique mix of skills and experience that would make her a superb queen.

Yet Rosanna was the woman he wanted for *now*.

That was the problem. With Rosanna in his home it was impossible to think about other women.

His mind and body betrayed him by continually focusing on his stern, sexy siren. Replaying the passionate kiss that had been a promise of carnal pleasure. Even her tight control and prim corporate suits only emphasised the alluring dichotomy of a capable woman whose businesslike exterior hid sultry ardour.

'I need your frank thoughts on the women you've met. Otherwise, how can I tailor my search to your requirements?'

Dark pewter eyes held his and he read determination there. Unfortunately he still yearned to see them silver with passion.

He shot to his feet and stalked to the window, looking out onto the city, fighting the adrenaline surge in his blood. Every muscle tightened, ready for decisive action. As if he weren't a modern monarch but one of his ancestors, men famous for taking what they wanted and negotiating later.

Salim breathed deep and kept his gaze on the rooftops, turning bronze and gilt as the sun waned. 'What do you want to know?'

'Who would you like to see again? There are limits on getting to know people in formal settings. In a more relaxed atmosphere—'

'None.'

'What? You don't want to spend time with *any* of them?'

He turned and saw her composure had cracked. Her mouth hung open for a second until she snapped it shut.

Her eyes sparked fire and, despite his best intentions, Salim felt satisfaction curl deep inside. He liked watching Rosanna flare up like that, even in anger if he couldn't have anything else.

He disliked it when she hid all that passion. Even if it was the correct, cautious thing to do, the sort of thing he was trying to do himself. It felt like fraud.

Salim put his hands behind his back, standing taller, knowing he was on dangerous ground. He felt it in every pore. As if he'd wandered into a treacherous bed of quicksand that looked innocent but could devour an unwary man.

When Rosanna spoke her voice was perfectly modulated. 'It would be helpful, Your Majesty, if we could go through each one and you told me why they weren't suitable.'

They were back to *Your Majesty*?

He shouldn't be surprised. He'd called her Ms MacIain today, careful to observe the formalities in public. But it had been more than that; he'd been angry with himself, and with his feelings for her. He'd done all he could to avoid being alone with her.

Face it, Salim. You were running scared!

It was a first for him. One he didn't like.

So he'd snapped at her. Done his best to distance himself at the museum, channelling his brother at his most haughty. Yet it hadn't worked. He'd still wanted her.

'As you wish. Run through the list.'

'Right then. Let's start with Lady Charlotte.'

'She's allergic to the Dhalkur.'

'Sorry?' Rosanna goggled at him. 'How can she be allergic to a country?'

'When we drove to the edge of the desert she was worried about getting sand blown into her hair. Plus she fretted that such a dry climate would dehydrate her skin.' He watched Rosanna's expression grow horrified.

'I'm so sorry. I had no idea. She sounded so good on paper, and when we talked. She didn't mention anything like that.'

Rosanna frowned, clearly blaming herself for not picking that up earlier.

'It's not the sort of thing you could discover from a search.' Yet that frown didn't shift. He let his mouth curl. 'She did assure me that she functions perfectly as long as she has twenty-four-hour air-conditioning.'

Salim watched a ripple soften the line of Rosanna's flattened lips. Then he heard a gurgle of laughter.

He felt it like a trickle of heat winding through his body, leaving him even more aware of the fact they were alone in his private space. 'You weren't to know. I expect she deliberately kept some things to herself until she got here.'

She shook her head and made a note. 'How about Jazmin?'

'A lovely woman and on paper she met my criteria. Especially with her first-hand knowledge of the region.'

'And in person?'

'Even though she's cousin to a king and grew up at his court, she confessed she's not comfortable with formal events. She's happier mixing with people in the country than at official receptions. That won't do for my wife.'

Rosanna sighed. 'Another who wasn't quite straight with me. I do apologise.'

She looked so downcast Salim felt sorry for her. She'd worked hard and done a good job. But he was determined to take only the right woman as his bride.

He needed someone who could hold her own in both formal and informal settings. Someone who could appear soignée yet welcoming at formal functions.

His thoughts strayed to Rosanna in misty green at that recent reception. She'd been beautiful and assured but engaging. He'd seen her talking animatedly with many of his guests and wished he could join her.

But even an outsider as confident as Rosanna would find it impossible to adapt a royal life full-time. He needed someone whose family circumstances or training equipped them for the demands of royal life. He'd spent a lifetime preparing for it and still sometimes his new position felt overwhelming. As if, just for a short space, he craved the chance to be simply Salim, not the ruler everyone looked to for solutions and leadership.

Salim snapped his mind away from fruitless thoughts. 'Who's next?'

'Princess Eliana.'

'No.' He saw Rosanna open her mouth ready to protest and raised his hand. 'She's pretty and clever and probably very nice, but she finishes my sentences. Do you have any idea how annoying that is?'

'I—'

'Very annoying. I couldn't live with someone who did that.'

'I'm amazed she had the temerity.'

Salim stared at Rosanna with her downcast eyes and nimble fingers making yet more notes. Was she laughing at him?

But even Rosanna's snarky observation was nothing compared to the frustration of having someone put words into his mouth.

'I don't mind a spirited conversation.' He drew himself up. 'But not someone pretending to know my thoughts.'

'No, of course not.'

Yet he read the smile lurking at the corners of her mouth. To his chagrin he felt his own mouth curl. His was a valid complaint yet Rosanna made him see the amusing side of it.

'What about Ingrid—'

'The doctor,' he said flatly. He'd had hopes of the beautiful, aristocratic Scandinavian, but they'd been deflated. 'Definitely not.'

'It would help to know why. She's beautiful, talented, presents well and speaks several languages.'

Salim shrugged. 'She's totally focused on her research.'

'You said you admired women who pursued careers.'

'Not to the exclusion of all else. Whenever someone raised a subject that wasn't to do with her specific area of interest she listened politely but had nothing to say. I want a wife who's interested in people, makes them feel welcome.'

'I'm sure if you gave her another chance…'

Salim shook his head and turned back to the window. 'No. I've made my decision. She's not the woman for me.'

'Okay then. What about Sylvie? She's got the diplomatic and linguistic qualifications you wanted and is very capable.'

Salim shook his head. 'She won't do. All the time I was with her I felt like I was being assessed so she could tailor her conversation to fit. I could almost hear the wheels turning in her mind.'

Rosanna didn't say anything and her silence eventually made him turn to look at her. She was looking across at him, frowning, her mouth a flat line.

'That's unfair. Of course she was thinking about what might interest you. She was trying to get to know you.'

'It was more than that. It just felt too…contrived. She lacked spontaneity.'

When he'd met Rosanna, for instance, their conversation had been easy and entertaining and felt as natural as water bubbling from a mountain spring.

Rosanna's frown didn't shift. 'So conversation is important. You want someone who talks easily and is interested in a lot of subjects.'

Put like that it sounded very basic, but that was precisely what he wanted. 'That's right.'

'So, then there's Natalya.'

'No sexual spark.'

Rosanna's eyebrows shot sky-high. 'Sorry?'

'She's a nice woman, I'll give you that. She's friendly and intelligent and not at all fazed by life at court, but I wasn't attracted to her.'

'But she's a model. She's the face of a multi-million-dollar cosmetics campaign!'

Salim shrugged. 'She's beautiful. But not for me.'

For some reason her ice-blonde beauty didn't move him. He'd spent several hours with her and felt not the least stirring of sexual awareness.

Whereas, he realised, he just had to be in the same room with Rosanna MacIain for his libido to throb into life. He set his jaw, determined to get this over. 'Who's next?'

They dealt with several more on her list. Salim's answers grew shorter and Rosanna's mouth tighter as she noted his objections. Everything from shyness to an annoying, high-pitched giggle, to one who'd tried to seduce him at their first meeting and whom he labelled too pushy.

Rosanna drew a slow breath and made yet another note. She looked grimmer than ever.

'So, you want a woman who's aristocratic, preferably royal, or used to mixing in such circles. She must be beautiful, but in a way you can't specifically describe. She has to be confident but not too confident. Able to satisfy you sexually but not be sexually predatory. You'd like a competent, career woman but not so focused she isn't interested in other things. She needs to be able to talk with anyone, but not presume to put words into their mouth. Someone who's at home in a formal setting but not just there. She must have a sense of humour and warmth but not an annoying laugh or any sort of verbal tic. Plus she has to like Dhalkur, be an accomplished linguist with not a whiff of scandal about her and be eager to have children.'

Salim nodded. 'Excellent. You've described her well.'

As he watched, Rosanna pinched the bridge of her nose and squeezed her eyes shut. She drew a deep breath then busied herself making another note. But she didn't raise her eyes to his.

'Right, what about Maryam, the last woman you met? She meets a lot of those criteria.'

Salim was already shaking his head. 'On paper she seems right, but in reality…' He paused, remembering those big doe eyes looking up at him. 'She deferred to me all the time. Even when I asked her a straightforward question she was reluctant to commit herself in case it wasn't the answer I wanted.'

'With respect, Your Majesty, that's not surprising.' He didn't miss the snap in Rosanna's voice, as if she held her temper by a thread. 'You can be quite daunting.'

'I told you to dispense with my title in private.' The way she said it, as if it tasted sour on her tongue, irked him. Or maybe it was the judgemental way her mouth flattened as he gave his completely legitimate reasons for each rejection. 'As for your *with respect*, that's what you say when you're feeling not at all respectful.'

She met his eyes, her stare fulminating. Yet she retained her composure and said nothing. Salim realised he was trying to crack the barrier she'd erected around herself. She challenged him yet pulled back at the final moment.

That was a good thing. It was safer that way, for both of them. Yet it frustrated him.

He wanted more from her.

'If you feel you're not up to the job…'

'Are you sure there really *is* a job?' She set aside her laptop and stared up at him, her gaze probing.

He frowned. 'What are you talking about?'

'Your requirements keep changing and expanding. I

bring you one of the world's most beautiful women and you claim you don't find her attractive.'

'I didn't say that. She is attractive. I just don't *want* her.'

Because, infuriatingly, his body and mind were fixated on Rosanna MacIain. The knowledge made him grit his teeth in annoyance. He was lord of all he surveyed and the one thing he wanted was the one thing he shouldn't want. Because she was his guest, his employee…

And the source of more frustration than he'd ever felt in his life. When he was with her he didn't feel like a king or her employer. He felt like a man lost in the desert, thirsting for a single taste of pure, lifegiving water.

'Are you playing some sort of game?' Emotion coloured her voice. She sounded fed up. 'Are you sure a tall, blonde aristocrat will meet your needs—'

'Why, Ms MacIain? Do you think a medium height brunette from Australia might be a better fit for my needs?'

Her gasp was loud in the thrumming silence. She shot to her feet, eyes flashing pure silver, hands curling into fists beside her. 'If you're implying—'

'I'm not implying anything, just pondering.'

And, despite his better judgement, enjoying the fact she was no longer treating him like a professional challenge. He much preferred her honest emotions, though he wouldn't accept such insolence from anyone else.

The air sizzled with the energy she radiated. Salim felt it like a shower of sparks peppering his skin. And in the heavy weight settling in his lower body. The strain of clenching muscles.

'I'd never…' She shook her head as if words failed her, but not for long. 'No, *you're* the one sabotaging this process. *I'm* the one trying to keep it on track.'

She dragged in deep breaths, her breasts rising against her blue dress. Valiantly Salim refocused on her face, flushed and vibrant.

'That's the problem. This project isn't on track at all. It's going off the rails.'

It was his fault for agreeing to have her here. He should have known better that night when she'd stalked into his office as if she owned it, demanding to know what he was doing there. That stirring excitement hadn't left him since. He'd been on tenterhooks, trying to do the right thing, curbing a reaction to her that was as undeniable as it was inconvenient.

She hiked up her chin, at the same time cocking her hip and planting her hand on it in an attitude of pure, feminine provocation that was impossible to resist.

'Okay. I'll bite. Why, in your opinion, is it going off the rails? Tell me straight. Don't waste any more of my time.'

'Why? Because of this, of course.'

Salim took a single stride that brought him right up to her. He saw her narrowed eyes widen but not, he saw, in dismay. He slipped one arm around her waist, drawing her against him, and cupped the back of her head with his other hand.

For an instant he was lost in the white-hot flare of light in her eyes, then he bent his head and his mouth met hers.

CHAPTER SEVEN

ROSANNA HAD SENSED the kiss coming in the static charge that made every hair on her body stand up. In the elation that had ramped up the longer they were together. She'd *seen* it coming, Salim's head lowering towards her in slow motion as if daring her to push him away.

Yet she hadn't done a thing to avoid his kiss.

She hadn't turned her head or pushed him back or said a word in protest.

How could she when this was exactly what she'd craved all these months?

Instead she'd grabbed his shirtfront and watched, breathless, as those dark eyes came closer and she tumbled into their midnight depths.

Finally, as his lips covered hers, it hit her. The most overpowering relief. As if she'd waited all her life for this moment.

Despite the energy running through her, Rosanna sagged a little, knees giving way and legs trembling with reaction. All because she experienced again the taste of his mouth on hers. As if she'd hungered all this time for the indefinable flavour that was pure Salim.

But even that weakness brought its reward as his hard frame pressed against her, his hold enveloping her, and joy burst free.

Salim's fingers moved, pulling her tight bun free and

channelling through her hair in a bold caress that was sumptuous and delicious.

Almost as bold and delicious as the way he kissed, knowing and satisfying, yet full of promise.

They were like lovers parted too long. Lovers who knew each other intimately. Salim *did* know her intimately. The stroke of his tongue, the angle of his mouth and the hard but not too hard pressure aroused and captivated her. As if he knew exactly what she wanted.

Rosanna squirmed closer, pressing herself against him, revelling in the contours of his body, his powerful thighs wide around hers. And all that glorious heat.

Salim caressed her scalp, gently tugging her hair so her head tilted backwards, giving him better access, and she couldn't prevent a muffled groan of pleasure.

Instantly his grip around her waist tightened, pulling her so close she registered his arousal, potent against her abdomen.

A shiver ran down her spine and across her skin. At her core was a melting sensation as if she softened, ready for his possession.

Yet, kissing him back, her hands tugging him closer, Rosanna didn't feel weak or overwhelmed. She felt as if she'd met her other half. As if they were designed for each other in some elemental way.

This was how she remembered that night in Scotland. Pure passion, the promise of wonderful things to come, the sense of union between like souls and a sheer carnal arousal such as she'd never known.

Salim lifted his mouth and Rosanna almost cried out in dismay. Except he wasn't moving away, just giving her a chance to breathe while he peppered kisses to the corner of her lips, her jaw, then the spot just below her ear that made her jerk in his arms and press closer, hunger reaching impossible levels.

'Salim!' Was that keening, breathless voice hers?

He said something deep and low in a language she didn't understand, his lips brushing her neck, his hot breath a caress that sent a quiver of longing through her.

He straightened, glittering eyes holding her in thrall. 'You want me to stop?' His voice hit a harsh note.

'No!'

Rosanna blinked as her instinctive denial sank in. They teetered on the brink of something far bigger than a kiss and they both knew it.

'I...'

She struggled for something to say. To remember all the reasons this shouldn't happen. But while her brain was scrambled her body was awake and too, too responsive. Salim drew a deep breath and that movement created friction against her breasts. Her nipples were tight, hard and needy and she wanted him to touch her there.

Rosanna gulped.

Madness, this was madness.

'Madness or not, it feels right. You can't deny that.'

Rosanna stared. She'd said it out loud?

'This is why our search isn't working,' he went on, his voice a gravel rumble. 'Because all I can think about is you, Rosanna.'

The way he said her name, his voice dipping, made something unravel inside her.

Or was it the way he held her, with an easy possessiveness that she shouldn't like yet revelled in? Then there was the way he looked at her. Gone was that haughty superiority, replaced by searing intensity and an honesty that cut through every common-sense reason to keep her distance.

Or perhaps it was the stunning import of his words.

All I can think about is you.

She soaked that up like a flower absorbing sunshine.

Greedily. Delighted to discover she wasn't alone in this forbidden longing.

'We can't,' she mumbled, her throat closing convulsively as desire waged war with professional ethics. 'I work for you.'

Salim straightened, his head rearing back, his hold loosening though he didn't relinquish her. 'You think I'm pressuring you to—'

Rosanna stopped his words with her fingertips to his mouth. Arousal ran through her at the feel of his lips against her skin. Reluctantly she dragged her hand away. 'No! Not that. This isn't harassment. Nothing like it.'

This was utterly consensual and she couldn't pretend otherwise. 'But I have a job to do. I have to find you—'

'At this moment I don't care about finding a bride.' His low voice held a savagery she'd never heard before and it sent a thrill through her bones. Never had she felt a man's need for her like this. Not even the man she'd once planned to marry. 'All I want, all I've wanted for weeks, is you.'

His hands moved, gathering her closer. Rosanna knew she only had to step back and he'd release her. But that act of will was beyond her. She stood trembling not from fear or outrage but from excitement.

What did that say about her?

That you need him just as much as he needs you.

The discovery that their longing was mutual swept away all the arguments she'd used to tell herself there couldn't be anything between them but a contract of work.

It changed everything.

Her heart hammered and her breathing turned shallow. Her head spun with Salim's cedar and spice scent and the feel of his body, primed yet waiting for her answer.

'I can't think about other women. I can't concentrate. I'm continually struggling for control because every time

I see you, even when I *can't* see you, I'm fighting the urge to do all the things I know I shouldn't…with you.'

'Really? But today—'

'Today I was in a temper. I apologise for being so short with you. I shouldn't have taken my foul mood out on you and I'm sorry.' He scowled and, instead of deterring her, it made something in her chest roll over as she sensed his internal battle. 'I've tried keeping my distance and not see you alone but it makes no difference. I'm not used to being unable to control my reactions.'

'*That's* why you refused to meet me?'

It threw a whole new light on his actions.

Salim nodded grimly. 'Much good it did me.'

He sounded sulky, like a man used to getting his own way and suddenly discovering he couldn't. For some reason Rosanna found that almost endearing. Or maybe it was just the confirmation that he too had suffered.

Salim shifted his weight and the brush of hard muscle against her body made her feminine core tighten needily.

'I want you, Rosanna.'

She watched him swallow, his Adam's apple jerking and the muscles in his bronzed throat working. The movement emphasised both his strength and the extremity of his tension. It made her feel suddenly strong, a *femme fatale* wielding seductive power. Except the power flowed both ways. Everything about Salim called to her, making her weak with longing.

'I need you.'

Even then he didn't plead but stood proud and tall, like a warrior of old.

Rosanna squeezed her eyes shut. Her imagination was on overload. She did *not* need to start imagining his as some romantic hero of the desert, swooping in to claim the woman of his dreams.

'Rosanna?'

His arm dropped from around her back and her eyes snapped open in dismay. He was releasing her?

That's when it truly struck her. That despite the pair of them together being a terrible idea, the alternative—to walk away—was impossible.

'I need you too.'

She hadn't meant to say it, but looking into those dark velvet eyes the truth just tumbled out.

Rosanna saw him absorb her words, not with a smile but with a clenching jaw and flared nostrils. Far from leaning in to scoop her closer he seemed to straighten still further, towering above her.

Never had she been more conscious of his power, of the fact that he was all hard, male muscle, honed by his desert heritage and military training into a force far stronger than she could ever be.

Yet that didn't scare her. It thrilled her. For the look in his eyes, hunger melded with something she couldn't name, told her he wouldn't use that power against her. It was himself he battled.

The knowledge, sudden and sure, made her feel like a different woman, as assured as a queen, any doubts fading to nothing.

She lifted her hand, intending to caress that clenched jawline, but he moved faster, long fingers wrapping around her wrist before she could touch him.

'Not here.'

His voice was thick, almost unrecognisable, but Rosanna understood, because she felt the same. They needed absolute privacy for what was to come. Because one touch would lead to another then another...

Rosanna's breath hitched and a smile trembled on her lips.

Did she imagine his eyes dilated? Before she could be sure, he turned, still holding her wrist, stalking away from the window. They passed groups of sofas and occasional tables, heading for a door on the far side of the room.

Salim's stride didn't seem hurried but Rosanna took two paces to each of his, her pulse ratcheting faster with each step and each hasty indrawn breath.

Through the door they passed a book-lined study on one side and what looked like a media room on the other. They swept past a gym that gave out onto a courtyard with a massive swimming pool. Past a couple of closed doors and finally through double doors into his bedroom.

Salim paused to close the door behind them yet didn't let her go.

Heat encircled her wrist and a shivery feeling of euphoria shot through her, tinged with just the tiniest bit of trepidation.

Rosanna wanted Salim more than she could remember ever wanting anyone or anything. Yet such intensity of feeling was outside her experience.

The snick of the door shutting them in his private domain was as loud as a gong echoing through the silence.

Rather than look at Salim she focused on the high, domed ceiling, painted the colour of the sky just after sunset, azure darkening to indigo at the top. She just had time to register a sprinkling of silvery stars against the blue when Salim led her forward.

Two large, elegantly arched windows gave views towards distant mountains. Between them stretched an embroidered coverlet of blue and gold, covering the biggest bed she'd ever seen.

Her breath caught in a gasp she couldn't prevent.

Moments ago she'd thought of Salim as a warrior of old, stern and uncompromising, sweeping his chosen woman up and away. This massive bed perfectly fitted that desert fantasy.

'It's a bit over the top, I admit,' he drawled near her ear, 'but it's tradition and it's comfortable. A new one is made for each new sheikh.'

'Imagine trying to launder the sheets.' Rosanna's voice sounded stretched. 'It must be a nightmare.'

She snapped her mouth shut, realising she was babbling. The enormity of this moment thickened her breathing and revved her heartbeat to a staccato rush.

She didn't dare look at Salim.

In case he sees how profound this feels for you?

Or in case he changes his mind?

He'd said he needed her and she felt the same. But out of nowhere, doubts assailed her. Rosanna wasn't gorgeous or gifted. She didn't speak five languages or heal sick children or negotiate international trade deals like the women Salim had rejected. She was ordinary, so ordinary that her ex had needed more in his life, dreaming of a glamorous life beyond their means.

Salim's thumb stroked a tiny circle on the pulse point at her wrist, making her shiver. But instead of taking her in his arms and kissing her, he stood beside her, radiating heat and that delicious spicy scent of warm male flesh.

'I confess, I've never thought about it,' he said, 'but I suppose you're right. I don't think I've thought about laundry since my days doing national service, washing my own clothes.'

'You washed your own clothes?' She turned to find him watching her, his expression unreadable.

'Naturally. Even the son of the sheikh gets no special treatment when it comes to doing his duty. In fact, I'm sure my father instructed that the year's military service should be as taxing as possible. He believed in toughening his sons to meet future challenges.'

Salim paused, his expression enigmatic. 'Is this too much of a challenge, Rosanna?' His voice dropped, the sound scraping through her, proof again of her visceral response to him. 'Have you changed your mind? You seem nervous.'

This was her chance to back out. Because it didn't make any sense, her with a man like Salim.

But that was the old, hurt Rosanna trying to wrest control. The one bruised by what Phil had done and crushed by guilt over his actions. The Rosanna who doubted too easily and second-guessed her judgement.

She didn't want to be that Rosanna any more. It had been testing, but she'd revelled in the stimulation of her work for Salim and the chance to prove herself. She liked feeling competent and strong.

She liked the way Salim made her feel.

Rosanna nodded. 'I am nervous.' She'd never had sex with anyone but her ex-fiancé, but that would be too much information. 'I don't...share myself easily or often.'

'Neither do I. There's been no one since before the night we met in the Highlands.'

Rosanna's eyes rounded. She hadn't expected that. A man like Salim could have his choice of eager women.

She thought of all the things she might say. Except if she opened her mouth now she didn't trust herself not to babble out more inanities. Besides, it wasn't talk she wanted.

Rosanna turned to face him, planting her free hand on his broad chest. Feeling the quickened thud of his heart beneath her palm eased her tension a little, because it proved he was nowhere near as sanguine as he appeared.

She splayed her fingers and leaned in. 'Kiss me, Salim. I don't want to talk any more.'

His mouth curled into a smile that stole her breath all over again. 'Your wish is my command.'

Rosanna caught the indulgent humour in Salim's eyes as he deliberately played into that fantasy, and suddenly her nerves dissipated. She was grinning up at him as he gathered her close and kissed her with a deliberation that left no room for second thoughts.

She wanted him. *How* she wanted him.

Her fingers scrabbled at the tiny buttons on his collarless shirt even as she lost herself in the sensual exploration of mouth on mouth, of bodies straining together, eager for more.

She felt Salim lift one hand at the back of her dress, then the slow, tantalising slide of the zip that was a caress in itself. She arched against him, eager for more.

'Drop your arms, sweetheart,' he murmured against her mouth and she felt strong fingers wrapping around her wrists, pulling her hands to her sides. Moments later her dress pooled around her ankles, leaving her in underwear and high-heeled sandals while Salim was still fully clothed.

Rosanna kept her gaze on his face as he captured her hands again and drew them wide, away from her body. He looked down, surveying each swell and dip with an attention so exquisitely sharp she felt it like the skim of fingers across bare flesh.

She might have felt uncomfortable under that scrutiny, like some slave girl being inspected by a potential buyer. Except she *wanted* this with every particle of her being. Besides, watching Salim through half-closed eyes, she registered the dusky heat slash across his high-cut cheeks. Saw the convulsive swallow and felt the needy way his hands tightened on hers.

He said something soft and low that sounded like treacle poured over grinding stones. The unfamiliar words were lush and rich yet harsh with emotion as if his larynx had seized.

Then ebony eyes met hers and something heavy swooped inside her. 'You're stunning, Rosanna.'

A tiny part of her brain told her Salim must be as desperate with need as she was. She'd never been called stunning and she knew she was average. Yet she responded unthinkingly to the accolade, standing taller, breasts swelling and nipples budding so tight the ache almost made her cry out.

'I want to see you too.'

She didn't consciously form the words but suddenly they were out and she was glad.

Salim released her hands but not her gaze as he made short work of a couple more buttons then hauled his shirt off. It was incredibly arousing, having him watch her as he undressed.

Finally, though, she had to follow the movement of his hands downwards.

Her breath stalled on the sight of a honed body that seemed all lean strength. The shift of muscles beneath golden skin mesmerised her. The dusting of dark hair across his wide chest invited her touch and she found it surprisingly silky and tempting beneath her fingertips.

A gasp filled the silence but whether it was from Salim or her she didn't know.

Was there anything in the world as wonderful as the feel of hot, sculpted, male muscle twitching against her touch?

Salim's hands dropped to his trousers and Rosanna's eyes widened. In what seemed like one urgent shove he dispensed with the rest of his clothes and his footwear as well, leaving him utterly naked.

Rosanna blinked, her mouth drying.

She'd never seen such male perfection. Had never thought to in real life. Salim's tall body was perfectly proportioned with wide shoulders, narrow hips, solid thighs and a jutting erection that made that soft spot low in her body turn molten. Even his bare feet were sexy.

But it was the invitation in his eyes that stole her breath. That and the little flare of his nostrils that told her he too struggled for control.

'Come.' He held out his hand palm up in invitation. She

put her hand in his and instantly long fingers encircled hers, drawing her to him.

Now she was surrounded by his heat, soaking it up eagerly, pressing closer, kissing his collarbone and throat. He tasted of spice and salt with a deeper note that was intrinsically, excitingly, pure male.

So entranced was she that she barely noticed him remove her underwear until they stood, naked flesh to naked flesh, and it felt as if her body sang out loud.

In one easy movement Salim lifted her then lowered her to the bed, following her so fast she was cocooned between his hot body and the silken coverlet. The sensations were so delicious it was a sybaritic overload. Desperately she stroked his bare body, shifting against him, revelling in the friction between them and the fascinating new delights.

Salim kissed her again, as easy as a long-term lover and more thrilling than anything she'd known.

Rosanna lifted her hands, channelling her fingers through his thick hair to cup the back of his skull. She shifted her legs wider so he sank against her, all magnificent heat and shockingly potent arousal.

'Please,' she whispered against his mouth. 'Please, Salim.'

Sex had never felt like this before. With Phil she'd never known this out-of-her-mind urgency. Never this sharp pang of need as if she'd die if she didn't join with Salim soon.

She lifted her hips, tilting against his erection, and it felt so good. Her breaths came in gasps and the fire in her blood concentrated where their bodies met.

Salim moved, his weight shifting to one side, and Rosanna felt his hand on her body. But instead of going straight to her breasts as she expected, those long fingers delved, down her abdomen and lower, following her slick heat to the cleft that hid the centre of her need.

Rosanna shuddered as electricity jolted through her, emanating from the press of his fingers against her clitoris. She snapped open eyes she hadn't realised she'd closed to see Salim watching her, gaze intent, his mouth taut and his breathing as harsh as her own.

She opened her mouth to say she wanted more than his touch. She wanted all of him. But he stroked her again, circling that sensitive bud, rubbing harder then deeper, testing her slick channel. Her pelvis rose of its own volition, drawn by a power stronger than thought.

His gaze held her captive as he lavished her with words of encouragement, urging her to let go.

A cry choked off her breath as everything within Rosanna coalesced into a single shining burst of energy. It was shockingly sudden, so quick she scarcely believed it. She felt it rise and expand, her blood sizzling, flames licking her bones, and joy, stunning and incandescent, consumed her.

Her taut body collapsed, boneless and weightless, and her eyes drifted shut, her brain overloaded by pleasure.

Salim moved away and dimly she assumed he was getting protection. Rosanna stretched languidly, her body buzzing still. Soon he returned. She felt the bed dip beside her then furnace heat as satiny flesh slid against her.

'Thank you,' she whispered.

'You're very welcome.'

How could that warm, husky voice sound so arousing after her monumental climax? She opened her eyes and felt instantly guilty that while she lay relaxed and sated, Salim was on edge. She saw it in the bunched muscles of his shoulders and the razor-sharp lines of his jaw and cheekbones, as if his flesh had been scraped to the bone.

'Salim.'

His name was magic on her lips as she reached for him. He settled between her legs, taking some of his weight on his arms. His erection felt impressive against her inner thigh but Rosanna didn't feel nervous, despite a relative lack of experience. She wanted to give him pleasure such as he'd offered her.

She wrapped her arms around him, lifting her mouth to his.

'Take me,' she whispered against his lips. 'I want to feel you come inside me.'

She might have lit a fuse on dynamite.

One moment Salim was holding himself back, as if concerned not to rush her. The next she heard and felt his deep groan of need as he kissed her hard, pressing her down into the pillows. He kneed her thighs wide then, with a single sure thrust, slipped in right to the heart of her.

Rosanna gasped, her breath failing as she struggled to absorb every delicious sensation. She'd never felt so full. So intimately connected to another. As if she hovered on the brink of some secret world, hitherto unknown.

'Rosanna. Did I hurt you?'

She shook her head. 'No.'

Her brain worked furiously, suddenly awake after that blissful lethargy. It told her these feelings were due to simple physics. That Salim was bigger, in all respects, than Phil. Plus he'd already given her an amazing orgasm, whereas, in the past, she'd struggled to climax. That had to explain why this union felt so profoundly different.

'Open your eyes, Rosanna.'

She did and it felt as if she fell into black velvet. Could Salim's eyes actually be so dark? Just looking at them excited her. As for breathing in his rich, addictive scent and feeling his body against hers…

'I need to be sure you're okay.'

A cracked laugh escaped her lips. 'I'm more than okay. I'm… I don't have the words.' Because even this, just lying together, joined, felt utterly miraculous.

Still he didn't move though that was what she craved.

Rosanna lifted her legs, winding them over his hips, hugging him to her and feeling him slide even deeper.

She felt a quiver ripple through Salim, felt his muscles bunch, and a second later he withdrew and thrust again.

Rosanna's head pressed back into pillowy softness as she arched up to him, his name a raw gasp on her lips. Her hands clutched, nails digging into cushioned muscle as she felt, impossibly, arousal stir anew. Tendrils of heat unfurled and twined through her, tightening at each erogenous zone.

Salim thrust again, deeper and more emphatic, and his hand closed around her breast. In the past when Phil had caressed her there it had sometimes been nice but often he'd squeezed too hard, too eager to read her body well as he sought his own relief. Salim's touch wasn't like that. She wanted more of it, more of everything.

'Like that?' His voice was gruff, almost unrecognisable, and she loved it. Loved knowing he too was on the edge.

'Exactly like that.' Rosanna struggled to find her breath as their bodies arched and thrust together as if they weren't virtual strangers but long-term lovers. 'Please,' she gasped. 'More.'

Something flared in Salim's eyes. His tempo quickened and his movements grew less measured, as if he too felt that primal beat in his blood. Rosanna met him, thrust for thrust, caught up in that surging tempo, until it burst upon her, an explosion of rapture that carried her to a place she'd never known.

She heard Salim shout her name, a long, deep groan of completion so raw it sounded almost like pain. Her climax should be dying but the quick, insistent pulse of his ejaculation drew her muscles into spasm again and her brain into paradise.

Rosanna felt utterly, wonderfully complete.

CHAPTER EIGHT

SALIM DISPOSED OF the condom then doused his head under the cold tap, trying to shock his brain into action. He stood, arms braced on the bathroom counter, head sunk between his shoulders, trying to think.

It had never been so hard to concentrate. His thoughts kept straying to Rosanna, luscious and inviting in his bed, so unconsciously seductive.

Unconsciously? He was imagining things.

Yet while she was innately passionate, Rosanna Maclain wasn't a practised seductress. More than once he'd caught her look of surprise. At her loss of control? At her multiple orgasms?

That was his ego talking. Wanting her to be blown away by how good they'd been together, as if no other man had made her feel anything comparable.

Salim's rueful smile died on his lips.

It was true. That's exactly what he wanted.

He lifted his head and looked in the mirror. A frown corrugated his brow and the lines carved around his mouth spoke of tension, despite the lingering echoes of bliss in his body.

Because no matter how good sex with Rosanna had been—and it had been phenomenally good—it had also been a mistake.

He employed her. It went against every rule to mix business with his personal life. Even though it had been consensual, he was her boss and he didn't like the disparity in power.

Salim's mouth rucked up in a wry grimace. Now he was sheikh there would always be a disparity in power between himself and any woman, wouldn't there?

His situation had changed so much, and though his upbringing had been designed to prepare him for such a possibility, the change sideswiped him sometimes.

He needed to be careful, behaving with decorum as well as decency. The example set by his brother, of reckless enthusiasms, inconsistent and questionable decision-making and personal cruelty, still lingered in the public psyche. Salim was doing his utmost to reassure his people that he wasn't like Fuad.

His brother's enthusiasms hadn't run to women but to fast cars, high-stakes gambling and a never-ending series of expensive whims. He'd siphoned funds earmarked for public programs to his private, lavish expenditure. As a result, Salim was particularly cautious of any actions that hinted he put his personal interests ahead of his duty.

Plus Salim had always kept his sexual liaisons private. In the days when he'd lived part-time in his father's palace and part-time elsewhere, he'd never invited a lover here, and there'd been no lovers since he took the throne because the needs of his nation had come before his own.

Because there was no woman you wanted as much as the stranger you left behind in the Highlands.

His mouth flattened in response to that truth. It made him restless and uncomfortable. Because, even now he'd had her, he still wanted Rosanna. Too much.

On every level he could think of, sex with Rosanna Maclain had the potential for disastrous consequences. It was wrong, or it should be wrong.

Yet it felt utterly right.

The glow of wellbeing that suffused his body and clouded his brain was testament to that.

Salim scowled at his reflection. He needed a solution to the problem that was his yearning for this woman.

She was here to find him a spouse. How could he expect her to continue now they were sexually involved? Even considering it made something sour roil in his belly, as if he were being unfaithful to a woman he hadn't yet met. Or to the woman who'd just shared his bed.

Yet he'd committed to the search for the sake of his people who had been through so much in recent years. He didn't have the luxury of choice. He *couldn't* turn back now.

How could he proceed while his thoughts were filled with Rosanna? When he hadn't had a full night's sleep in weeks because of his craving for her?

There had to be a solution. And he had to find it *now.*

Rosanna heard Salim get out of bed then the snick of a door closing.

Her breath escaped on a sigh that was part bliss and part wonder. She'd never felt like this in her life. Boneless, weightless and buzzing with absolute pleasure.

She'd been engaged, had been with Phil for a couple of years. Yet what she'd just shared with Salim was totally new territory. She felt wrung out, her body well-used and exhausted yet at the same time trickles of rapture still coursed through her and a sense of absolute rightness filled her.

Salim had taken her to places she'd never known and brought spectacular, unrivalled joy. He'd called her *sweetheart* in a way that had melted her heart. He'd given her tenderness as well as shockingly raw carnality. She felt like a different woman, sexy and powerful as never before.

And conflicted.

The smile curving her lips faded as the real world crowded in. The world beyond this vast, decadent bed.

Rosanna opened her eyes and saw afternoon light slanting across the room, picking out the gold embroidery on the rich coverlet. It was daylight and she was lolling on the sheikh's bed.

Would staff come looking for him? What if he had more meetings? Or if not, would they bring refreshments to his rooms?

She had to leave before she was seen.

Yet, with her body lethargic from bliss, she found it hard to move.

Dazed, she lay there, telling herself she'd move in a moment, when she gathered strength to stand. Staring up, she realised the stars on the ceiling weren't some painted, regular pattern. They sparkled like gemstones, and instead of being in neat rows, they were scattered across the vast space in what she realised now was a star map showing constellations she'd seen in the night sky.

The sight distracted her. That someone had taken the time to create a virtual starry night especially for their sheikh was amazing. And that they'd done it with…no, surely they weren't real gems…

That thought brought her back with a thud to reality. Naked and ravished to within an inch of her sanity by Salim, her body gently throbbing from his possession. No wonder she was grinning again.

Except Salim wasn't simply the man she'd yearned for. He was trouble. A client. A king. Surrounded by watchers and commentators. A man who could snap his fingers and have whichever woman he wanted.

What had she been to him?

Rosanna wanted to believe she was more to him than an afternoon's indulgence, but that would be a problem of monumental proportions. Neither of them was suited to an affair. Salim because he was searching for a wife. Rosanna because she wasn't into short-term flings. This was her first. A liaison had the potential to wreck her mission here and through that both her reputation and her aunt's business.

She snatched in a sharp breath that caught between her ribs. She catapulted off the bed then paused a moment, knees trembling and heart pounding, but she couldn't afford to linger. Hurriedly she stumbled forward, snatching up her crumpled dress. A puddle of gleaming anthracite grey silk caught her eye and she lunged for her underwear near the foot of the bed.

Where was her bra? And her shoes? Had they been kicked under the bed?

She was hunched over looking for them when warm fingers shackled her wrist. Instantly she froze.

'Not so fast, Rosanna. Where do you think you're going?'

Slowly she straightened, her pulse quick and high in her throat. Excitement stirred but she struggled to fight it, knowing she couldn't afford to be dazzled again by carnal enticement.

Rosanna turned and there he was, looking even bigger, more handsome and imposing than when he was fully dressed.

She fought the urge to forget common sense and lean against him so he could gather her close. She wanted the comfort of Salim's body wrapped around hers so she could ignore for a little longer the harsh realities that faced her.

'I'm going to my room, after I find all my clothes.'

His raised eyebrows told her he hadn't expected that. 'You think you can just walk away?'

That superior stare cut through her dazed thoughts. It was a timely reminder that her exciting, wonderful lover was an autocratic ruler, used to having everything he wanted.

Including women?

The idea dimmed Rosanna's lingering joy. He'd convinced her that he too had been affected by their meeting in Scotland. That he'd been fighting their attraction.

Yet how well did she really know him? Her track record with men was terrible. She'd trusted Phil and planned a future with him but he'd turned out to be nothing like the man she'd believed him. He'd made a mockery of her vaunted skills at sizing people up.

Rosanna swallowed hard. Maybe, despite what Salim had said, she'd just been convenient.

She straightened, tossing her hair over her shoulder, trying to ignore the fact they were both naked and that her traitorous body was stimulated by having him so close. She tugged at his hold but he didn't let go.

'Of course I can walk away if I choose. I'm not your possession. I'm not here for your convenience. If I want to leave that's my choice.'

Her stare dared him to disagree.

Salim released her and held up his hands, palms towards her as if emphasising that she was free.

The trouble was she didn't feel free. She felt bound to this man in ways she couldn't even begin to name.

'If you go, where will that leave us? With nothing resolved, that's where.' He paused as if to ensure she took in every word. 'You still want me, Rosanna. I know you do. And this cuts both ways. I want you too. What we shared has only increased the wanting.'

Her pulse hammered faster, her breathing turning fast and shallow. Salim felt the same. Stupid to feel pleased but she did.

'If you walk away now we'll still have the same problem. We can't keep our hands off each other even though this is the last thing either of us wants.'

Well, that was her told. Rosanna's pleasure dimmed.

Maybe her hurt showed for his expression softened. 'Come, sit with me. We need to talk.'

He bent to reach for his discarded clothes and Rosanna's tongue stuck to the roof of her mouth as she watched the mesmerising movement of his honed body.

He held out his shirt to her. She took it in stiff fingers, watching as he yanked on his trousers, not bothering to do up the top button, then sat on the side of the bed and patted the mattress beside him.

Rosanna breathed deep, drawing in the scent of exotic spices, of lemon soap, warm male flesh and sex. It was a heady mix, so heady she knew he was right. He was impossible to resist. This attraction was too strong and she had no idea how to fight it.

Even if she wanted to.

Her dress dropped to the floor as she put his shirt on, doing it up with trembling fingers then rolling up the sleeves. It covered her yet she was supremely aware of her nakedness beneath the fine cotton. Strange that after what they'd just done together, she felt overwhelmed by the intimacy of wearing his clothes.

Carefully she sat beside him, striving to keep her gaze off his bare torso.

Salim nodded encouragingly. 'This has crept up on us both. The connection, the desire, and it's so strong it feels unstoppable.'

Rosanna was taken aback by his frankness. She was simultaneously gladdened and scared because if they were both weak in the face of this attraction, where did that leave them?

She wasn't naïve enough to believe this could end with flowers and promises of happy ever after. She and Salim came from different worlds with different expectations. Their paths would only cross for a brief time.

She could never be the sort of woman he needed and

even in her wildest dreams she couldn't imagine living in a grand palace. Yet the thought of walking away from Salim tore at something vital inside her.

Rosanna had a job to do but this, between them, was a devastating roadblock.

'I tried to resist,' he continued. 'But keeping my distance and throwing up barriers didn't make a difference. Nor did the fact that you've been the epitome of efficiency and productivity. It made me wonder if you were trying to distract yourself from us too.'

The way he said that one syllable, *us*, with a deep scrape of his baritone, sent a shiver of longing through her.

He twisted towards her and suddenly he was touching her, the lightest of caresses, a single finger stroking the underside of her forearm, yet Rosanna felt it like an earthquake, shattering the foundations of her world. She trembled, her nipples puckering towards him and a ribbon of heat swirling through her core. Her lips parted and she had to stop herself from leaning closer.

'I don't think either of those tactics will work again, do you?' His voice was soft, sneaking beneath her tattered defences and winding around her heart. 'Even if you're superefficient and focused and I try to avoid you or treat you like a stranger, the truth between us is too big. We've let the genie out of the bottle and there's no way to push it back inside and pretend it doesn't exist.'

That light touch skimmed down to her hand, circled her wrist then slipped across her palm and a great shudder of longing racked her. Just that tiny caress and she needed him. She swayed towards him then caught herself and sat straighter, yet she didn't have the strength to pull away.

'So,' she finally managed in a voice turned uneven with emotion, 'if we can't go back to being strangers, how do we go forward?'

Salim's hand closed around hers and he nodded, a half-smile forming on his face. 'I like that you don't waste time in pointless argument,' he said. 'That you're always looking ahead to what needs to be done.'

It was the sort of accolade Rosanna was used to hearing on a professional front. It was something that had stood her in good stead in the commercial world. Now though, Salim's compliment felt personal.

It made her realise how much she craved positive reinforcement, after the tough time she'd had back home in Australia. Her family had said she'd taken on too much personal blame for events she couldn't have prevented. She didn't agree. But maybe she'd been too hard on herself since such a simple compliment felt so important.

'Thank you. And I like the fact *you* don't prevaricate. You say what you're thinking.'

Even though his straight talking sometimes tested her patience, like when he found fault with every one of the women she'd brought to Dhalkur.

But how would she have coped if he'd taken a shine to one of them? Rosanna tried to imagine herself watching him woo and possibly seduce another woman and her stomach tied itself in knots. Something sharp jabbed her chest, twisting deep, and she had a horrible feeling it was jealousy. For something that hadn't even happened!

'So you want me to be straight with you?'

'Of course.' This was no time for guessing games.

Salim nodded. 'We can't go back to the way we were and the way we are now—' his hand tightened on hers '—isn't sustainable long-term. Agreed?'

'Agreed.'

Because if this relationship continued long-term it would make Rosanna his mistress. The idea was anathema to her. She had no desire to be a convenient lover on the side, especially when he married. Rosanna respected marriage vows and hoped one day to find the right man with whom to spend the rest of her life.

She'd thought Phil was that man. Her disillusionment at her mistake had put her off dating ever since.

'Then I can think of only one solution. We become lovers for a short time.'

Salim's thumb stroked across her wrist and onto her palm, creating ripples of erotic delight that made her breath stall. Or was it the idea of being his lover?

'How will that make a difference? It would just complicate things.'

Nausea churned in her stomach. She couldn't imagine working daily to find his perfect spouse then spending each night in his bed.

'We'd have to put your work on hold. It wouldn't feel right, continuing that while we shared a bed.'

Rosanna looked into his sternly sculpted face and felt relief flutter through her with each heartbeat. Relief and enthusiasm at the idea of them as lovers.

She'd wondered if he shared her scruples. It was good to hear that he did. The thought of finding him his perfect match while they were intimate had a distasteful edge to it. As if she really were some disposable mistress and what they shared meant nothing to him.

'I'm glad you feel that way. I couldn't do this—' she gestured to the lavish bed '—and be your matchmaker at the same time.'

Strange that it hadn't even occurred to her to say no to becoming his lover. But Rosanna wasn't into self-delusion. She couldn't turn her back on this, no matter how she tried. He was right, the genie was well and truly out of the bottle. How much harder would it be, being around him, trying to work, when all the time her thoughts were veering to sex?

'It would be wrong to ask that of you. I've already found it too tough trying to do justice to the women you've brought forward while my thoughts are focused on you. It feels deceitful both to them and you.'

Rosanna put her hand over where he held hers. 'Thank you, Salim. I've been tying myself in knots over this. It's a relief to know you have the same concerns.'

Their eyes met and something powerful passed between them. Understanding. Relief. Respect. All that and more.

Slowly his taut features eased into a hint of a smile that sent warmth easing through her. 'So we're agreed. Now we just need to do something about it.'

Rosanna didn't miss the eager glint in his eyes. 'But I don't see how an affair will solve our problem.'

'It's the only solution. We have a short, intense affair and this attraction will burn itself out.'

'But will it? How do you know?'

He tilted his head as if to read her expression better. 'It's what always happens with an affair. Passion and fun and pleasure, then it fades and we move on.'

'Really?'

'Of course. Surely you've found the same.'

Rosanna thought of not answering but this was too important. Besides, it wasn't anything to be ashamed of. 'I've never had an affair before so I don't know.'

Shock showed in those dark eyes and his hand tightened reflexively around hers. 'But you weren't a virgin.'

It was a statement, yet she heard the echo of a question there.

She shook her head. 'No, but I was in a long-term relationship. I'd planned to marry and in the meantime…' She shrugged.

There was silence for a moment. 'So you've only been with one man before me?'

Salim looked so serious, so surprised, almost as if he'd never heard of such a thing, that Rosanna fought a smile. 'What can I say? I've always been more interested in finding a man I can love rather than someone for a short fling. It's not a crime, you know.'

He blinked and sat straighter as if suddenly realising how close he'd leaned towards her. 'Of course not. I admire you.'

'But that's not your experience.'

'Searching for love? Never. Until now sex without commitment has been enough for me.'

Well, she'd wanted honesty. Rosanna opened her mouth to ask if he expected love to grow in his marriage, then thought better of it.

'And from your considerable experience, you believe that if we have an affair, this—' she waved her hand in an encompassing gesture '—will burn itself out?'

Perhaps she was naïve but it didn't feel like something that would disappear fast. But then she was a novice, she had discovered, to such extreme sexual pleasure. She'd have to rely on Salim's expertise.

'Definitely.'

He sounded absolutely certain. That was a relief, though a tiny part of her almost regretted it.

'Good. That's good to know.'

'You don't sound convinced.'

She shrugged and looked away. 'You're right that we need to move on. But at the same time I rather liked…'

'Oh, so did I, Rosanna.' His voice ground to a rough note that ran through her middle like suede brushing sensitive skin, making her quiver. When he spoke again there was a hint of amusement as well as a definite promise in his tone. 'But don't worry. There will be plenty more pleasure before we're finished, I can absolutely promise that.'

Her head snapped around and their eyes met. What she saw in his expression made her chest grow tight and her body soften.

Rosanna swallowed hard, trying to appear calm despite the heat flushing her cheeks and the suddenly altered atmosphere. Was it a new scent in the air? A thickening weight to the momentary silence? Or the burgeoning excitement through her whole nervous system as she fought not to lean into him and offer her lips to his. She was aware of the air caressing her skin with each breath she took, of the sensitivity in her breasts, belly and lower still that spoke of arousal.

It wasn't just a kiss she wanted. Sitting half-naked next to Salim was torture. She wanted to touch him. Wanted that powerful body moving with hers, the sound of his breathing hoarse in her ear as he came, and took her with him into ecstasy.

'You're doing it again,' he growled.

'Doing what?'

'Looking at me the way you did before. Like you want me to ravish you.'

Yes, please.

But she didn't say it, because her mouth had turned desert dry at the gleam in his dark eyes.

'How long will it take?'

'Sorry?' He looked startled and she couldn't blame him. Dragging her mind back to the thread of their conversation was almost impossible.

'This affair. How long till we can…conquer this?'

'Ah. The time frame for our affair.' Did he move closer or did she imagine it? 'I'd like to say a month but I don't have much time available. What we need is to be together day and night, sating ourselves. A stolen hour here or there just won't do it.'

Rosanna took a slow breath and nodded, trying not to look shocked at the prospect of *sating themselves*. It sounded decadent and intoxicatingly tempting.

'I suggest a week.' His eyes held hers as if daring her to disagree. 'A week where we'd be totally alone.'

Rosanna couldn't help it, she shivered in pleasure at the prospect.

What was happening to her? This was totally outside her realm of experience, yet instead of being shocked or hesitant, she couldn't wait.

Rosanna moistened her dry mouth with her tongue. 'When?'

Salim's attention lifted from her lips and she was thrilled to read arousal in his hooded eyes.

'As soon as I can manage it. I'll get Taqi onto it straight away. It will take a little time to reschedule everything and clear my diary so we can go away together.'

'We're going away?'

'Definitely. We want absolute privacy for what I have in mind. Only one or two people whom I trust absolutely will be aware that we're together. That way we can protect your reputation and not give rise to gossip.' He paused. 'Does that sound okay?'

More than okay. The fact that he wasn't just considering the need to slake his desire, but aiming to protect her privacy, meant a lot.

In many ways Salim had the qualities Rosanna appreciated in a man. He was thoughtful as well as decisive and he cared about others. From what she'd gathered his decision to choose a bride was prompted by the need to allay others' fears over the lack of an heir. He took his responsibilities seriously.

'You think it will solve our problem?'

'I do.'

'Then,' she admitted, 'I think it's a great idea.'

The only difficulty would be trying to keep up the appearance of professionalism in the meantime.

'Excellent.'

He looked like a man who'd just sealed a great deal.

Suddenly Rosanna felt uncomfortable, sitting here, calculating how to have an affair. She wanted it yet at the same time she felt…

What do you expect? To be swept into his arms as if the world didn't matter? To be wooed with promises of happy ever after?

Instantly a metal wall clanged down in her brain.

No more false promises. No more hazy romantic daydreams. This was the real world.

She slipped her hands from Salim's and wrenched her gaze away too. She found herself looking down at her bright blue dress, discarded on the floor. She still had to find a way back to her room without anyone seeing her looking as if—

'It's time I left. I'll get my clothes and go.'

As she watched a large hand covered hers. 'Soon. But there's something we need to do first.'

'What's that?'

Rosanna made the mistake of looking up. Her pulse stuttered as she read the heat in Salim's expression and the curling smile on his lips.

'We need to seal our deal.' He paused, then lifted her hand, skimming his lips over her knuckles and watching as she tried and failed not to quiver. 'After all, it could be days and days, not to mention long nights, before we're alone again, Rosanna. I think we deserve a little indulgence now to keep us going. Don't you?'

Salim leaned close, one hand on her shoulder, and she found herself lying on the bed looking up into that hard, handsome face, all thoughts of leaving disintegrating.

Beyond him a shaft of dying daylight hit a constellation of stars on that beautiful, indigo ceiling. A reminder that she was totally out of her depth, playing dangerous games with a powerful royal in a world she didn't fully understand.

But none of that mattered as Salim undid the buttons on the shirt that covered her and straddled her hips. When his mouth found hers Rosanna sighed and clutched him close. Time enough to worry about it all later.

CHAPTER NINE

'HE'S A DIFFICULT client then,' Marian mused.

'Hmm.'

Rosanna's reply was noncommittal as she shifted on the seat of the rose-covered arbour in what she thought of as her private courtyard. The warmth of the day lingered, producing a honey-rich scent that urged her already relaxed muscles towards torpor.

A day after that life-altering afternoon in Salim's private rooms and she still felt the aftereffects. She'd gone there impatient at his determination to find fault. But after his confession that *she* was the reason he couldn't focus on the beautiful women brought before him, it was hard to remain angry.

'You don't think he's difficult?' Marion sounded surprised.

'He certainly knows what he doesn't want,' Rosanna said carefully. 'But as well as choosing a life partner he's picking a consort. She will have to be someone quite special to fulfil those royal duties.'

The more Rosanna saw of Salim's work and responsibilities the more she appreciated he had to choose wisely. Especially with the country's traditionalists trying to direct his choice.

For the first time she found herself feeling sorry for those born royal. He couldn't simply choose for himself.

'That's a relief,' Marian interrupted her thoughts. 'I was afraid you might feel overwhelmed by the task. Not because you're not up to it,' she hurried to explain. 'But because it was always going to be difficult.'

'You knew that? Why didn't you warn me?'

Rosanna thought of the hours she'd spent second-guessing herself, wondering how she could have done better.

'I didn't want to scare you. Especially as it was your first solo effort since I'm still stuck here. I've only done one royal match but I remember how tough it was. It wasn't just the bridegroom who had to be satisfied but his family and any number of powerbrokers in the kingdom.'

'I'm sure Salim will make the final decision.'

'Salim? You're on first-name terms? That's a good sign.'

Rosanna was grateful her aunt couldn't see the guilty heat climbing her cheeks.

She thought of what she'd been doing this time yesterday in Salim's bed and had to draw a calming breath. He'd led her back to her room via a private passage, one that went directly from his suite to the cluster of apartments in what he'd informed her used to be the harem.

She'd been both horrified and thrilled at being led along a route made solely to give the ruler easy access to the women's quarters. She was thankful it saved her from being seen by palace employees in her crumpled clothes. But it reinforced the disparity in power that had always existed between the sheikh and his lovers.

Now she was one of them.

She was torn between illicit excitement and dismay. That hadn't stopped her disappointment when he'd led her to her room, kissed her hand in a courtly gesture of dismissal and disappeared the way they'd come. She'd hoped he'd make love to her again and through the night she'd found herself looking at the concealed door, wondering if it might open and he'd come to her.

The fact that he hadn't had made Rosanna wonder, once more, if he needed her as much as she needed him. When she'd agreed to an affair she'd felt empowered. Yet now she felt uncharacteristically unsure.

She grimaced. Her experience with Phil had knocked her confidence more than she'd thought. Either that or this attraction to Salim was more powerful than she'd imagined.

'Rose?'

She gathered her scrambled wits. 'He's only formal in public. But it doesn't make him any easier to please.'

That was a downright lie, she realised. Sexually they were very attuned indeed and she'd pleased him very easily.

'Sheikh Salim has to be particularly careful in his choice. My sources tell me the country was troubled while his brother governed for their ill father. There were whispers of power abuses and shady dealings. The country even came close to war with its neighbour Nahrat until the Nahrati king married Sheikh Salim's cousin.'

'I didn't know that.' Rosanna had heard about the previous king and his elder son who'd acted as regent when he became ill but not much more.

'Ah well, I have my sources.'

She sure did. Marian's insider knowledge of the rich and famous was second to none.

'And those sources tell you there's pressure on Sheikh Salim?'

Strange how protective that made her feel. As if she could do anything to protect Salim!

'Absolutely. He's trying to get the country back on track after the damage his brother did. That would be part of the reason he needs a wife with no scandal in her past. He'll also need a woman who can hold her own in a traditional country as it modernises.'

Rosanna's curiosity about Salim's brother grew. The man was dead but his shadow lingered. It wasn't in her remit but Rosanna couldn't help wondering how Salim's odious brother had affected him personally. The man she knew was capable, focused and at times arrogant but he seemed remarkably level-headed.

'Now,' Marian said. 'Run me through his preferences again so we can consider how to broaden our field.'

Rosanna moistened her lips, her self-consciousness growing. 'Salim is planning a break. He's going to take a week off and doesn't want to be bothered with matchmaking during that time.'

He'd been adamant that while they were together he didn't want even to think about other women and that suited her completely. She paused, trying to still the telltale wobble inside. Her aunt was a clever woman and would grow curious if Rosanna sounded nervous. 'I thought I'd take a few days off at the same time. See something outside the palace.'

Rosanna held her breath. She had a wonderful relationship with Marian and part of her yearned to confide in her and seek her advice. Except she feared she knew what Marian would advise. That she leave Dhalkur and Salim immediately. No matter how much she loved and respected her aunt, Rosanna couldn't do that. Not yet. Not while she felt this way about Salim.

'Excellent. A short break will do you good. But all the more reason to review our progress now.'

For Salim the days since that afternoon with Rosanna dragged.

Because he'd made himself keep his distance, knowing that if he didn't there'd be no keeping the secret of their liaison. While his reputation wouldn't be affected, he didn't want her embarrassed.

So that afternoon, against every personal inclination,

he'd led her to her room then left, despite the shimmering invitation in her eyes.

He hadn't seen her since.

That had taken more determination, more stoicism in the face of physical discomfort, than his whole year of military service. He was on fire with wanting her. His body grew more taut and cramped by the day as his unrelieved tension built.

He'd known it would be impossible to take a break immediately. A royal schedule wasn't easily cleared. But his patience wore thin as the days passed, each seeming longer than the last. The nights longer still.

Usually he had so much to do that the days were too short. Before he'd become sheikh he'd kept a hectic schedule, seeking out and developing international partnerships that could benefit his country. He'd been away on one such mission when his father took ill.

Since taking the throne he'd been busy, not merely with the normal business of the country, but undoing the morass his brother, Fuad, had made of the public finances and taking steps towards the changes he wanted to make.

Which meant every day was packed with meetings, paperwork, consultations and public events.

Yet now they dragged.

Had his father ever felt like this? Strung too tight and distracted because of a woman? It was hard to imagine.

Salim missed the old man. They hadn't always seen eye to eye. His father had been cautious about many innovations Salim wanted to pursue, but he'd been a decent, dedicated man.

He'd have appreciated his father's perspective right now.

Grimly Salim laughed and opened the last document before him. His father wouldn't approve of his son making time for an affair with a foreigner when he should be choosing a spouse. His father had been a great one for ensuring the stability of the nation. Even Salim, who had no desire for a wife, knew it was imperative that he marry and start a family. He'd seen how dangerous instability could be and understood the mood of his people.

But the thought of wife-hunting made him feel sick in the gut. The only woman he could think of was Rosanna.

He glanced towards the window. The sun would be up soon and he wanted to finish his work before taking Rosanna to their secret rendezvous.

His pulse quickened as anticipation stirred.

Finally they could be alone. A whole week with her beckoned. He couldn't recall ever feeling such elation at the prospect of being with a woman.

Maybe the anticipation was heightened because these days he was so hemmed in by court traditions and royal rules. Because he was no longer a private citizen.

Yet ever since the night he'd met Rosanna something had felt different.

Salim shoved aside such notions and read through the document to appoint a High Court judge. He signed with a flourish then added it to the pile.

As he sat back and rolled his stiff shoulders, he caught the first glimmer of grey lightening the eastern sky. A smile broke across his face. It was time.

Rosanna hunched into her jacket as the four-wheel drive sped along the highway, grateful that she'd known enough to understand that a desert could get cold at night.

Not that it was cold in the air-conditioned vehicle, yet her skin prickled as if from the dawn chill.

'You're warm enough?'

Salim didn't take his eyes off the road but he was attuned to her. Rosanna didn't know whether to be pleased or disturbed by that.

'I'm fine. Besides, it will be warm when the sun's up.'

'True, but not as warm where we're going as in the city.'

She nodded, hoping the casual clothes she'd packed would be suitable.

Who was she fooling? The way Salim had looked at her as he invited her into the vehicle made her wonder how often she'd get to wear clothes at all. His dark eyes had been as black as ebony. Just as when he'd made love to her. Despite the morning chill she'd felt distinctly overdressed. And delighted.

Rosanna focused on the road rather than the man beside her. For the first time since they'd met she felt close to being tongue-tied. That worried her. He might be a king but she was her own woman. She couldn't afford to be cowed by Salim. He already dazzled her too much.

'It's glorious here.' She swallowed, her throat dry. 'The mountains look wonderful in this light.'

The dawn light painted the peaks in a wash of gold turning to apricot, the deep clefts a dark indigo that made her think of the beautiful ceiling above his bed.

Her mouth lifted in a crooked smile. Clearly she had a one-track mind around Salim.

'I'm glad you think so. Dawn and dusk are my favourite times in the desert.'

'You come here often?' There was a moment's silence then they both laughed. 'That sounded so stilted. I'm not sure why when I'm interested in the answer.'

Salim lifted one hand from the wheel and placed it briefly on her denim-covered thigh. Instantly heat radiated from his touch and she shivered at the delicious sensations.

'I know why. You're nervous.' Rosanna frowned, about to deny it, when he added, 'So am I.'

'You are?' She forgot her determination not to watch him and twisted in her seat, taking in his proud profile as he put his hand back on the steering wheel. 'What have you got to be nervous about?'

He was the one with all the experience. She was the novice when it came to an affair.

He knew the place they were going. They were in his territory. She was the outsider.

More, he looked the epitome of calm control. Just as he did whenever they met in his office or at some function.

Salim shrugged and for the first time she registered that the movement didn't have its usual fluid ease. As if his shoulders were stiff.

'That you'll change your mind about this. Why do you think I'm breaking the speed limit to get there?'

His voice was light yet there was something about it that sounded like truth.

She glanced at the speedometer. 'You're not speeding.'

He shot her a smile that undid her and left her glad she was sitting down. She knew her legs wouldn't support her after that loaded grin.

'Not now because we're turning off the tarmac.'

On the words, he slowed and took a fork onto a gravel road that wound around a low hill. There was no evidence of a town ahead, not even a signpost marking the road.

'Where, exactly, are we going?' She'd imagined everything from a nomad tent to a vast, modern home. 'Wherever it is,' she said as the vehicle bumped over a dry gully, 'it doesn't look like they encourage visitors.'

'We don't.'

He sounded smug.

'We?'

'The royal family. This is our private road. Only the locals and our security staff know about it. It's not on any maps.'

'And it takes us where?'

The mountains ahead looked wild. Maybe they were going to camp in a cave. Though that didn't seem a good venue for a week of decadence.

'Up there.'

She followed his pointing hand towards the foothills of the mountain range. Tucked in the curve of a ridge, perched above a ravine, she saw a blob of pale pink. As they drove closer she made out straight lines and realised it was a building, though it seemed to grow from the natural rock.

'What is it? It's too big for a house.'

'It's the Queen's Palace and it is, actually, a house, albeit a fortified one. Don't worry, it's comfortable. The royal family has been using it as a private bolthole for generations.' He paused. 'I've known the caretakers all my life. They're utterly discreet so you don't have to worry about news of your presence leaking out. They won't come inside unless we send for them. We can be utterly private.'

There it was again, that note of complacency in his deep voice. Rosanna was glad they'd be alone. That's what she craved. Yet she couldn't prevent that tiny tremble of nerves.

She wanted to be with Salim. There was no question of that but she wondered if this scheme would cure her infatuation. What if an affair only cemented it? Strengthened it into something more than lust?

The thought scared her into speech. She didn't care if she was babbling, she had to break the silence and her thoughts.

'But it's pink. Is that because it was designed for a queen? It doesn't look like a place a sheikh would choose for a getaway.'

A chuckle rolled across her skin and loosened her clenched muscles. 'You think it's not macho enough for fearsome desert kings?' He shook his head. 'It's made of pink granite, one of the strongest local materials, and I can tell you it withstood at least one siege. But over time it was redesigned from a fortress to a private retreat. It's known as the Queen's Palace and the royal family comes here for pleasure.'

Did she imagine the way his voice dropped on the word

pleasure? Or the connection between pleasure and the sheikh's consort?

It seemed to Rosanna that all those dry reference texts describing the power wielded by hereditary Dhalkuri sheikhs should include a note specifically about them as dangerous seducers.

Salim only had to drop his voice to that baritone rumble, or unleash a sexy chuckle, and she turned to mush.

How would she fare after a week in his company?

She told herself she was doing the right thing. That at the end of their week they could move on. Besides, what alternative did she have?

Half an hour later Rosanna stood in the most beautiful bedroom she'd ever seen.

It was airy and spacious and it felt so welcoming. Like a hug embracing her as she entered.

The walls were pale, except for the one behind the canopied bed which was painted with a gorgeous mural of a garden, complete with trellises, fountains, arbours and butterflies flitting between flowers. The furniture looked comfortable and inviting with plenty of plump cushions.

She could imagine herself curled up on that vast divan with the amber-and-gold throw, reading a book or looking out onto the internal courtyard garden. There were beautiful rugs, the sort for which Dhalkur was famous, in shades ranging from cinnamon to amber, dusky rose and dark garnet red.

Along one wall, tall arched windows gave out onto a broad terrace edged with crenellations beyond which, far below, stretched the vast southern plain of Dhalkur and the capital, a blue smudge in the distance.

The scent of roses was everywhere, from the potted plants on the terrace to the embossed gilt bowls in the room, filled with blooms of every shade.

Through an open doorway she spied a vast, sunken tub

in a bathroom that glowed in the early light with shades of amber, gold and mother-of-pearl.

'I've died and gone to heaven,' Rosanna murmured as she stepped inside, her hand automatically reaching for a bowl of perfect roses, some of which, she realised, still held beads of dew. She inhaled, shutting her eyes against a sudden overload of joy.

She'd agreed to a week of sex with Salim. They could have gone to another city, or left the country for an anonymous hotel. Instead he'd brought her somewhere so romantic she had trouble swallowing over the lump rising in her throat.

Over the past four days she'd alternated between exhilaration and a nagging fear that this attraction wasn't as significant for him as it was for her. He'd proven her wrong, bringing her to a place that was clearly special to his family. That showed a level of respect and thoughtfulness that banished her doubts and created an overwhelming surge of emotion.

His thoughtfulness made her feel special. As if she mattered to him.

At the same time she felt more vulnerable than ever. She wrapped her arms around her middle, trying to hold back her swelling emotions.

'I'm glad you like it.'

Salim's voice came from just behind her, making her shiver as his voice hit that rumbling note that never failed to soften her feminine core and scramble her wits.

He stood close. She felt his breath feather her hair and his body heat against her back. Just that was enough to make her breasts feel fuller and damp heat form between her thighs.

Rosanna snapped her eyes open and focused on the beautiful room, rather than the urge to swing around, plaster herself against him and beg for him to take her.

'It's very special. It radiates welcome and wellbeing.'

And Romance with a capital *R*, but she didn't mention that. Because it would be dangerous thinking of Salim and romance together.

This was about lust, she told herself firmly. It was a pragmatic choice to scratch a physical itch and get it out of their systems. She couldn't afford to weave any other fantasies about Salim.

Rosanna blinked, horrified to discover that from joy her emotions had swung abruptly to distress.

'Would you like tea after our journey? Or breakfast? You must be hungry.'

She should be. They'd left so early that she hadn't eaten. Presumably their early start had been to avoid being seen together.

Rosanna pressed a hand to her suddenly churning stomach. She wasn't used to the idea of a secret relationship. As if it, or she, were shameful. 'No thanks, I'm fine.'

Silence. Was it imagination or did her skin tighten as she waited for Salim to speak?

'Perhaps you need to rest. We had a very early start.'

'No!' The word was out before she realised she'd formed it. 'I'm perfectly fine and wide awake.'

Still he didn't touch her. Why?

Because he's giving you the courtesy of time and space to adjust. Because he's a decent man who won't pounce on you the moment you're alone together.

Rosanna swallowed, her throat aching with tension. 'There *is* something I want.'

'Yes?'

She felt him move closer, his body mirroring hers, his breath tickling her ear.

'Make love to me, Salim.'

CHAPTER TEN

It was exactly what he planned to do. Yet Rosanna's words were a cold blast to his overheated libido.

Make love, she'd said, and for a second he'd been in total agreement. Till he read the nuance of her words.

He'd brought her here because it was one of his favourite places, plus it was close enough to the city that he could return quickly in an emergency.

He'd given instructions that the place be prepared for them and he'd enjoyed planning to please Rosanna. He'd instructed that the suite be filled with roses because he thought she'd enjoy them, and because they reminded him of her. Her skin was as velvety as any damask petal and as fragrant. She could be thorny too but at heart there was a honeyed sweetness that was irresistible.

Yet, now they were here, he realised how she might misinterpret things. He planned a sybaritic week of sex and relaxation. What he'd given her was a romantic bower.

Worse, though she had no way of knowing, he realised it had never been a place where sheikhs dallied with passing lovers. It had been transformed into a special place by one ruler for the queen he loved. Only queens and their families stayed here.

Yet how could he hold back from Rosanna? He'd already lashed his arm around her waist and hauled her back against him.

He breathed deep, trying to summon restraint. The whole drive here he'd fought a hard-on that had made driving a chore and tested his patience to the limit.

Salim bent his head and used his free hand to drag her hair out of the way so he could nip at her neck. She shuddered in response, her head lolling to one side in invitation.

He loved her eager passion. Rosanna might be a feisty woman and in business matters a formidable negotiator, but when it came to intimacy her instant responsiveness was everything he could want.

Yet he hesitated to take her to the bed which, he realised now, was strewn with blush-pink petals.

Because this wasn't the beginning of some sweet romance that would end with a happy ever after. He didn't want her misinterpreting.

He needed to dispel that fantasy, though he had no intention of giving up Rosanna and all the pleasure they would share over the next week. On the contrary, he intended to use them both to the limit and squeeze every possible erotic pleasure from the time they had. Because he already knew a week would barely be time to take his fill of this remarkable woman.

She moved, her backside swaying from side to side as if inviting him to take her, and fire shot through his groin.

Salim licked her earlobe then nipped there, harder than before, and she gasped, her hands grabbing his encircling arm. She was as turned on as he.

'Is this what you want?' he whispered against her ear as he shoved his other hand between her legs, cupping her mound hard through her jeans.

'Yes.' Her response was a raw groan that lifted the hairs at his nape and made his jeans grow uncomfortable.

A taut smile dragged at his facial muscles as he widened his stance to take her weight a little more. In the process he caught sight of their reflection in the mirrored wall of the bathroom through the open doorway and his pulse stopped. He saw Rosanna, head back against his chest, eyes closed in an expression of bliss, gasping in pleasure as he rubbed his hand between her legs.

'More. Please, Salim.'

'As you wish, my rose.'

Still keeping one arm wrapped around her middle, he flicked open the button of her jeans, then dragged down the zip. He tugged at the denim and it slid down but snagged on her hips. 'Help me.'

She lifted her hands from his arm and shoved her jeans down.

'Now the rest,' he murmured, inserting a finger through the side elastic of her underwear. She grabbed the other side and together they slid the lacy triangle down.

Salim's chest tightened around his snared breath. She still wore her plain white shirt, not some diaphanous lingerie. Yet the sight of her bare, sweetly curving hips and that glossy dark swatch of pubic hair cupped between her slender legs was one of the most arousing sights he'd beheld.

He swallowed, fighting the impulse to rip his own jeans off and power into her without any preliminaries. He owed her more than that.

Her eyes fluttered open and he caught a dazed silvery gleam as she frowned and made to turn towards him. 'Salim?'

'No. Stay like that.'

He cupped her again, this time with no constraining fabric between them and felt her feminine heat, the tickle of soft hair and a dampness that made him smile. Rosanna shuddered, her eyes drifting shut as he slid his hand lower, curving back between her now open thighs. She shifted against him, allowing him access, and once again gripped his supporting arm with both hands.

'Easy, sweetheart.'

Though even as he said it he realised there was no need to wait. No reason at all. Hard and fast would be some consolation after the tortured loneliness of his empty bed. And it might help dispel any misunderstanding about this being a romantic tryst.

Salim pulled her closer so Rosanna leaned back against him as he slipped his hand again between her legs, into that cleft where he found her sensitive bud. She jolted and pressed against him as he slid into her wetness, probing gently.

Rosanna's hips moved in a telltale twist of need as his fingers slid further, deeper.

'You like that, Rosanna?' he whispered in her ear.

He could tell from every movement of her body, and by her desperate expression in the mirror, that she was close. Maybe she'd been as aroused as he on the trip here, anticipating the moment when they came together again.

She might have read his mind. 'Yes. But I want more.'

This time, instead of leaning into his hand she tilted her pelvis back, grinding her buttocks against him, drawing all the blood in his body to his rock-hard erection.

It would be the work of a moment to strip free of his jeans and plunge into her. Except he wanted more too. He wanted her absolutely frantic for him.

So Salim gritted his jaw and dragged the arm at her waist higher so he could cup one luscious breast while sliding his other hand along the slick track of delight between her soft thighs.

Her legs trembled. Her breathing turned to a series of gasps as her head lolled back against him. Salim read the signs of approaching orgasm. Her jerky movements, the rush of moisture against his hand, the musky perfume of female arousal. He bit down at the base of her neck where she was so sensitive.

Rosanna's whole body shuddered. He felt her convulsions from his buried fingertips right down to the soles of his feet as she fell into ecstasy, calling his name. He'd never heard anything so heartfelt, so mesmerising.

And through it all he watched her in the mirror and felt something stronger than satisfaction. It felt much darker than gratification that he'd given a lover pleasure. It felt like possessiveness.

Which was nonsense. It was just a masculine response to the delicious sight of Rosanna in the throes of bliss.

Yet he battled the feeling that this was more than simple sex. She captivated him.

It was just that the wait to claim his lover again had been too long. He wasn't used to waiting for any woman. His liaisons in the past had been much less complicated. The illusion would pass once he'd reached his own climax.

Rosanna was still shaking when he slipped his hand into his back pocket and drew out a condom.

'Here, lean against this.'

His voice was guttural with repressed need as he gently moved Rosanna sideways so she could grasp the back of a high sofa. As soon as he knew she could support herself he undid his jeans and sheathed himself. Even that practised movement was fraught with danger. He was so aroused he feared he mightn't last.

So instead of lifting Rosanna over onto the sofa, he moved behind her, bending his knees and positioning himself at the centre of her feminine heat.

Any fear that she'd had enough after that orgasm faded as she shimmied her hips, drawing up higher to accommodate him more easily. There, he nudged her entrance and lightning jagged through him.

'Ready?'

For answer she pushed her rump towards him, enclosing him in damp heat.

That was it. Salim couldn't wait. He grabbed her hips and thrust long and true, on and on, right to her heart.

The sensation of her tight, wet heat folding around him like a closing fist sent a tremor of raw excitement down his spine and through his groin.

'Yes,' he hissed, barely able to hear the word over the pounding in his ears. She felt so good he had to wait, gather his control, before moving again.

But Rosanna was moving. He opened his eyes and saw her wrenching open her shirt buttons, then struggling free of the fabric. She leaned forward enough to slip a hand between them and flick her bra undone. A second later it was gone too and in the mirror he saw her pink-crested breasts bob free.

Salim swallowed a groan. He wasn't going to last long enough to enjoy this as he wanted.

Then she grabbed one of his hands, tugging it free of her hip, and dragged it up her body, planting it with a breathless sigh on her breast.

Yes, that was better. So much better that Salim's thighs were rock hard with the effort not to buck harder.

'Look in the bathroom, Rosanna.'

His voice was so thick it took her a moment to understand. When she did, their eyes met in the mirror, hers widening at the erotic sight they made. Yet she wasn't dismayed. Salim felt the pulse of pleasure through her body.

That was enough to crack his control. He moved, withdrawing so slowly it was exquisite pain, then pushed up hard, into her sweet depths, his hand tight on her breast, his gaze holding hers.

He heard her snatched hiss of breath. Or was that his? He saw her eyes grow hooded with pleasure as she bucked her hips back against him, lodging him deeper still.

She looked so beautiful with her hair loose around her bare shoulders, her skin flushed and mouth panting with every quick breath. Salim slid his other hand from her hip, watching in the mirror as his hair-darkened arm contrasted with her pale skin, and he took the precious weight of her other breast too.

A voice inside cried out in triumph and he moved again, this time not pausing, simply following the dictates of his animal brain that pushed him higher and deeper, stronger and harder.

But most profound of all was the sense of shared purpose. The diamond-bright glitter in Rosanna's eyes as she met him thrust for thrust. The arch of her body, the way she pushed her breasts into his hands and quivered when he hit that sweet spot deep inside.

He liked that so much his attention turned from his own needs to finding that spot again and again till, like a desert storm appearing out of nowhere, she convulsed around him.

He had an instant's satisfaction that he'd brought her to another pinnacle, then the storm smashed in and tore him free of the mundane world. Salim hung on, pumping frantically in ecstasy, teetering on that knife edge of need so exquisite it veered towards pain. Then, with a roar of shocked completion, he slumped over her, gathering her to him and burying his face in her scented hair.

Rosanna woke, smiling, to a feeling of warmth and luxurious wellbeing that had become familiar over the past few days.

Salim lay entangled with her, his powerful body encompassing her in the way she adored. He was fast asleep, which wasn't surprising given how little rest they'd had. And how very active he'd been a short time before.

Her smile widened into a grin. She could count on the fingers of one hand the hours Salim had spent away from her since they'd arrived. Then it had only been because even on holiday a sheikh needed to maintain contact with his staff in case anything vital cropped up.

The rest of the time he'd devoted to her.

Sex with Salim had been an eye-opener. Not only did it cast Rosanna's experience with Phil into the shadows, but Salim had made her aware of her sensuality in a way she never had been before.

The morning they'd arrived here was the first time she'd had sex outside a bed. With Phil they'd always been horizontal, in the dark, usually after a long day at work.

But tiredness alone didn't explain the difference. Salim worked long hours too, and he was definitely not getting enough sleep. Yet he was sexually vigorous and demanding, passionate and adventurous. She revelled in it. Not once had he pushed her to do something she didn't want. In fact, she'd revelled in the freedom to follow her needs fully, making her own demands.

Rosanna shivered, thinking of all the ways they'd enjoyed each other these last few days.

Behind her Salim stirred but didn't wake. Yet even that tiny movement made her hyper-aware of him, his chest against her back, one hairy thigh between her knees and his hand lax on the nest of curls at the apex of her thighs. As if, even in sleep, he claimed her.

She adored the way he never tired of touching her. Often with bold, sexual intent, but not always. How often had he swept her hair from her face then tangled his fingers there, as if fascinated by its softness? Or reached out to brush her cheek or hand in a passing caress?

He took her hand often, especially when they left the palace to explore the surprisingly fertile if rugged landscape.

This morning he'd led her up a narrow mountain path to watch the sun rise. They hadn't gone far but it had felt like another world with the spectacular plain spread before them, gilded by the light.

He'd taken her to a ravine where cyclamens and lilies grew wild and a carpet of other flowers she didn't know. She'd been lost in wonder at the sight of such natural beauty.

Then, still holding her hand, he'd led her to a natural spring, its water bubbling from a cleft in the rock to tumble into a deep pool high above the valley.

Inevitably Salim had persuaded her to join him naked, in the cold water, and they'd made love there, looking out over his land as the sun lifted. The place and the moment had felt magical. Rosanna knew the memory of it, and of how it felt to be cherished by Salim, would last the rest of her life.

That's how she felt. Cherished.

Salim showed her in so many small ways, each day, that she mattered.

Like when he personally brewed tea for her each morning, after learning it was her favourite and that she only drank coffee once she was well into the day. The way he shortened his stride to match hers as they walked together. How he was so solicitous, always offering her choices, like whether she wanted to swim in the palace's mosaic-lined pool, or to go out exploring in the four-wheel drive. Or have sex. He respected her need for rest and never expected her simply to accept what he wanted to do.

They might be having a short, steamy affair. They might spend most of their time naked and sometimes her legs were so weak from prolonged bliss that Salim had to carry her to the sunken tub and stay, in the warm, scented water, to carry her out again. But never had Rosanna felt cheapened or taken for granted.

Salim wasn't that sort of man. She wouldn't be here if he were. That was one good thing to come out of past trauma. She wasn't a woman who'd let herself be taken for granted ever again. They were equals here, no matter what differences society placed on them.

It was heady and wonderful. Salim made her feel strong

and special, as if their lovemaking forged a new power in her. A new confidence that she'd lost somewhere in the last couple of years.

Sexually, he might hold her in thrall but that didn't make her weak. Because she'd seen evidence, time and again, that she had the same effect on him. She mightn't have his experience but Salim needed her as desperately as she needed him. That showed no sign of abating.

Rosanna frowned. This was their fourth day together yet if anything she felt bound more closely to Salim than before. There was no fracture in the ties between them, certainly no boredom or lack of interest.

'Are you all right, my rose?'

Salim's voice was husky with sleep and, she guessed, arousal, since she felt his erection stiffen behind her.

Instantly that frisson of not-quite-anxiety disintegrated, replaced by a familiar coil of anticipation deep inside.

She revelled in that pet name he used so often. As if he saw her as delicate and precious, something she'd never imagined herself to be. It fitted the romantic ambience of this wonderful place, so special with its rich silks and decadent luxuries, its bountiful walled garden and exquisite frescoes. It made her feel as if she belonged here, though she knew that could never be.

'Of course I am. I was just thinking of getting up and leaving you to rest.'

'Alone?' No mistaking his disappointment. Or his intent as he dipped his hand into the downy curls between her legs and found her already damp with wanting. 'Ah, Rosanna.' His voice burred across her skin like the rub of roughened velvet. 'You do like to tease me, don't you?'

Salim shifted, his proud erection solid against her buttocks, and Rosanna found herself arching back, pressing against all that exciting hardness while his fingers delved deeper and her breath caught.

'You need your sleep,' she gasped, even as her eyes rolled back in sheer bliss. She loved being wanted by this man. She loved that he insisted on pleasing her, every time, often several times, before his own release.

'I was dreaming of you. And no wonder.' His questing fingers made her gasp as delight shimmered through her. 'You can't ask me to go back to sleep now.'

Yet he moved away, all that lovely warmth gone in a second, and Rosanna opened her mouth to protest. Except gentle hands pulled her onto her back and he was above her, the excitement in his eyes contrasting with his almost sombre expression. As if suddenly this wasn't a matter of teasing but something much more serious.

Her feverish buzz stilled as she sensed a change in him. 'Salim?'

Rosanna reached up, wondering at that sober look. Her hands skimmed his chest and shoulders but before she could embrace him, he sank low, settling further down her body. He wrapped his arms around her thighs, pulling them up over his shoulders, and she couldn't stifle another gasp as his hot breath tickled her damp curls.

'Salim, I…'

She lost whatever she'd been about to say as he kissed her intimately and once again made the world fall away.

Salim looked across to Rosanna lying on a padded sun lounger. She was naked but for the diaphanous red caftan she'd insisted on throwing on after their swim. His gaze traced the lines and entrancing curves of her body enticingly revealed through the sheer fabric. He couldn't imagine ever wanting to be anywhere else.

For the first time it occurred to him to wonder what it would be like if he hadn't been born royal, with a nation's expectations on his shoulders, and could please himself with what he did and who he chose to be with.

Hurriedly he thrust away the thought. That could never be.

'Tell me about this place, Salim. It's obviously very old but it has such a warm feel to it. Not grim like a fortress.'

Rosanna's voice was soft and her eyes closed as she lay on her stomach, her cheek pillowed on her folded arms. Even this late in the day it was warm enough for her to settle in the shade rather than bake in the direct sunlight at the edge of the long pool.

'What do you want to know?'

She looked like she wasn't far off sleep and he couldn't blame her. They'd had a vigorous, wholly satisfying afternoon.

He couldn't remember ever feeling so good, fizzing with energy, despite the weighted laxness of his well-used body. Rosanna tested him to the limit, urging him to peak after peak when common sense decreed he should be sated.

A dull clamour of warning sounded in his brain. Like a cracked bell ringing off-key in paradise. He felt the discordant jangle too in the hollowing of his belly.

Salim frowned, trying to identify it. He'd experienced it earlier in bed. He'd rolled her over and looked down into eyes as bright and beguiling as moonlight and felt…

That was it. The temptation to feel too much, read too much into their compatibility, though he knew they'd soon go their separate ways.

Salim ignored the pain stabbing his rib cage. That, he assured himself, was for Rosanna. He worried about her. He'd seen her dreamy expression as she watched him and feared maybe she was building unrealistic hopes about them.

Yet whenever they talked about the future, Rosanna was as sensible as she'd always been. Expecting nothing from him but this single week.

He wanted more than a week. Seven days wouldn't be enough to sever the bond between them.

But it had to be. He'd already gone beyond the limits of what was reasonable.

'Tell me about the queen it was made for,' she said sleepily, and he was reminded irresistibly of himself, years ago, begging his mother for another bedtime story. Time alone with her had been such a treat.

'It wasn't built for a queen but as a clan fortress centuries ago.' His lips quirked up in a smile. 'Times have changed. These days local power struggles are confined to politics.'

Rosanna opened her eyes and surveyed him. He read the dark pewter colour, so different to the bright blaze of silver when she was aroused. This was her assessing look, as if she weighed his words. He knew she was still thinking of the queen, not old power struggles.

Salim shrugged and relented. What harm would it do to tell her? 'It came to the crown when one of our country's greatest sheikhs married the daughter of the clan chieftain of this region. She brought the fortress as part of her dowry.'

'It must have been a powerful clan to give up such a strategic position.'

He nodded, surprised at how quickly she'd grasped its significance. 'It was. Winning her as a bride was a political coup for the sheikh. The irony is that she refused him, not once but twice.'

Rosanna's eyes widened. 'I've heard about her!'

She pushed herself up on her elbows, inadvertently giving Salim a glorious view of her breasts.

A clenching weight in his groin banished that phantom sensation that something was amiss. His palms itched with the need to cup those lovely breasts and caress her till she purred with pleasure. She was so beautiful.

Yet he'd known more classically beautiful women. There was something about Rosanna that he couldn't explain but *felt* at a visceral level.

'The sheikh made those three wonderful gates to the palace to celebrate when she finally agreed to marry him.'

Salim looked into Rosanna's face and knew she'd fallen for the old tale.

Slowly he nodded. 'So the story goes.'

'You don't believe it?' She studied him intently then shrugged, her mouth turning down at the corners, and lay down again.

Instantly Salim regretted puncturing her fantasy. Not because he couldn't see her breasts any more. The view of her back, buttocks and legs was one of the finest vistas he'd ever enjoyed. But because he'd erased that smile.

'I'm not a romantic. But you're right, that's the story. In fact, the story goes that sheikh after sheikh since then married for love.'

Until recently.

Her smile was back, mischievous this time, and he liked that too.

'I love it! All those fierce rulers, so autocratic and powerful, turning weak at the knees for just the right woman.'

Of course she did. It was the sort of fantasy women adored.

'After he acquired the fortress, the sheikh set about turning it into a private retreat for himself and his wife, and eventually their family. Tradition has it that he was the one who ordered the courtyard to be planted with flowers as well as the usual fruit trees and medicinal herbs. In every generation since, changes have been made, introducing more luxuries. Now the only real evidence of the fortress are its thick walls and the crenellations along the top.'

'I like the fact it's become a retreat for the royal family. It must be special to you.'

Salim nodded. 'It is. I've been coming here for as long as I can remember.'

The caretakers here were like family to him, though

on this visit he'd barely seen them, spending all his time with Rosanna.

'So,' Rosanna mused. 'You come from a long line of romantics. I find that hard to believe.'

She didn't need to mention his businesslike search for a wife. It was there between them, the elephant in the room. Time enough for that when they returned to the city.

'You're right. But I'm not actually descended from them.'

'You're not?' Her eyes snapped open. 'I thought the title passed from father to son?'

'It does. Usually to the elder son, though in my case the Royal Council chose me over Fuad.'

An action which had sent his brother storming from the capital in a fit of fury. Straight to his death in a mangle of metal when his too-powerful car had crashed on a road not built for Formula One–style racing.

What would have happened if Fuad had survived? Salim couldn't imagine him quietly sitting on the sidelines while his younger brother ruled.

'How is it that you're not from the same line?'

Salim hauled his thoughts back from Fuad's death and his own conflicted feelings. He'd have done anything to save his brother, but he had no illusions about his character. There'd never been anything like love between them.

'Two generations ago the sheikh had only one child, a daughter. But under our constitution a woman can't inherit the Dhalkuri throne. His wife died and he was urged year after year to take a new wife to get a male heir and secure the succession.'

He paused, checking to see that Rosanna understood, which she clearly did, given her attentiveness.

'The sheikh refused because he'd loved his wife and didn't want to replace her. Eventually he relented when he realised how worried his people were about instability if he had no clear successor. So he married the respected widow of his best friend. A woman who already had one son. He adopted the boy as his legal heir and that boy grew up to be my father.'

'That's so romantic, that the old sheikh didn't want to marry after he lost his first wife.'

Salim nodded. Seeing that dreamy look in her eyes he didn't add the story he'd heard privately, that the old sheikh's second marriage hadn't been consummated because he couldn't bear to sleep with a woman other than his first wife. That would only cement Rosanna's romantic imaginings.

'What happened to his daughter? The one who couldn't inherit?'

'She married. They're both dead now but their daughter, Tara, my cousin, is still in the region. She married the Sheikh of Nahrat, across the border. I saw her recently and she's very happy.'

He was glad for her. He'd always liked Tara and it was good to see her thriving.

Salim looked at Rosanna's tender smile and the glow in her eyes. It was a shame but he couldn't let her weave romantic imaginings. It was too dangerous.

'I missed the romantic tradition. My parents' marriage was an arranged one. My mother was a princess from a nearby kingdom and brought a lot of valuable resources with her. Fuad and I were raised to expect something similar. To choose brides who would benefit our nation, not someone we fell for.'

'You don't believe in love?'

Her tone wasn't wistful. In fact, he couldn't catch any inflection there, yet Salim sensed there was more to her question than simple curiosity.

Which wouldn't do. It was too dangerous.

He lifted his shoulders in a shrug. 'I believe romantic

love exists because there are people who swear they've experienced it.'

Actually, watching his cousin, Tara, Salim *knew* it existed. She and Raif were head over heels in love. But she came from a different background.

'No one in my immediate biological family has experienced it. Not me or my brother. Not my parents or my parents' parents. I suspect susceptibility to love might be something you inherit or acquire from your family. But in my family…' He paused and shook his head emphatically, watching Rosanna closely to be sure she got the message. 'No. Definitely not.'

CHAPTER ELEVEN

ROSANNA LOOKED UP from the book she was trying to read and shut it with a sigh.

She couldn't concentrate. Salim's revelations about this place and his family kept circling in her head.

The tale of a long-ago king, consumed with love for his proud bride who wasn't easily won. The romantic in Rosanna responded to the idea of him planning a dynastic marriage and instead succumbing to love. And all his descendants too. She didn't know much Dhalkuri history but even she had heard that its leaders were famed as fierce and indomitable.

Yet it wasn't the long-ago past that occupied her thoughts. It was Salim. The sharp, assessing look he'd given her when he carefully explained he was *not* descended from the same stock. That his family didn't marry for love.

Rosanna understood.

It was a reminder that Salim would marry sensibly. He'd choose a partner who met his exacting criteria, to satisfy him and the needs of his country. There was no question of him falling in love.

No question of him falling for *her*.

Which was a good thing.

Neither of them wanted that sort of complication.

After Phil she wasn't ready for a long-term relationship.

The thought of falling in love scared her. It would take a lot for her to give her trust to another man.

Plus she didn't need Salim to warn her of all the reasons why she wouldn't make a suitable match for him. She spoke only English and a few phrases of schoolgirl German. She had no diplomatic experience. She didn't feel at home mixing with royalty or national leaders. As for being tall, blonde and free from scandal in her past…

Rosanna shifted abruptly and the book slid from her lap to the ruby-coloured cushions of the window seat where she was curled up. She reached out and pulled the carved wooden screen further open so she had a clear view across to the next mountain peak.

The sun was setting, bathing the world in an apricot glow. Light caught the spray from a tiny mountain stream, creating a hazy rainbow that turned the nearby ravine into a magical place.

A weight pressed down on her lungs.

She didn't believe in magic.

Since Phil she barely believed in romance, despite her fondness for stories with happy endings. Which was why she'd been able to accept Salim's proposition. It was the only way forward. The only way to survive her all-encompassing fascination with this man.

She had to believe that by sating this hunger she could conquer it and move on. Having this honest relationship, where she and Salim shared the truth unvarnished by the trappings of romance, made her stronger. She was taking control of her pleasure and her life choices.

When it was over she could return to getting her life back on track after the disaster she'd left behind in Australia. She could focus on her career and eventually, maybe one day when her soul had healed, she'd meet a man she could trust and care for.

It all made eminent sense. Why then had she felt hurt

when Salim excused himself to visit the family of caretakers here? He'd explained that he'd known them since childhood and it would be rude not to see them.

Rosanna had watched him leave for the house tucked into the walls on the outside of the palace and felt…desolate.

Didn't he believe her good enough to meet his friends? Was he ashamed of her?

Rosanna's fingers tightened on the intricate carving. The screen was beautiful and provided a filter for the sunlight. Yet it was a reminder of a time when women lived restricted lives. Such screens had sometimes been a barrier between them and the outside world.

It was fanciful but suddenly Rosanna felt isolated and lonely. Not because of the palace's secluded location, which actually appealed, but because Salim chose not to take her with him.

She frowned. She was used to looking after herself, holding down taxing jobs and keeping busy. She was happy in her own company. Yet none of that mattered against the fact Salim chose not to introduce her into this tiny fraction of his personal life.

She was good enough for an affair but not to meet his friends.

Rosanna's mouth flattened. She couldn't even be angry because Salim was right. It wasn't that he was ashamed of her but that he was avoiding unnecessary complications. Introducing her to his friends would raise expectations and the need for explanations in the future.

He was saving both of them discomfort.

Yet it didn't sit well with her.

Even so, it was a timely reminder of why they'd come here. And what would happen when they left.

Nothing. Nothing but the conclusion of her work then her return to London to more work for Marian.

She had to focus on that. And getting Salim out of her system as soon as possible. Because the alternative, of this affair not curing her need for him, was too frightening to consider.

'Are you sure you feel up to a hike this morning?'

Normally Salim welcomed any opportunity to get outdoors, especially here where he had the luxury of almost guaranteed solitude. But Rosanna must be exhausted this morning. He felt the delicious lassitude that came after great sex. He wouldn't mind basking in bed then having a late breakfast with her, and then starting all over again.

'Of course. I'm looking forward to that view of the mountain villages you promised.' She paused in the act of getting out of bed and slanted a look over her shoulder before her gaze slid away. 'Unless you'd rather not.'

Rosanna's voice didn't sound right.

She sounded diffident.

Surely not. Not after the way they'd spent the last hour, sharing incredible intimacies and a level of bliss that astounded him. Diffidence was the last thing he expected from Rosanna. She was competent, assured, sexy and eager to make the most of this week. This woman wasn't meek or shy.

He thought of how she'd greeted him on his return yesterday afternoon. He'd felt uncomfortable, almost guilty, returning from the warm embrace of his friends and feeling that he should have invited Rosanna to join him.

Not that she'd pushed for that. But her curiosity about his country and its traditions, plus the fact she was a guest alone in his country with little opportunity to make acquaintances, had weighed heavily on him. It had been selfish not to invite her. Because, he realised, she was *his* secret and, like a miser hoarding gold, he didn't want to share her with anyone.

Maybe too he'd needed some distance because with Rosanna he'd felt unsettling emotions stir.

He'd returned, half expecting to find her brooding or sulky, maybe a little cool with him.

Instead she'd sauntered up to him with a provocative sway to her hips and a hooded, sensual look in her eyes, and invited him to join her for a naked dip. The fact she'd worn nothing but that gauzy scarlet caftan had decided the matter.

Guilt had receded, replaced by instant lust. They'd spent the rest of the evening teasing and pleasing each other. Rosanna's single-minded focus on exploring their mutual passion had brought him undone several times. It was a miracle either of them had the energy to slide out of bed this morning.

Yet there she was, on her feet by the bed, a question in her eyes.

'Of course I—' he began.

'We needn't go as far as the villages—'

They both stopped. She thought he was afraid she'd insist on visiting a mountain village?

A bitter tang filled his mouth as he realised she thought he didn't want to be seen with her. His chest tightened. Did she think he was ashamed of her?

'We can go as far as you like,' he offered. 'I thought you might be tired.'

As he was. Not that it stopped him greedily devouring the sight of her nakedness. He'd never tire of her body. Even clothed she had a grace that caught at something high in his throat, and, he admitted, deep in his groin.

She shrugged one shoulder, making Salim marvel at how she could turn a casual gesture into something that made his whole being clench with desire. Not just physical desire either, but something more puzzling.

The desire to keep her with him. As his.

Shock slammed into him, jerking his head back. Something cleaved through his gut. Warning? Or fear?

He was imagining things. He was just feeling the after-effects of hours of erotic play. A connection that seemed profound because of its intensity. But soon it would begin waning.

'Okay then, I'll have a quick shower and dress. I'd like to get out into the countryside.' She paused. 'But I'll understand if you change your mind. I could always go for a stroll by myself.'

There it was again, that hint of diffidence. It didn't sit well with the indomitable, fascinating woman he knew.

Before Salim could answer she walked quickly to the bathroom. To forestall further discussion?

He opened his mouth to stop her then closed it. What would he say? Apologise for leaving her yesterday? But it had been the sensible thing to do, protecting her privacy and avoiding speculation.

Yet he found his jaw was clenched and his belly cramped. He didn't like leaving the conversation that way, feeling he'd done wrong by her.

Salim forked his fingers through his hair, unaccustomed to this indecisiveness.

But one decision was obvious. No matter how much he wanted to make amends and see Rosanna's glorious smile, he would *not* follow her into the shower. It would scupper anything like clear thought for a long time to come.

Salim needed all his wits about him.

What had begun as a simple solution to inconvenient lust felt far more complex than he'd anticipated.

An hour later, after breakfast at Rosanna's favourite spot on the terrace, they were ready to set out. Rosanna was bright and seemingly full of energy.

Too much energy? Was her good cheer a little brittle?

Salim shook his head, annoyed at his imaginings, and led the way around the building and past the empty stables. Next time he visited he'd ensure the stables were restocked. The area was perfect for riding and Salim missed it.

He imagined riding with Rosanna through the mountains to some of his favourite places. Until he remembered they wouldn't come here together again.

'Your Majesty.'

Salim paused as a tall, familiar figure emerged from the last stable door.

'Murad! It's good to see you.'

The older man bent deep in a gesture of obeisance, reminding Salim abruptly of all that had passed since they'd last met.

'Please rise.'

In other circumstances he would have embraced the old man, but Murad would feel uncomfortable since they weren't alone. Salim had seen his gaze flick to Rosanna.

'My sympathies on your loss, Your Majesty. Your father was a good man and an excellent ruler.'

'Thank you, Murad. He was indeed. I hope to fulfil his expectations of me.'

'You will, Majesty. That's certain.' He smiled and Salim couldn't hold back any longer. He grasped the old man's hand in both his.

'I feel better for seeing you, my old friend.' He turned to Rosanna. 'This is Murad Darwish. He used to be caretaker at the Queen's Palace until he retired a few years ago. I've known him all my life.'

He was like a de facto grandfather.

'Murad, I'd like you to meet Ms Rosanna MacIain, who's visiting from London.'

He watched with pleasure as the two shook hands, and Rosanna surprised him by greeting his friend in his own language then observing in the same language that it was a fine day. Naturally Murad was delighted.

'You came to visit your family?' Salim asked, continuing to speak English. He didn't want Rosanna feeling excluded.

Murad's son and daughter-in-law were now the palace caretakers while Murad lived in his village several kilometres away.

'I'll see them, but I came to see you, Your Majesty.' He gestured to the open door beside them. 'If you will.'

Knowing it was useless to protest the formal title, Salim entered the stables.

'Oh, how gorgeous!'

Rosanna saw the puppies at the same time he did. Murad opened the stall and she hurried forward as a tumbling bundle of fur resolved itself into a couple of puppies. They already showed fair to mature into the elegant, long-legged hunting dogs so familiar to him. At the moment their plumed tails seemed out of proportion, like their oversized paws.

Memory hit Salim. Of the pedigreed dogs who'd always lived at the royal palaces. They'd been his father's pride and joy. To Salim, who'd spent hours in the kennels and stables, they'd been playmates. His chest tightened as he recalled being abroad when Fuad cleared both stables and kennels in their father's last days.

'They're fine-looking animals.' He bent to stroke one silky ear then watched indulgently as the pup wriggled enthusiastically and tried to nip his fingers.

'Bred from your father's finest stock.'

'Really? You managed to save them?'

'Some.' Murad shook his head sadly. 'Some trusted people helped rescue others.'

Rosanna looked up from where she squatted, playing with a pup.

'Thank you, Murad. I appreciate it.'

Murad inclined his head. 'Since they're from the royal kennels I wanted to present one to you. That's why I'm here, with the two finest pups of the litter.'

Strangely, Salim felt his throat tighten. The gift was generous when a dog with such a pedigree would fetch a lot of money. More, it was the reminder of his dead father and of times gone by that hit him. And recognition of Murad's role in his own life as mentor and friend.

'Thank you, Murad. That's a generous gift indeed.'

'I'm pleased you think so.' Murad paused. 'If you permit I'll let my family know I've arrived while you make your choice.'

The old man might have been a diplomat, for he'd surely guessed at Salim's sudden upsurge of emotions, though Salim was sure his expression had revealed nothing. He'd been taught to conceal his emotions as befitted a prince. But the old man knew him better than most. He knew how much he admired his father, despite the formality that had existed between them.

Salim hunkered down and was immediately mobbed by two eager puppies. He grinned, his hands sinking deep into soft fur.

'You're a dog person.'

He shrugged. 'We always had dogs and horses in the palace.' He looked up to see Rosanna's keen-eyed stare fixed on him. 'So are you. You're a natural with them.'

'With four children in the family there were always pets at home. Always at least one dog and a couple of rabbits. There was a blue tongue lizard too at one stage and several mice.'

Salim like the sound of it, informal and fun. 'It sounds like quite a menagerie.'

'Says the man who grew up with kennels and stables.'

Her generous smile conveyed only humour, not jealousy. That set her apart from many. Often people's view of him was tinged by his privileged upbringing. It was true he'd never lacked for food, shelter or money. Yet the demands of royal life and expectations meant he'd missed out on the more informal joys of normal family life. Not that he was complaining. It was just a difference between him and others. Yet Rosanna teased him as easily as if there were no gulf between them. He liked that.

'Did you have a dog of your own?'

The question dimmed his burgeoning smile. 'For a short time.'

It had been a pup like these, with bright eyes and feet too big for its body. Salim had adored it.

'I'm sorry. Not a good memory?'

Salim shrugged as a pup, the one with the remarkable black colouring so rare in its breed, licked his hand. The raspy caress unlocked something inside him he'd almost forgotten. Or maybe it was Rosanna's silence. He knew she was curious but she didn't push for details. Whatever the reason, suddenly he wanted to share.

What could it hurt? He owed precious little loyalty to Fuad. Plus he knew Rosanna would never tell anyone. Salim settled more comfortably, his back against the stall wall.

'I was given a pup for my fifth birthday. I loved dogs and my parents thought it would be a good way to learn responsibility. Unfortunately that made my elder brother jealous. He'd never been given a dog.'

He saw Rosanna frown. He knew it sounded like favouritism, and Fuad used to accuse him of being their mother's favourite because she'd sometimes sit with him when he had nightmares. 'He hated dogs so it would have been pointless giving him one as a pet.'

'That's sad. Had he been bitten by one?'

'Not that I know of.' Salim scratched the belly of the pup now lying on its back before him. 'He didn't like animals of any sort and they didn't like him.'

Salim remembered horses shying when Fuad approached and dogs barking aggressively or cringing away. As if they sensed the cruel streak that he seldom bothered to hide when he was alone with his little brother.

'My dog went missing and was eventually found at the bottom of an old well in the courtyard.' He met Rosanna's stare. 'No one could understand how he fell in when there was wire mesh over the top. Until a stablehand came forward to say he'd seen Fuad drop the dog in.'

'Oh, Salim!' Her eyes rounded and she leaned forward, grabbing his hand with hers. She looked aghast. 'That's horrible! Was it true?'

'Fuad denied it but he was never allowed alone in the kennels or stables after that. Not that he minded.'

But their father had found other punishments for him. Fuad had blamed Salim for that, taking out his anger on his younger brother whenever he could, knowing Salim wouldn't run crying to their parents. Even as a child Salim had had more pride and foolhardy obstinacy than to admit weakness before his brother.

'I'm so sorry.' Her remarkable eyes glittered in sympathy. 'It must have been tough growing up with a brother like that.'

'We weren't close,' he said eventually.

But Rosanna wasn't finished. He should have realised she'd guess. 'You said your father's dogs needed saving. Because of your brother?'

He looked at her, sitting cross-legged with a now sleepy dog in her lap. Its pale grey pelt reminded him of the prize hounds of which his father had been so proud. Anger stirred at Fuad's petty vengefulness.

Finally he nodded. 'When our father's terminal illness worsened Fuad assumed control, acting on his behalf. I was abroad getting investors for some development schemes in

Dhalkur and didn't realise how ill my father had become. Neither he nor Fuad mentioned it whenever I rang home.'

Salim still felt guilty over that.

'And something happened while you were away.'

He released a slow breath. 'Fuad ordered the stables and kennels emptied. The horses were sold but the dogs… He gave instructions that they simply be got rid of.'

'You mean killed?'

Salim nodded. 'I knew most of them somehow escaped but not what happened to them.'

Her fingers squeezed his. 'Your friend Murad is a good man. No wonder you like him so much.'

'I'm lucky to have him in my life.'

Salim paused, thinking of how he'd resisted the urge to quiz Rosanna about *her* past, trying to keep some distance in their relationship.

Distance! What a laugh. He felt closer to Rosanna than to anyone he knew.

That realisation rocked him.

He had friends and people he'd known all his life, but no one close enough to talk with like this.

'Salim? What is it?'

'Nothing important. Tell me more about the menagerie at home and all your siblings. Are you still close?'

It turned out they were and Rosanna didn't mind talking about her family in the least. She described her three brothers and her childhood in suburban Sydney. She spoke of backyard games and netball competitions. Of swimming lessons and holidays on the coast. Of her beloved border collie who'd finally died just as she left home for university.

Salim sat, relaxed, stroking the dog beside him, and felt transported to a world that felt exotic and appealing. Because of the warmth and charm Rosanna exuded as she reminisced. He wanted to see the old apple tree where they'd built a treehouse and taste her mother's best ever roast and apple crumble. Hear more about the compassion and common-sense values instilled by her social worker father and school librarian mother.

It was a far cry from his own upbringing.

'And the man you planned to marry? What about him?'

As soon as he said it, Salim realised he'd destroyed the relaxed mood. Rosanna stiffened, her hand poised in mid-stroke over the dog nestled in her lap.

'Phil? He's no longer in my life.'

'How did you meet?'

'At work. I was employed to recruit senior staff for a major financial institution. He worked there and we hit it off.'

Salim watched her mouth flatten and felt inordinately pleased that there was clearly nothing now between her and her ex-fiancé. Not that it was any of his business.

'You were together long?'

She shrugged. 'Long enough to think of marriage.'

'So you were obviously compatible.'

Rosanna shot him a look from under lowered brows. 'I thought so but I was mistaken.'

It was clear she didn't want to discuss this and Salim should do her the courtesy of stopping. Yet he needed to know more. Because if he wasn't mistaken, that was pain he read in her expression and he didn't like the way that made him feel.

'He hurt you?'

She looked away. 'I trusted him and he betrayed me, so yes, he hurt me.' She turned back, meeting his gaze almost defiantly. 'I'm more wary now. I thought I knew him but I was wrong and that undermined my confidence. But I've adjusted my expectations. I won't make the same mistake again.'

Her lips turned up in a smile that didn't meet her eyes

and she began talking of the dogs, of how hard it would be to choose between them.

Salim listened but with only half an ear. He was far more interested in Rosanna's revelations and what they told him about her.

Her ex had betrayed her. With another woman?

The man had poor taste. How could he want another woman when he had Rosanna?

Salim thought of her professionalism and competence and wondered how she'd coped when her ex undermined her confidence. She never gave any indication that was the case, standing up to Salim and challenging him to be realistic in his requirements. That only strengthened his admiration.

But what made him most curious was her statement that she'd adjusted her expectations. Had she closed off her heart, not believing she could trust a man after that betrayal?

That saddened him. This woman deserved more. She deserved not just honesty but a man who would devote his life to her.

Salim's thoughts turned to what *he'd* offered her. A week's carnal pleasure. A chance to gratify his yearning for her before they returned to the capital and he set her to work finding him a wife.

Suddenly his actions seemed not pragmatic but selfish. Not clear-sighted but crass. Even after their affair ended, to expect her to help him choose a bride…

Distaste churned in his belly at the idea he'd taken advantage of a woman who'd already had her hopes and expectations destroyed by a man.

Salim should have treated her better. Not that Rosanna complained. But the very fact that she'd agreed to his proposition, and that she responded so fully and generously to him, made him feel less than the man he wanted to be.

But what else could he have offered her? It was this short affair or nothing.

And despite what honour urged, *nothing* hadn't been an option. He was a man of strong self-control but even one more day together in his palace and he wouldn't have been able to keep his hands off her.

Salim watched Rosanna smile as she stroked the silvery puppy that he feared would always remind him of her beautiful eyes. He thought of the day, soon, when she'd return to Britain. He'd never see her again unless she attended his wedding to the nameless woman who would hopefully meet his all-important criteria, because his country needed her.

Strange. In the past he'd thought of his bride with the resignation of a busy man who saw her as another job to be ticked off.

Now he actively disliked that faceless woman.

CHAPTER TWELVE

ROSANNA LAY, PANTING and flushed, across Salim's heaving chest. Their lovemaking had been vigorous and satisfying and something else too. But she refused to analyse why it had felt different. Meaningful. Profound.

No, she wasn't going there!

She'd promised herself not to weave fantasies about Salim. She couldn't afford to begin now.

No matter how tempting.

What did it matter that today in the stables, and later when he'd taken her to a village where they'd been warmly welcomed, she'd felt special? Because Salim had shared so much with her. Because he'd drawn her into his world on yet another, personal, level.

He'd let her glimpse a slice of his private life that she could tell he treasured. She hugged that to herself like the precious gift it was.

Salim had taken her first to the palace caretaker's home where he'd introduced her to Murad's family and pleased the old man by accepting the beautiful black hound as a gift, before purchasing the other pup at a very handsome price.

Then the two men had led her to Murad's village. She'd drunk sweetened tea and eaten almond and honey sweets. She'd exchanged halting pleasantries with the locals and been rewarded with wide smiles. The women had proudly shown her their weaving and the roses they cultivated to sell for their fragrant essence. She'd had fun with the children too. They'd invited her to join in a local version of hopscotch, teaching her to count the numbers in their language and crowing with approval at her success.

Rosanna had left with a smile on her face and a warm glow inside.

'The people here are so friendly,' she murmured against Salim's chest. 'I had a wonderful time today.'

'They love visitors,' he murmured, wrapping his arm around her back. 'Guests are always welcome.'

Rosanna thought about the small but scrupulously clean homes she'd seen. The rough but magnificent terrain that didn't yield easily to the plough yet supported the scattered villages. The sense of community.

'They seem very happy.'

He stroked her hair over her shoulder and she stretched into his touch. He made her feel like purring.

'Dhalkuris are hardy and resilient, and we love our country.' He paused. 'They appreciated that you spoke their language. When did you learn?'

'You make it sound like I'm fluent. I only know greetings and a couple of other words.' Yet Salim's acknowledgement felt like high praise. She'd worked to perfect her few phrases. 'I had free time in the evenings.'

Maybe those lonely nights were part of the reason she'd so fixated on Salim.

'Your assistant, Taqi, helped. I asked him to correct my pronunciation. He's a stickler but it paid off when the villagers understood me.'

She felt proud. Before coming to Dhalkur she'd never conversed in another language outside a classroom and it felt amazing when she actually communicated. Maybe she'd continue learning when she left here. But instead of pleasing her, the idea flattened her smile. She didn't want to think of leaving.

Just as she didn't like the trill of Salim's phone. She knew that ringtone, knew it meant a call he wouldn't ignore.

Sure enough, Salim excused himself and slid out from beneath her, rolling to the far side of the bed and rising to sit with his back to her as he reached for the phone.

Rosanna lay, drinking in the sight of his powerful frame, his rumpled dark hair and wide, straight shoulders. For now at least he was hers and—

Something about his stillness caught her attention. The way he suddenly sat straighter, raking his hand through his hair in a gesture of impatience or frustration.

Slowly he lowered the phone and put it on the bedside table. He didn't turn immediately but sat as if staring at the view beyond the window. Except the sun had gone and the panorama was in darkness.

A chill crept along Rosanna's bones and her happiness froze into a hard lump, heavy inside her.

'Salim?'

Her voice sounded surprisingly normal. Not as if it emerged from a throat constricting with fear.

Then he swivelled around, his eyes meeting hers, and every unvoiced fear was realised.

Her heart crashed against her ribs as shock ran through her. 'It's bad news, isn't it?'

He shook his head. But in the few minutes since he'd slid out from beneath her, he'd altered. He looked sterner, his gaze shuttered. There was a distance between them far greater than the width of the bed. Salim was back in regal mode and she hated it.

Because she knew what that meant.

'Not bad news. Actually, it's good. There's been an unexpected breakthrough in some international negotiations.'

Rosanna said nothing, waiting for what she knew was coming.

'But it means I'm needed. This final stage of the negotiation will be between heads of state.' He paused and she saw a fleeting expression that looked like regret. 'Either I go to the capital or I bring the negotiations here.'

Which he wouldn't do. This was his private bolthole. Nor would he want to advertise her presence.

'When do you leave?'

For a long moment he didn't answer.

'Now.'

Salim watched her flinch and had to brace himself not to lunge across the bed and gather her close. He wanted to bury his head in her fragrant hair, bury himself in her warm, lush body and forget about the outside world.

He wanted to ignore duty and the peace treaty that had been his priority since taking the throne.

He wanted to curse and throw his phone across the room and stick his head in the sand.

He wanted to stay here.

He wanted Rosanna.

That was the problem. He still wanted her as much as he had when they'd arrived. More so. If anything their time together had strengthened their bond.

How could he have fooled himself that this short interlude would satisfy him? That he could easily put her aside and move on with the future he must embrace for the sake of his country?

Dhalkur would accept his choice of bride but he owed it to his people to choose someone with the skills and background to help him achieve what needed to be done. Someone ready for life as a royal, ideally with some understanding of their language and culture or able to promote his renewal projects.

Not a woman whose prime asset was the fact that he wanted her and she made him feel good. *A woman he cared about.*

His parents had taught him duty and responsibility. To sacrifice personal desires for the greater good. That had been reinforced by the debacle of Fuad's time in power.

Yet for the first time he wondered if the greater good justified the personal sacrifice. Parting from Rosanna *was* a sacrifice. The idea caught him by the throat. The floor shifted beneath his feet and he was glad when Rosanna's terse words fractured his thoughts.

'I see.'

She sat up and shuffled back against the pillows, her breasts jiggling delectably, and Salim's mouth dried. Then she lifted the sheet and tucked it under her arms, something she hadn't done in all the time they'd been here. Salim felt something sharp scrape through his chest and plunge into his belly.

She spoke again, her voice cool and measured. 'You won't be back, will you?'

He stared. Had he *wanted* her to cling and beg him to stay? 'No. It will take some time.'

And their time here was due to end in two days. He had a full schedule lined up after that.

Rosanna nodded. 'You shower while I start packing.'

Salim frowned. He should be glad she was taking this with good grace. That she was being practical.

Instead something like fury ignited. At the negotiators who'd done their job too well. At the foreign king who'd proved ready for a treaty. At Rosanna for not caring that their time was done.

He couldn't imagine driving with her back to the capital. He didn't have enough command of his emotions to act for an extended period as if none of this mattered.

The pain searing his gut was proof it *did* matter. To him

at least. Though it wasn't supposed to. Though his lover looked as calm as if he'd commented on the weather, not broken up their affair.

'Don't bother.' He surged to his feet, unable to sit still. He watched her gaze trawl over his bare body and felt a flare of satisfaction at the interest she couldn't hide, but not enough to temper his mood. 'There's no need to pack. Stay the rest of the week as planned and have a holiday. A car will come for you in a couple of days. I'll have a shower and be on my way in ten minutes.'

He turned and strode to the bathroom. Because he knew that even now there was a danger he'd weaken and haul her into his arms.

CHAPTER THIRTEEN

ROSANNA HAD BEEN back at the capital for four days when she realised something was wrong.

At first she thought she was imagining things. Since the evening Salim had left so abruptly she'd struggled. Every action, every conversation, took so much effort, but nowhere near as much as it took to conceal her hurt.

She'd watched him walk out that night without so much as a farewell kiss and realised she'd made the biggest mistake of her life.

Once she'd assumed that had been trusting Phil, the man who'd duped her. But that paled into insignificance compared with the disaster of falling in love with Salim.

Totally, irrefutably in love with Salim.

The man who'd seen her as a convenient sexual partner till their passion ended. Now he presumably expected her to find him the perfect wife.

Not that he'd deigned to see her since she'd returned. She'd tried and failed to schedule an appointment. As if she were an importunate petitioner instead of a valued worker. Or ex-lover.

Rosanna snatched a fractured breath and told herself hearts didn't really break. Yet she grabbed the doorjamb of the office she'd been assigned as she swayed. Her knees had gone soft.

Like her heart and her head.

Because even when Salim had left abruptly, even when he'd thanked her formally for their time together, she'd waited for him to add something. A promise of time together back in the capital, for after all they'd only had five of their seven days. Or some sign that their intimacy had been special to him.

She'd waited in vain.

Five days with Salim had enmeshed her deeper in her feelings for him, while it appeared that he'd been cured of his desire for her. Just as he'd predicted.

Their time together had ended his desire but nearly destroyed her.

That's how she felt, lost and hurting. Unable to work because Salim didn't have time to see her. And because she didn't have the heart to find more possible brides.

Now, on top of that, something else was wrong.

The palace employee who'd just brought her afternoon coffee and pastry, a woman she knew and usually enjoyed chatting with, had blushed and stammered when Rosanna spoke to her. She hadn't met Rosanna's eyes and had scurried away so fast Rosanna wondered if she'd offended her.

This morning something similar had happened with another staff member. She'd wondered if word had leaked out about her affair with Salim. She'd sought out Taqi and asked if she'd done something wrong but he'd refuted the idea.

She firmed her lips. She might be in limbo waiting for Salim to see her, but she could at least get to the bottom of this mystery. Ignoring the tantalising scent of coffee wafting from the tray on her desk, she left her office. Taqi *must* know what was going on.

Moments later Rosanna pulled up short at the large waiting room outside the sheikh's offices.

There on the other side of the room was one of the secretaries who worked with Taqi. Walking beside him in a flowing gown of lustrous amber was Zarah, one of the potential candidates for Salim's attention. The one who, it had turned out, was niece to the Minister for Finance. And there was the Minister, entering the sheikh's office with his niece, a satisfied look on his face.

Rosanna withdrew a couple of steps, putting her hand on the cool decorative wall tiles beside her, needing support.

Salim had halted the matchmaking while he was away with Rosanna. He'd insisted she couldn't resume her work until she spoke to him and he decided how they'd proceed.

Yet here was one of the marriage candidates being ushered, with a member of her family, in to see the sheikh.

Had Salim grown impatient working with Rosanna? Had he decided that, given their intimacy, he couldn't trust her to continue her work?

Obviously he had. He was meeting Zarah without discussing it with Rosanna.

A storm of emotions bombarded her. She told herself not to jump to conclusions. Perhaps Zarah was here for some other reason.

Yet Zarah's work as a photographer wouldn't bring her in contact with Salim. She didn't do portraits. Besides, if they were discussing her work why was her uncle here?

Rosanna recalled the man's antagonism and Salim's comment about him wanting his niece to become queen. No matter how Rosanna considered it, it seemed Zarah was here for that very reason.

Salim had cut Rosanna out of the process. Maybe it wasn't that he didn't trust her but he felt uncomfortable having her involved now they'd been intimate.

No wonder she hadn't been able to get an appointment!

Rosanna slumped, her shoulder to the wall.

Zarah was graceful and pretty, a local who knew Dhalkur. Who had important family connections. She'd make Salim an excellent wife. She even had gorgeous dark honey-coloured hair courtesy of her foreign mother.

Did Salim find her attractive? Desirable?

Rosanna pressed a palm to her stomach as nausea churned. Nausea and distress.

And an anguished scraping hurt, like claws drawing blood.

Jealousy.

She didn't remember stumbling to her room. She didn't remember sitting, staring at the courtyard till darkness closed in. The afternoon was a nightmarish haze, punctuated by the occasional sickening rush of blood when she thought she heard footsteps in the concealed passage to the sheikh's suite. But she'd imagined it. Salim didn't come to her.

Now she faced the truth she'd known for four days yet not quite believed. He would never come to her again.

The realisation made her hollow inside. As if she were nothing but an empty husk.

Except she wasn't completely empty. She still had the capacity to hurt. And to yearn.

Rosanna considered what she knew about Salim. His pride and determination. He'd needed both to survive life with his sadistic older brother. He hadn't said much about Fuad but the things he'd let slip painted a picture of constant alertness around his brother. And of parents more focused on their royal duties than creating a warm, loving family.

Not that Salim complained. He'd spoken of the valuable lessons learned via military service and royal training and it was clear he'd cared for his parents. Yet his curiosity about her family, his fascination with so much that she took for granted, hinted that his experience of love and even trust were different to hers. Just as his expectations of marriage were completely different.

Yet despite telling herself not to, she'd begun to believe Salim felt more than lust for her.

The trouble was he'd been brought up not to believe

in love. He'd made it clear love didn't factor in his world, warning her not to expect too much of him.

That last day when he'd taken her to meet Murad's family and then to his village, Rosanna had been seduced by the heady feeling that Salim shared part of himself. That he really cared for her.

His actions since disproved that.

Rosanna stared at the now moonlit courtyard, the scent of roses rich and heavy in the night air. How many women over the centuries had sat here, pining for a man who would never return their feelings?

For surely the story Salim had told her about the sheikh who fell in love with his chosen bride, and all those generations of descendants who married for love, was no more than a fairy tale.

This wasn't a place where happy ever afters came true.

Even if they did, Rosanna MacIain wasn't the woman to find one. She'd thought she'd loved Phil, only to discover he wasn't the man she'd believed him to be. Then, despite her caution, she'd fallen for Salim and been rejected.

There wouldn't be a third time. Rosanna refused to open herself up to such hurt again. She was done with love. Or would be as soon as she could take her wounded heart away from here and lick her wounds in private.

She had a horrible feeling it might take years but she *would* get over Salim.

But first they had unfinished business. He'd signed a contract with Marian's company. Rosanna couldn't allow her mistake, agreeing to an affair, to affect that. She knew how much time and money had already been invested in this project and how vital its success was to Marian.

Rosanna would see the job successfully completed no matter what.

The first step was seeing Salim.

All she had to do was find a way to get past all his protective staff and then treat him like a stranger, not the man who'd broken her heart.

Her huff of laughter sounded suspiciously like a groan of pain.

CHAPTER FOURTEEN

'MY APOLOGIES, YOUR MAJESTY. It won't happen again.'

Salim shook his head. 'One apology was enough, Taqi, and please, stop using my title.' They usually worked informally when alone. 'I've had enough of it for one day.'

The Minister for Finance had been at his most obsequious and had left Salim fuming with frustration. He'd have enjoyed kicking the man out, except his niece, Zarah, didn't deserve such rough treatment. No matter how foul a mood her sheikh was in.

Salim had to give the man credit. He'd known enough to wait until Taqi was away from the office before persuading a less experienced staff member to admit him. Presented with a *fait accompli* it had been easier for Salim to see the pair.

After all, Zarah was one of the candidates Rosanna had selected for him to consider. It made sense to meet her.

Yet it had felt wrong. Even now Salim's gut roiled with distaste. Not at Zarah, who it transpired was a lovely woman, but at the notion of considering a bride.

Because he was still fixated on Rosanna.

He'd avoided seeing her since her return from the Queen's Palace because he needed time to shore up his defences. He'd had his time with her and now it had to be over. Though it didn't feel like it.

It felt… No, it *had* to be over. He had a duty to find the

most suitable queen for Dhalkur. He wouldn't dishonour Rosanna by continuing their affair while he shopped for a wife.

'There's something else you need to know,' Taqi said. 'The reason I was out of the office so long.'

Salim looked at his aide and friend and read the worried furrow on his brow. 'Take a seat and tell me.'

'It's about Ms MacIain. Rumours are circulating at court about her.'

Silently Salim berated himself. He'd tried to ensure their affair wouldn't become public but it seemed he hadn't been able to protect Rosanna as planned.

'It's said she's a criminal. That she and her ex-fiancé stole huge amounts of money from unsuspecting investors. Some elderly people lost their life savings.'

'What?' Salim braced his hands on his chair. 'That's nonsense.'

'She told you the truth then?'

'No. This is the first I've heard of it. But I know Rosanna. She's no thief.'

Taqi gave him a speculative look which he ignored. Salim knew Rosanna and this simply wasn't true. 'Who's spreading the rumours and what are they using as evidence?'

His staff had checked her references and qualifications but that was all. He hadn't ordered a full investigation and didn't know all her past.

Yet he knew her in the ways that mattered.

Anger seethed through him that people were maligning her.

'That's what took me a while. I put someone onto digging into Ms MacIain's past—' Taqi glanced at Salim as if expecting a protest '—while I followed up the source of the rumours. They originated with the Minister for Finance's staff.'

Salim sat back, pondering. The man was a nuisance. Good at his job but always looking to increase his power. His current focus was promoting his niece as a royal bride, not knowing Zarah was already on the list of candidates.

'The rumours began with Ms MacIain's return to the palace. From something a staff member let slip, I suspect the Minister guessed where she spent last week.'

Salim nodded. No doubt he'd made it his business to know. Had he assumed, as Salim had, that theirs would be a short affair, soon over? Rosanna's return to the palace would make him see her as a serious threat to his niece's prospects. That must have prompted his smear campaign.

'What are they saying?'

'That millions of dollars were stolen from investors. That she and her fiancé were in it together. He went to prison and she only escaped sentencing because of an unscrupulous lawyer and a legal loophole.'

Pain clamped Salim's skull as he ground his teeth. 'I knew her ex had misled her but not like that.' He'd imagined infidelity.

'He channelled the funds through a joint account they'd set up, which is why she was investigated. But she was cleared of involvement. There was never any question of charges being laid against her. She lost money too, and though I still need to check this, it seems she tried to pay back some money to a couple of elderly victims, even though she wasn't to blame.'

That sounded foolhardy but noble and all too possible. For all her professionalism he suspected Rosanna had a soft heart.

'Does she know about the rumours?' he asked.

He had to squash them before she found out. The idea of her suffering for what her ex had done, and because of her involvement with Salim, was unbearable.

'I'm not sure. She wanted to see me this afternoon but I've been too busy.'

Salim nodded, his thoughts racing. 'We need to deal with this. Straight away.'

Rosanna surveyed her wardrobe.

She needed something elegant enough for the gala gallery opening and eye-catching because she refused to let Salim ignore her any longer. But she refused to spend her hard-earned money on new clothes just to confront *him*.

Emotions churned but she told herself it was impatience she felt. And determination. Not hurt or regret.

She reached for a scarlet top and a pair of silky white palazzo pants that she'd packed at the last moment. The top had a straight boat neck and its long chiffon sleeves gave an air of elegance. It was perfect, demure because it covered her totally, yet provocative with its unmissable colour and the way it moulded her body.

She'd had enough of fading into the background at Salim's convenience.

What she'd say when she saw him, she had yet to decide. A public event wasn't ideal, but if it was the only way she could see him, she'd make it work.

Rosanna had an invitation to the event because she'd originally planned to introduce some potential brides today. Before Salim decided to postpone her work.

Rosanna's heart lurched. The search was continuing without her.

She hated the idea of continuing the role of matchmaker but she'd despise herself if she let him dismiss her both personally and professionally without making a stand.

The event was crowded. There were locals in traditional clothes, foreigners in suits and designer fashions and enough jewels to dazzle the unwary.

Rosanna ignored them all as she made her way towards the central atrium where the crowd was thickest. Soon she was rewarded with the sight of Salim, half a head taller than most of the men around him and more compelling than any of the art on the walls.

Her heart stuttered and she pressed her hand to her breastbone.

This wouldn't do. She wasn't even close yet she felt a flurry of nerves.

Determined, Rosanna forged a path towards him. Finally she was close enough to hear the deep burr of his voice, and feel it like the memory of a caress stroking her abdomen, breasts and lips.

Despair assailed her.

She couldn't do this. Couldn't march up to him and demand a meeting. She'd done it before but that was when she hadn't known the truth of her feelings for Salim. To face him before all these curious eyes and pretend she felt nothing…

Rosanna was turning away when a voice stopped her.

'Ah, there she is. Ms MacIain, the very woman.'

What was he playing at? He'd avoided her for days yet now he singled her out in this crowd.

She swung around, her breath shallow as that dark, impenetrable gaze snared hers.

Something pulsed between them. Recognition, memory, desire.

No! She might feel that but she had to stop imagining he did too. What for her had been a primal connection had been for Salim simple lust, now eradicated.

'Your Majesty.' As the crowd parted she sank into a deep curtsey.

'This is very timely,' Salim said, beckoning her as she rose. 'My friend here was just mentioning you.'

Rosanna approached, her heart sinking as she recognised Zarah and her uncle with Salim.

'Mentioning me?'

She couldn't imagine why and, seeing the discomfort on Zarah's face, suspected something unpleasant.

Salim nodded. 'The Minister has taken an interest in you and especially your relationship with your ex-fiancé.'

At his words Rosanna froze in horror. She felt again that terrible plunging sensation, as if her stomach went into freefall. Once, back in Australia, she'd felt that way all the time.

'I was about to enlighten him about the actual situation but since you're here perhaps you'd care to.'

Salim knew about Phil? She hadn't told him any details. It was a part of her life she preferred not to remember.

Yet as she stood gaping she registered the tension in the small group before her and the martial light in Salim's eyes. Yes, he knew about Phil. The question was whether he knew the truth. Was that anger directed at her?

Suddenly she realised how quiet it was. Conversations around them petered out as people leaned closer. Heat flushed her cheeks as she realised it wasn't only the Minister for Finance who'd heard something of her past.

Taking a deep breath, she said slowly and clearly, 'I was once engaged but I broke it off. I discovered the man I'd trusted was a thief and embezzler. He's now in prison and I have no contact with him.'

The minister frowned, still looking supercilious. 'I'm surprised you weren't implicated too, given your close relationship. Wasn't it true that you were questioned by the police?'

Rosanna swallowed down the sour taste on her tongue. She read malice in his stare and knew he was deliberately making trouble.

But before she could respond Salim spoke, his deep

voice carrying. 'Since you're so interested, I can tell you the police investigation discounted that possibility completely. There was never any question that Ms MacIain was involved. She was a victim too. To suggest otherwise is slander.'

Rosanna suppressed a gasp. She wished she'd had such powerful allies at the time when there'd been speculation about her involvement.

'Of course, Your Majesty. Forgive me.' The man gave a half-bow. 'I'm naturally concerned that anyone working in the palace is entirely trustworthy.'

He turned to Rosanna, his mouth tight. She hadn't liked him the first time they met. Now his stare made her shudder. 'It's strange you were taken in by him. You work in recruitment. Surely that requires the ability to judge character.'

'It does.' Rosanna held his eyes, her chin lifting. 'I've learned a lot since then. I've learned not to trust too easily and definitely not to let my emotions cloud my judgement. I let a person's actions speak for them, not the lies they tell or insinuations they make.'

You could have heard a pin drop in the silence. But Rosanna refused to back down, despite his scowl. He knew she referred to him as much as to Phil.

Just as she expected another verbal attack, she felt warmth encompass her fingers. She looked down to discover Salim had moved closer, his hand enfolding hers.

Did she imagine a hushed murmur through the crowd?

Her pulse beat hard and fast, pumping heat through her stunned body. She didn't dare look at him but that touch, that reassurance, meant everything.

Rosanna had fought her own battles for so long she wasn't used to having others stand up for her. Her family had been a thousand kilometres away when the debacle with Phil broke. They'd been supportive but she'd faced each day alone.

Salim spoke, his voice cold and carrying. 'That's an important skill. To mistrust plausible, unctuous people who are motivated purely by self-interest rather than the common good.'

Now there was no mistaking the whispered conversations around them. Or the way the minister's face paled.

He'd been assessed and publicly found wanting by his sheikh. No one listening to Salim could be in any doubt that he was referring to the minister.

Stiffly the man bowed and withdrew, taking his niece with him, and Salim turned to the curator standing nearby as if nothing untoward had happened.

Except he kept hold of Rosanna's hand as he introduced her to the curator and others. Nor did he release his hold as they moved through the building, viewing the exhibition.

Rosanna barely spoke, her emotions too close to the surface as she struggled to maintain her poise. But she couldn't miss the way others reacted to the sight of her standing close by Salim, her hand tucked in his.

Surely aligning himself with her complicated everything?

He'd dumped her. He'd also made it clear earlier that he didn't relish the idea of being associated with a woman who brought scandal in her wake. Admittedly he'd been talking about a wife, not a short-term lover, but surely the same principle applied.

Rosanna found herself biting back a slew of questions as they slowly progressed through the building and spoke with what seemed every VIP in attendance.

She might love this man but she found him impossible to understand.

CHAPTER FIFTEEN

SALIM KEPT HER by his side through the rest of the event, even leading her to his limousine for the return trip to the palace.

Through it all Rosanna's sense of unreality grew stronger and her body more tense as she fought to appear at ease. She wanted to spurn Salim's touch and demand an explanation. She wanted to curl up against his solid shoulder and take her first unfettered breath in days. She wanted…

She couldn't have what she wanted.

Even though he'd stood up for her publicly against one of his most influential advisors.

Rosanna's gait was stiff and her heart bruised as Salim ushered her through the palace and into a large sitting room.

When she recognised it she stumbled to a halt.

Her breath shuddered out. Salim's private apartment. Over there was the spot they'd first kissed. Where he'd told her he couldn't think about any other woman because he could only think of her.

Rosanna's gaze slewed to the door on the other side of the room. The door that led deeper into his private realm and to his bedroom. Horrified, she slammed that memory shut and stalked away from his silent presence behind her.

Salim hadn't said a word since they left the exhibition, presumably because they hadn't been alone. But that silence unnerved her.

She swung around to face him when she reached the window. 'Are you going to explain?'

That took him by surprise. His eyes widened and his jaw firmed. Why? *She* hadn't been the one to make a scene. His friend had done that. Then Salim had compounded it, ensuring everyone saw them together as if they were…

'First you refuse to see me. I presume because I'm an embarrassing complication. Then you parade me around as if I'm some prize VIP for everyone to stare at.'

For several seconds Salim said nothing while the atmosphere between them thickened.

'You don't embarrass me. And I find it hard to believe you don't like being stared at.' His gaze trailed down her body, igniting sparks everywhere it touched.

Rosanna's chin hiked up as she planted her hands on her hips. 'I'm covered from neck to ankle.'

He shook his head and moved closer. 'Maybe so, yet I can see every delicious curve of your body.' His voice hit a deep, growly note that she felt in her marrow. 'And that red screams for attention.'

He was right. She'd been desperate for him to notice her. But she didn't understand what was happening. That fed her annoyance.

'So, are you going to explain?'

There it was again, that glint in Salim's eyes that spoke of temper fiercely leashed.

'You think *I* have something to explain?' He paused, his stare piercing. 'Why didn't you tell me about your lover?'

'*Ex*-lover. And I did, I told you he'd betrayed me.'

'You didn't mention how. You didn't tell me the trouble he'd caused you.'

Rosanna drew in a deep breath. 'It was no one's business but mine. *I'm* the one he hurt, not anyone here.'

'You think that doesn't matter?' Then before she could process that Salim continued. 'And you're wrong. It's now my business since you work closely with me and reside at the palace.'

Abruptly all her indignation seeped away like air from a punctured balloon. She sagged against the window frame, guilt eating at her. 'You're right. I'm sorry. I never thought my past could reflect on you or your administration.'

'You think I'm worried for myself?'

Rosanna couldn't read Salim's expression except she was sure fury was part of it. This really was the end.

'You're going to break the contract, aren't you? You're going to send me away.'

Suddenly she felt overcome. She'd kept her head up through that interminable public event but now her hurt at Salim's rejection and her fears for Marian's business felt like stone after stone being piled on top of her, crushing her into the ground.

'Come.' His voice was brusque. 'Sit. You look done in.'

'No.' She blinked and tried to gather her strength. It didn't help when Salim was kind. That only fed her weakness for him. 'I'd rather stand.'

Rosanna watched his fingers clench at his sides then stretch out as if he deliberately tried to relax. 'You're one obstinate woman, Rosanna.'

He should know. He was the same. It was something they shared.

'It's how I survive,' she murmured.

She'd need every bit of tenacity and determination to get through the ordeal to come. Leaving Dhalkur. Never seeing Salim again. Knowing she'd damaged her aunt's business at a time when Marian needed her help more than ever as she recuperated.

Finding a way to patch up her splintered heart.

Rosanna sucked in a quick breath that sounded horribly like a sob and forced her gaze from his. Yet she felt the phantom touch of his hand on hers as if he still held it. Just as she still smelled that intoxicating scent of virile man mixed with cedar and spice, though it wasn't physically possible when he stood so far away.

How long before those memories faded? Or would they haunt her the rest of her life?

'What was the idea, holding onto me like that in front of everyone?'

She needed something concrete to focus on. Preferably something that made her angry, because the alternative would be to reveal how sad and weak she felt.

Rosanna frowned, remembering the way people had stared while trying to look as if they didn't. Her flesh tightened. 'It was totally unnecessary.'

'Oh, believe me, Rosanna, it was necessary.'

Staring into his midnight eyes she felt a familiar beat of connection. That infuriated her as did the fact he was holding back. 'But people stared, as if you'd done something significant.'

Salim's guarded expression grew even more unreadable and Rosanna felt her eyes grow round. Her nape prickled in premonition. 'It *did* mean something! Are you going to tell me or am I going to be the only person in the dark?'

She folded her arms around her middle, as if that could prevent the hurt building inside. She didn't know what was going on and felt like she was riding an out-of-control roller-coaster.

Salim spread his hands and lifted his shoulders. 'In Dhalkur the sheikh shakes hands with other heads of state. Other than that, in public he would only touch a member of his family.'

Rosanna digested that. Clearly she wasn't a member of his family. She surged forward, closing the distance between them. 'You mean you were putting your *mark* on me?'

She'd *known* that touching him in public, or allowing

him to touch her, was wrong. Except it felt so right that she hadn't been able to pull away.

'You can't just reach out and...and...claim me like a chattel!'

'You're right.' Yet he didn't look in the least abashed. 'Would you be less angry if I said I was primarily thinking about the need for comfort?'

Rosanna jerked back. Had she looked so forlorn? She hoped not, but Salim knew her well. He'd probably read her distress. 'I don't need you to comfort me.'

Salim's mouth lifted in a rueful way that twisted her insides into knots. 'Maybe I was the one who needed the connection.'

Salim watched Rosanna's stormy eyes turn blank with shock.

He was shocked too. Admitting to weakness went against his character. Even as a boy he'd avoided it, with Fuad ever ready to pounce on any weak point. Salim had grown into a man who drove himself hard to do his duty and relegate personal feelings to the back of his consciousness.

He didn't *do* personal feelings.

Until Rosanna.

'What do you mean, Salim?'

Her voice wobbled and he felt an answering tremor rip through him, as if the very earth shook beneath their feet.

'It means I didn't care how it looked or what people thought. I saw you hurting and I wanted to comfort you. Because watching you hurt caused me pain too.' He paused. 'And I wanted to protect you.'

That had been a revelation to him, though not a surprise.

'You already protected me. You championed me. You made a government minister look like a snivelling bully.'

'And so he is.'

It had taken all Salim's discipline not to punch the man in his smarmy face. The fact that Salim had already been poleaxed by the sight of Rosanna marching towards him, sexier than ever and sparking with the latent energy of a lit firecracker about to explode, hadn't helped. He'd wanted to hustle her away from all those avid looks and gossiping mouths. But it had been imperative he deal with the rumours first.

Rosanna opened her mouth and shut it again. For such a forthright woman it was a sign of either confusion or superhuman restraint. Salim suddenly found himself nervous, trying to gauge her reaction.

'When did you find out about Phil?'

'That he'd embroiled you in his crimes? Late yesterday.'

'You heard the rumours and believed them.'

Rosanna's downturned mouth was eloquent.

'No. Taqi came to me with news the Minister for Finance and his staff were spreading rumours that you were a criminal who'd escaped justice on a technicality.' He saw her turn pale and hurried on. 'I knew it wasn't true but had my staff dig for any details on the public record ready to refute the rumours.'

'You *knew* it wasn't true?'

When he nodded Rosanna shuffled across to the sofa and collapsed onto it. She looked stunned.

'I had no idea about Phil's crimes,' she murmured. 'Not until everything fell apart.'

'You don't have to tell me.' Salim wanted to know but not if it caused her more pain.

'There's not much to tell. Phil always had expensive tastes but when he changed jobs he started mixing with people who had serious money and liked to spend it. He was on a good wage but nothing to compare. He told me later that he'd taken the money *for us*.'

Her mouth turned down in disgust. 'He wanted a fancy

wedding at the most expensive venue. A honeymoon at an ultra-exclusive overseas resort. To buy a prestige apartment. I kept telling him I was happy with what we could afford. We put a percentage of our incomes into a joint account to cover the wedding and save a house deposit but I didn't check the balance. I thought I knew how much there'd be.'

She sighed and looked down at her hands clasped in her lap. 'Meanwhile he developed a taste for high-stakes gambling with his friends. He lost and stole more in hopes of winning enough to hide what he'd stolen.'

'And he got found out.'

Rosanna nodded. 'I'd actually been going to call the wedding off. Phil had changed so much from the man I knew.'

Salim sank onto the lounge beside her. He longed to pull her close but held back.

'Thank you for believing in me.' Her eyes, dark as a stormy sky, held his. How he longed to see them glitter brilliant with joy. 'I'm sorry to taint you with my past.'

He shook his head. 'It's a storm in a teacup.' Or it would be once he was finished.

'Nevertheless, I appreciate you standing by me.' She paused. 'And it did help when you held my hand. I felt a bit wobbly. Just as well it actually didn't mean anything.' Her gaze darted to his. 'You didn't really mean it about people thinking you'd claimed me.'

Salim reached for her hands. His chest constricted as he felt how unsteady they were. Deliberately he lifted them from her lap and threaded his fingers through hers.

'Everything I said was true. By now half of Dhalkur knows you're the woman I want in my life.'

Her eyes were huge and troubled but she looked too exhausted for outrage. 'You mean, they know I'm your lover?'

'Some will speculate. But I meant they'll see the action as a clear token of my intention to marry you.'

Salim had been wrong about her exhaustion. Rosanna snatched her hands back and shot to her feet in a single move. But he was just as fast. He stood before her, toe to toe, forcing her to look at him.

'Rosanna?'

She looked stricken. Not what he'd intended or hoped for. Salim was used to women eager for his attention. Women who'd jump at the chance to be his bride.

But Rosanna had never been like other women, had she?

Why had he imagined this would be straightforward?

His gut twisted. She couldn't surely reject him?

She shook her head, her lovely dark hair slipping around her shoulders. 'What a mess. How are we going to get out of this?'

Salim's spine stiffened. 'We don't have to get out of it.'

'You mean I just leave quietly and everything eventually dies down?'

How could she even think it? 'Absolutely not.'

Her head jerked up. 'What *are* you saying, Salim?'

Nerves gnawed at Salim's belly. He felt unsure of himself. Unsure of Rosanna.

But he wasn't a man to dither.

'I'm saying we marry.'

'You've got to be kidding! To avoid gossip? Just because you held my hand? That's pretty extreme.'

'Not as extreme as losing you.'

That stopped her rant. Her cheeks flushed and her questioning look scored him to the bone. He grimaced, fully aware of how he'd publicly put himself and his feelings on the line. 'Don't worry, Rosanna. You can always refuse. That's your prerogative.'

'Why are you doing this?'

Salim hauled in a sustaining breath. 'I thought that was obvious. Because I *want* you, Rosanna.'

She backed away a step. 'That's just lust—'

He took a step towards her. His pace was longer than hers and it brought him into her personal space.

'Not just lust. A whole lot more. Things I never expected.' He paused, searching for some sign she felt the same. 'Your happiness matters to me and when you hurt, I hurt. I want to protect you from harm, but I love watching you succeed at whatever you set your mind to. Did you know I find your competence incredibly sexy?'

Given the way she gaped up at him, clearly not. He smiled through taut facial muscles. It was rare that he found Rosanna lost for words.

'I've fallen in love with you, my darling.'

'That's impossible. You don't believe in love.'

'I didn't. I never expected it.' Which was why he'd been slow to understand what was happening to him. 'But there's no other explanation for the way I feel. I want to make you mine for always.'

Yet Rosanna didn't smile or sink into his embrace. Salim fought not to reach for her, knowing he needed her to come willingly, not because she was seduced by passion. Not because he was the sheikh and he commanded it.

'This is crazy talk. You need an aristocratic wife. Someone who understands diplomacy and Dhalkur. Who speaks the language and can be useful. Not a woman with a tainted reputation.' Suddenly she was blinking. 'Not a woman who doesn't understand the culture or politics.' The blinks came faster and his heart hammered against his ribs. 'Not someone who's brunette and only medium height and—'

'My love.' Salim pulled her into his arms and held her tight against him. Was that a sob? She was shaking, her head burrowed against him so he couldn't see her face. 'Does my proposal make you so unhappy?'

'You didn't propose.'

He slid his hands up her arms and stepped back, holding her at arm's length. Her overbright eyes shone misty grey and Salim felt excitement stir.

'Beautiful Rosanna. Will you do me the honour of marrying me? Will you be mine for the rest of our lives? I promise to be faithful and supportive and to love you always.'

Her mouth crumpled and abruptly his welling satisfaction disappeared. Had he got it wrong? Did she not feel this amazing connection between them?

'Even though your people won't respect you for choosing someone with a past?'

He shook his head. 'I thought I needed a bride who met all those criteria because I never understood what I really needed was a woman I could love. My people will welcome the woman I choose, because she's brave and true as well as beautiful and kind.'

Her arrested expression told him he'd finally got through to her.

'Even though you risk getting a crick in your neck from kissing me?'

Salim's heart gave a great thump of relief. 'I'm willing to risk it.' He swallowed, his mouth as dry as Dhalkur's mighty desert. 'How do you feel about me, Rosanna?'

'You know far too much about seducing a woman until she can't think straight.' Salim grinned. 'You're also too good at giving orders and expecting to get your own way.' She paused. 'You have an important job and I'm scared I'll be a liability.'

'Never. We'll make a perfect team. You can temper my autocratic tendencies and I can teach you everything you need to know about being royal. I predict you'll become one of Dhalkur's most popular queens. You're honest and decent. You're clever and capable. And you're right for *me*.'

That was what mattered.

She blinked up at him. 'You didn't let me finish.'

Salim held his breath. Surely she wouldn't deny him. Surely she cared. He willed it to be so.

'You're proud and obstinate but you're a good man who really cares about people. You have a kind heart and…' Salim felt as if he was stretched on a rack, tortured, as he waited to hear her judgement. 'I don't think I can be happy without you. I love you, Salim.'

He didn't wait for more. He swept her off the ground and into his arms, her words ringing in his ears and his heart overflowing.

'I should have known from the start,' he murmured against her mouth. 'You bewitched me from the first. I couldn't get you out of my head. When you arrived in Dhalkur it seemed like fate.'

'I doubt it. You were angry with me that first night.'

He shook his head as he strode across the room with her in his arms. 'Not angry. Thrilled. Disturbed. Worried. Desperate.'

Her misty smile made his heart turn over. 'I felt the same.'

'Didn't I tell you this was meant to be?' He shouldered the door open and headed down the hall. 'But we'll take this slow. We'll have a long engagement.'

Rosanna nodded. 'That's a good idea. That will give people time to adjust.'

'Exactly. I'll announce it tomorrow. A month from today.'

'A month! That's barely time to organise a dress, let alone a wedding!'

Salim smiled down at her as he carried her over the threshold into the bedroom. 'It's more than enough time when we have a palace full of staff to organise it. Besides, I can't wait any longer.'

His bride-to-be regarded him seriously then slowly nodded. 'In that case we'd better not delay.'

She reached for the top button of his shirt and Salim laughed with pure, exultant joy. He really had found his perfect match.

EPILOGUE

'You look like a fairy princess!'

Rosanna looked from Salim's cousin, Tara, to the full-length mirror.

'I *feel* like one.' She swallowed. 'I can't believe this is happening.'

The reflection before her showed a poised princess wearing cloth of silver, heavily embroidered in more silver, and wearing diamonds at her throat and ears and in a circlet over her unbound hair. Her dress had a dramatic, mediaeval feel with a fitted bodice that gave way, around her hips, to the heavy folds of her full-length, jewel-encrusted skirt. The long sleeves widened from the elbow to reveal linings of exquisite cloth of gold, embroidered with gold thread and studded with rubies.

Rubies to match the simple but beautiful ruby she and Salim had chosen together for her engagement ring.

Rosanna lifted her hand to her throat, feeling her pulse flutter with nerves.

'Believe it, Rosanna. It's happening and I couldn't be happier for you.'

She turned to meet Tara's glowing green eyes. Her soon-to-be cousin, Her Most Royal Highness the Sheikha of Nahrat, resplendent in a gown of green and gold, looked genuinely thrilled.

'I've never seen Salim like this,' Tara went on. 'He's beside himself with pride and nerves.'

'Nerves?'

He'd admitted to nerves on their way to the Queen's Palace the first time, but she'd assumed he was just trying to allay her jitters. Salim took everything in his stride, even winning around his people to accepting his unexpected bride as their new queen.

Far from spending the month of their engagement busy with wedding plans, Salim had taken her around the country, showing her off like a proud fiancé and giving her a chance to get to know her new home.

'Of course, nerves. The man's head over heels in love.' Tara squeezed her hand. 'It's a new and overwhelming concept for a man like him, strong yet sensitive and raised to think only of his duty. Believe me, I know.'

Her smile turned soft and she smoothed her hand over her just discernible baby bump. Rosanna realised she was thinking of her husband, the rather overwhelming yet surprisingly kind sheikh of neighbouring Nahrat.

'Then he'd better get used to it. I'm looking forward to a very long, very happy marriage.'

'I'm glad to hear it.'

That deep voice, husky with emotion, made her swing around.

'Salim!'

He stood in the doorway, the dearest, most handsome man in the world. He too wore silver, with discreet traces of gold edging, as if he'd dressed to match her.

'What are you doing here?'

'You didn't think I was going to make you walk down the aisle alone, do you, in front of thousands of people and all that press?'

For Rosanna's father was on crutches with a sprained ankle and couldn't accompany her. Rosanna's mother had considered doing so but knew it would lead to her husband hobbling down the aisle on his bad foot too and probably damaging it more.

'Hey, she wouldn't be alone, she has me, remember?' Tara piped up, but there was a smile on her face.

'I remember, cuz.' He bent and gave Tara a swift peck on the cheek. 'But this is all new to Rosanna and I want to make it as easy as possible.'

'But surely that's not the tradition?' Rosanna queried.

Salim turned and the warmth in his expression undid the knot of nerves inside. She could do anything, even marry with the cameras of the world's media turned on her, when Salim looked at her that way.

'We'll make our own traditions.' His voice dropped to that low, raspy note she knew signified profound emotion. 'My sweet love.' He stepped towards her but, instead of embracing her, took her hand and pressed it to his mouth. 'You look wondrous.'

'So do you, my darling.'

He looked as if he were about to say more when there was a burst of sound from the next room.

'What's that?'

Rosanna turned as the noise coalesced into a babble, broken by the sound of barking.

Salim's hand clasped hers. 'I didn't think you'd want to wait till after the ceremony to see them.'

Through the open door streamed her parents, siblings and her little nephews and nieces, all exclaiming. Then she was in her mother's arms and her father's, careful of his crutches. She was passed from one family member to the other, engulfed in familiar banter and loving reassurances until Salim announced it was time for the ceremony.

Finally, she and Salim were alone.

'That was close,' Salim said. 'Layla and Qamar almost sneaked in with your family. My fault, your nephews begged to see them.'

Rosanna grinned, the two pups, named for the night and the moon, were still learning obedience. Qamar, her coat the silvery colour of moonlight, had been one of Salim's engagement gifts and more precious to her than the fabulous heirloom jewels she wore.

She reached up and straightened Salim's collar even though it was already perfectly aligned. Because she needed to touch him and reassure herself that he was real. All this felt too good to be true.

He lifted his hand, drawing his knuckles softly down her cheek, and she sucked in her breath.

'I love you so much, Rosanna.'

'You stole the words from my mouth.'

A slow smile spread across his face. 'We're going to be so happy together.' He paused, giving her a chance to blink back tears of joy.

'I know.'

Then, hand in hand, they walked together towards their beckoning future.

Every Dhalkuri who saw them together that day knew for certain that it was true after all. Tradition had been restored. The Sheikhs of Dhalkur married only for true love.

* * * * *

THE POWERFUL BOSS SHE CRAVES

JOSS WOOD

MILLS & BOON

CHAPTER ONE

CAT MEME…RECIPE for lentil and lime salad…picture of a sunset…motivational quote…another cat meme…

Ella Yeung skimmed through her social media, bored to tears. She only had three weeks left at Le Roux Events—thank God—and the last month had been the longest of her life. She'd have stayed at home, as her boss wanted her to do, but pride had her clocking in to work every day. As long as she was an employee of Le Roux Events, she wanted Winters and his pet snake, Siba, the Human Resources officer, to see her face every day, to be reminded of how they'd failed her and, as she'd heard, a handful of other women over the years.

Being the cowards they were, if she walked into a room, they walked out of it.

Lately, Le Roux Events hadn't been a fun place to work but, in three weeks, when she was out of their hair, Ella had no doubt she and her complaints, would soon be forgotten.

Until Neville Pillay, their best client and beloved family entertainer, sexually harassed another woman working at the company. For how much longer would they protect him by sweeping his actions under the already filthy rug?

How—from Winters to Siba, to the Director of Human Resources at Le Roux International to the owners, the Le Roux brothers—could they live with themselves?

Over the past month, she'd tried to shed light on Pillay's

despicable actions, but her complaints had gone nowhere and she hoped it didn't give him the confidence to be bolder, to push for more. Ella knew that he got off on feeling powerful and invincible, and prayed he wouldn't progress to serious sexual assault when the next event planner, secretary, make-up artist, backing singer or PA caught his attention.

It was only after her accusation had become public knowledge—within the company, at least—that she'd discovered he'd sexually harassed at least three other women at Le Roux Events. They'd all subsequently resigned, and Ella had no doubt he'd done the same elsewhere. But how was she supposed to stop him when upper management dismissed her claims and refused to take her seriously?

And, God, she was tired of trying. Tired of fighting. Tired of feeling alone and desperate to be believed. She'd taken her complaints to her boss, Winters, and then to Siba, the Human Resources officer. When it had been put to her that she hadn't actually been raped, that nothing *that* serious had happened—nothing serious? The man had put his hand up her skirt!—she'd emailed the Director of Human Resources of Le Roux International, the sprawling international company that owned the company for which she worked, along with many others.

That fine individual had told her to pipe down, not to make trouble, and that if she kept quiet she'd be given a raise. When she'd refused to do that, she'd been offered a great package to resign. After she'd refused again, she'd been moved from her corner office to a small, cramped office at the far end of the building, which she shared with at least twenty dusty boxes, and had been given low priority events to organise—the events that were usually handed to interns for them to gain experience. Her Wi-Fi access was routinely cut off and her company car had been taken away.

It was obvious that they were trying to push out the trouble maker and, after six weeks, she'd finally cracked and submitted her resignation. Ella wasn't sure whether to feel relieved or angry that she'd buckled. But what she did feel was battered, powerless, less than.

Leaning back in her chair, Ella looked out of her window at the not-so-fabulous view of the car park, wondering yet again how her life had gone off the rails.

Not so long ago, she'd been a well-respected event planner in Durban with a reputation for getting the job done on time, within budget and with flair and pizzazz. She'd been working at a small start-up and, after successfully pulling off a couple of high-profile events, she'd been headhunted to join Le Roux Events, one of the best event-planning companies in the country. She'd be based out of Johannesburg and her new salary and perks would be triple her salary.

It was, so they said, an opportunity not to be missed.

She'd accepted their offer and now, a year later, after having been promoted to Senior Event Planner, she was on her way out. Company management had closed ranks on her, and her colleagues avoided her. Oh, she knew they sympathised with what she was going through—and her female colleagues had sent her messages of support—but times were tough and nobody wanted to get on Winters' bad side. He was a 'you're either with me or you're my enemy' boss and nobody was prepared to risk losing their job by siding with her.

She got it—she did—they had mortgages to pay and families to feed. But it still hurt that she stood alone, fighting this battle not only for herself but also for the past, present and future female employees of the company. But such was the influence, spending power and star power of the company's biggest client.

Ella now knew—in a way she'd suspected before, but only now fully understood—that people only believed what they wanted to, that she couldn't rely on anyone to listen to her or to believe her, and that the only person she could rely on was herself.

Her dad had brushed off her opinion once and his inaction had been a factor in her mother's death. Now her boss refused to entertain her accusations against everyone's favourite client and the bigwigs of Le Roux International put profit and business ahead of their employees' welfare.

Her mum was dead and Predatory Pillay was still on the loose, free to make sexual, offensive comments to other women, to push them up against walls in empty conference rooms and shove his hand up dresses and between their legs…

Ella felt her throat close and her hands prickle and the papers she held fluttered to her desk. She would never have to have anything to do with him again. She was safe and, quite frankly, she'd been lucky. She had no doubt that, had that door not slammed, had they not heard the rumble of a cleaner pushing a cart, Pillay would've done worse…

She wondered if she'd missed any signs, something to suggest that he turned into a monster when no one else was around. But, as hard as she tried, she couldn't think of one instance that made her think he'd assault her; that he was anything other than the perfect gentleman he was reported to be.

Not only had she had been pinned against a wall and subjected to his roving hands but, because she refused to keep quiet, she'd been forced to quit her well-paying job and been branded a trouble maker. How could she be alone with a man again? Would she always be second-guessing herself, scared to take a chance, constantly wondering if this was another situation that would go south? How was she ever going to date a man again, take him home, go to bed with him?

Her faith and trust in people, never good, was now lost. Her trust in herself was shaky at best.

But, worse, what if Pillay did it again? What if the next time, someone didn't interrupt his assault and he raped a woman? Could she live with herself if that happened? But what more could she do? She'd tried to report him, tried to stop him. But she was just one person and Le Roux International was a multi-billion-dollar international company with tens of thousands of employees. She'd tried. That had to be enough.

But it wasn't.

Feeling helpless, and being disbelieved and dismissed made her remember what had happened fourteen years ago, when she'd screamed at her dad to listen to her. She'd begged him to take her mum to hospital, convinced something was very wrong with her suddenly sleepy, drunk-sounding mother. She'd begged, cried and yelled but, because her mum liked the odd lunchtime gin and tonic her father had opted to let her mum 'sleep it off'. Hours later, she had died dead from a massive brain bleed.

She couldn't help wondering, then and now, whether she'd used the wrong words or whether she hadn't expressed herself clearly. Had she been too emotional, not concise enough? Did it matter? Her mum's death had caused her to build strong, high walls. But the Le Roux management, by not believing her, had managed to scale what she'd thought were pretty good defences and flood her still sliced-up soul and unhealed open wounds with the emotional equivalent of hydrochloric acid.

Ella heard a door slam down the hallway and it jerked her out of her cycle of self-pity. Straightening her spine, she told herself to look to the future.

She didn't think anything remained for her in South Africa. The event planning world was interconnected, and Winters had bad-mouthed her to anyone who would listen, from clients to suppliers and competitors. She'd been told that she now had a reputation for being difficult and a trouble maker. There was little chance she'd pick up another job at the same salary and level in the city. She could return to Durban—her father was still there—but what was the point when they didn't talk? Durban would also mean taking a massive cut in salary and smaller projects. It would be a step backwards.

No, her decision to emigrate to the UK was a good one. In a month, she'd be overseas, in a new city and, hopefully, in a new job. She'd have six thousand miles between herself and her dad, and she wouldn't feel obliged to see the man who didn't want to see her. London or Dublin would be a new start, some place where she could breathe and be herself again. And maybe, in a hundred years or so, she might find a man who'd support and believe her.

Then again, she might find a unicorn guarding a pot of gold first.

Through her open window, Ella heard the low growl of a powerful engine. Intrigued, she stood up and gasped when she saw a silver Bentley Bentayga turn into the car park. Before their relationship had fallen apart, Ella and her dad had shared a love of cars, with Ella spending many a Sunday attending car shows with him. The Bentayga was an exceptional SUV, stunningly expensive and, given its stratospheric price, there were only a few in the country.

She'd love to see one up close and personal and she'd give her eye teeth to drive one. Ella watched as the driver expertly spun the huge car into a tight parking space. The door opened and a man exited, and Ella took a moment to admire his height: he had to be six-three or more, with wide shoulders, a broad back and a truly excellent butt. He wore a white shirt, his sleeves rolled up tanned forearms. His shirt was tucked into navy chino pants, held up by what looked like a soft leather belt the same colour as his leather brogues. His short, loose curls were expertly cut, a natural combination of light brown and the darkest blond.

From the back, he was gorgeous. If his face matched his body, he could easily feature on the cover of *Men's Health*.

He turned to walk towards the entrance of their building—was he a potential client?—and Ella saw the thick stubble on his square jaw, strong eyebrows and sexy mouth. Yep, he had a masculine, fallen-angel face…

As if sensing her eyes on him, he abruptly stopped and tipped his head up, scanning the windows. Ella didn't pull back quickly enough and his eyes zeroed in on her, dark and dangerous. She couldn't tell the colour, but saw the intensity in his gaze, and she felt her skin prickle and heat.

She was so busted…

Ella blushed, lifted her hand in half a wave and saw his lips quirk upward in a 'I'm so hot what can I do?' smirk. He lifted two fingers to his temple in a cocky salute and Ella frowned, unimpressed with his attitude.

Sick of men who thought they were God's gift, she opened her window and peered down. 'Get over yourself, I was just admiring your car,' she called to him.

Those strong eyebrows lifted and his smile broadened. Was that a dimple in his left cheek? *Yep, definitely overkill, God.*

'Really? I'm sure you don't even know what it is.'

Oh, God… His voice was warm and deep, a voice that spoke of an excellent education and old money. It was a bedroom voice…

Concentrate, Ella!

He'd just issued a challenge and it was one she could easily win. She intended to take Mr Cocky down a peg or two.

'It's a Bentley Bentayga, S-model and powered by a six-hundred-and-twenty-six horsepower, twelve-cylinder W-shaped engine. It has an eight-speed automatic transmission and is rated as the fastest SUV in the world. Although Lamborghini might dispute that claim, as the Urus SUV is also pretty exceptional.' As she expected, his mouth fell open and his expression changed to astonishment.

'Newsflash, Hotshot—girls can be interested in cars too,' she told him, before pulling her window closed.

God, she was so sick of being dismissed and underestimated! Sick of men who thought the world revolved around them.

Ella turned at a rap on her door and smiled when Janie, her closest friend at Le Roux Events, stepped into the room, her face alive with curiosity. 'Something big is going down,' she announced, her light brown eyes alive with curiosity.

Since she only had three weeks to go, Ella didn't much care. 'Has Paul in accounting received new hair plugs or did someone steal Eva's parking spot?' Ella asked.

'Neither,' Janie said, her eyes wide. 'Apparently the big boss is in the building!'

'Big boss?'

'Micah Le Roux, one of the owners!'

Ella frowned. The Le Roux brothers owned the events company but she'd never seen them on the premises. Her boss went to their offices, not the other way round. Janie walked over to the window and pointed to the car park below. Ella looked over her shoulder and saw a group of about five men standing by the Bentayga, discussing and admiring the car.

'That's his car, and Naomi just confirmed that he's here to see Ben. I wonder why?' Janie mused. 'Do you think it could have anything to do with your complaint?'

So the hot guy in the cool car was one of the owners of the company. Interesting. Ella recalled Janie's question and shook her head. She was too sensible to assume that. 'I doubt it. Even if he could be bothered, men like him, when discussing issues like mine, would demand a meeting in his office. He wouldn't drive across town weeks after the incident.'

'Then why do you think he's here?'

'I couldn't care less,' Ella answered. Why should she? She'd worked twelve-hour days for months and months, organised some incredible events and had come in on time and budget on every project. Le Roux Events had made money off her hard work but when she'd asked for support, to be believed, they'd metaphorically punched her in the face.

It wasn't fair…and it most definitely wasn't right.

And, because he was on the premises and she had the opportunity, maybe it was time that someone told Micah Le Roux that straight to his face. Ella frowned, mentally asking herself if she really intended to confront the company owner…

For her peace of mind, she had to.

Would anything change? Probably not. Would she get an apology? That was wishful thinking. But Micah Le Roux would know exactly what she thought about his company, his managers and their abysmal attitude towards sexual harassment.

And maybe, just maybe, something she said would cause him to review their HR policies; to take the subject seriously.

She sent Janie what she hoped was a confident smile. 'Wish me luck.'

Janie's eyes widened. 'What are you going to do?'

'Ambush Micah Le Roux and give him several pieces of my mind.'

If he did nothing, changed nothing—as she expected him to—then she could leave this job and city, knowing she'd done everything she possibly could to prevent the same thing, or worse, happening to another woman.

Micah only allowed his smile to bloom, the first in days, when he knew he was out of sight of the gorgeous brown-eyed woman. A woman who knew a thing or two about cars, which upped her sexy factor by a good ten per cent.

He also liked her feisty attitude. He'd been firmly put back into his box and he couldn't remember the last time that had happened. As a Le Roux, one of the most powerful businessmen on the continent, that didn't happen often.

Or at all.

He'd felt her eyes on him the moment he'd left his car, had clocked the prickle on the back of his neck, the tingle in his palms. He'd scanned the building and quickly found her, standing at a window on the second floor.

He hadn't meant anything when he'd flashed her a smile and saluted her. He'd been acknowledging her presence but she'd taken it as him being flirtatious… Hell, maybe he had been. It was just what he did, a part of his charming persona. His twin, Jago, was meant to be the stand-offish and temperamental one, whereas Micah was seen to be more laid back, charming and personable.

That couldn't be further from the truth, though. He was the one who had to keep his temper leashed, his impulsivity in check, his quick tongue tempered. Charm and geniality were a cloak he could pull on and remove at will.

The woman at the window hadn't appreciated his casual, flirtatious attitude. Her eyebrows had pulled together, her wide mouth had thinned and she'd gripped the edge of the window sill a little tighter. He'd just stood there like an idiot, head tipped back, unable to walk away, entranced by her loveliness.

She was a startling combination of cultures—Chinese, white and maybe Indian. Her straight hair was the rich, deep, dark brown of imbuia wood. Her cheekbones were high, her mouth sensuous and her chin stubborn. Her body, the little of it he'd been able to see, was thin but curvy. She looked young—twenty-four, twenty-five—but her confidence and wit suggested she was older, probably in her late twenties or early thirties.

As he walked to the entrance, he wondered who she was. That she was one of his employees was indisputable—she was in his building, on a floor occupied by Le Roux Events staff. He didn't expect her to recognise him; few at this level did. Was she a clerk, an event planner, an accountant or did she work in admin? Did she like working at Le Roux Events? How long had she worked for them?

The urge to stop, to log into the Le Roux International server—the one that only he, Jago and a couple of their most senior and trusted employees had access to—and pull up her file was almost overwhelming. Since this small subsidiary only employed thirty or forty people, he'd find her quickly. In five minutes, he could know her age, her history, her credit score, her salary and see her work reviews.

Micah shook his head and ran his hand up and down his jaw. He'd never—not once since he'd started working for his father after graduating university—used his power and access to spy on an employee. Doing that would be a serious breach of trust. It was his and Jago's view that they only pulled an employee's record when they had damn good reason to.

And that reason had never occurred because they'd never interfered in the day-to-day running of the companies they owned. He and Jago had too many enterprises to do anything but look at company performance and balance sheets. He was only here because he had a very specific problem: he needed to find a new wedding venue for his sister's prestigious wedding in two months' time.

He didn't have time for an out-of-the-blue attraction, neither did he have the inclination. He had a company to run, deals to do, money to make. His responsibilities at Le Roux International required him to work sixteen-hour days as it was. Micah had no idea how he was going to fit in the search for a wedding venue on top of his insane workload. But he was, once again, taking responsibility for a problem that wasn't his…

But that was what he did, who he was. Whenever anything went wrong with his family, because of what he'd done twenty years ago, he assumed the responsibility of fixing the problem. Because he couldn't fix what had happened to Brianna…

Micah felt his breath catch in his throat and, needing a minute, he changed course and walked away from the entrance and down the side of the building, slipping round the corner and into a small alley between his and the next building. He leaned his back against the red brick wall, lifted his foot and placed it on the wall, tipping his face to the sun.

This month would be Brianna's twentieth year of being in a persistent vegetative state, two decades of being non-responsive. She'd spent nearly seven thousand, five hundred days in that hospital bed on a feeding tube.

And it was his fault. He'd put her there.

Why the hell had he phoned her when he'd stormed out of Hadleigh House? Why had he dumped his hurt and anger on her? He knew the answer to that question: because she'd been the one person, besides Jago, who understood the screwed-up dynamics of the Le Roux family, and Jago hadn't been around. Their parents had been long-time friends. She'd grown up with Jago and him and had been part of the family. She'd seen Theo's temper, his need for control, and had often told Micah that his frequent fights with his father would end in tragedy.

She'd been right but she'd been the one who'd paid the price for his lack of control and blinding anger. Because she'd loved him, because she'd needed to rescue him, Brianna had followed him, and on a busy Johannesburg road had met her future. Or non-future.

The events of that night had changed everything. By far

the worst consequence was Brianna's catastrophic head injury. But there'd been other consequences too: for the Pearson and Le Roux families, for his siblings and, obviously, for himself.

Naturally, he'd personally taken more than a few major hits. In the aftermath of the incident, he'd drunk far too much, flirted with drugs and had looked for any respite from the swamping guilt and unrelenting pain. Jago had got him some professional help—his father and stepmother hadn't bothered—and he'd cleaned up his act. He'd learned to control his temper and reckless streak, and had vowed that he'd do anything and everything to make life for his siblings flow smoothly—he'd be polite to his stepmother but she could take care of herself—vowing he'd never disappoint Jago or Thadie again. He'd also promised himself he'd never hurt another woman, in any way, ever again. As a result, he only ever engaged in shallow affairs, one-night stands.

Brianna had wanted the big family, the husband and the picket fence. At one point he'd wanted the dream too, but he didn't deserve to have what she couldn't, what he'd taken from her.

Guilt was his constant companion, his ever-faithful friend.

Micah gripped the bridge of his nose and squeezed. Standing here, thinking about the past—how he'd messed up so many lives—wasn't going to get his immediate problem solved.

His sister was getting married in two months and, a couple of days ago, some swamp rat had called the hotel hosting the wedding, somehow convinced everyone working there that he was representing Thadie's wedding planner and had cancelled the wedding reception. The organisation, believing the fake calls and emails, had immediately rebooked the space and now Thadie, Clyde and their thousand guests had nowhere to celebrate their union.

Thadie and her very expensive and famous wedding planner, Anna de Palmer-Whyte, had spent the past two days frantically calling round to find another venue but had yet to find anything suitable in and around the city. Seeing their rising panic, Micah had offered his assistance and to co-opt one of the event planners they employed to work with him to find a venue outside of the city. Yeah, he had deals pending and an overflowing inbox, but Thadie could ask him to pluck the moon from the sky and he'd find a way to do it. Thadie, her twin toddler boys and his own twin, Jago, were the most important people in his life, and he'd do anything for them. And apparently 'anything' included finding a five-star wedding venue.

Micah headed back to the entrance, his hands in the pockets of his trousers. Over the years he'd paid little attention to this business, one of many that was part of the empire he and Jago controlled. The place turned over a decent profit and it was handy to have a group of professionals on call to organise company events, which they did with efficiency and aplomb. He could've summoned the manager to his penthouse office in Sandton, but a personal visit would impress the urgency of the situation.

Hopefully, someone within the building would be able to find him that elusive, and exclusive, venue. Pulling open the front door, he glanced up to the second floor and felt a moment's regret at not seeing the gorgeous brunette again.

But he couldn't afford the time to be distracted.

CHAPTER TWO

BEN WINTERS DIDN'T have any event planners he could spare.

Micah sat across from his manager in his messy office—the guy needed to do some filing—and listened to him explain that his planners were all juggling two, three, sometimes even five projects in various stages. He couldn't spare anyone to research possible venues outside of the city and then travel to see whether they were suitable.

'The best I can do is to ask my planners whether they have any ideas, any contacts. Of course, it would help if I knew what type of function you are wanting to host…' Ben suggested.

He was fishing for information—obviously curious as to what could be so important and imminent to demand his involvement—but Micah rarely explained his actions. And it was a family rule that they never discussed personal matters with anyone who didn't share their DNA.

The sole exception to that rule was Jabu, their long-term butler, confidant, father figure and friend.

'Capacity to hold a thousand guests, sophisticated, upmarket. Ample accommodation in the area. Money is not an object,' Micah stated. He saw Ben scrunch up his face and shrug his shoulders, and realised that he'd wasted his morning visiting Le Roux Events. If Winters reflected the people he employed, then he'd receive no help from them.

He needed someone to think creatively, to be innovative, and he didn't think he'd find that someone here.

Micah stood up. 'Thanks for your time,' he said, holding out his hand.

'I'll walk you out,' Ben said and mouthed a curse when his phone rang. He picked it up and looked at the screen and it was obvious to Micah that he wanted to take the call. He told Ben he'd see himself out.

Leaving his office, Micah ignored the flirty smile the receptionist sent him and pushed his hand through his hair. He genuinely didn't know what to do next, an unusual situation for him.

He'd head back to his office and maybe he and Jago could brainstorm some ideas. Two heads were always better than one. Pulling open the door, he stepped outside and felt the slap of the midday, somnolent summer heat. He pulled his phone from his pocket and checked his messages as he headed back to his car, desperate to climb inside and blast the air-conditioner. The vehicle had cost him a quarter of a million pounds—being an international company they only thought in pounds, not rands—but, right now, all he wanted from it was its ability to blow frigid air at his overheated body.

Micah used the key fob to open his driver door and looked up from his phone to see the brunette from earlier leaning against his door. She wore a sleeveless pale-pink top tucked into a slimline black skirt that hit just above her knees, and killer heels. Some time in the last fifteen minutes she'd rearranged her long hair into a twist pinned to the back of her head with a clip.

Their eyes collided. Micah saw the rolling emotion in hers and sighed. She was great-looking—slim and lovely—but he didn't have the time to dally, or for a dalliance, right now.

And he was surprised that she was down here, waiting

for him. He thought he'd annoyed her, but it wasn't the first time his surname had changed a woman's mind about his level of attractiveness. Sad but true.

'Can I help you?' he asked, keeping his tone cool.

'I doubt it,' she replied, her tone snippy. He looked again and saw that the emotion in her eyes wasn't desire but annoyance. Maybe even anger.

Right, he'd read her wrong. Which begged the question: what had he done to upset her?

'I'm Ella Yeung,' she stated, looking at him as if he should know her name.

He shrugged. 'Have we met before?'

'No, but I thought you would've read about me somewhere along the line.'

He had no idea what she was talking about. 'Look, I don't have time to play guessing games with you, Ms Yeung. If you have something to say, get on with it, because I have things to do and somewhere to be.'

Confusion and frustration ran across her face and Micah watched as she seemed to collapse in on herself. She lifted her clenched fist to her mouth and the last remaining colour in her face faded. 'You don't know what happened to me, do you?'

Whatever it was, it was serious. He didn't know why or how but Micah knew he needed to hear it. He nodded to the entrance. 'Let's go inside where it's cool. I'll commandeer an office and you can tell me what's on your mind.'

Ella shook her head. 'No.' She crossed her arms and nodded at his driver's door. 'We can talk in your car.'

Micah walked her round to the passenger side, opened the door and waited for her to settle in the passenger seat. When he was behind the wheel, he turned the ignition and blasted the air-conditioner. The smell of new leather filled the car and he watched as Ella took in the interior, with its real wood trim and metal accents. She suited the car, he thought—classy and elegant. And, up close, she was sexier than he'd initially realised.

Micah took in her creamy complexion touched with a hint of magnolia, the exact colour of the flowers his mum so adored. He'd been right about her heritage, Chinese and Caucasian mostly, and stunning. Her cheekbones were high, her eyes an intense brown and shot with hints of gold and green. Her nose was long and straight. Her full mouth was covered in a pale pink lipstick, and even that hint of make-up was unnecessary.

Micah, used to attractive woman and not normally caught off-guard, swallowed and tried to ignore the way she ignited his desire. What the hell? Yeah, she had good hair—thick and a deep, dark brown—and a great body, but he'd dated supermodels, sports stars, actresses and aristocrats and nobody had ever, *ever*, caused his world to tilt, to knock him off-balance like this.

Calm down, Le Roux.

Ella leaned forward, adjusted the vents and ran her hand over the sleek dashboard in front of her. He expected her to compliment the car but the next words out of her mouth rocked his world.

'I've recently resigned from my position as an event planner for Le Roux Events. I did that because our biggest client, Neville Pillay, sexually accosted me.'

Pillay? He'd met him a few times and had liked the guy. He was said to be the most popular entertainer in the country and was respected as a philanthropist and actor. He looked at Ella and saw that her fists were clenched. Her expression was blank but the muscles in her neck were tight with tension. He'd lived with a consummate liar his entire life and could spot BS from a mile away. Micah knew Ella was telling the truth.

He chose his words carefully. 'I'm so sorry that happened

to you, Ella. Did you report it to the police? To Ben Winters, Human Resources?'

Her laugh was high and false. 'Yes, I reported it. The police said that because there were no witnesses, and because it wasn't what they termed a serious assault, it was a "he said, she said" situation. Ben and Siba, our HR guy, suggested I gave him the wrong signals and asked me to forget it.'

They said fury was coloured red but to Micah, it was a deep black, and endless. He closed his eyes and asked another question. 'Start at the beginning and tell me everything, Ella. Every little thing.'

By the time she was done, Micah had learned that the company had been covering up Pillay's misdeeds for years, and that every single person to whom Ella had taken her problem had disappointed her.

He'd always been proud of the work he and his brother did and was proud of the company they'd built. Right up until this moment. He felt sick, ashamed and soul-deep, skin-exploding angry.

'I don't expect you to believe me—you have absolutely no reason to—but neither my brother nor I knew anything about this. It was never brought to our attention,' Micah told her, conscious of how weak his explanation sounded.

'I just wanted you to know, in the faint hope that you'll do something so that it doesn't happen again,' Ella told him, her hand looking for the door handle. 'I've resigned, so I'm out of here, but he might do something else, something worse, to someone down the line.'

'That won't happen,' Micah told her. 'I will fix this, I promise.'

She looked at him, her eyes deep and fathomless. 'I'd like to believe you, Mr Le Roux, but I've heard too many empty words and insincere promises from your company, and throughout my life, to believe anyone about anything.'

She slipped out of his car and, without looking at him, slammed the door closed. Micah watched as she walked back to his building, her spine straight and her chin up.

How the hell was he going to fix this?

He didn't know but he would. He'd do it for that proud young woman and, as she'd pointed out, for his future employees.

Micah instructed his on-board computer to call Jago and, when his twin's face appeared on the screen in front of him, he spoke. 'Do you know about a sexual harassment claim made by Ella Yeung, employed by us as an event planner?'

Jago frowned and shook his head. 'No. Should I?'

'Our Head of Human Resources does.'

Jago shrugged. 'Were our protocols followed and, more importantly, did our employee get counselling? Is she okay?'

Micah rubbed his temples with his fingertips. 'No. Nobody believed her, Jago. Because of the fame of her accuser, not one person in our organisation took her seriously.'

'Who harassed her?'

Micah told him and Jago's eyebrows flew up in shock. 'Well, he wasn't on my list of most likely offenders.'

'Mine neither but I believe her, Jay.' Damn, he hoped Jago stood with him on this, but if he didn't he'd go it alone. Their people had disappointed Ella but he wouldn't.

'Good enough for me,' Jago replied.

'I plan to take Pillay down, but that will take finesse,' Micah told his twin, his tone resolute. 'But I intend to find out what went wrong in our organisation first. They branded Ella as a trouble maker and pretty much forced her to resign.'

'Right.' Jago's expression darkened and his navy eyes turned black with anger. 'What the hell, Micah? We have a policy, a protocol, and our employees' wellbeing always come first!'

'Not this time. Maybe you should alert the board, Jago, because heads are about to roll.'

Jago sent him a tight smile. 'Last time I checked, we own this company and we set the policy. Screw the board. I'll start sharpening the swords.'

Back in her office, Ella dropped into her chair, placed her elbows on her desk and pushed her fingers into her hair.

What on earth had happened out there? Instead of reading Micah Le Roux the riot act, instead of tearing off ten strips of skin, she'd caved and in fits and starts, told him the whole story.

Where had her fire gone? While she'd been waiting for him to appear, she'd built up a huge head of steam, but as soon as she looked into his Persian blue eyes her anger had faded and embarrassment strolled in.

Oh, she wasn't embarrassed about what had happened with Pillay; none of that was her fault and she refused to take any blame for any part of his appalling actions. But she felt embarrassed that her first conversation with Micah Le Roux had revolved around her being sexually accosted. She hadn't wanted him to see the tears in her eyes, to hear her halting voice.

She would've far preferred the big boss to be eighty years old and portly, not young, fit and gorgeous. She would've liked their first conversation to have happened at a bar, over a glass of chilled champagne, or at a restaurant over perfectly grilled fish. Or at a club with a sexy beat pulsing in the background.

All of which was insane. Even if Pillay was a choir boy, there would've been no chance of her meeting Micah Le Roux! She was just another working woman, one of the millions in the city; he was South African royalty. Their paths were never destined to cross again so why was she thinking about clashing gazes across champagne flutes, dancing with him in a nightclub or sharing getting-to-know-you dinners?

Why was she fantasising over his lovely blue eyes, his masculine face and stunning body? Maybe because she'd had so little to fantasise over lately…

But she should focus on his reaction which, to be honest, had been surprising. She'd expected him to find excuses, to play down what happened to her, but he'd seemed genuinely angry—completely horrified, in fact. Ella did not doubt that her claims had been a surprise to him: she'd seen his shocked, then furious, expression.

But what she did doubt was his promise to fix the situation. She didn't believe him, she couldn't. She'd been let down too often by too many people to put her faith in a stranger, even if he was rich and sexy, made her stomach pitch and roll and her heart flutter.

Besides, what would he fix? Sure, he could fire everyone who'd ignored her claim—not a likely scenario, admittedly—but there was little he could do about Neville Pillay, as going after him would be a PR nightmare. He was a very popular entertainer, known to be a loving family man, and nobody would believe that a snake lurked beneath his designer clothes. Micah publicly accusing him of sexual harassment would damage the Le Roux brand and that wasn't something a successful billionaire businessman would do. Not on the word of one mid-level employee.

It was done and she should just try to put the last few months behind her. There wasn't anything more she could do and it was obvious that she'd never see Micah Le Roux again.

It was time to focus on the future, to make a new life somewhere else. She just needed to hang in here a little longer. If she did, she'd be paid her bi-annual performance bonus.

She'd endured so much already. She could handle another fifteen working days spent in this cramped and stuffy room.

Two days later, Micah was back at Le Roux Events. After checking that Winters' office was empty, he walked up the stairs to the second floor, ended up in a dull grey hallway and looked at the numbers on the doors in front of him. Ten, eight… He was going the wrong way. Ella Yeung was in room sixteen, so he changed direction, ignoring the curious glances from people behind their glass half-walls. Twelve, fourteen…

Sixteen…

At the sound of his quick rap on her open door, Ella turned and a long, lovely leg caught his attention. He was tempted to look for longer—and couldn't help noticing her white skirt and emerald-green sleeveless top—but he knew he had to rein in his admiration and act as professionally as possible, even if there was something about Ella Yeung that made his head spin.

With her, given what she'd recently endured, he had to be ultra-professional. Difficult when all he wanted to do was run his eyes over her…

He lifted his eyes to her face and was happy to see some colour there.

Judging from the curiosity in her still cool eyes, she'd heard that Winters and the HR guy were gone and was perhaps wondering how that had come about. She was the only person who was entitled to some answers.

'Can I come in?' he asked, after greeting her.

'Sure,' she replied, gesturing him inside her office. She walked past him to sit on the edge of her desk. He wasn't invited to take a seat, he noticed.

Micah looked around her space and noticed the stack of dusty boxes in the corner, some old chairs and two broken filing cabinets. A laptop rested on the surface of a scarred wooden desk.

He'd learned a lot about Ella Yeung over the past forty-eight hours and the thought of her being banished to this dreadful office, wasting her considerable talent, annoyed him. Thank God Winters was gone or else he'd have fired him just for that.

'I thought I'd give you a personal update on the changes here,' he said, sliding his hands into the pockets of his trousers. Hands that wanted to touch her hips and her butt, hands that wanted to cradle her face, cup her breast. Of all the women in the world, he had the luck to be fiercely attracted to someone who was completely, solidly off-limits.

He'd heard the emotion in her voice the day before yesterday when she'd recounted her awful experience but he'd been impressed by her strength and admired her determination to stop Pillay's reprehensible actions. Ella Yeung had hidden depths…

Depths that would remain unexplored.

'The office gossip has been working overtime,' Ella replied. 'They're saying that Ben took early retirement, but I suspect you fired him.'

'I did.' And he'd do it a hundred times over. During the man's exit interview, Micah had ascertained that Winters was a raging misogynist. When he'd suggested that Ella had 'asked for Pillay's attention', Micah had nearly lost it. Micah refused to condone his repulsive world view by allowing him to take early retirement instead of having his employment terminated.

He'd also fired their Director of Human Resources, and the Le Roux Events Human Resources officer, as he told Ella.

Ella nodded, folded her arms and tapped her fingernail against her bicep. 'Thank you.'

He shook his head. 'It was the right thing to do. I'm just

sorry it took so long for this to be resolved. We will be placing a temporary manager in Winters' place and, should you wish to resume work at your old position, we'd be grateful to have you,' Micah added. 'You'd return to a hefty pay rise and better perks.

'I've done my research, talked to some of your clients, suppliers and your colleagues. You work hard and you are damn good at what you do. The salary increase is what other event planners of your experience earn. I'm sorry to tell you that equal pay for equal jobs was another one of our policies that Winters did not follow.'

Ella grimaced. 'That doesn't surprise me.'

'We're overhauling this company and we will be making big changes. We'd like you to be a part of that.'

'Have you fired Pillay as a client?' Ella demanded.

He grimaced. 'I want to, and so does my brother, but our lawyers want us to hold off until we gather more evidence. I've hired a private detective to track down other women he's harassed—'

'I can give you some names of women who left the company because of him,' Ella said, interrupting him.

Micah nodded. 'That would be great. If my PI can get them to make a statement, we'll add their experiences to the case we are building against him.'

'Intellectually I understand that, but my word should be enough.' Ella's voice shook with anger.

He wanted to touch her, to pull her into him to offer her some comfort, but knew he shouldn't. However, he couldn't resist taking her hand and squeezing gently before releasing her quickly. 'It absolutely should be but, unfortunately, it isn't. I want to nail him, Ella, I really do, but we need to be patient just for a little longer.'

She stared at him, her unusual brown eyes bright with frustration. He knew she wanted to argue, to protest, and was grateful when she took a deep breath and nodded. 'I'm in the process of moving to the UK and plan to fly out a couple of days after I finish working out my notice here. If he hasn't been fired as a client by that time, I will not consider returning to work here. And, once I get on that plane, I'm not coming back.'

She'd put him on notice as well. Good thing that he worked well under pressure because he had no intention of losing her. Losing her *skill set*, he corrected himself… Good people were hard to find.

Her eyes dropped and he followed her gaze, surprised she was looking at his hands. What was she thinking? Could it be she wanted him to touch her? A fireball of lust skittered up his arm and fired its way down his spinal cord. It took all of his willpower to keep his expression implacable, to casually drop his hands when all he wanted was her sexy mouth under his, his hands on her slim body.

Or, and much more likely, she was wondering why the hell he was touching her—an employee, and someone who'd recently received unwanted male attention. Was he insane? What was he thinking?

He clenched his fist. 'I'm sorry, I shouldn't have touched you.'

Ella shook her head. 'It's fine…um… I know you were just trying to reassure me.'

Reassurance…sure. Let her think that. She certainly didn't need to know that he'd been slammed by the most intense sexual attraction he'd ever experienced in his life. No big deal.

Feeling hot, he looked around for the remote control to the air-conditioner. Finding it on that credenza, he picked it up and realised that this wasn't his space—well, technically it was, but it was *her* office—so he asked her if he could drop the temperature in the room.

She agreed and Micah put it on cold and high, and then, remembering Ella's sleeveless top, settled on a temperature they could both live with. Tossing the remote control on her desk, he pulled up two old office chairs and gestured for her to sit. He sat opposite her and leaned back in his chair, linking his hands across his stomach. He casually lifted his ankle to rest it on his bended knee.

Now came the difficult bit… But he was the company trouble-shooter and it was his job to sort out problems. And, in Ella's case, that was finding out whether she intended to sue Le Roux International or not. She had a case, and she deserved some sort of compensation, which he was happy to pay her, but he'd like to avoid the enormous legal bills.

He could try and tease the answer from her but he was exhausted and decided on a direct approach. 'Look, Ella, we both know that if you wanted to you could sue my company, and we'd end up paying you a large settlement because of how badly this was handled. Do you intend to do that?'

She nodded. 'I've thought about it but I haven't made up my mind yet.'

Fair enough.

Ella stared at a point behind his head. 'Your offer for me to return to work—provided Pillay is no longer a client—is tempting. I love my job. But I couldn't work for a company I'm suing. That would be, well, uncomfortable. And, if I emigrate, I do want to leave all this behind me.'

Micah thought this was a perfect chance to segue into making her an alternative offer. One that would provide her with a serious amount of cash without going through the legal system. A solution that would also give him the help he so desperately needed.

Micah pushed his hand through his hair and then tapped the wooden surface of her desk, his fingertips moving at a rapid beat. He saw Ella look down and, when she cocked her head to the side, he clenched his fist. He only ever tapped his fingers when he was nervous and, for goodness' sake, there was really no reason to be nervous.

'How would you like to spend the next three weeks doing something other than twiddling your thumbs?' Micah asked.

Interest flickered in her eyes, along with wariness. 'And what would that be?'

Now came the tricky bit: How much to tell her? Thadie was a paparazzi's dream subject—gorgeous, lovely, rich and successful, and she was newsworthy. So far, they'd managed to keep the news of her wedding venue cancellation a secret, and they'd like to keep it that way. If the story was leaked, it would make a splash. *How had this happened? Why couldn't Le Roux organise something as simple as a wedding reception? What was happening behind the scenes?*

Thadie was one of the country's richest women and Clyde, her ex-rugby-star turned commentator fiancé, was a national hero, so the interest in them was sky-high. He needed to keep his cards close to his chest and that meant telling as few people as possible.

But keeping this a secret from someone whose help he needed was going to hamper her efforts. How could he get her cooperation as well as ensure her silence? Micah considered some strategies and discarded others, one thought tumbling over that other. He decided to tiptoe through this minefield.

'If you agree not to sue us, I'll pay you a hundred thousand pounds—we work in pounds, not rands—to do some work for me.'

Her eyebrows flew up as shock brightened her eyes. 'And what work would that be?'

'Event planning work. I need a venue on a specific day, fairly soon. If you manage to secure one, I'll pay you another hundred thousand on the proviso that nothing appears in the press about our search, the venue and us working together. If you choose not to do the work, I'll still pay you the first instalment to compensate you for how badly you were treated at Le Roux Events. I know that money can't change what happened but…' He shrugged. 'Unfortunately money is all we can offer.'

Ella tipped her head to the side and looked at him, intrigued. 'We both know that any lawyer I hired would demand more.'

Money was no object. 'Then hit me with a figure,' he suggested.

She took a couple of minutes, no doubt doing some mental arithmetic. He was expecting her to ask for millions and was surprised when she only asked for another hundred grand—three hundred thousand altogether. Too low, he suddenly decided, she deserved more. A lot more.

'What about two-fifty up front and another two-fifty once it's all complete?'

Her mouth dropped open and her eyes widened. 'Five hundred thousand pounds? With that sort of money, I could set up my own events planning company and maybe even buy a venue suitable for luxury events. I want to specialise in intimate family occasions, weddings, birthdays and events I like,' she explained. 'I'm good at those.'

'From what I've heard, you are good at everything you do,' Micah murmured.

She blushed, and her gaze clashed with his, but she immediately looked away. Micah sighed. Ella was trying hard to remain cool and unmoved but he knew that she was feeling anything but. He knew women, knew them well, and he'd had a lot of experience in picking up non-verbal cues when his attraction was reciprocated.

Ella liked what she saw. She wasn't being obvious about it, licking her lips or tilting her head. If anything, she was fighting her reaction to him. But the rapid beating pulse point in the side of her neck, her small, tight nipples under her shirt and the pale pink tinge to her skin gave her away.

He rubbed his hand over his jaw, mentally cursing the situation. He'd found an event planner, which was excellent news. Not so excellent was their immediate, compelling and dynamic reaction to each other.

It was just his lousy luck that the one woman who caused him to feel like this was his employee, and the last woman he should get involved with right now. Even if that hadn't been a factor, he and Jago had a deal that they never played where they worked. Their father, Theo, had no problem sleeping with his secretaries, marketing managers, accountants and in-house lawyers. It made for some uncomfortable workplace situations, and had cost the company a bundle in lost talent over the years, because his lovers always moved on to other employers when Theo dumped them.

Over the last twenty years, Micah had trained himself to be less impulsive, more patient. To think before he spoke. Now it took all of his willpower not to lean forward and capture that sassy mouth. To discover her taste, to feel her luscious skin under his arms, to slide inside her warm heat…

Micah stood and walked to the window, forcing it open and pulling in some fresh air. He kept work and sex miles apart. Negotiating with a woman to whom he was attracted was a fresh hell, a place he hadn't visited before.

His week was just getting more and more complicated.

CHAPTER THREE

THE POSSIBILITY OF half a million pounds? Was she having an auditory hallucination?

No, Micah didn't look as though he was teasing her. Those bright blue eyes were sombre and his expression was heart-attack serious.

Ella opened her mouth to say yes, then snapped it closed and shook her head. What, was he the snake charmer and she was being hypnotised into doing what he wanted? Ridiculous!

Ella dropped her eyes and they came to rest on his strong wrist, sporting a vintage Rolex from the sixties. The watch suited his he-man, too-cool-for-school, rabble-rouser vibe. There were more hints of his rebellion; on his other wrist, he wore two bracelets, one a thick, braided leather and the other a series of alternating black and blue beads interspersed with silver. His stubble was too thick to be designer and his nose—she could tell by the bump in the otherwise straight ridge—had been broken more than once. She could see the tiny holes in his earlobe that suggested he'd once worn earrings and through the material of his shirt she caught the outline of a bold tattoo covering his right pec.

Underneath his designer threads and his CEO persona, Micah Le Roux was a rebel and the thought—and the man—made her hot.

Ella watched as he stood up and walked over to the window, the same one she'd used to watch him walk across the car park. When he'd stepped into her office earlier, he'd brought with him an electrical storm. Lightning fizzed, thunder rumbled and thunderheads whirled and swirled. She felt primal, elemental, as if she were the original Eve and she was about to taste rain for the first time. Nothing much had changed in the fifteen minutes since.

She still felt like she was surfing the bands of a hurricane. Dear Lord, what was wrong with her? Ella pulled her tongue off the roof of her mouth and looked around for a distraction. She needed time to think rationally and carefully.

Ella pushed back her chair and glanced towards her office door.

It was shut.

The door was *shut.* And she hadn't noticed. She lifted her hand to her throat and stared at the panelled door, panic climbing. She needed to get that open as soon as she could.

Bad things happened behind closed doors when she was alone with strange men.

Ella stood abruptly and moved towards the door. She felt his eyes on her back as she opened it wide before picking up a box and wedging it in front of the door so that it couldn't blow shut.

He pushed his hand into his hair, looking uncomfortable. His eyes bounced between the open door and her, his expression thoughtful. Then he surprised her by picking up the bottle of water that sat on her desk and twisting the cap open before handing it to her.

Who *was* this man?

Ella sipped her water, hoping that her pulse would soon drop to not-about-to-have-a-panic-attack levels. Her anxiety receded and her breath evened out but her heart was still skipping around her chest, acting as if she'd never seen a good-looking guy before.

The truth was she'd never met anyone like Micah Le Roux, who was both straightforward and, seemingly, sensitive. And had she mentioned sexy?

Do try to focus on what is important, Ella.

Ella rolled her shoulders, intrigued despite herself about his offer. She'd told him a little white lie earlier; she'd never seriously considered suing Le Roux International. Mostly because it sounded expensive but also because, as she'd said, she did want to put these last few months behind her.

But if Micah was willing to compensate her, provided she find him a venue, she'd be a fool to turn down his offer. Especially since it would give her the capital to start her own business…

'Okay, so you want me to find you a particular venue on a particular date and you're prepared to pay me a lot of money to do that. What's the catch?'

Micah's expression hardened. 'It's imperative that you do not leak any information about the venue, the function or anything we discuss.'

Ella felt her skin shrink, feeling like a caterpillar encased in a too-tight cocoon. She prided herself on her integrity and she'd never, ever let slip a detail about any function. And she now knew, personally, what it felt like to be the subject of office gossip and speculation.

'I'm not going to say anything, Mr Le Roux. You either believe me or you don't.' She wasn't going to beg him to. She'd done that before, both times with far more at stake than five hundred thousand pounds. She couldn't put a price on her mum's death or being pushed out of her job. From this moment on, people either believed her or they didn't; she wasn't going to beg them to.

After a brief pause, Micah explained how his sister had lost her wedding venue and that she and her wedding planner—Anna de Palmer-Whyte, wedding planner to the rich and famous—hadn't managed to secure another venue.

Ella was outraged by what had happened and felt awful for Thadie Le Roux for losing her booking at the utterly lovely venue. It was a favourite amongst the elite of the country, and for good reason. It was a fairy-tale place with an amazing, ornate ballroom, amazing gardens and facilities. Weddings were so stressful at the best of times and to have this happen was catastrophic.

'I'm so sorry,' Ella said, genuinely upset by the news. 'Do you have any idea who could've done something so horrible?'

Micah shook his head, looking thunderous. 'God help him if I find him.' He pushed his hand through his curls. 'The important thing is to find Thadie a venue.'

Ella frowned, confused. 'So, you are wanting to pay me a lot of money for me to spend a few days looking at suitable venues in and around Johannesburg, checking whether they are available and arranging for you to visit them? But isn't that something Anna should be doing? And, if she is doing that, and I'm pretty sure she is, why would you hire me to duplicate her efforts?'

His eyes turned darker, bluer. If that was at all possible. 'Anna hasn't been able to find anything yet, so I suggested that we extend our search. If you agree, we will visit various venues outside of the city…together. The Drakensberg, Clarens, the Midlands. We might fly to some, drive to others. If we find any venues suitable, I'll pay to secure the date, and at the end we'll narrow it down to three. Then we will visit them again, this time with Thadie and Anna, who will make the final decision.'

He wasn't playing around, Ella thought. He expected her to spend long hours, in cars, planes and confined spaces, with a stranger. She couldn't do it. Not even for half a million pounds. God, she couldn't even be in a room with a closed door with him, some place where there were colleagues down the hall.

You were fine with the closed door until your brain kicked in and told you that you should be feeling scared. Up until then, you were fine being alone with him... Why can't you trust yourself any more? Trust your gut?

Ella ignored her inner voice and waved it away. Her gut was unreliable, so she intended to be sensible and to err on the side of caution.

Sure, the money would be nice—very nice indeed—and she desperately wanted to do something besides sitting in this office but…she couldn't.

It was too much of a risk.

'You'll be staying in five-star accommodation, flying on luxury planes or driving my brand-new Bentayga—'

'I'll be driving it?' Ella asked, surprised.

'I'll need to work occasionally so, yeah, I'd expect you to drive,' Micah said.

Wow. To her, driving his fantastic car was a perk. And, judging by his small smile, he knew it.

'You'll be eating excellent food and drinking great wine,' Micah continued, ignoring her interruption. 'You'll be out of this dismal office and seeing some beautiful parts of the country.'

Except that she'd be alone, for an extended time, with a stranger.

God, she was tempted, so tempted. She was ninety-five per cent sure that she'd be safe with Micah, that nothing would happen that she didn't want to—nothing would happen, full-stop!—but that damn five per cent of uncertainty held her by the throat and wouldn't let her go.

But that wasn't the *only* reason she was hesitant to take him up on his offer. Honesty had her admitting that another part of her *wanted* something to happen between them.

The truth was that she was startlingly, crazily attracted to Micah. She wanted to step into his arms, nuzzle her nose into his neck and pull his shirt from those dark, smart designer jeans. After being groped by Pillay, she didn't think she'd ever feel lust again, but here she was, wondering whether he tasted as good as he looked, whether his muscle had muscles and whether he had those sexy hip muscles she so loved on men. She wanted him, harder and hotter than anything she'd experienced before. She didn't know how to handle feeling so off-kilter, unbalanced, so thoroughly, crazily turned on.

And what if something happened, something she asked for, and at the last minute, she freaked out? What would he think of her? How would they work together after that? No, it was easier, safer, to walk away, so that was what she'd do.

She would still receive two hundred and fifty thousand pounds, a cracking amount, but she had to protect herself in every way possible.

Forcing herself to meet his eyes, she twisted her lips. 'Sorry, but I'm not the right person for this job.'

Ella saw the frustration in his eyes, and a little bit of panic, and realised how important it was for him to solve this problem for his sister. In fact, it was a lovely thing for him to do, but she couldn't let that sway her. She had to protect herself, and that meant not putting herself in positions that could backfire. He was asking her to be alone with him for long stretches of time, to stay overnight at venues out of the city, and her comfort zone. He was a fit, strong guy and she wouldn't have a chance in hell against him. While she was reasonably sure that he was one of the good guys, she couldn't take that chance.

Ella was about to refuse again when his phone rang, breaking their tense silence. Micah jerked the device out of his trousers pocket and scowled down at the screen. She watched as tenderness replaced anxiety, affection chased away frustration. He held up his finger, silently asking her to wait, and answered his video call.

'Hey, how are my two favourite guys?'

'Hi, Unca Micah.' A very young, piping voice drifted over to Ella. Unable to resist, she craned her neck to see the source of the high pitched voice. Instead of the one child she'd expected, she saw two, both with bright blue eyes, lovely light-brown skin and curly hair. They wore different coloured T-shirts and shorts but it was obvious they were twins.

'Why aren't you guys smiling?' Micah asked, sitting on the edge of the desk. 'Did Mummy send you to the naughty corner again?'

'Mmm-hmm.'

Ella watched, fascinated by the half-smile that caused Micah's lips to twitch. His eyes, lighter and brighter, were full of amusement and he looked years younger. When he did it properly, Ella was fairly sure his smile could blister paint.

'We said dammit and Mummy put us in the naughty corner for five minutes!'

Micah swallowed and Ella suspected he was biting the inside of his cheek to keep his expression sober. 'Guys, that's a bad word. You shouldn't say it,' Micah told them, his voice serious.

Their response was quick and hot. 'Then why don't you go to the naughty corner, because you say it all the time!'

'It's not fair!' the other twin added.

Ella slapped her hand over her mouth to stop herself from laughing. 'You're right, I should go to the naughty corner, maybe even for *fifteen* minutes.'

'But that's for ever!'

Micah nodded, his expression still serious. 'Don't repeat my bad words, guys, and listen to your mum. I've got to go but I'll talk to you guys later.'

He disconnected the call and gently banged the face of his phone against his forehead.

'Ugh, my sister is going to tear a strip off me again,'

he told her, finally allowing his smile to bloom. It creased the corner of his eyes, showed off his white, even teeth and dropped another few years off his face. Ella glanced at the wall, disappointed when she didn't see the paint bubbling.

'I think they won that round,' she pointed out, unable to resist teasing him just a little.

'I do try to watch my language around them but I'm not always successful.'

Ella was surprised Johannesburg's favourite bachelor billionaire had even taken their call—which had to have been authorised by their mum, so she couldn't be too mad at her brother—and was also shocked he sounded so at ease with the twins. It was obvious that he spent a lot of time with them and spoke to them often.

He was smart, nice to kids and far too attractive, Ella thought, and she needed to leave his presence before she did something stupid and agreed to spend three weeks with him hunting down a venue.

It took a lot of effort for her to stand up and hold out her hand. 'I'll take the two hundred and fifty thousand but I'll pass on your other offer. Anna de Palmer-Whyte is amazing; I'm sure she'll find you a venue.'

Ella turned and hurried towards the door, knowing that if she stayed, if he smiled, she might just say yes. And that wasn't something she could afford to do.

She definitely couldn't return to her old job at Le Roux Events, Ella decided at the end of what had been a long, interesting, weird day. And, with the quarter million pounds Micah had promised to pay her as a settlement, she could take some time to decide what she really wanted to do, where she wanted to be.

It gave her some breathing room but she'd still emigrate. If she was going to start a new life it might as well be in another country, Ella thought as she headed to her leased car on the far side of the staff car park. The UK would be a blank slate, some place to start afresh, to reinvent herself.

To start again…

How many more times would she have to do that? She'd had to pick herself up after her mum's death and grieve on her own, recover on her own. Her father had supplied her with a place to stay and money, but he'd stopped emotionally engaging with her, and in time had stopped talking to her altogether. She'd spent the past decade trying to bash through the steel plate he'd erected around him, to no avail. She could only give him so much time, so much energy, and she was done. He didn't want her in his life so she was giving him what he wanted.

After university, she'd returned to the coastal city, found an apartment and a job and in time had received the offer from Le Roux Events, which necessitated her moving to Johannesburg, a fast-paced and cutthroat city. She'd embraced the new start and the challenge but then her world had fallen apart…

Hopefully, this third reset would be the charm.

'Seven hundred and fifty thousand pounds and nothing will happen.'

Ella jerked her head up to see Micah Le Roux leaning his butt against the door of her hatchback, its cherry-red paint glinting in the sun. Designer sunglasses shielded his eyes from the still potent late-afternoon sun and she could see the streaks of deep gold in his hair. Earlier she'd given him thirty minutes to vacate her office and then had spent the rest of the afternoon reading up on him online. She now knew his tan and streaked hair came from spending as much time as he could outside and that he spent his free weekends running triathlons, sailing or doing adventure-trail running.

He adored his family—his twin, Jago, and his much younger sister, Thadie, socialite and social media influencer, the mother of the twin boys she'd seen on his screen. According to the all-knowing Internet, he wasn't dating anyone at the moment and didn't do serious relationships. Micah Le Roux liked variety and wore his single status like a badge of honour. He liked red wine, lived in his wing of the famous, historical family mansion in Sandhurst and had been voted as one of the most influential men under forty on the continent.

And he was standing by her car, waiting for her. Ella's heart bounced around her ribcage and she felt her breathing turn shallow and her skin prickle with awareness. What was it about this man that caused her brain to stop working and her joints to liquefy? She'd dealt with many wealthy, good-looking guys but no one had made her feel so off-balance, so aware, so feminine, as Micah did.

'What do you think, Ella?' Micah asked as she used her car's remote control to unlock it. She walked past him to open the boot and tossed her bag inside, scowling at her seldom-used gym bag. His muscled, fit body was a reminder that she needed to start exercising again…

Holding her phone and her car keys in one hand, she slammed the boot lid closed and cursed when it didn't catch. She slammed it again, harder, taking some of her frustration out on the car.

Ella joined Micah by the driver's door. 'I'm not interested, Micah.' What a lie; of course she was interested. And scared.

'Except that you are.' She started to protest and stopped when he held up his hand. 'I saw it in your eyes; you want to help me. And the additional money interests you too.'

Ella wrinkled her nose. Of course it did; she wasn't a saint.

Micah leaned his hip into her car again, his eyes connecting with hers, so deep and such an incredible shade of blue.

'You're scared to be alone with me,' he murmured. 'I'm sorry it took me so long to figure that out but I got there in the end.'

Ella's head shot up at his sympathetic statement, her gaze flying across his face, trying to see if he was mocking her. No, he looked and sounded genuine.

'I need your help, Ella, but I understand why you can't trust me or the situation,' Micah softly stated. 'You have every reason to feel that way. But I *do* need your help.'

Frustration passed through his eyes. 'I don't know how to reassure you except to tell you that I'd never hurt you, or any other woman, and that you can trust me. You're my employee, and I never play where I work.'

Ella felt herself wavering, wanting to believe him. But that could be her insane attraction to him clouding her reasoning.

'I instinctively trusted you earlier, Ella, when you told me about Pillay. Can you not do the same for me?'

She considered his words. He was right. He hadn't hemmed or hawed, he'd listened and sprung into action. He hadn't changed his mind upon hearing who had accosted her, even though Pillay was part of his A-list social circle and she was sure they'd met.

Could she trust herself, trust her gut feeling that Micah would never make an unwanted advance? Would she miss out on a huge opportunity because she was five per cent scared, maybe even less?

'I believed you. Can you do the same for me?'

Micah believing in her was huge, a balm to her battered soul. After so many defeats and disappointments, she was intensely grateful to be taken seriously.

So grateful that she could kiss him…

Ella sighed. That wasn't breaking news. She'd wanted to kiss him from the moment she laid eyes on him again a few hours ago. But kissing wasn't on the agenda, and if she accepted his offer she would be there to work, not play. Pity, she thought. In another life, at another time, if she'd been someone different—someone confident and self-assured—Micah Le Roux, she was sure, would be a fun way to pass some time.

'Well? Do you? Trust me, that is,' Micah demanded, and she heard a hint of impatience in his voice.

She did. She knew she did. Her gut had never yelled this loudly before, so she nodded. 'Yes, I do.'

'Thank God,' Micah muttered.

Ella smiled at him. 'You know, all the articles about you all mention how charismatic you are, how you can charm anyone, anywhere. I think that's true but I don't think that's who you really are. I think you are more impatient and demanding than most people realise.'

Micah's eyes widened in shock, and his mouth fell open. Then he laughed, a deep belly-laugh that raised the hair on her arms and created heat between her legs. If his smile was potent, then his laugh was dazzling and delightful on a million different levels. She wanted to dance in it, roll around in it, wrap herself up in it…

'You're right. I am all those things, and most people never suspect that. How did you?'

She didn't know how to answer his question, she just did. To her, it was as obvious as his blue eyes and his wide shoulders.

'So, knowing that, are you prepared to spend the next three weeks on and off in my company?' Micah asked her, suddenly serious.

'I am,' Ella told him. 'But can I ask you one more thing?'

Amusement flashed in his eyes. 'A million pounds is my highest offer,' he told her with an easy smile.

Ella shook her head. 'I'm not asking for more money, Micah.'

'Okay, we'll settle on seven-fifty for now, Ella. What's your question?'

Three quarters of a *million*… The mind boggled. But her request wasn't about the money. This was one last test, one more hurdle for him to jump over and, if he managed it, she knew she'd never spend another moment worrying about him. She gathered her courage. 'You keep looking at my mouth. Does that mean you want to kiss me?'

He didn't hesitate to nod. 'Yeah, of course I do,' he answered in a gruff voice.

She knew he'd say that but he hadn't dropped his head or moved closer to put his words into action. So far, so good. 'Why?' she asked, pushing him, loving his direct way of answering her question.

'Because I'm so damn attracted to you it actually hurts. I'd love to know how you feel in my arms, what you taste like, whether your skin is as soft as I think it is.'

Oh, God. His gaze darted between her mouth and eyes and she felt her back arching, her body betraying her.

'But I won't, because I gave you my word.' He lifted his hand, as if to touch her mouth or cheek, but dropped it before he could make contact with her skin. She was both relieved and disappointed. Relieved because he'd kept his word, disappointed because she wanted nothing more than to kiss him. 'You said that you keep your word. I do, too.'

Micah reached past her to open her car door and, when he spoke again, his tone was brisk and business-like. 'I'd like you to spend the day tomorrow researching possible venues in areas not too far from here. I'm thinking Clarens, Parys—places like that. If you find any options, set up appointments for tomorrow and we'll drive down.'

Her mind was spinning but she managed to nod.

'I'll confirm a pick-up time with you tomorrow, but it'll be early.'

'I'm not good at early,' Ella confessed, sliding behind the wheel of her car. 'If you give me your number, I'll send you a GPS pin for my address.'

He asked for her number, punched it into his phone and a few seconds later her phone rang. 'That's my private number—save it.'

Oh, and he was bossy too! Ella resisted the urge to salute.

Micah closed her door and bent down so that their heads were level. 'We'll talk tomorrow, Ella.'

She nodded and cranked the key to start her car. She turned her head to look into Micah's eyes and couldn't help her gaze dropping to his sexy mouth. She sighed and, when she lifted her eyes again, saw amused frustration on his face.

He sighed. 'It's going to be a long, long three weeks, isn't it? Because you want to kiss me as much as I do you.'

He was so honest, and she liked it. She was also so busted. 'Yes, but we're adults. We'll cope.'

'Speak for yourself,' Micah muttered before walking away.

She grinned at his broad back and shook her head. He was the only person she knew who could be both charming and grumpy. She rather liked it. She liked him.

He was right, she thought as she drove away, it was going to be a very long three weeks.

CHAPTER FOUR

MICAH PARKED THE Bentayga in his parking bay within the Hadleigh House garage and lifted his hands, noticing his trembling fingers. He switched off the ignition and leaned forward, placing his head on his custom-leather steering wheel. On the way home, a forty-five-minute drive, he'd ducked in and out of traffic, his entire concentration on the road and Johannesburg's crazy drivers. But, now that he was home, he couldn't avoid thinking of Ella.

He hadn't had this strong a reaction to a woman in what seemed like a hundred years. Or, frankly, ever. From the moment he'd laid eyes on her, he'd imagined her head on his pillow, her naked body on his white sheets. He wanted her in the worst way and couldn't work out why. She was lovely, but more wholesome than glamorous, more down to earth than fabulous. Because he was as shallow as a puddle, and he liked being that way when it came to relationships, he wasn't normally attracted to anyone who wasn't glamourous and over-the-top fabulous.

He desperately wanted to take Ella to bed and do wicked, wonderful things to her while he had her in it. But he'd made her a promise and he intended to keep it—keeping his word was vitally important to him. He'd be a monk around her. A frustrated monk, but a monk none the less.

Micah looked around the detached eight-car garage they shared with his stepmother, Liyana. His 1967 Jaguar E-type was covered with its custom-made tarpaulin and the fabric was covered in a thin layer of dust. He hadn't driven it for months. Then again, neither had he taken his Ducati out for a spin either. He couldn't remember when last he'd used the speedboat he shared with Jago, and it had been even longer since they'd taken the jet skis out on the water. There were ATVs and dirt bikes, and none of them had been touched in years.

They had too many toys and too little time, too much work to do.

Micah saw that Jago's car was gone. He glanced towards Liyana's end of the garage and noticed that both her cars were in residence, which meant that Liyana was…somewhere. London? Milan? It was hard to keep up with his stepmother, not that he wanted to.

He and Liyana had what could be described at best as a frosty relationship, and at worst as a long-standing cold war from the moment they'd met when he'd been nine, just a few weeks after his mum's death. The next nine years had been a raging battle between them. The two years after Brianna's accident had been filled with silence, and these days they didn't talk more than they had to. Too much had happened and she'd hurled too many acid-tipped accusations at him.

'Brianna's condition is your fault.'

'You are a bad influence on Thadie and I should keep you away from her.'

'You don't deserve to be part of this family after what you did.'

Leaving the garage, Micah headed to the house but made a detour to a wooden bench at the base of one of the oldest oak trees on the property, where he sat and rested his forearms on his knees, childhood memories rolling over him. In the space of a couple of months, he'd lost his mum, acquired a stepmum, seen the family house stripped of his mother's possessions and been told that it was time for a new start, a new chapter. Within a year, he'd also acquired a half-sister, and it had been too much to deal with. He'd been upset, grief-stricken, confused and angry, and he'd acted out…

He'd been an absolute terror, obstreperous and defiant, rebellious and lost. He'd pulled Jago into pranks, some of which had been downright dangerous. He looked at the two-storey-high roof of the garage and his blood iced at the memory of the two of them sliding down the roof and off its edge to land on a stack of mattresses on the grass below. He could've broken a leg, Jago could've broken his spine… If the twins even thought about doing something like that in the future, he'd ground them for life!

But back then he hadn't cared, he'd just been looking for trouble, for attention good or bad. His relationship with his father, when he was around, was terrible. Unlike his siblings and his late mother, Micah didn't hesitate to call his father out for acting like a jerk, something Theo excelled at—and, when she wasn't yelling at him for being impulsive, reckless or for doing something stupid, Liyana ignored him. Jabu, their family butler, had been more of a parent than his father and stepmother put together.

It had all come to a head a month or two after his eighteenth birthday. He'd been on his own at Hadleigh House—Jago had been away on a rugby tour and Micah had been suspended from school for the third time that year. He had been rubbing on his father's and Liyana's last nerve…deliberately, he was sure. His father, he of the volatile temper, had started yelling at Liyana and him. Then Theo had focused all of his ire on Micah and their argument had rapidly escalated. Theo had pushed him and he'd pushed back. Then Theo had thrown a punch, his fist breaking Micah's nose and spilling his blood on the ancient Persian carpet. Despite being constantly at loggerheads, he'd never imagined, not once, that his father would physically hurt him.

Shocked, stunned, emotionally eviscerated, the physical pain had been secondary, almost an afterthought. Knowing he had to leave, he'd stormed out of the house and, out of habit, called Brianna.

While Jago never hesitated to call him out, Brianna had always, *always* agreed with him and taken his side. He'd told her what had happened and that he planned to get drunk and stoned. She'd begged him not to go, told him that the bar he intended to visit was in a dangerous area and that he might get hurt. He'd brushed her off, never thinking that she'd follow him to that bad area of town, and had proceeded to get drunk, then high. When he'd finally made it home the next morning—he had vague memories of an older blonde who'd taken him home and into her bed—he'd been met by his father and Liyana, red-eyed and weeping.

Brianna had been in a head-on car accident, he'd been told, had massive head injuries and was on life support. Nobody had understood why she'd been out at night, why she'd been in that area of town. Her parents then accessed her mobile phone and they'd quickly established, by the numerous voice messages she'd sent Micah, that she'd been worried about him, upset that he hadn't returned her calls or messages. Her last message had been that she was going to look for him. Not used to driving at night, she'd lost control of her zippy car and had veered into the oncoming lane…

Brianna had eventually been moved off life support and onto a feeding tube and she had been moved to a private long-term-care medical facility. To this day she remained in a profound state of unconsciousness, had minimal brain activity and her prognosis for recovery was slim to none. Yet her parents continued to hold out hope that, with the field of neuroscience advancing rapidly, someone, somewhere, would find a way to bring their only child back to them. And her parents had never stopped blaming Micah for her condition.

That was okay, because he blamed himself too.

His first year at university had been a blur, a lost time period of bouncing between lectures, lawyers and sessions with a psychologist to help him deal with his guilt and grief. After the court case had been dismissed—he'd not been found *legally* liable for her injuries—he'd slowly started to turn over a new leaf. It had taken time, but he'd managed to get his temper under control and learned how to think before reacting. He'd also made a couple of vows to himself—most importantly that he'd never again be a source of pain for anyone he loved and cared about. That meant never putting himself in a situation where he risked hurting anyone, especially a woman, again.

It was simple: if Brianna could never have her greatest wish fulfilled—to have a family and kids—then neither could he.

Micah heard a familiar clearing of a throat and looked up to see Jabu standing on the path, his hands linked behind his back. His face radiated dignity, and within his dark eyes Micah read his concern.

'*Sawubona*, Mkulu,' he said, greeting him in Zulu, and using the word for 'grandfather'. It was also a word used for elderly men held in high regard, which Micah did.

Jabu lifted his grey eyebrows. 'As a child, when you were upset I could usually find you up this tree. Is everything all right?'

Micah stood up and walked over to the shorter man, gently gripping his shoulder. He knew Jabu worried about him and, since he'd caused the man enough grief, he forced a smile. 'Everything is fine, Mkulu.'

Jabu sent him a disbelieving look.

'Your stepmother is asking for a report. She wants to know if you've made any progress on finding a wedding venue,' Jabu stated as they walked to the side entrance of Hadleigh House. Instead of using the massive front hall, with its hand-carved double-wide staircase and impressive paintings, he and his twin accessed their suites via a back staircase. Jabu punched in the code to open the door and Micah stepped back to allow him into the house first.

Did Liyana honestly think he could magic a venue out of thin air? Before he could reply, Jabu spoke again. 'I told her that you are working on it and that I'm sure you'll find something soon.'

'Thank you. If she asks again, tell her that I have help and that I am on it.' He and Liyana had been passing messages to each other for twenty years through Jabu and he'd never once complained. It was childish and immature but it was also a habit that kept the peace. Life was better for all of them when he and Liyana ignored each other as much as possible.

'I had another job offer today,' Jabu told him, pulling a drooping rose from the vase on the hall table.

Micah, about to run up the stairs, stopped and turned to face his favourite person. He was reasonably sure Jabu would never leave them, and that he used his status of being the most headhunted butler in the country as a means of manipulating Jago and him to settle down and start families.

Micah, knowing the drill, just waited in silence.

'The family has three young boys under the age of ten. They entertain a lot, both here and at their home in Switzerland. The couple seems to be very happily married but busy; they need help.'

Translation: neither you nor Jago has provided me with grandchildren, you don't entertain enough and you need a woman in your life. 'Jabu, come on…'

Uneasiness flashed through Jabu's eyes. 'I don't earn the enormous salary you pay me, Micah.'

Ah, so he was worried about that again. It was a subject that, along with their single status, raised its head occasionally. He and Jago travelled a lot and when they were at home they were very self-sufficient. These days, Jabu's duties were limited, and they knew he felt guilty about living in the large apartment above the garage, his huge salary and the use of a company car.

'Mkulu, I know that my father never paid you what you were due when we were kids; he was a notorious skinflint and you earned the bare minimum. Jago and me—mostly me—were terrors, Theo was volatile and Liyana was demanding. You dealt with all of us without a word of complaint and with incredible dignity. Jago and I agree that you've earned an easy semi-retirement.'

'But—'

'Got to go,' Micah said, running up the stairs. On the landing, he looked down to see Jabu still standing in the hall, his eyes on a black-and-white photograph of Jago, Thadie and himself. Jabu straightened the photograph, nodded once and touched the edge of the frame with his fingertips.

Crisis, Micah thought, averted. But if Jabu was feeling restless then he'd ask Thadie to request his help with the twins for a day or two. He'd come back exhausted after running after those bundles of energy, and his requests for a busier Hadleigh House would die down for a month or two.

He loved Jabu, but his own children running round the rooms of this old house would never happen.

The next day, Ella stood on a wooden deck of The Gate boutique hotel, entranced by the sandstone cliffs of the Golden Gate National Park. The multi layers of the cliff and outcrops fascinated her, with each layer sporting a different colour ranging from black to gold, to red, to orange and ochre. She remembered visiting this area as a child and wondered why she hadn't been back to the park since then or visited the quaint and artistic town on its doorstep, Clarens.

It was only a three-and-a-half-hour road trip from Johannesburg and they'd left the city at eight that morning. She'd waited for Micah on the pavement outside her apartment block and he'd swung his expensive car into a parking spot a few feet from her. He'd tossed her small suitcase into the boot of the car, handed her the keys and told her he needed to work.

While she drove his car through the city's traffic and onto highway, busy with trucks and empty of cars, he'd spent the next three hours and twenty minutes on his phone and laptop, frequently both at once. It was only when they'd approached Clarens that he raised his head, closed his laptop and looked around. The on-board navigation system instructed her to bypass the town and head for the Golden Gate National Park, and they turned to the right not far from the towering cliffs and the park's entrance.

This was their first appointment; they had another this afternoon and one tomorrow morning. They'd toured the grounds of the hotel, looked at the sweet chapel, inspected the kitchens and the function rooms and peeked in on the bride and groom and honeymoon suites. Micah, surprisingly, allowed her to take the lead on questioning the functions manager, and she'd covered all aspects of staging a huge event without letting the owner know she was looking for a wedding venue. Ella looked back into the function room, saw Micah shake the manager's hand and sighed at the hopeful look on the guy's face. A Le Roux function would put this place on the map and would be a stunning advertisement for the hotel. Unfortunately, she couldn't recommend it as an option for his sister's wedding.

Micah stepped onto the deck, closed the glass door behind him and joined Ella at the railing, holding two bottles of water in his hand. He opened one for her, handed it over and took a long sip. When he lowered the bottle, he sent her an easy grin. 'Hi,' he said softly.

'Hi back,' she replied equally softly, leaning her forearms on the railing, enjoying the mild breeze coming off the mountains. 'God, it's beautiful here.'

Micah nodded. 'I love this area. It's one of my favourite places to do trail runs and hike.'

'It could be one of my favourite places to sit on a deck like this and read a book,' Ella told him, smiling.

'I like to be busy,' Micah told her. That wasn't news to Ella, as he hadn't taken a breath for the entire trip from the city, either taking calls, giving orders or banging away on his laptop or phone. She hadn't minded being ignored. She'd needed the time to think.

When he'd collected her this morning, he'd acted cool and professional and she hadn't picked up a hint of the attraction she'd seen yesterday. Ella turned over his words about him being attracted to her, wanting her in his arms. Had he meant them or was he just being kind? Had he changed his mind about finding her attractive?

Maybe his attraction was a one-off, one-day thing, a soap bubble hitting a thorn or a piece of spun sugar. There one moment, gone the next. The problem was that his attraction to her might've faded, but hers was still raging.

Ella placed her tablet onto the glass-and-wood table to her right. She caught Micah looking at it and tipped her head to the side. 'What?'

'Are you sure you've got enough space on that to hold all your notes?'

She blushed a little, knowing that her habit of taking down reams of notes, most of them probably a bit unnecessary, was a source of amusement to her work colleagues. 'I don't like to miss anything.'

'Ella, you nearly wrote the equivalent of Proust's *In Search of Lost Time* in two hours.'

She didn't get the reference so she asked him to explain. 'It's supposedly the longest book in the world,' he said.

'Ha-ha, funny,' she said, but her tone lacked heat. 'It's important to me that I don't miss any details, because you never know when a little detail might be important.'

Micah rested a hip on the table and his forearm on his thigh. He was dressed casually today in a pair of tailored blue Chambray shorts—almost the same colour as the sky above—a cream button-down shirt with its sleeves rolled back and a pair of trendy trainers. 'There's a story there. Will you tell me?'

It was such a direct question, no hesitating, fudging or judgement, so she shrugged. 'I lost my mum when I was sixteen and my life became a little chaotic. Order became very important to me. I like making notes and lists.'

'They make you feel safe, in control,' Micah observed.

She nodded, surprised at his perception. 'Yes.'

'You enjoy planning events, don't you?'

Ella leaned back against the railing and looked up into his face, noticing the fine lines around his eyes, no doubt from squinting in the sun, just as he was doing now. As if he heard her thoughts, Micah dropped his sunglasses from the top of his head and covered his eyes.

He didn't give her a chance to answer. 'I was watching you and you dove into the meeting, completely confident. You asked him a dozen questions I would never have thought about.'

'Well, it's what I do,' she pointed out, though pleased at the compliment. 'And, yes, I do love it.'

He leaned his forearms on the railing and looked at the scenery, watching three vultures lazily riding the thermal bands high above them. Standing in the sun, enjoying the quiet and the cool breeze, Ella could easily pretend they were on holiday, taking a mini-break, lovers instead of work colleagues. She wanted to step between his legs, lean her head on his chest and feel his arms around her. Taking the moment, being together in the present.

But that was impossible.

'So, what do you think?' Ella asked him, reluctantly turning her attention back to the venue. It was a pretty place, built from local stone, and the interior was exquisitely decorated. There was ample accommodation in the village and surrounding areas to accommodate the wedding guests but, sadly, the place was too small. The guests would be jammed into the venue like sardines in a can. And when a wedding was so upmarket and luxurious, space to move, dance and socialise—to see and be seen—was high on the list of priorities.

Ella still believed that Johannesburg was the right place to hold the wedding and was convinced that there had to be a private estate, a museum, a vintage hall or an industrial warehouse that could be prettied up. They just needed to think outside the box.

'Very pretty.'

Ella turned at his low, intense voice, and when her eyes connected with his she immediately realised that he wasn't looking at the view or the buildings but at her, his eyes hidden by his designer sunglasses.

'I like your dress,' Micah added in his still-businesslike voice. She'd wanted to look professional but to be comfortable too, so she'd chosen to wear a graphic printed white-and-brown Boho-inspired maxi dress, its halter neck leaving her arms bare.

'Thank you,' Ella replied, feeling a little at sea. He was saying the right words, but she still couldn't read him, and it was frustrating as hell.

She should stop this going-nowhere conversation, change the subject herself, but instead she dropped her gaze and idly noted that his beard was slighter thicker than it had been the day before and that his lower lip was fuller than his top lip. She wondered if he'd taste like the coffee he'd drunk earlier, or the apple he'd crunched as a mid-morning snack. Or a combination of both. She shouldn't be thinking of kissing him; he was her boss. She was advising him on a venue, trying to help him solve a pretty big problem…

But how could she concentrate when all she wanted was to be in his arms, to have his mouth on hers?

'Dammit.'

'Problem?' Micah asked and Ella cursed herself. Why did she let the mild curse leave her lips?

'No, I'm fine.'

He pulled off his sunglasses and hooked them in the vee of his shirt. 'Are you worried about being alone with me?'

God, no! Was that what he was thinking? Of course she wasn't! 'No, I'm not worried about you making a move on me.'

His mouth lifted at the corners in a sexy smirk. 'Then are you worried that *you* are going to make a move on *me*?'

Yes.

'No, of course not!' Ella scoffed, cursing her higher-than-normal voice. How did he know that? He slid his hands into the front pockets of his shorts and rested his hip against the wooden railing, his raised eyebrows silently calling her out on her lie.

'I think you want to kiss me but then you remembered that you are working for me, that we have a job to do,' he said, a hint of teasing in his voice.

Ella felt embarrassed that he could read her so easily. Why couldn't she play it cool, hide her feelings, be a little less transparent, dammit?

'We are allowed to be attracted to each other, Ella,' Micah pointed out in a reasonable tone.

Ella rubbed her forehead with her fingertips. 'Yes, I'm more attracted to you than you are to me. Happy now?' she asked, sounding belligerent.

Oh, why couldn't she keep her mouth shut? What was wrong with her?

'You think that I'm not as attracted to you as you are to me?' Micah demanded, genuinely astounded. 'Why would you think that?'

'Teasing voice, charming attitude, shuttered eyes…take your pick,' Ella replied.

His eyes caught hers and he allowed her—of that she had no doubt—to see the turmoil inside him, his hot desire, his burning need. Where did all that heat come from, and how did he manage to hide it so well?

Was charm a cloak he pulled on, one that shielded his emotions from the world? He had a reputation for being laid back and easy going, but she'd seen his irritation and impatience the other day. Was he just very adept at hiding his feelings? Maybe. Possibly.

'Did you not hear what I said yesterday about how much I want to kiss you?'

Ella dragged the toe of her shoe along a wooden beam of the deck. 'I thought you changed your mind, that it was a blip,' she admitted.

'A blip?'

'Um… Well, you were super-business-like when you picked me up, and you didn't say two words to me for more than three hours. I thought…'

'You think far too much, Ella,' Micah stated, pushing his hand through his hair.

'And you hide your thoughts too well, Micah,' Ella shot back.

'Touché.' Micah nodded. 'But understand this…nothing has changed. I still want you in every way a man wants a woman.'

Oh…right. Wow. That was pretty clear.

'But *I* can't make the first move here, *I* can't do a damn thing,' Micah said, his voice sounding strangled. 'My hands are tied because you work for me and *I* promised you—*promised* you!—that you were safe with me.'

He'd put a lot of emphasis on the 'I'...

'I've already resigned from your company, and I've decided that I'm not coming back to work at Le Roux Events, so I'll be leaving your employ in a little under three weeks. Does that make a difference?' Ella asked him, surprised at her question. She wasn't normally this brave. Correction: she was *never* this brave when it came to men.

He stared at her, his hands bunched in his pockets, his eyes holding hers captive.

'And what if I told you that I do feel safe with you, and I appreciate you making me feel that way? Most men would take my statements as a green light and would've been kissing me by now, trying for more.'

His eyes blazed but his stance didn't change. 'I'll say it again and I'll keep saying it: I don't force myself on women, ever.'

God, how was she supposed to resist him, fight against the rush of need and want? 'What if I kissed you? What if I placed my hands on your body, my lips on your mouth?'

The air shimmered between them, and it was as if lightning was striking all around them from the cloudless blue sky. 'You talk far too damn much, El,' he muttered.

Ella stepped closer to him, feeling mighty, potent and, best of all, in control. Something she hadn't felt for months. She placed her hand on his muscled chest, stood on her tiptoes and did what she'd been longing to from the moment she'd first seen him—and that was to place her nose in the space where his jaw and throat met. She inhaled his scent, cologne, soap and hot male skin, and her stomach rolled over. Cupping her hand around his neck, she noticed that his hands were still bunched in his pockets and his heart was pounding. He wanted her...

She knew that as she knew her own name.

Ella placed her lips on his and nibbled and licked her tongue across his bottom lip. He was stiff, tightly coiled, and she pulled back a little to look up into his fire-blue, narrowed eyes. 'Please kiss me, Micah.'

For a moment she thought that he was going to refuse, to reject her, but then one hand was on her lower back, pulling her into his body, and the fingers of his other hand held her jaw, gently but possessively. She expected him to cover her mouth with his, to drop them into a hot, deep, slide of a kiss, but surprisingly his mouth travelled from the side of her mouth, up her cheek and back down along her jaw. When he finally returned to her lips, he nibbled, then sucked, tracing his tongue over her bottom lip. It wasn't enough; she needed more. She needed to feel his heat, to taste him, to feel wholly connected to him.

And, right at this moment, she wanted more than a kiss—she wanted it all. Cool sheets, naked bodies, him sliding into her and making her whole…

In his arms, she felt pretty and perfect—sensational, as if her sole purpose in life was to stand in the African sun and kiss him. If only he'd do it properly. Ella opened her mouth to demand more but, before she could utter a word, he captured her open mouth and slid his tongue inside. And she was suddenly on a bullet train travelling through a kaleidoscope of light and warmth, sensation and emotion. On one level she took in the details—his soft hair, his clever tongue, his big hand cupping her butt, the length and thickness of his erection. On another level, she was pure sensation—heat and colour and warmth and emotion…

This guy, she thought, her mind spinning, could *kiss.* If he was half as good, a quarter as good, in bed, she'd never recover. Wow, was she thinking of going to bed with him? Yes…yes, she was. Why wouldn't she? She'd had a few miserable months; didn't she deserve a little fun?

Ella heard Micah's low groan as her hands travelled up and down his back, and his kiss deepened when she pulled his shirt out of the back of his shorts so that she could feel his warm skin under her palms. So strong, so masculine... She wanted to kiss him here, at the base of his spine; and here, on the deep valley above his hard butt. There were other places she wanted to kiss, intimate spots she'd never explored before...

Micah placed his big hands on her cheeks and his kiss turned gentle, softer, a gradual dialling down of his passion. He pulled his mouth off hers and kissed her cheek, her nose and each of her closed eyelids before resting his forehead on hers. Like her, he was breathing heavily.

'Wow,' he whispered.

'That bad?' Ella asked, even though she knew it was anything but. But a little reassurance never hurt a girl.

'That good,' Micah said, wrapping his arms around her and pulling her into a tight hug. 'Hold on to me for a sec. I just need a moment to recover.'

She knew he didn't, not really, but she was happy to stand in his arms, her cheek on his chest, looking out at the valley overlooked by those impressive cliffs and hangouts. Somewhere in the distance, she could hear the chatter of a stream and the melodious tones of two women talking in Sesotho. She could stand like this for the rest of the afternoon. Being held by Micah was better than she'd ever imagined.

But in a minute he'd break the spell, suggest that they go to their hotel and finish what they started. Because a kiss like that was just the start of a pleasure-soaked journey, one that needed completion. It was, obviously, the natural outcome...

He was her boss, but in a six-steps-removed type of way, so the boss-employee dynamic wasn't, to her, much of a factor. And sleeping with Micah would be the perfect way to get her back in the dating game, to put the ghosts that hovered around her because of Pillay's behaviour to bed. She wasn't the type of girl who could easily separate sex from love. She thought the act was better when emotion was involved, but maybe sleeping with Micah would be a good way to get her sexual mojo back. If she'd ever had any.

In a couple of weeks, she'd be out of his life, so there was no way she'd allow herself to fall for him. Being with Micah would be a way to replace those bad sexual memories of Pillay's hot breath and clammy hands with some good ones. If she started feeling confident and attractive—who wouldn't feel like that after being with Micah?—maybe that would translate into her feeling confident about her life, would make her feel more self-assured. Sleeping with Micah would give her a new lease on life and would be a great way to kick-start her new life.

She had no fears of sleeping with Micah. Nothing about being with him, being held by him as tightly as she was made her have any flashbacks. She didn't feel constricted, scared or flustered, she just wanted more. So, yes, she was interested in sleeping with him, of course she was. She'd initiated that kiss and she'd all but climbed inside him while they'd been kissing. To men like Micah, kissing was the first stop on the destination, but…

But maybe it was wise to slow down…just a little. To stop, think and work out whether she was heading in the right direction. Being around Micah was like stepping into a Category Five tornado, and she felt caught up in its turbulence. She'd prefer to make the decision to sleep with him when she was feeling a little less storm battered and more like the self-confident person she so wanted to be.

Ella waited for his suggestion that they go, that they pick this up at their hotel, but instead of going there Micah patted the top of her bottom and pulled back from her. 'I'm starving. Why don't we head into Clarens and find a place to eat? I need to check my emails and return some calls before we head a few miles out of town for our next appointment.'

Right, that wasn't what she expected to hear. So what else could she do but nod her head and follow him to his car? And why did she feel so intensely disappointed?

CHAPTER FIVE

MICAH, AFTER CONSULTING the hotel receptionist, took Ella to the most popular restaurant in town for dinner. He couldn't remember when he'd last been in anything but a modern restaurant, an upscale jazz joint or as a VVIP in a happening club, but this place was a pleasant surprise.

The owners of this high-class eatery seemed obsessed with quality, from the astounding art on the walls, to the extensive range of excellent spirits behind the bar and the daily menu. This included chic dishes such as roasted quail with grapes, fennel-roasted pork belly and whipped-honey and lemon ricotta. If he were in the market for a gastro pub—and he might be in the future—this place would be of interest. It also happened to be within the grounds of their hotel, so it was an easy walk from their chalets, and he didn't have to worry about drinking and driving.

The décor was a mix of styles—wood, concrete, slightly rusted iron sheets and boldly coloured walls. He approved of the linen table cloths and serviettes and the quality glassware. He narrowed his eyes at a games room attached to the back of the restaurant containing a fine, antique billiards table, a vintage pinball machine and—*ugh*—a dartboard. It was currently occupied by a group of youngsters. The owners were making a mistake by not filling the space with tables. The rest of the joint was a fantastic blend of luxury and laid back, but that games room hindered rather than helped.

Standing at the modern, brushed-concrete bar, his lips still scorched from their earlier kiss, Micah looked in the counter-to-ceiling mirror behind the bar and watched Ella, who sat at a small table at the back of the room. She'd changed from her feminine dress into a pair of tight jeans and a simple navy-and-white-striped top. Ballet pumps covered her feet and she'd twisted her hair up into a loose knot on the back of her head.

She looked amazing, and her clothes told him that his choice of a more casual place to eat was spot-on. If he'd chosen one of the elegant restaurants in town, she might have felt pressured to continue what they'd started earlier and that was something he was desperate to avoid.

She might be on her way out of Le Roux Events—and, as a businessman, he regretted losing her talents—but he was still her boss for now. And he was very aware that, when a boss and employee became sexually involved, life could quickly become complicated. No, if Ella wanted more, she'd have to make the first move. Hell, she'd have to make *all* the moves.

Micah leaned his elbows on the bar, accepting it would be a while before the bartender took his order, and found he was happy to have a moment to think. He knew women and thought he understood them but he found Ella both mystifying and fascinating. She was a combination of confident and skittish, scared and brave. She kissed like a dream and she could be either hellishly straightforward or very cagey. She was a study in contrasts—light and shade, monochrome and intense colour.

Initially, she'd been worried about being alone with him, but after just one day, and a hellfire-hot kiss, she seemed to have got over that. She now seemed at ease around him, thank God.

Their employer-employee relationship and her recent history were factors in his hesitancy about taking her to bed. But there was a bigger reason for his caution: for the very first time since Brianna's accident, he felt something more than lust, more than a man's normal desire for sex, for a release, for a few hours of fun on a mattress. Ella intrigued him, confounded him and made him want to know more...

Sure, he wanted to explore her beautiful body, but he also wanted to take a walk around her maze-like mind. And he wanted her to like him too—a terrifying thought and one he'd never admit to.

She'd seen past his act and had sussed out that he was a great deal more impatient and less charming than he generally allowed people to see. She'd ignored his stylish exterior and the cash in his wallet and had caught glimpses of the man he really was: abrupt and easily irritated. Ella innately understood that, under his surface, he was more driven and less charismatic, and his occasional prickliness didn't bother her.

But what was the point of letting her duck her head to see below his surface? Not only was she his employee—albeit not for much longer—but she was also leaving the country soon. He could give her some bed-based fun and physical pleasure, but nothing more because...

a) She'd recently been accosted by a person in power...
b) She'd made him feel too much far too quickly, and that was as dangerous as hell.

Not that he was thinking of her in terms of falling in love—that wasn't possible, given that he'd been vaccinated against that emotional virus twenty years ago He would never marry and have kids. How could he when he'd taken that away from Brianna, when his actions had resulted in her existing in a space somewhere between life and death?

He'd offloaded onto her, and then had cut off contact with her, and he should've known that she would be worried about him, that his silence would've driven her crazy. He should've anticipated her jumping in her car and trying to find him…

It was his fault.

'Sir, what can I get you?'

Micah ordered a beer for himself and a glass of excellent red wine for Ella and told himself to be sensible. He should ignore their attraction and stop thinking about that kiss, about how much he'd love to make love to her. No good could come of it. He didn't, after all, deserve good.

Micah heard a wave of noise coming from a small room adjacent to the main pub, and looked across the crowded room to see a group of young adults playing pool and throwing back their drinks. There were going to be a couple of very sore heads in the morning, he thought.

So young. So dumb.

Micah paid for the drinks and picked up a couple of menus, tucking them under his arm. He walked back to Ella, placed her glass in front of her and handed her a menu.

'I'm starving,' Ella told him, opening it. She made her choice and he summoned a waiter and placed their orders before leaning back in his chair. He closed his eyes and allowed the music, the general noise and the occasional shouts from the rowdy group in the games room to wash over him. Unfortunately, his day was far from done, he still had hours of work ahead of him tonight. Le Roux International work didn't come to a stop because he was out of the office. But being anywhere with Ella was a nice respite.

'Why are *you* looking for a venue for your sister?'

Ella's question made his eyes fly open and he stared at her, caught off-guard. Because he was the family troubleshooter, the guy who sorted out the drama, the one who had amends to make.

'Because my sister asked for help,' Micah told her, his tone warning her not to ask any more questions.

She chose not to hear it. 'Thadie has a very talented wedding planner and she strikes me as being smart. Her fiancé also has connections of his own. It's not *your* wedding so, again, why you?'

Everything snaked back to The Incident two decades before. Brianna was at the centre of that whirlpool but its ripples had affected so many people. Thadie had lost her heroine, the person she'd considered to be her big sister, her beloved babysitter. Theo and Liyana had lost their best friends, and they missed the vibrant girl who'd spent an enormous amount of time in their house. And he'd put Jago through hell as he'd not only had to deal with Bri's diagnosis but also Micah's own abhorrent behaviour.

Of course, he couldn't tell Ella any of that…but, for the first time ever, he wanted to.

Because he didn't want to spend the rest of the evening in awkward silence, Micah decided to give her an explanation he hoped would satisfy her curiosity.

'Thadie does some charity work, and, through her social media observations on being a single mother, has become one of the country's biggest influencers. But her full-time job is being a mum—her boys are her priority and looking after them takes up a lot of her time. She doesn't employ a nanny and Jago and me, our butler, Jabu, and Thadie's best friend, Dodi, are her back-up system. We are who she calls when she needs time away from the kids, which she seldom does.

'She wanted to come on this trip with me to look at venues, but it wasn't feasible, as she has two charity events she can't miss. And Gus, the older of the twins, has a surgery scheduled.'

Ella leaned forward, immediately concerned for the health of a child she didn't know. 'I hope it isn't anything serious?'

He shook his head. 'No, he's having his tonsils out. Apparently, it's a minor op when you are three.'

He caught Ella's shudder. 'It is, but it's hell when you're an adult. I had mine out five years ago and I thought I was going to die, it was so painful. I really missed my mum that week.'

He allowed his fingers to drift across her hand, over her wrist. 'I lost my mum when I was nine. Not fun.'

Their eyes connected and he saw the pain and confusion he'd experienced in those green-gold-brown depths. Here was someone who understood how the ground could drop away from under your feet without a moment's notice.

'No, not fun.' Ella waved her hands, as if to swipe her words away. 'So, what did you think about venue number two?'

He appreciated the change of subject; he didn't talk about his mum, his childhood or life in the Le Roux household with anyone other than his siblings and, as a family, they didn't tend to look back.

'Venue two was a little bigger than venue one, but not as upmarket.'

Ella tucked a strand of hair behind her ears. 'I still think the venue needs to be in Johannesburg. It just makes sense for it to be there.'

'Thadie's wedding planner, as you know, is the best in the business and has contacts a mile long. She's spent days looking for a suitable venue and there's nothing.'

Ella pursed her lips. 'I don't believe that. There's got to be something.'

'Well, if you have any ideas, let me know, but in the meantime we're going to keep looking for an alternative venue. We'll head back to Johannesburg tomorrow. Where else do you think we should look?'

'What about Parys?'

The arty riverside town situated on the Vaal River might

be a good option: it was a wealthy and stunning place with superb scenery.

'Look into it.'

Ella nodded. 'I will but I still think that—'

'That Johannesburg is where the wedding should be.' Yeah, he got it, but there was nothing, and he couldn't magic a venue out of thin air. What could he do? Not keep looking and hope like hell something turned up? No, he couldn't take that chance. He would fix this for Thadie. Fixing stuff was what he did. Who he was…

Another loud shout from the billiard room caught their attention and everyone in the bar looked over to where the kids were doing shooters. South Africa's legal drinking age was eighteen but at times like this Micah thought it should be raised to thirty or thirty-five.

Their food arrived and Micah was happy to see Ella tucking in with gusto. Unlike many women he knew, she didn't push her food around the plate, pretending to eat but not making a dent in her meal. No, Ella dove in and murmured her appreciation, closing her eyes in pleasure as she chewed. She was such a sensual woman but Micah knew she had no idea of her impact. She glided when she walked, her face lit up when she smiled and the corners of her eyes crinkled just a little when she laughed. She turned heads, both male and female. She had presence, an energy, that couldn't be ignored.

By the time they finished eating, the party in the billiards room had turned loud and obnoxious. Ella finished her second glass of wine and scratched the side of her head. She nodded to the young adults. 'They are so inconsiderate; they're spoiling the place for everyone else.'

Well, yeah, kids did that. They didn't think of other people and never when alcohol was involved. He couldn't judge them too harshly; he'd done far worse than party it up in a bar.

'Ten more minutes and they'll be out of here,' he told Ella. The leader of the group was looking restless and Micah knew that he was bored. And where he went the others would follow. He was the guy others listened to, the party animal, the leader of the crew.

'What sort of teenager were you?' he asked Ella, interested in the answer. He was interested in everything about her. Smart and studious, he bet. Responsible and thoughtful.

She confirmed his thoughts when she answered. 'I was driven, I guess. I wanted to get my studies over with as quickly as possible so I could go out and work, earn some money.' He suspected that part of her need had been to get out of her house; she'd mentioned it had been chaotic. Before he could ask her a follow-up question, she asked a question of her own. 'And you? What kind of teenager were you?'

He debated whether to answer her but then shrugged. What harm could it do? It wasn't as if he was going to tell her anything of consequence. At least, he hoped he wouldn't.

He picked up his nearly empty beer bottle and pointed it at the leader of the group. 'Do you see Mr Cool, the one with the ripped jeans, the *AC/DC* T-shirt and the designer trainers that retail at nearly three hundred pounds?'

The kid had his arm slung around a girl who wasn't as drunk as the others and looked as if she'd had enough. He'd seen that look on Bri's face often enough.

'I bet he has a very expensive car outside, something like a Range Rover, or an Audi TT, or a limited-edition Golf GTI. Something pricey and fast and red-hot. He clicks his fingers and girls come running and, if they don't, he shrugs off the rejection, calls them a waste of his time and moves on to the next in the line. If they do jump to do his bidding, he dumps them when he gets bored with them and, trust me, he has a very low threshold for boredom. He doesn't get told "no" often, or ever. He's out of control, and he knows it, but his pride won't let him admit it.'

Ella turned back to look at him, her expression puzzled. 'How do you know all that?'

'Because I was him,' Micah admitted. He shrugged and tried to smile. 'You asked me what I was like when I was young. I was like that.'

Ella started to protest but she'd barely started her sentence when Micah saw the older of the two bartenders cross the room towards the youngsters, a nervous look on her face. Micah pulled a face and mentally told her to look tough or else the kids would eat her up and spit her out. The kids noticed her approach and their expressions turned belligerent. This wasn't going to end well.

Micah looked around the room and silently cursed when he saw that everyone else was either eating or ignoring the situation. Mr Cool folded his arms and his male friends lined up behind him, a wall of arrogance and aggression. She was one person, not a knife-wielding group of thugs.

It was like sending in a poodle to deal with a pack of pit bulls. He stood and pushed up from the table. Time to get scary…

'Give me five minutes,' he told Ella. Slowly, hands in the pockets of his shorts, he meandered past the tables to the games area, coming to stand a few feet behind the bartender, who had no idea of his presence.

'I think it's time for you lot to go home,' the bartender said, her voice quavering.

'And how do you think you going to make us…?' Mr Cool's voice trailed off when he saw Micah and, yep, he paled just a bit. He was a big guy, far bigger than anyone in the room, and it was clear he knew that when he looked angry he could intimidate Satan himself.

'We'll quieten down,' he stated, his eyes darting to Micah and back to the bartender.

Micah shook his head and the kid winced. Mr Cool looked around at his mates, pushed back his chest and lifted his lip in a sneer. 'We might as well go, guys, this place is awful anyway. Never been so bored in my life.'

He pulled a set of keys from the back pocket of his too-tight jeans and tossed them up in the air. He fumbled his first catch, just made the second and Micah knew he wasn't in a fit state to drive. None of them were.

Micah had been as full of arrogance and self-importance and had made a stupid, impulsive decision which had had far-reaching consequences. Life-changing, heart-breaking consequences. He still lived with the guilt and would for the rest of his life. If he could save another teenager from tragedy, he would, and he didn't care if he had to some knock some heads together to do it. Not that this situation would come to that. None of these kids could meet his direct gaze so he knew nobody would throw a punch. If they did, well, they'd test his Krav Maga skills, honed over years of training.

After asking, he ascertained they were staying within walking distance of the pub and could easily walk home.

'I'm not leaving my Rover here!' Cool told him hotly. 'Not a chance.'

Micah saw an empty wooden bowl on a shelf, grabbed it and held it out. 'Car keys, *now*.'

One by one, sets of car keys dropped into the bowl and Micah engaged in a staring contest with Cool until he dropped his keys inside the bowl too. He glared at the bartender. 'My car had better be safe when I come back for it or else!'

Micah ignored him and handed the bowl to the bartender. He brushed off her thanks and waited for the kids to leave before returning to Ella and rolling his eyes.

'That was pretty hot, Le Roux,' she said, her eyes holding admiration and more than a little lust. 'I like how you got them to listen with just a scowl and one raised eyebrow.'

He smiled. 'It's one of Jabu's favourite tricks. He never screamed or yelled, he just glared at me and lifted one eyebrow and I did whatever he asked, as quickly as I could.'

'Who is Jabu?'

'Butler, friend, the only father I ever really had,' Micah said, wondering why words flew from his mouth when he was around her. He drained his beer and pushed his chair back so that it rested on its back legs, giving him a better view of the exit and the kids heading towards the road.

'Why did you interfere?' Ella asked him. 'Most people wouldn't, they'd let the staff deal with them.'

Micah gestured to the bartender. 'She's their age, and timid. Do you really think they were going to listen to her?'

Ella shook her head. 'That's not why I'm asking. Why did *you* get involved?'

He knew she wasn't going to drop the subject. The vision of Brianna popped into his head, lying in that hospital bed, and he tasted the acrid hospital disinfectant at the back of his throat. He remembered her still body and her eyes, so blue and so vacant, staring at nothing.

Ella's hand gripped his and she squeezed his fingers. The hiss of pain jerked him back to the present. 'Come back from wherever you are, Micah. It's not a good place for you to be,' Ella told him in a fierce voice.

It was where he should be, Micah thought. He deserved, like Brianna, to be in no man's land. He looked down and away, cursing fate that Bri wasn't living her life out in the world, laughing and loving. She could be married by now, with a family. But she was stuck in that weird half-life and, to an extent, so was he.

He worked, looked after his family and worked some more. He exercised. He didn't have a personal life. He wasn't worthy of having one… What the hell was he doing here, spending time with Ella, chatting to her over dinner and a drink, as if this had the potential to go somewhere?

Sex was necessary, a great way to relieve stress, and he treated the woman he slept with well, but he never emotionally engaged with them. He didn't kiss them on balconies, tell them anything about his past and hold them tight, enjoying their softness and their femininity, feeling for the first time in years at peace in someone's arms.

He pushed back his chair with such force that it skidded across the floor. He pulled cash out of his wallet, tossed the notes onto the table and, without a word, walked away. He caught the confusion on Ella's face and knew he was behaving badly, but he needed air, he needed quiet and he needed to get away from her…

She saw too much, and worse—much worse—made him feel far too much. She was dangerous and he needed to remember that.

CHAPTER SIX

ELLA LOOKED DOWN at the money on the table and stared at Micah's retreating back, noticing the tension in his neck and shoulders. He looked as if he was carrying the world on his shoulders.

What on earth had she said? What had triggered his switch from being a charming dinner companion to a man who looked like she'd kicked him in the solar plexus and then stamped on his heart?

Ella caught the eye of the waitress, pointed at the cash on the table—far more than what their meals cost—and pushed back her chair. Walking slowly, she stepped into the still hot, fragrant summer night and looked up at the sky. Because this was mostly a rural area, the stars hung low in the sky, like sparkly little apples ready to be plucked off an intergalactic tree with wide branches.

The moon was a sliver in the sky and she remembered her mum describing it as 'God's thumbnail'. It was at times like these—times of change and uncertainty—that she missed her mum the most. She'd do anything to be able to call her up and ask for advice or to simply step into her arms for a long 'I've got you' hug.

Her mum had given the best hugs and, until this morning, she hadn't had a decent hug since she'd been sixteen years old. Her previous lovers hadn't been the 'cuddle her close' types.

Ella ignored the burn of tears in her eyes and rapidly blinked them away. Her dad didn't engage with her. Why did she keep thinking about him? Why couldn't she forget him—he obviously wanted her to—and move on with her life?

Because he was her dad, the only person she could call her own… Ella walked past the reception to the hotel and stepped onto the path that would take her to the attractive building that housed Micah's and her adjoining rooms. Their rooms shared a veranda and looked onto the rolling lawn that ended at a pretty pond. In the pale light on the veranda, she saw Micah leaning against the door to his room, arms folded and head bowed.

The world thought he was this charming, carefree character; sexy, successful and sophisticated. Oh, he was all those things, but also so much more. Underneath the sharp clothes and the designer stubble, the fancy watch and the smart car, was a man of unexplored depths, someone who had demons running after him with pitchforks.

Ella stopped on the path a little way from him, wondering what to say or how to act. Should she pretend that nothing had happened inside the bar, ignore his flash of deep unhappiness, his burst of temper? After what happened with Pillay, she thought she'd be scared to be alone with any man, but she was convinced Micah would rather cut out his kidney than hurt her or any other woman, child or animal.

No, whatever had happened had nothing to do with her. His anger had been self-directed, and she knew he was doing some intense self-flagellation. Words wouldn't help, Ella decided. Nothing she could say could bring him back from that dark place he was currently visiting. She could stand beside him and wait for him to return to her on his own, but who knew how long that would take? Or she could try and reach him another way…

Ella walked up the shallow steps to the veranda, stepped

in front of him and gently pulled his arms apart so that she could wrap her arms around his waist and place her cheek on his thumping heart. He needed comfort, so she plastered her body to his, wanting to give him her heat and something to hang on to as he surfed those cold, dark winds.

He didn't touch her. His arms hung at his sides but after a minute, maybe more, she felt some of the tension leave his body and heard his deep sigh. She knew that he was coming back to her when he placed his big hands on her hips and when he turned his head to rest his lips in her hair. Knowing he needed more, that she needed more, she pulled back and placed her mouth on his, encouraging him to step out of the darkness and back into the light.

He tensed again so she probed the seam of his mouth with her tongue and, when he opened his mouth, she kissed him gently, silently telling him to concentrate on her, on how she made him feel.

Ella felt a long shudder run through him then his hand slid across her lower back and he pulled her into him. She felt his hard erection, the proof she needed that he was back with her, in the moment. He took control of their kiss and, with one swipe of his tongue, he pulled her into an alternative world, one where only he existed.

She didn't care that he was her boss, temporarily or otherwise, and that this might be awkward in the morning. All she knew for sure was that she wanted him.

And that maybe, just for tonight, he wanted and *needed* her. That was enough. That *had* to be enough.

Ella wrenched her mouth from his, pulled back and shoved her hand into the pocket of her jeans to pull out her electronic room key. She stepped around Micah, jammed her key into the slot and cursed when the room remained locked. She repeated the action, the door opened and she reached back to grab a handful of Micah's shirt to pull him into the room. As soon as he was inside, she wound her arms around his neck, found his mouth again and tried to tell him, in the only way she knew how, how much she wanted to see him naked, to know what it felt like to have his body on hers, in hers.

Micah groaned, pulled her closer and kissed her thoroughly, intensely, his hand in her hair to keep her mouth plastered to his.

She needed him in a way that felt both foreign and wonderful, scary and delightful. She was riding the world's most dangerous roller coaster, stowing away on a rocket ship, diving to dangerous depths without a mask…

And she was loving every second of it.

Micah gripped a handful of her hair, gently pulled her head back and, despite the darkness, she saw the look of intensity on his face, the heat in his eyes. 'Are we doing this, Ella? Having sex?'

Given her recent history, she understood that he wanted—*needed*—her verbal consent and she was happy to give it. It might be a mistake, but she'd face those consequences tomorrow. 'Yes, if you'd like to.'

His answer to that statement was to take her hand and place it on his erection. She sighed at how hard he was, how big. 'I'd like.'

Through the material of his trousers, Ella swiped her thumb across his shaft. She didn't drop her eyes from his and saw the flash of pleasure, heard his sudden intake of breath. He liked that, so she did it again.

Releasing a small growl, Micah bent his knees, wound his arm under her butt and lifted her. It felt natural for her to wind her legs around his waist, relishing his strength and power. She felt small next to him, completely feminine. His mouth closed around her nipple and he tongued her through the fabric of her top and bra. Annoyed by the barrier, she leaned back, trusting him not to drop her, and lifted her shirt up her chest and over her head. She kept her eyes on his face as she reached behind her and undid the snap of her bra, pulling it off to toss it to the floor. She saw his gaze lower to her chest to take in her pale skin, her breasts—smaller than she'd like—and puckered nipples.

His hand cupped a breast, lifted it up and his lips closed over her nipple, setting off another round of fireworks in her brain, down her spine, between her legs…

'Micah,' she moaned, spearing her fingers into his hair.

He lifted his head to look in her eyes, and she fell into all that blue. 'You are so beautiful.'

She wasn't but he made her feel that way. He was so big, completely and overwhelmingly masculine. But, as strong as he was, there was a part of him that could be bruised, that was tender, able to be hurt…

In Ella's eyes, that didn't make him less of a man, but more.

Micah carried her over to the bed in the centre of the room and gently lowered her down, stroking his big hands over her breasts before shedding his shirt and unsnapping the buttons of his jeans. His tattoo was a Māori-inspired design covering his right pec, and fabulously hot. He pushed his jeans down his hips, along with his underwear, and she saw his slim hips, those sexy hip muscles she'd imagined him having, the ridges of his cut stomach. Her eyes dropped down further but, before she could take in his length and thickness, he bent down to kiss her chest and her stomach. His hand played with the snap of her jeans. 'Let's get these off, shall we?'

He was checking in with her again, wanting to know if she was still on board, and Ella nodded. Micah removed her jeans and stared down at her lacy panties, a hand drifting over her hip and across her bare bottom. 'I love thongs,' he said, sounding hoarse.

She did too, but right now she wanted it off. Instead of removing the scrap of fabric, Micah stroked his finger over her, pushing the fabric down into her feminine lips where it soaked up her heat. Lying back on the bed, Ella placed her forearm over her eyes and, half-lifting up, tried to push Micah's hand to where she most wanted it—touching her in that special place.

He released a satisfied laugh before pulling the edge of her panties to the side and sliding his finger up and down, flirting with her core. Ella lifted her hips off the bed to increase the contact, needing more. Needing everything he could give her.

Micah lay down beside her, holding her face so that she looked at him. 'I want to go slow, but I need you, El.'

Ella found his erection and wrapped her hand around his girth, surprised when he hardened even more. 'I need you too. Now.'

'Condom,' Micah said, sounding desperate.

She didn't have any but, God, she hoped he did. Micah rolled off the bed, grabbed his jeans and yanked his wallet out of the pocket. Bank cards, cash and credit card slips fell to the floor. He swore creatively and then she heard his relieved sigh. He dropped his wallet and, still standing up, completely unselfconscious, ripped open the condom and rolled it down his shaft, a normally prosaic action made erotic by a sexy man.

Micah placed his knee on the bed and dropped his head to place his mouth on her, licking her once in a slow, hot slide. Ella gasped then released a heated groan and Micah slid into her, stretching her and filling every inch of her. He placed his hands on either side of her head and stared down at her as he pulled back and re-entered her, slowly, stunningly.

Ella licked her lips, needing his mouth. 'Kiss me, Micah.'

Micah dropped down and she caught a flash of intense blue before his tongue entered her mouth, echoing the movements of what was happening down below.

Ella felt as though she was both inside her body and out of it, a part of Micah but not, playing on the stars as well as riding the biggest of the ocean's waves. She was sex and sensation, on the bed and not; herself, but Micah too.

Sensation steadily built and she felt tears in her eyes, her heart filling with an emotion she couldn't identify. She'd had sex before but nothing like this, nothing so crazy wonderful, so startlingly sensational.

She felt herself standing on the edge of a cliff but not scared to walk off it, knowing she'd be caught and tossed up into the heavens, into that starry sky she'd admired earlier.

Ella dug her fingernails into Micah's butt and arched her hips, silently encouraging him to go faster, to take her higher. He responded immediately and pumped his hips, driving deeper into her, commanding her to feel all of him, to take every bit of pleasure she could.

His voice faded away, a wave of pleasure shoved her into the void and she tumbled and fell, rolled over and ignited in a fireball that was all heat and no pain, filled with colours she'd never experienced before.

She exploded and, a long time later, she floated down, idly gathering her shattered pieces, slowly putting them back together.

When she was done, she realised Micah's face was on her neck, his arms cradling her head and his weight pushing her body into the mattress. It didn't matter that she couldn't breathe; he felt amazing.

As though reading her mind, Micah rolled off her onto his back, his hand patting the space between them to come to land on her thigh. Ella turned her head to see that his eyes were still closed and that he was breathing rapidly, his chest pumping up and down. A fine layer of perspiration covered his neck, shoulders and chest.

He looked like a Greek god who'd just run a marathon. So sexy…

Micah rolled his head to the side to look at her. 'Wow.'

He'd said the same thing when he'd kissed her earlier. 'That bad?' she asked, knowing it wasn't.

He squeezed her thigh and sent her a long, slow, skin-melting smile. 'I don't know. I might have to do that again so that I know it wasn't an aberration.'

Ella smiled, happy to see that his ghosts were gone. 'I'm happy to help you come to a definite answer.'

He grinned and kissed her briefly before rolling off the bed. He walked into the bathroom and, when he returned, he bent down to pick up his jeans and swiftly pulled them on. Ella sat up abruptly. 'Are you leaving?' she demanded, confused.

Micah kissed her nose. 'We need more condoms, sweetheart. Do you have any?'

Condoms? No! She hadn't thought she'd be having sex any time soon, so it wasn't something she'd stocked up on. 'Uh…no.'

'Didn't think so. I'll be right back.' Micah straightened and pointed a finger at her. 'Your only job is to remove those panties.'

It was only then that Ella remembered that she had them on.

Ella woke up and wasn't surprised to find herself alone in her big double bed. She rolled over and peered off the end of the bed but, as she expected, Micah's clothes were gone too.

Ella stretched, arched her back and pointed her toes before slumping back into the mattress. The bedside clock said it was twenty past six and, through the gap in her closed curtains—though she didn't remember pulling them closed last night—she saw that it was raining steadily. What she most wanted to do was to roll over and go back to sleep but, having failed to find a suitable venue in Clarens—they'd heard that venue three was even smaller than the others—

they were heading back to Johannesburg this morning. She assumed she would be driving, and she'd need a vat of coffee and a few energy drinks if that was the case.

Still naked, Ella sat up and wrapped her arms around her bent knees, staring at the water colour of the mountains on the wall across the room. She'd made love to Micah Le Roux last night and it had been…

Well, fabulous. Divine, wonderful, amazing.

They'd made love twice, and done some hot exploring in the shower afterwards, and she'd loved every minute with him. He hadn't banished the memories of Pillay's hot breath and sweaty hands, of him pinning her against the wall and trying to force his hand between her legs, but they weren't as oppressive any more. They'd somewhat faded.

From now on, when she thought of being intimate with a man, she'd remember Micah's sexy mouth and broad hands sliding across her skin, the way he'd turned her blood to hot syrup and how he'd raised fireworks on her skin. She wasn't one to rush into relationships—she was terrified of rejection and broken expectations—but she'd no longer be driven by fear. She was, thanks to Micah, in a different place now.

But Ella also suspected that any man she dated in the future, every future lover, would always be compared to Micah. She genuinely didn't believe last night could be improved on. It was the perfect first night with a new lover, both hot and sweet, tender and tempestuous.

But Micah didn't want a relationship and neither did she. It was a one-night stand, something that wouldn't be repeated. She now knew she could date again, maybe even sleep with a man again, and that was a relief.

But Ella still doubted she could have a relationship again. Because some scars didn't heal as quickly as others. Her father had mentally and emotionally disappeared on her after her mum had died. He had, in a sense, chosen to emotionally abandon her. Yes, he'd provided for her, and paid her school and university fees, but as she'd got older the gap between them had widened.

She'd always thought that, at some point, they'd find their way back to each other, but after years of trying she now knew they never would because it took two to reconnect. Being disappointed by your dad was a special type of hell and one that caused deep scars that would take a lifetime to heal. If they ever did.

And, if she couldn't trust her father—the one man who was supposed to love her, listen to her, to be there for her, to believe in her, to support and protect her—how could she trust any other man? Her father had taken away her trust in men, Pillay her trust in herself.

But maybe, thanks to Micah, she was regaining some of her self-confidence. There was something incredibly empowering about having a good, sexy-as-sin man interested in her. He wasn't the charming, charismatic man the world thought he was… No, that wasn't right, of course he was charming and very charismatic. But he wasn't *only* that man. He was deeper and more complicated than people suspected.

Micah had, she was sure, lived a thousand lives and not all of them were good. Things had happened to him that had caused deep, wide wounds, injuries that still made him ache and seethe. He was both hurt and angry, wounded and wishful.

But she couldn't get involved, couldn't let him get to her. She already cared far too much about what Micah thought about her. If she spent more time with him—assuming that he wanted a repeat of last night—she'd be in trouble, the 'losing her heart' kind of trouble. Even if she hadn't been planning to emigrate, there'd have been no hope of a relationship developing between Micah Le Roux and her. He didn't do relationships. According to social media and the press, he'd never had a girlfriend who'd lasted more than a few months, and she couldn't risk having someone she cared for disappoint her again. She was a normal working girl; he was a fast-moving billionaire businessman. Their lives had temporarily intersected but life would, as it inevitably did, pull them apart.

She had to be sensible, smart and protect her heart. She was the only one who could do that. Because, if she didn't look after herself, no one else would.

Knowing his concentration was shot, and that he wouldn't get much work done if he tried, Micah elected to drive them back to Johannesburg. Never before had a woman managed to pull his focus off work but Ella was one of a kind.

She was a series of firsts, he decided as he pulled over to pass a fuel tanker. The first employee he'd got naked with, the first woman he'd spent most of the night with—he'd only left her room when the red numbers on her bedside clock had flipped to six a.m.—and the first he'd wanted to keep in bed for the rest of the day.

The Bentayga's fancy computer flipped the windscreen wipers onto fast and Micah raised his eyebrows as the sound of thunder drowned out his favourite radio station. Rain fell in heavy sheets and, because the visibility was terrible, he slowed down. At this rate, it was going to take them for ever to get home.

He glanced to his left and saw that Ella was busy on her phone, looking at pictures of a grey-blue building. Judging by her cool but friendly attitude this morning, no one would've guessed they'd spent the night together or that he'd, in turn, made her scream and sigh. When she'd appeared in the dining room for breakfast, she'd acted as if nothing had happened and he was both grateful and irritated. Grateful because he didn't want her to start acting like his girlfriend, and irritated because she was behaving as if she hadn't rocked his world.

Micah ran a hand over his face, knowing that he sounded like an insecure kid. They'd had sex, great sex, and if she wasn't going to make a big deal of it, neither was he. He was older, and better, than that.

'What are you doing?' he asked, needing for some stupid reason to hear the sound of her melodious voice.

She looked up quickly before looking back down at her phone. 'I'm still trying to find a Johannesburg-based option for your sister's wedding.' She obviously caught something on his face because her lips twisted. 'I know you think it's a fool's errand, but I'm convinced there's something out there that would be a brilliant venue.'

'I can't stop you from looking but I don't think you're going to find anything. Thadie's wedding planner is—'

'The best in the business and she has incredible contacts...blah, blah, blah,' Ella muttered, eyes on her phone. 'I'm still wrapping my head around her losing the booking at The Gables.'

'I don't think it's fair to blame her,' Micah said.

'Oh, I blame everyone involved,' Ella quickly responded. 'The whole thing was badly handled.'

Really? 'Why do you think that?'

'Firstly, if I were the owner of the hotel, or the hotel's function manager, on receipt of those emails I would've got on the phone, or even driven to the wedding planner's offices, and demanded a face-to-face meeting to find out what went wrong. I can't understand why they didn't, because they've blotted their name with every wedding and event planner in the city now.'

'So you think the hotel messed up?'

Ella pushed her straight hair back over her shoulders. She wore another dress today, this one fitted to the waist and flaring over her hips in a navy-and-white polka-dot print.

'Of course they did. Badly. If you can't trust your vendors to call you when a problem arises, how can you use them ever again? Trust me, The Gables are going to regret this. And I can't understand why Anna didn't scream and shout and dance on the hotel manager's desk until they reinstated the original booking. I think she let The Gables off the hook far too easily.'

Interesting. When he'd heard about the cancellation and the snafu, he'd gone into problem-solving mode and, after hearing that it would be impossible to hold the wedding there, hadn't given The Gables another thought. His entire focus had been on finding a new venue, sorting out the problem and keeping everyone happy.

And maybe Anna de Palmer-Whyte wasn't as hot as everyone thought.

Micah saw a herd of cattle at the side of the road and, knowing how unpredictable they could be, slowed down a little more. 'What's your favourite type of event to organise?' he asked, interested in everything about her.

Ella half-turned to face him and smiled. 'Weddings, of course. But, as I said yesterday, I'd like to specialise in family events, like Anna does. That's the dream, but specialising takes connections at the highest level, connections I don't have. Maybe when I get to the UK I can look at doing smaller, more intimate events. I'm good at those.'

He believed her. 'Why are you emigrating?'

Ella removed her water bottle from the cup holder and tipped it up to her mouth. Micah remembered those lips under his, sliding across his chest, down his stomach. Lower…

He squirmed in his seat but Ella seemed oblivious to his discomfort. 'There's nothing and no one left for me in South Africa.'

That was a hell of a statement. 'At all?'

Ella replaced her water bottle and tucked her leg behind her knee, her torso angled towards him.

'I'm an only child of only children. My dad still lives in Durban but we don't talk.'

'Why not?' he asked.

'After my mum died, our relationship significantly deteriorated.' It was an answer but not an explanation.

'We're not on speaking terms any more. His choice,' Ella added.

Micah knew that something major had happened for all communication to end. He'd lived a scenario exactly like that. And he knew how painful it was to see your family ripped apart. He at least had Jago and Jabu and, although she'd been so young at the time, Thadie. Ella, it seemed, had nobody. His heart ached for her.

Ella turned the silver ring on her right middle finger round and round. 'I just want a new start, another one. He—' She abruptly stopped talking and turned to sit in her seat properly, staring out of the side window.

'Will you tell me what happened?' he asked quietly. 'Between you and your dad?'

'I don't want to rehash it, Micah.'

She shrugged and bent down to fiddle in her bag. When she sat up again, she slid sunglasses onto her face, despite it being a grey and wet day without a hint of a glare. She didn't want him to see her eyes, to catch a glimpse of her thoughts.

Why did Ella hiding from him cause him such frustration? Why did he want to explore her mind as well as her body? He wanted to be the one person she could open up to, to feel safe with...physically and emotionally. Why her? And why now? What was it about Ella that made him forget why he was the way he was—an extroverted loner? There were few people he let into his inner world... Jago, Thadie and Jabu. Brianna, back in the day. People had to earn a place to eat at his table and he seldom gave anyone the chance to do that. But here he was, asking Ella to open up, and considering doing the same for her.

And it was funny how, since meeting Ella, he was thinking about Brianna more than he had in years. She would've liked Ella, and vice versa. He could see them being friends, laughing together over something he did or said. Missing Brianna came in waves and, right at this moment, he felt as if he was drowning. His eyes burned, his heart felt like a petrified piece of wood and he couldn't get enough air into his lungs.

Ella's hand on his leg, her fingers tightening on his thigh, pulled Micah out from under that cold wave.

'You've gone to that dark place again,' Ella stated quietly. 'As I said last night, it's not a good place for you to be.'

He sent her a look and, when she didn't ask a follow-up question, when she didn't push or pry, he sighed. 'You are the least curious, least pushy woman I have ever met.'

'I'm not sure if that's a compliment or a criticism. Do you want me to push and pry?'

Micah shuddered. 'God, no!'

Ella pushed a strand of hair behind her ear. 'It's raining hard, and the road is busy. I don't think it's a good time for deep and intense conversations, Micah.'

Right. Okay then. Maybe it was better if they didn't talk; he did need to concentrate. But after five minutes, curse him, he did start to miss the sound of her voice. He turned to look at her, thinking they could discuss something, anything, but found her curled up on the seat, fast asleep.

She remained like that until they hit the outskirts of Johannesburg.

CHAPTER SEVEN

ELLA PULLED UP next to a BMW convertible, top down, and lifted her bag off her passenger seat, hauling in a series of deep breaths to calm her racing heart. Micah had dropped her at her flat yesterday and kissed her goodbye without making arrangements for them to meet over the weekend. Ella had tried hard, really hard, not to feel disappointed. They'd only slept together, she reminded herself, they weren't in a relationship.

So she was surprised to get a text message that morning, demanding her presence at a meeting at Hadleigh House at ten. Ella had thought she'd spend her Saturday morning researching venues in Parys but here she was, ten minutes early, at one of the oldest and most historic estates in the city. Ella stepped out of the car, slammed the door and looked up at the magnificent, massive double-storey house with its shingled roof and ivy-covered walls.

Curious, she ignored the imposing front door, walked round the side of the house and sighed at the magnificent English-style country garden, the old and dignified oak trees and the dark-blue swimming pool.

It would make the most magnificent wedding venue, Ella decided. If Thadie pared down her guest list and decided to have a garden wedding, she could maybe accommodate two, three hundred people here, maybe more. Back in the day, this house had been the gathering place for the elite of Johannesburg mining society, and the house had played host to soirées, balls and tennis parties. She could see a huge, romantic tent on the deep-green swathe of lawn to her right, fairy lights in the trees, a gazebo holding a dance floor, roses floating on the surface of that huge pool…

But the idea of having a wedding here sparked a memory. She dimly recalled another house, old and lovely, somewhere in this area. It was another old Victorian, one of the grandest mansions in the city. She'd read about it when she'd first come to the city and for some reason—she knew not what—it floated into her brain when she thought about a garden wedding.

The Le Rouxs could make another fortune hiring out Hadleigh House. With its thick, lush lawn, extensive, colourful rose garden and magnificent trees, it was the perfect venue for an intimate wedding. But Thadie and Clyde didn't want intimate, they wanted a glitzy, glam, see-and-be-seen wedding. And there were few places that weren't soulless convention centres that could give them what they wanted—romance and soul, luxury and loveliness.

'Welcome to Hadleigh House.'

Ella smiled, turned around slowly and saw Micah standing on the cobbled path behind her. His hair was damp and pushed back from his face, which still hadn't seen a razor, and he was dressed in a navy linen shirt, white tailored shorts and expensive leather flip-flops. He looked as though he could star in one of those glamourous adverts for perfumes Ella couldn't afford, which always seemed to be set in the Ionian Seas.

She wanted him to take her to bed. Right now.

Ella gave herself a mental slap and pulled what she hoped was an impersonal smile onto her face. 'Nice place, Micah.'

He looked round and she caught the flash of affection in his eyes, pride on his face. 'It's home. I love it here.'

He didn't make a move to usher her into the house so Ella stayed where she was, happy to feel the sun on her bare shoulders. She wore a pale-blue and white sleeveless jumpsuit today and flat-soled sandals. She'd pulled her hair up into a messy knot on top of her head and wore minimal make-up. It was, after all, a Saturday.

Ella looked up and counted ten windows widely spaced on the second floor of the mansion. 'Big place,' she observed.

He nodded his agreement. 'I live here with my twin, Jago. We recently renovated the house and we have separate, private apartments in each wing, though we currently share the kitchen, downstairs entertainment areas, the deck, pool and, obviously, the garden. If either of us decide to bite the bullet and marry—'

'A fate worse than death,' Ella said, her tongue in her cheek.

He lifted his eyebrows. 'For me, it would be.'

It was a warning, Ella thought, a subtle way to remind her that, while they'd slept together, there was no possibility of more. The warning was unnecessary because trust was impossible. And a relationship without trust was a bird without wings.

Not waiting for her to comment on his answer, he continued. 'As I was saying, if we want more privacy, Hadleigh can provide enough space and distance to make it feel like two separate homes.'

Micah gestured for her to join him on the path and she followed him around the corner of the building to a vast, covered entertainment area featuring an outdoor kitchen, bar, gas barbecues, a dining table that could seat twenty and many plump couches and outdoor chairs.

Nice. Very nice indeed.

'Are you and your twin close?' Ella asked him, smiling at the two hammocks strung from the beams in the far corner of the veranda.

'Very,' Micah told her, placing a hand on her back as they hit the slate steps leading up to the veranda. Ella wished she could simply hang out in the space, maybe lie on one of those luxurious loungers beside the pool, take a dip, or sit in the ten-man hot tub.

'Jago won't be at this meeting. It'll just be Thadie and her bridesmaid Alta, Clyde's stepsister.'

She followed Micah across the veranda into another outdoor seating area, which could be closed off from the elements with bi-fold doors. This room sported black-and-white-striped couches, cherry-red armchairs, bold cushions and even bolder art on the walls. Ella, in sensory overload, was finding it difficult to concentrate. There was so much to look at and take in.

'Where's her fiancé? Her maid of honour? Actually, who is her maid of honour?'

'Dodi Lewis. She owns Love & Enchantment, the wedding dress salon. Dodi has a busy morning at work and I'm not sure what Clyde's excuse is.' Ella caught the bite of irritation in his voice and wondered if he approved of his sister's fiancé.

Then again, Thadie was a grown, independent woman and didn't need her brother's approval.

'We're meeting in the library.'

Ella followed him down a hallway, stopping briefly to take in the magnificent hall, with its Harlequin tiled floor and matching, hand-carved staircases, and caught a peek through a doorway of a sleek, glossy, gourmet kitchen with acres of granite countertops.

Exceptional art decorated the walls and massive bouquets of roses, hand-cut and probably from the garden, perfumed the air. Sculptures, bronzes and ceramics sat on antique tables and Ella kept her arms folded and her bag tucked by her side so that she didn't knock anything over. They'd have insurance but some of their objects looked irreplaceable. This was, by far, the grandest house she'd ever visited.

Micah stepped back to let her precede him into a double-storey library, shelves extending up so high that a ladder was attached to a railing twenty feet in the air enabling the reader to get a book from the top shelves. A big wooden desk dominated one half of the room and, at the other end, two fat, dark leather couches sat in front of a pair of French doors which opened into the garden.

She immediately recognised Thadie Le Roux, with her big eyes, flawless light-brown skin and her famous mother's incredible cheekbones. She turned at their entrance and her smile was Julia-Roberts-wide. God, she was gorgeous.

The woman next to her with gold hair, pasty skin and narrow eyes paled beside her. Thadie wore a bright-yellow sundress and sandals whereas the other woman wore a revealing top, a far too short black mini-skirt, and three-inch heels. Not to mention pursed lips and a scowl…

Thadie jumped to her feet and Ella took in her height. She was close to six feet and curvy. As she held out her hand in greeting, their eyes connected and, within those dark-brown depths, Ella saw warmth, a hint of panic and maybe a touch of *what the hell am I doing?*

Micah introduced her to his sister, and then to Alta, Clyde's stepsister, who didn't bother getting to her feet.

'Are the twins still with Jabu, Micah?' Thadie asked him as she sat down and crossed her long, slim legs.

'Yes, they are in the greenhouse. Mkulu's probably got them filling pots with compost or digging for worms in a flower bed.'

Alta gasped, horrified. 'But that's unsanitary!'

Thadie smiled. 'Little boys like dirt and digging in the

soil, and being outside helps build up their immunity. Ella, please take a seat.'

Thadie gestured her to the couch and Ella sat down, placing her tote bag at her feet. Micah offered her something to drink, and when she asked for coffee he nodded. A solid-silver tray sat on the coffee table and held a Chinese-looking teapot and thin-as-paper teacups on equally thin saucers.

'I'll just go make you a fresh cup,' Micah said.

'Just ring for the butler,' Alta told him.

Micah's lips tightened at being told what to do in his own house. 'As I said, Jabu is with the twins in the greenhouse and, even if he wasn't, I would never interrupt what he was doing to demand he bring me a cup when I could so easily get it myself. I'm rich, not spoiled,' Micah told her with an easy smile, his good humour restored.

Ella knew that Alta wanted to ask him what the point was of employing a butler if he didn't buttle. Was that even a word?

Thadie waved at a plate holding exquisite looking, one-bite cakes covered with a mirrored chocolate glaze. 'Please have one. They're divine, and I've already eaten three, so help me out here.'

Ella grinned, loving her honesty and, because she hadn't had breakfast and adored chocolate, took a tiny cake. 'Thanks.'

'You're not going to fit into your very expensive wedding dresses if you keep eating those,' Alta said, sounding snide.

Thadie just grinned. 'Of course I will! I run ten miles a day on the treadmill and another ten chasing the boys. And life is too short not to eat chocolate!'

Ella instinctively liked her. She just as instinctively didn't like Alta, with her plummy accent and cool eyes. For Thadie's sake, she hoped Clyde was a lot warmer than his stepsister.

Thadie leaned forward and briefly rested her fingers

on Ella's arm. 'Thank you so much for helping Micah to find a new venue.'

Ella was about to respond when Alta spoke. 'If your very experienced, unbelievably connected wedding planner can't find you a venue, Thadie, then I doubt Bella—'

'My name is Ella,' Ella mildly corrected her.

Alta didn't miss a beat. 'Will be able to find you a suitable venue. I strongly suggest you postpone the wedding and rebook the venue and vendors.'

Ella looked from Thadie to Alta and back again. Alta sat up straight and was as tightly wound as piano wire. Thadie, who'd kicked off her sandals and tucked her feet up under her bottom, looked relaxed and unfazed. This was, after all, her childhood home.

'I have complete faith in Micah,' Thadie told Alta, before flashing Ella her mega-watt smile. 'And you, of course, Ella.'

Ella thanked her but refrained from telling her that her faith might be misplaced. And optimistic. She wondered if she should try to temper Thadie's expectations but, before she could decide, Micah walked in, holding an enormous mug in his hands.

He handed it to Ella. 'Milk, no sugar. Strong.'

They'd often stopped for coffee on their trip to Clarens and back and Micah had surprised her by not having expected her always to do the coffee run. He'd asked her how she took her coffee and remembered. It was such a little thing and it shouldn't make her feel tingly. And special. Most of all, special. Micah, she told herself, was a super-smart guy and no doubt he remembered lots of little things, often.

Ella took the mug, wrapped her hands around it and took a grateful sip. Great coffee, she decided. Expensive coffee. Yum.

Micah ignored Alta's gesture for him to sit next to her—

ah, so that was the way that wind blew!—and sat down on the leather ottoman at a right-angle to Ella, their knees inches apart. He rested his forearms on his thighs. Ella looked at his broad hands with their long fingers, and was transported back to how those hands had stroked her from hip to breasts, how his fingers had slid between her legs…

'Don't you think so, Ella?' Micah's question was accompanied by a nudge to her knee, and she jerked her head up to look into those amused blue eyes. He was laughing at her, as if he knew exactly where her thoughts had wandered to. Dammit, she hated it when he seemed to read her mind.

'Sorry, I missed that,' she apologised, blushing.

'Micah was just saying that none of the venues in Clarens was suitable,' Thadie explained. 'I wanted to know whether you agreed.'

Ella crossed her legs, leaned forward and nodded. 'There are some lovely venues, but some aren't big enough, some aren't luxurious enough, some are just blah.'

'So what's the bottleneck?' Thadie asked, her intelligent gaze meeting Ella's. She narrowed her eyes the same way Micah did when he was focused on a problem—or making love to her—and tapped her index finger on her knee, the same way her brother did. They looked nothing alike, but both had similar mannerisms and a no-nonsense way of looking at a problem.

'The problem is that you don't have enough time, Thadie! If you postponed the wedding, you'd give everyone some breathing room!'

Thadie didn't acknowledge Alta's outburst, but Ella noticed her pinched face and the hard twist of her lips. Why was Alta one of Thadie's bridesmaids? They didn't seem to be friends, or in any way close. Was she just there because she was Clyde's stepsister?

'Ella?' Thadie asked, steel in her still sweet-smile.

Right, business. 'I think it's a combination of all three

issues. You want a huge venue that is special and luxurious, able to accommodate many people. And you want it soon, when most venues have been booked for a year, sometimes two.'

'She's Thadie Le Roux,' Micah said. 'She's one of the most famous women in the country and that should count for something.'

He said it as a statement of fact, without a hint of elitism or boasting, and Ella couldn't take offence at that.

'Yes, I am. I am also marrying one of the most famous men in the country,' Thadie said, sitting up and dropping her feet. She sent Ella a rueful smile. 'But hotels are not going to bump a bride for me, especially at this late date. And they shouldn't. I'd hate for a bride to lose her big day because of me; that would be dreadful.'

'Not finding a decent venue would also be dreadful, a complete disaster. Really, you should postpone!'

Wow, Alta really wasn't bringing anything to this conversation. Ella decided to follow Thadie's lead and ignore her. 'Micah mentioned looking for a venue somewhere in the Drakensberg or the KwaZulu Natal Midlands…'

'But you don't think there's anything,' Thadie stated.

Ella wrinkled her nose. 'There are some big operations, and maybe something will turn up; it's worth a look.'

But how on earth was she going to be able to spend more time with Micah without being in his arms, in his bed? It was supposed to have been a one-night thing but, man, she wanted more. But Micah wasn't a 'more' type of guy and, even if he were, he'd never look at her in a 'let's have a relationship' way. She came with too much baggage. She had daddy and trust issues, disappointment issues, being believed issues. Finding her confidence issues.

A relationship was impossible.

Ella looked at Micah. 'If you like, I can go drive down

myself, scout out the venues and report back. If there is anything viable, you could then come down.'

Thadie sent Micah a guilty look. 'I know how busy you are, Micah, and that you can't afford to take time away from the office. Ella seems sensible and straightforward, so I'd be more than happy to trust the search to her.'

Micah surprised her by shaking his head. 'No, I said I'd do this, and I'm doing it. I'll—*we'll*—find you a wedding venue, Thadie. I promise.'

Ella winced, wishing he hadn't said the P-word. She didn't know if she could fulfil that promise. But maybe this was a good time to raise another option. 'Would you be open to doing something different?'

Thadie shrugged. 'Like?'

'I'm thinking of a flower-filled atrium within a botanical garden. An old house or a mansion, a warehouse or an industrial building.'

Ella waited for the response to her out-of-the-box suggestions and, while Thadie and Micah thought about her suggestions, Alta erupted. 'My brother will never agree to exchange vows in a factory!'

Thadie ignored Alta again—something, Ella was convinced, she did quite often. 'Actually, Anna and I were just talking about that—exploring alternative ideas. We even thought about trimming the guest list so that we could be married here, at Hadleigh House—it's always been my dream to be married at home—but Clyde and my mum vetoed that idea. As they pointed out, it's too late to un-invite people to our wedding.'

But maybe, since both she and Anna were exploring other options, and if the wedding gods were on her side, Thadie would still have an incredible reception in a beautiful, unusual place.

'On Clyde's behalf, I absolutely insist on having the reception somewhere decent!' Alta spluttered.

Decent, to Alta, meant a five-star hotel, upmarket and luxurious. Thadie caught her eye and Ella suspected she wanted to do a massive eye-roll. As the bride, Ella thought she was being remarkably patient.

Thadie stood up, smoothed down her dress and slid her feet into her sandals. 'I need to get going.' She kissed Micah's cheek before turning to Ella and holding out her hands. Ella was surprised when Thadie squeezed her fingers and dropped a kiss on her left cheek, then her right. 'It was so lovely meeting you. Thank you for your help. I'm so appreciative. Maybe you, Anna and I could meet and we could throw some ideas around.'

Ella knew how possessive planners could be about their functions and internally winced. 'I don't think Anna would appreciate my input.'

'Anna is lovely, and not at all pretentious or protective of her turf. And, since this is becoming a wedding from hell, she'd welcome any input.'

Yeah, but not from someone so far down the events-planning ladder. But, God, being able to say that she'd worked with Anna de Palmer-Whyte, even for a day, would be a great, gold shiny star on her résumé.

But she wouldn't wait for Anna's call, that would just be setting herself up for disappointment.

Seeing that Alta was also preparing to leave, Ella concluded that the meeting was over and picked her tote bag up off the floor. Micah didn't suggest she hang around so she followed his sister into the hall. Thadie said goodbye to Alta and told them she was going out of the back door to fetch the boys from the greenhouse. Ella, Alta and Micah walked in silence to where Alta's and her cars were parked.

At her convertible, Alta kissed Micah's cheek, placed her hand on his chest and looked up into his face. 'It really will be so much better if Thadie postponed the wedding, Micah. So much easier, less *messy*.'

Ella looked away and swallowed her growl as Alta stroked Micah's chest as she would a fur stole. Hot and sticky jealously lodged in her throat.

'It's Thadie's wedding and she calls the shots, Alta,' Micah told her, not bothering to remove her hand from his chest. *Grr...*

'But you can persuade her, I'm sure,' Alta said, lowering her voice an octave. Then she stood up on her toes and dropped another too-long kiss on his cheek. 'Call me.'

Ella bit the inside of her own cheek as Micah opened Alta's car door and she deliberately flashed him most of her slim thigh as she settled into the seat. She gunned the engine, sent Micah another sultry smile and reversed, narrowly missing Ella's car.

What a…

'Wow. She's…prickly, isn't she?'

And she's got her eye on you...

'Alta? She's okay, she's just highly strung.'

Guys often used that as an excuse for a woman who was a complete witch. 'She doesn't like your sister much, does she? Why is she one of her bridesmaids?' Ella asked.

Micah looked genuinely surprised. 'What are you talking about?'

Oh, come on, it was *so* obvious. 'She does not like Thadie. At all.'

'You got that from one meeting?' Micah asked, and his amused and dismissive tone irritated her.

'Yes, I did.' Ella tipped her head back to look up at him. 'Be careful of her, she's not good for your sister.'

'She's harmless,' Micah scoffed. 'You're overreacting.'

You're crazy, you're overreacting, you're nuts. I don't believe you. I can't trust what you say.

She'd heard all the comments and every variation of the theme made her clench her jaw and grind her teeth.

How could he so easily have believed her about being

sexually accosted but not believe her about this? His rejection of her opinion reminded her of how her dad refused to believe her when she'd said her mum was sick, of Winters brushing her off when she'd told him his best client had forced his attentions on her. She opened her mouth to argue her point, to stand up for herself, but the words stuck in her throat, creating an acidic slick.

Alta was Thadie's friend, and the wedding party had nothing to do with her, so she should just leave the subject alone and shrug off Micah's casual dismissal.

But it still made her stomach knot and her lungs burn. And, even if she'd had a right to an opinion on Thadie's and Alta's friendship, she knew that she didn't have the confidence and self-assurance to defend her judgement.

Before Pillay and her experience with the Human Resources people at Le Roux Events, she'd been able to stand up for herself, to defend her point of view. Ella knew that she wasn't the most confident person in the world but at least she'd been able to function. These days, she overanalysed everything and overreacted and, whenever she found herself at odds with someone about something—even something as small as Alta's and Thadie's relationship—she felt like a balloon collapsing in on itself as it lost air.

She hated it, hated feeling less than, feeling small, rejected. Hated that even the smallest thing could affect her so much.

Needing to leave, Ella spun round, climbed into her car and pulled on her seatbelt, forcing it into its catch. She turned the key in the ignition but it didn't catch, so she banged her fist against the steering wheel and cranked it again.

'Ella, hold on! What's going on?' Micah demanded, bending his knees to look through the open window.

'Nothing,' Ella muttered. It was a weak response, a cop-out, but what else could she do? Blub on his shoulder, moan about how unfair life was, how she was still affected by Pillay's actions, how *less than* she felt? He'd find excuses and explanations and then pat her on the shoulder.

No, thank you.

Just once, just once in her life, she wanted to feel less isolated, to feel as if she had someone on her side, someone who always took her seriously and cherished her. But that wasn't going to happen, not any time soon. And Micah wasn't that person. Shaking her head, Ella turned the key again and this time the car fired up. Ignoring Micah, she slapped it into gear and turned to look behind her so she could start reversing.

'Come back inside, Ella.'

She heard the irritation in his voice, along with a healthy dose of *I don't know what just happened.*

Ella pushed the button to raise her window and ignored him calling her name. She reversed, shoved the car into gear to go forward and out of the corner of her eye saw Micah slap his hands on his hips, confused.

Talking wouldn't help. This was her issue, not his, and he was her lover, not her therapist. No, it was better to leave, to deal with her feelings in her way and on her own. After all, it was what she did best.

She was tempted to stop and explain but he wouldn't understand. Nobody did. So she drove on.

CHAPTER EIGHT

MICAH THREW UP his hands and watched Ella roar down his driveway, gravel kicking under her tyres.

Why was she upset? Micah replayed their conversation in his head, frowning. She'd told him Alta didn't like Thadie and he'd disagreed. He honestly didn't know how they'd gone from what he thought was a minor difference of opinion to her belting away from him.

Women. They were complicated characters.

Micah heard his name being called and spun round to see the twins hurtling across the lawn towards him, Thadie trailing behind them. He understood three-year-old boys. Sexy, complex woman? Not at all.

Micah dropped to the balls of his feet, opened up his arms and braced himself for the attack. As they connected with him, he gathered them up, tucked them under his arms and spun them around. They yelled their approval and, when he felt himself getting lightheaded, stopped. They demanded more and, because he was a sucker, he did it again.

When he dropped them to their feet, he noticed two *hadidahs* pecking at the grass on the far side of the lawn and suggested they try and catch the birds. They never would, but it would give him the chance to talk to his sister.

When they were out of earshot, Micah turned to Thadie. 'For someone who is getting married soon at a still-unknown venue, you are looking remarkably relaxed.'

Thadie raised her shoulders. 'Me worrying about it won't help. And I have a feeling we will find a venue.' Thadie tucked her hand into his elbow and rested her temple on his bicep. 'I like Ella, Micah.'

He knew she was fishing for more information on whether they were more than work colleagues, but he wasn't going to touch that comment with a barge pole. Yes, he liked Ella but she hadn't changed, and wasn't going to change, his mind about marriage and commitment.

As she'd slid behind the wheel earlier, he'd caught something in her eyes. Hurt and sadness… Had he let her down in some way? He couldn't think of what he'd said to make her feel like that. It couldn't be because Alta had come onto him and Ella was that insecure or petty. No, her pain went deeper than that…

And why did he care? She was leaving. They couldn't have a relationship because he didn't deserve one, but neither would he risk hurting her in any way.

But, damn, no woman had ever tempted him this quickly and this much.

Thadie tapped her sunglasses against her bicep and pulled her lower lip between her teeth. She glanced at the twins, who were on their bellies trying to stealthily approach the birds, and gestured to the bench underneath his favourite oak tree. 'Let's sit down for a moment.'

He knew that tone of voice and recognised the look on her face. She had something on her mind, was wrestling with a decision. They sat down on the bench and he flung his arm around her shoulder. 'What's up? How can I help?'

'I'm thinking of asking Alta to step down as my bridesmaid.'

His eyebrows shot up. 'Okay, that wasn't what I expected you to say. Why?'

Thadie turned to face him. 'She's so negative, Micah. Nothing is ever good enough for her and I'm so sick of what she calls "constructive criticism". She also doesn't like me,' Thadie added.

Huh. So Ella was right.

'If that's the way you feel, then boot her. But Clyde might not like it,' Micah warned his sister. Alta was, after all, Clyde's stepsister and brand manager.

'I've asked him to talk to Alta, to ask her to tone down her attitude, but he hasn't, so he's left me with no choice. I won't be miserable on my wedding day,' Thadie replied, her tone fierce.

'No, that would be unacceptable. Fire her, and know that you have our full support,' Micah assured her.

'I'll call her later,' Thadie said, grimacing. 'It's not going to be a pleasant conversation. Alta can be quite fiery.'

Micah kissed her head. 'My money is on you, kid.'

Across the lawn, the *hadidahs* took flight with their trademark indignant squawk and the twins rolled in the grass, laughing with complete abandon. 'Isn't that the best sound?' Thadie asked, her hand on her heart and her eyes misty with emotion.

'I remember you laughing like that,' Micah told her, kissing the top of her head. 'Good job on raising happy kids, sweetheart.'

And, talking about sweethearts, he needed to head across town and find out what had turned Ella from sweet to sad. He'd never get any work done this weekend if he didn't. Not that he would anyway, since thoughts of Ella were constantly front and centre and consistently distracting.

It had been two sentences—*She's harmless. You're overreacting*—but it had spun her off her axis, tilted her world. Ella paced her all but empty apartment, cursing herself. Those few words shouldn't have had the power to wound her. She should be able to shrug them off, let them go.

She had to get past the mental trauma of the past two months and come to terms with the fact that people weren't always going to agree with her, listen to her, take her seriously.

She understood it on an intellectual level but she couldn't make her stubborn heart see reason. Despite thinking she'd made progress in coming to terms with being accosted and then not believed, that tenacious organ was still sulking, still feeling battered and bruised. She knew that a large part of her trauma had to do with her dad not listening to her about calling an ambulance for her mum, and that experience, and the events of the past months, had created a psychological fog she was trying to find her way through.

But she couldn't keep feeling like this and reacting badly when a conversation didn't go her way. If she did, her life would be hell. Maybe, if those words hadn't come from Micah, she would've reacted more calmly. But they'd come from the mouth of a man she admired, respected...someone she liked.

A man she could, in another life and at another time, fall in love with.

Think, Ella, don't just feel. Be sensible.

Was there a chance she was confusing attraction with gratitude because he was the only person who believed her about what had happened with Pillay? Was she feeling indebted to him because he'd leapt into action and righted a wrong, acting like a modern-day knight?

No. While she was grateful for him for resolving her issues with Le Roux Events, she wouldn't have slept with him if she didn't feel something for him, if she wasn't crazy attracted to him. Ella rested her forearms along the back of the couch and dropped her head between her arms, feeling flustered and frustrated. She'd only met him a few days ago. Nobody should have this much effect on her so quickly!

But, as she was coming to realise, Micah didn't do what people expected him to.

With most people he was startlingly suave and appealing, quick with a smile but with her he was different. With her he occasionally discarded that cloak of geniality and allowed himself to be mercurial, impulsive, occasionally grumpy, more real. He'd even opened up a little: she knew that his butler was a father figure to him, that he didn't like the person he'd been as a teenager and that he'd do anything and everything for his family. She knew that he was a brilliant, creative, considerate lover and that he had a streak of integrity a mile wide.

Despite only knowing him for a little less than a week, she felt connected to him, as if he was an old friend or a lover from a previous life. Ella pushed her fingertips into her forehead, rolling her eyes and her fanciful thoughts. Simply put, she liked him. In bed and out. A lot.

A hell of a lot.

His opinion mattered to her. And she wanted hers to matter to him. And she wanted to feel strong enough, confident enough, to challenge him when she disagreed with him. Not to argue or to be proved right, but self-assured enough to defend her corner, as she knew he would his.

This had very little to do with whether Alta liked Thadie or not. It was about her own reaction to Micah disagreeing with her and—God, this was hard to admit—about the balance of power. Micah had most of it. Not because he wanted it but because she lacked the confidence to grab her share.

Oh, why was she even thinking like this, contemplating a life beyond the short time they had left together? She was over-thinking, over-analysing.

Overreacting.

Ella's head snapped up at the hard rap on her door and she frowned. Janie knew where she lived but her friend was out of town this weekend.

There was only one other person who had her address…

Ella stood and walked slowly over to her door, looking through the peephole just to make sure. She sighed, released the chain, flipped her locks and opened the door, leaning against the door frame.

'I thought you had work to do,' Ella told him, trying to sound bored.

'I do,' Micah replied. 'And it concerns you. Want to tell me why you stormed away earlier?'

'No.' It was a truthful answer because she didn't want to tell him. Kiss him, make love to him, sure. Talk about her hang-ups? No, thank you.

'Can I come in?' Micah asked, looking over her shoulder into the emptiness beyond.

She didn't want him to see her empty flat, to take in the bare, cold, white walls. Her flat was soulless, and she didn't want him to think she was too.

Before she could find the words to answer his question, Micah cupped her face in his hands and gently kissed her mouth. It was a soft kiss, an *I've got you* kiss, a kiss that brought tears to her eyes. Because she'd had so little tenderness for so long, it had the ability to drop her to her knees.

Micah dropped his hands, gripped her waist and quickly, with no effort at all, picked her up and walked her into the flat, kicking the door closed with his foot. He put her back on her feet and looked around the open-plan lounge, diner and kitchen. When his eyes met hers, they were shot with steel.

'You told me that you are emigrating, so I'm presuming that you've been selling your stuff?'

'Yes.'

'That explains the empty flat. But if you've been sleeping on a mattress, I will lose it,' he warned her.

'I still have my bed,' Ella told him, trying to sound cool.

God, he looked so big in this space, and he sucked up the air and energy.

He frowned at her and turned around in a slow circle before walking over to the fridge and yanking it open. Ella winced; it was mostly empty, as she'd planned to run down to the supermarket a block away to stock up on food for the weekend but hadn't got round to doing it. Her small freezer held nothing but a couple of ice trays.

Micah opened a few more cupboards, growing considerably more tense. Slamming a door shut, he shook his head and, without saying anything to her, stomped across her flat to open the door to her bedroom and disappeared inside. Ella frowned and followed him.

When she got there, he was lifting her small suitcase—the one she'd used on their trip to Clarens—onto her bed.

'What the hell are you doing, Micah?'

'I'm taking you home to Hadleigh House.'

He was? This was news to her.

'You don't have any food in this house, no furniture... you don't even have a TV for entertainment! You have a couch and a bed!' he stated, his tone grim.

She knew that; she lived here. 'I'm only buying what I need so I don't have to throw anything away when I leave. And it's only me, so a couch is more than adequate, and I have a laptop on which I can work or watch movies or listen to music,' Ella replied, bemused by his annoyance at the way she was living. 'I'm perfectly comfortable, Micah.'

'Well, I'm not, Ella! I'm not comfortable with any of this!' Micah stated, looking irritated. 'I'm not comfortable with how much I want you, how much I hate seeing you live like this.'

She wasn't living rough, for goodness' sake.

Micah pushed both his hands through his hair. 'And I'm sure as hell not comfortable with whatever it was that sent you flying away from Hadleigh like a bat out of hell.'

He pointed a finger at her. 'And we are going to talk about that, by the way.'

God, she loved it when he sounded a little out of control, fractionally uncivilised.

'Come back to my place with me, El. Come and lie by the pool, eat great food prepared by an excellent chef, watch movies in our media room. I need to work, as I have quite a bit to do, but I won't get a damn thing done knowing you are here…'

Ella tipped her head to the side. He seemed genuinely stressed by her living here, surrounded by white walls and her few boxes. 'I'm not on the verge of homelessness, Micah.'

A look of pure frustration crossed his face. 'I know that; I'm not that much of a snob,' he snapped. He held up his hands, annoyed and frustrated. 'I want you with me, okay? I want to know that you are around, that I can find you when I'm done with work. I want us to spend time together.'

Aw...

'And when we make love—and we will, often—I'd prefer to do it in my enormous bed, where we have space to move.'

Oh, that did sound amazing. Ella rubbed the back of her neck. But should she spend the rest of the weekend with him? She was tempted, of course she was—who wouldn't want to spend time with Micah in his glorious house?—but, given that she was a conflicted mess of too-hard-to-handle emotions, *should* she? It was one thing to have a one-night stand, another to spend hours with him, lounging around, eating his food, drinking his wine, swimming in his pool. Exploring his delicious body…

He'd already turned her world upside down. How would she be after spending concentrated time with him?

She was just making it harder to leave him, to say goodbye. But leave she would, so why not make a couple of memories she could hold on to? Decisions, decisions…

She nodded. 'Okay, I'll spend the weekend with you.'

Ella turned back to her cupboard to grab some clothes but Micah's hand on her arm kept her in place. 'Not so fast, sweetheart. What happened earlier?'

She wrinkled her nose, thinking of what to say, how to explain.

'It doesn't matter,' she told him.

'It does to me.'

Micah walked to the nearest wall, leaned his shoulder into it and crossed his ankles. He didn't push her to speak, just waited her out. And she knew that he would stand there until she told him what had upset her earlier.

She couldn't think of an excuse and she wouldn't make up a story. So that meant telling him the truth. As much as she could. But would he understand? Could she trust him with this?

Ella sat down on the edge of her bed and placed her hands down beside her, her fingers digging into the fabric of her cotton bed cover. 'As I said, my mum died when I was sixteen on the most stunning summer's day. A day much like this one, actually.'

Micah didn't drop his eyes from hers, neither did he speak, so she carried on. 'My mum liked to drink at lunchtime over the weekends and she had a couple of G&Ts that day. She stood up from the lunch table and, basically, her legs crumpled. She dropped like a stone. I rushed around the table and she was muttering, speaking but making no sense.'

Ella rubbed her fingertips across her forehead. 'I knew, at that moment, that there was something wrong with her. I told my dad to call an ambulance but he said no, that she was drunk—he hated her drinking—and that she just needed to sleep it off. I knew she wasn't drunk, but he wouldn't budge. I screamed, yelled, pleaded and, when I tried to call for an ambulance on my phone, he pulled it out of my hands. He put her to bed to sleep it off.'

'But she wasn't drunk.'

'She died later that afternoon, a few hours after she collapsed.' Ella shook her head. 'She had a massive brain bleed, some sort of stroke. Apparently, the worst thing to do when that happens is to go to sleep.'

Micah didn't issue any platitudes, didn't fuss. She appreciated that. 'Is that why you and your dad don't speak, because he didn't call an ambulance?'

'I was upset that he didn't call an ambulance—still am—but I've never blamed him for her death. Not really. How could I when he blamed himself? He fell apart so completely when she died,' she explained. She shrugged. 'I don't know why he's cut me out of his life. Maybe it's because he feels guilty, maybe I remind him too much of her. Maybe it's because he wishes I'd died, not her.'

Micah's eyes widened in horror. 'El, don't say that!'

Pain spiked and flared. 'Why not? He doesn't want anything to do with me and doesn't care what happens to me.'

She heard her voice rising and winced. It was time to pull back, to take control of her emotions. After taking a few deep breaths, she spoke again, and was happy to hear her voice sounded normal. 'All I know is that I lost two parents that day. Because my dad didn't believe me and, having recently experienced being disbelieved and diminished, I'm currently super-sensitive when I think my opinion is being dismissed.'

He nodded. 'And you thought I did that when we were talking about Alta and Thadie?'

She nodded. She fought the urge to apologise for being silly, to mock her feelings. And she prayed that he wouldn't either.

'I'm sorry.'

It was a straightforward apology, and she saw the sincerity in his eyes. Tension flowed out of her body and her shoulders dropped from just below her ears.

After a few seconds of silence, Micah rubbed the back of her neck. 'Talking of your recent past…'

Oh, God, where was he going with this?

'Were you okay with everything we did in Clarens? I think you had a good time but I just want to make sure that you are completely okay. Maybe I was too demanding, maybe you needed me to be—'

'You… It was *perfect*, Micah,' Ella rushed to reassure him, touched that he'd asked. She stood up to walk over to him and placed a hand on his chest, needing to feel connected to him.

'I was lucky, so lucky. I spoke to a therapist after it happened and I've worked through it. You gave me exactly what I needed, Micah, a fantastic experience. I don't have any hang-ups about sex, I promise you. Even before I spoke to my therapist, I never equated what he did to me with sex. It was about power and control.'

He gently brushed her hair back from her forehead. 'You didn't deserve that, Ella.'

'No, I didn't.'

Micah's thumb skated over her cheekbone. 'If I ever do something, make you feel something that…well…that reminds you, will you tell me?'

That he'd even thought to make that offer heated Ella's blood and made her heart flutter. Kind, gruff, occasionally edgy…now she could add 'sweet' to her list of descriptors for Micah she had running in her head.

Because he still looked worried, and because she wanted to prove to him that there was no link between how he made her feel and Pillay's actions, Ella linked her arms around Micah's neck and placed her lips on his. There had been too much talking and not enough kissing, in her opinion.

She felt Micah's hesitation, knew that he was debating

whether to push for more information, so she pulled his bottom lip between hers and nibbled softly. He sighed and she slipped her tongue between his open lips, seeking his. Ella wound her tongue around his, and his fingertips pressed into the skin above her knees. Micah held her against his body, so tightly that the buttons of his shirt dug into her chest. One arm banded around her, and his other hand came up to cup her head, holding it in place as he took their kiss deeper to hot, undiscovered depths.

Her hands skated up and down his sides, over his broad back, her fingers playing in his hair. She touched his jaw and ran her hand down the cords of his neck, down his chest. She couldn't get enough of him and she couldn't wait, not one second longer, to have him have her again.

In every delightful way possible.

Forcing herself to wrench her mouth off his, she grabbed his hand and tugged him back to the bed.

Lying down next to her, Micah's fingers danced over her clavicle before coming to cover her breast. Ella arched into his hand and groaned. She flung her thigh over his hip and went to work on the buttons of his shirt, ripping some in her frustration to get to his bare skin.

Micah's hand on her thigh tightened and he pulled away from her mouth to haul in a couple of deep breaths.

Ella frowned. 'Why did you stop? What's the problem?'

His eyes blazed with blue fire. 'The problem is that I'm trying to slow this down because I am this far—' he lifted his hand to show her an inch-wide space between his thumb and index finger '—from ripping your clothes off and plunging inside you.'

Ella fumbled for the zip on her jumpsuit. 'Why don't you do just that?'

Micah held her eyes for a moment, nodded and went on to do exactly what he'd said.

CHAPTER NINE

HOPING NOT TO wake Ella, who slept on the pool lounger under the shade of a huge umbrella, Micah quietly slipped into his pool and started to swim, pulling through the water silently and effortlessly. Every time he turned his head, he caught a glimpse of the lounger where Ella slept and told himself that he should let her sleep, that he needed to exercise, that he couldn't wake her up by kissing her instep, dragging his tongue up the inside of her calf, nibbling her knee.

In the four hours he'd spent in his office, he'd managed to complete what he called his 'zombie work'—tasks he could accomplish without needing much brain power or concentration. Most of his focus was on what Ella had told him, and now and again he had to push aside the images of her being manhandled, to breathe through his anger. He had to remind himself, often, that she hadn't been hurt, that things hadn't gone that far…

She was right: she'd been lucky. But it should never have happened in the first place.

He was astounded at how much Ella had had to deal with and how well she was handling the events of the past few months, especially since the actions of his employees dug into an old, personal wound. She'd already had issues with not being believed, but being sexually accosted and then having her allegations dismissed and derided must've rocked her world.

Must be still rocking her world. No one recovered from that sort of trauma quickly. And she'd done it alone. He'd heard her mention a Janie from work and, while it sounded as if they were friends, he didn't know if they were close enough for Ella to confide in her. He could be wrong but he suspected that Ella walked through the world solo, and that was a dark and desperately lonely path.

Even at his lowest points, he always had Jago standing behind him. He knew that his twin would never let him down, would always be at his side and would help him slay any and all dragons. Now that she was an adult, Micah also had Thadie's full support, and Jabu had been the rock he'd rested on many times throughout his life. Ella didn't have anyone.

The thought made him want to weep. And howl. And fix…

She'd crawled under his skin and was banging on the door to his disused, mangled heart. And he wasn't the only one to realise the impact she'd made in such a short time. Thadie had also noticed. Why else would she tell him she liked one of their many employees? No, it was Thadie's way of giving him her blessing, of telling him she approved.

After lunch, when Ella had gone upstairs to change into a swimsuit, Jabu had informed him he'd set up the lounger by the pool for Ella and that he intended to make her as comfortable as possible, supplying her with water and fruit. He'd even taken a quick drive to Thadie's house and borrowed a couple of her magazines in case Ella wanted them.

Leaving the premises to borrow magazines was a pretty big deal, and he'd asked Jabu why he was going the extra mile.

Jabu had sent him a steady look. 'How many people

offer their hand to a butler and say, with complete sincerity, how happy she is to meet me? No one, that's how many.'

Right. Ella had Mkulu's seal of approval. Not that she needed it, because their relationship wasn't going anywhere! How many times would he have to repeat that before it started sinking into his suddenly stubborn brain?

Micah felt a small hand grip his ankle and he whirled around to see Ella hanging on to the side of the deep end of the pool, her hair off her face brown and glossy. She gave him an open and lovely smile. It was obvious that she had no idea he'd spent the last ten minutes fantasising about how good it would feel to rearrange Pillay's handsome features.

He planted his feet on the bottom of the pool and pushed his hair off his face. 'Did you have a good nap?'

'Mmm,' Ella said, moving towards him, wrapping her arms around his neck and her legs around his waist. She felt so good in his arms, so feminine. A wave of protectiveness rose within him; she was his to protect.

His to keep. His to love…

For the next week or so at least.

Confused by the unfamiliar emotions washing through him, Micah dipped his head and covered her mouth with his, smiling as she sunk into him, falling into the kiss. Passion flared between them, as hot and fiery as a rocket launch. He'd never felt this way before. Sure, he'd felt desire, but as soon as that was sated he lost interest. But, with Ella, she fired up his mind and his heart, as well as his body.

It was a potent combination…

Ella pulled back from his mouth to drop little kisses along his jawline, slowly meandering her way to his ear. She kissed the spot where his neck met his ear before whispering directly in his ear, 'Let's go upstairs and roll around in your bed.'

He loved the fact that she was so forthright and had no qualms about telling, or showing, how much she wanted him.

'I can't wait that long,' Micah told her, his hand coming up to cover her breast. He dragged his thumb over her nipple and Ella sighed. A second later she stiffened and he felt her legs releasing their grip around his waist.

'What's the problem?' Micah asked, frowning.

'I am.'

Hearing that voice, Micah cursed. Under the water, he clenched his fists. He told himself to find his implacable expression and, when he thought he had it, he slowly turned around.

His stepmother stood between the loungers and the pool, dressed in a pistachio jumpsuit, three-inch heels and a gold chain as thick as his finger. She wore braids today, and she'd pulled them back from her face, highlighting those world-famous cheekbones. She was in her fifties now but she could still pass for a woman twenty years younger.

'Jabu isn't in the house,' Liyana stated, her eyes locked on his. So far, she hadn't even acknowledged Ella's presence.

'It's his night off,' Micah told her, widening his stance and folding his arms. He lifted his eyebrows.

'Jago?' Liyana demanded.

'He's out for the evening,' Micah replied, trying to keep the impatience out of his voice.

This was his stepmother, for God's sake, a woman who'd been around for most of his life. How much longer were they going to keep up this cold war? It was so stupid and it didn't serve any purpose. But he was stubborn and she was stubborn…

She was also looking stressed, Micah decided. On closer inspection, the grooves next to her mouth seemed deeper, the frown between her eyebrows wider. Liyana was seriously tense, upset about something. Thadie's wedding problems? Maybe. Whatever it was, she was worried enough to come across from her house to find him. Well, to find Jabu and give him a message…

Micah swiftly crossed to the wall, hauled himself out in one easy movement and walked around the pool to stand a few feet from Liyana. Out of the corner of his eye, he saw Ella holding out a towel and he took it, nodding his thanks.

'I'll see you inside,' Ella said softly as he wound the towel around his hips.

He shook his head and pointed to the lounger, silently asking her to stay. If they had company, there was a good chance that they'd rein in their tempers and behave themselves. Liyana hated making a scene. Ella wrapped her sarong around her waist and sat down on the edge of the lounger. Just seeing her there made him feel stronger, more in control. Better.

What was she doing to him? Why did she have this effect on him?

Turning his attention back to Liyana, he spoke again. 'I can see that you are upset, Liyana. And the fact that you are still here tells me that you have something to say. What is it?'

Liyana played with the solid gold bracelet on her arm. 'I don't talk to Brianna's mother any more. I haven't since…' She trailed off, looking away.

Yes, he got it. Since the night he'd run out of the house.

'But Kate and I do have mutual friends, as the society we keep is a very small one,' Liyana continued.

Micah clenched his fists, trying to keep his temper. His stepmother was a complete snob and considered herself Johannesburg and African royalty. If you wanted to be friends with Liyana Le Roux, you had to be either stupendously rich, famous or powerful. Preferably all three.

Liyana hauled in a deep breath and he noticed that she seemed genuinely upset. 'I have it on good authority that Brianna has a serious respiratory infection. She's not responding to the antibiotics and they don't think she's going to make it.'

A cold hand encircled Micah's heart and pushed ice into his veins.

'Kate is preparing herself for the worst.'

Micah gripped the bridge of his nose with his thumb and index finger. 'Do they still have a DNR policy in place?' After Brianna's father, Phil, died he'd heard that Kate had put a Do Not Resuscitate order in place. In essence, it said that if Brianna had a heart attack the staff would not resuscitate her.

Liyana nodded. 'Yes. Kate won't remove her feeding tube but she did put the DNR in place.'

Micah hunched his shoulders. He didn't know what to say or how to act. He never did. Eventually, he spoke again. 'Thanks for coming to tell me. Will you let me know if...?'

Liyana nodded, opened her mouth to say something else and shook her head. Then she ducked her head and briskly strode away, back to her house and her life as Theo's rich widow and society maven.

Was it wrong to wish that the infection would take Brianna, that she'd just slip away? He'd hoped, for years and years, that she'd recover—medical miracles did happen, after all. But, as he'd aged, he'd prayed that she'd be released from the space she occupied between life and death.

It was no place for someone to live, especially someone as vibrant as Brianna.

Micah felt Ella's hand rubbing his back, then she linked her fingers with his and led him to the veranda. He sat down on the first piece of furniture he encountered, a four-seater couch, spread his legs and dropped his head, drops of pool water dotting the non-slip tiles.

He heard Ella opening the door to the fridge behind the bar, the snap of a beer bottle cap being removed and then he felt the cold bottle against his bicep.

He took it, downed half the bottle and rested the icy glass against his forehead. Ella sat down next to him, her small shoulder pressing into his upper arm.

She sat there silently, offering him comfort, making no demands for an explanation. But he wanted to tell her, wanted to shine a spotlight on the darkest, scariest time of his life. Somehow, though he knew not how, she'd crow-barred her way into his life, opening doors that were long closed.

'That was Liyana,' he explained, sitting up.

'I gathered,' Ella quietly responded. 'She's stunningly beautiful.'

'She's also stunningly high maintenance. We don't talk,' Micah admitted. 'That was the most we've spoken in months, maybe years.'

Ella took a sip from her water bottle and didn't ask the obvious follow-up question: Why? She'd pulled on her tank top but her pretty feet remained bare. He could turn and face her, kiss her until he forgot about Liyana's news, until he was lost in her. But while that appealed—and always would, he suspected—his urge to unburden himself was stronger than his desire.

Another first.

'Liyana married my dad six weeks after my mum died. I don't know if they fell in love quickly or whether they were having an affair before my mum passed away. It's not something I need an answer to.'

He went on to explain that his father had had a terrible temper, that he'd been incredibly volatile and that, while Jago had tried to keep the peace, or at least tried to avoid the eruptions, he'd run head-first into the volcano. He'd argued, fought and bucked the system.

'I was a nightmare child,' he confessed.

'You were angry and grieving and it doesn't sound like you were given the time and space to mourn your mum.

It sounds like your feelings were dismissed and you were forced to accept the status quo.' Ella bumped his shoulder. 'I don't think you've accepted the status quo a day in your life, Le Roux.'

That was true. It was in his nature to question, to dissect. He rarely took anything at face value.

Ella's hand on his thigh, a gentle squeeze, was her silent way of telling him to continue. 'The older I got, the more out of control I became. I was the ultimate rich-boy rebel.'

He stopped, not sure if he could carry on. If he told her about The Incident, there would be no going back. He would be sharing with her, someone who was little more than a stranger the event that had defined his life. How would she react? Would she say something trite, or go into a deep psychological analysis? He didn't want either, he just wanted her to listen, to be on his side, to look at him kindly.

He didn't know if she would.

'Who's Brianna, Micah? And why is she on a feeding tube?'

Micah drained his beer, put the bottle on the table next to him and gripped her hand in his. 'She was my, *our*, oldest friend. Her parents were my parents' best friends and we grew up together. She loved me.'

'As a sister or as a lover?'

'Initially, as a sister, but then as we hit our late teens it was obvious that she was in love with me. I didn't love her like that but, being the young, spoiled bastard I was, I didn't have any problem with stringing her along. I'd make out with her, then move on to the next girl. I later learned she spent many nights crying over me. I'm not proud of that.

'But she was the person that I could always talk to about everything. She knew about my relationship with Theo and Liyana, how lost and unloved I felt. Jago was the oldest, and perfect, you know? Bright and sporty, and he worked the system rather than bucking it. Thadie was a ray of sunshine, sweet and lovely. I was the middle child who caused grief. I wasn't really necessary.'

Ella made a sound in her throat that sounded like disagreement. He stared out at the row of oak trees at the bottom of the garden. He told her about the argument with his dad and Liyana, that Theo's punch had broken his nose and his need to get out of the house. He explained that he'd called Brianna, had told her that he was heading for a sketchy bar, that he was going to get wasted and stoned.

'She knew where I was going. I'd told her about the place before. She hated me going there because it was a bad area…the bar was filled with lowlifes and known for vicious fights. At the time, I guess I felt at home there.'

Ella rested her temple on his shoulder. *'Micah.'*

'She told me not to go…begged me to come to her place instead. I cut the call but she kept calling, texting, leaving voice messages. I didn't read or listen to them, I just wanted to be alone. She blew up my phone and I switched it off.'

'Did she follow you?'

'Yeah. She wasn't an experienced driver and hated driving at night. She had a head-on collision, which resulted in severe neurological brain damage. She's been in a permanent vegetative state since she was eighteen years old.'

Ella half-turned to face him, placed her forehead on the ball of his shoulder and closed her eyes. 'God, that's horrible.'

Needing to tell her everything, Micah explained how his parents had blamed him for the accident, that they hadn't spoken to him for two years, and that Brianna's parents had sued him but the court case had ultimately been dismissed. That, if not for him, Brianna would likely be married by now, probably with a heap of kids.

Ella scooted backwards so that she could look at his

face without tipping her head back. 'You blame yourself,' she said.

'My actions led to her spending her life in a hospital bed, unresponsive,' Micah stated.

Ella frowned at him. 'No, your actions led to your dad punching you—which is unforgivable, in my view. No matter the circumstances, no parent should hit a child, *ever*.' She saw that he was about to speak and shook her head. 'Don't even try and say you deserved it, Micah, I won't accept it. Your father was the adult in the room and him punching you is indefensible.'

Jago had told him that before—so had the therapist—but the words seemed to resonate today, when he heard them from Ella's lips. He did not doubt that he'd been revolting, but Theo punching him really *had* been unacceptable…

'As for Brianna, it was her choice to follow you to a bad area in town and to drive at night when she wasn't experienced. She was reckless, Micah, and very foolish.'

'But…'

Ella shook her head. 'I'm not done. Your parents should've stood by you, not isolated and ignored you. They could've hated what you did but still loved you.'

Hated what…? 'Sorry, say that again?'

'I said that Theo and Liyana could've hated your actions but still loved and supported *you*.'

That. That made sense. He'd done something ridiculously reckless and stupid, had been out of control and irresponsible, but his father and stepmother had made him feel rotten to the core, as if he deserved no love and support.

For the first time, Micah could look back and see the boy he'd been—lonely, lost and desperate to feel connected to his family. Theo and Liyana hadn't known how to handle his in-your-face personality and, instead of talking calmly to him, rationalising as Jabu had, they'd screamed, shouted and tried to impose their will on him.

'And I suppose you have this notion that, because you were the reason Brianna jumped into her car and had an accident, you now have to atone for your sins by solving the world's problems or, at the very least, the Le Rouxs' problems?'

Well, yeah. He darted a look at her and she lifted her eyebrows, waiting for his response. What else could he do but nod?

'And you believe that, because Brianna can't have a life, neither can you?'

'I have a life!' Micah protested.

Ella rolled her eyes. 'You live in the shallows, Micah. You don't fall in love, you don't commit… I presume you have no intention of marrying and having children?' Ella demanded.

'I don't,' he admitted.

'Okay, I'm not going to tell you how nonsensical that is—' except that she just had '—but I'm going to ask you one question, just one.'

Micah tensed.

'What would change for Brianna if you fell in love, married, had kids?'

He didn't understand her question. 'What do you mean?'

She placed her hand on his cheek. 'Would Brianna's condition improve?'

'Brianna is never going to wake up,' Micah said coldly.

'And that's my point, Micah,' Ella gently told him. 'Whether you live your life fully or skate along the surface, nothing is going to change for Brianna. She won't know, she'll *never* know. You are punishing yourself when you are not to blame for her accident, and your denying yourself happiness will never change Brianna's condition. Micah, don't you see? You're also in a coma, but yours is an emotional one, and you placed yourself in it. It serves no purpose but to feed your guilt.'

Ella leaned forward, placed her lips on his cheek and then pulled back. 'I'm sorry about Brianna, Micah, I am. But you're a good man who deserves to be happy. You've punished yourself long enough. Enough, now.'

Micah watched, his brain whirling as she stood up and walked into the house, her hips swaying. When she disappeared, he stood up and went to the bar fridge to get himself another beer, idly popping the top. He sipped and looked onto the rose garden, the one his mum had loved so much.

He was an adult and, for the first time in his life, could look back on the child and teenager he'd been without wincing and cringing. Theo had been a bully and had had no idea how to be a dad, and Liyana had been a young herself, not yet twenty-four when she'd met and married his much older dad. What had she known about raising twin boys and dealing with Theo's volcanic personality?

Ella was right—his father punching him had been unforgivable. No matter how badly behaved he'd been, he hadn't deserved to get his nose broken.

He'd been a lonely, lost and rebellious kid with too much money and freedom and not enough love. He'd made some stupid decisions but Ella had nailed it—it wasn't his fault that Brianna had followed him to that pub. That had been her decision; he'd never asked her to.

His parents, and her parents, shouldn't have laid all the blame at his door. But when the unimaginable happened people needed a place to put their anger. He'd been disliked, misunderstood and difficult, and it was easier to blame him than to apportion any blame to the angelic-looking girl being kept alive by a feeding tube.

He got it; he did.

You're also in a coma, but yours is an emotional one...

Ella was correct—he was. And he was the only person who could pull himself out of it, to start to live again properly and fully. And he wanted to do that with Ella.

He tightened his grip on his bottle, wondering if he was just confusing lust and gratitude with a need for permanence, to create the family he'd always wanted. Was he imagining himself in love with her—or something close—because she'd cracked open some emotional doors and made him look at things differently?

In the space of a few short days, she'd changed his life but, bombarded with emotion, he didn't know what was real or false any more, what was true and lasting or ephemeral.

Before he said something he couldn't take back, before he did anything that he couldn't unravel, he needed to make sure of his feelings.

Very sure.

Ella went upstairs and walked into Micah's shower, turning the powerful jets to cool. She stripped off her clothes and stepped under the spray. When the first blast of water hit her skin, she started to cry.

So much made sense now, things she hadn't understood were falling into place. Micah wasn't meant to be alone, he had too much to give, but he'd taken himself away and made himself emotionally unavailable because he felt as though he didn't deserve to be loved, to be in love.

He was a guy who took responsibility, too much of it. Yes, he'd been a stupid kid, but his girlfriend had chosen to run to Micah's rescue—out of love, friendship, a need to protect and save…who knew? The result of that decision had been catastrophic but Micah wasn't to blame… and how dared his and her parents do that to an already messed up kid?

Despite the life blows he'd been dealt as a young adult,

he'd managed to become an incredible man. So many kids would've lost themselves in alcohol or drugs, but Micah had just absorbed the blows, got an education, become a successful businessman and looked after his family. He was amazing, she thought, tears mingling with the shower spray. How was she going to stop herself from falling in love with him now?

How was she going to leave?

Ella heard the shower door opening but didn't turn around, not wanting Micah to see her red eyes. She felt his arms encircle her waist and he pulled her back and touched his lips to her hair. His big body enveloped her and, for the first time since she'd been sixteen, she felt completely safe. He'd stand between her and the world; he was that type of guy.

A guy she needed, enjoyed, possibly loved. *Probably* loved.

Micah's big hands came up to cup her breasts and his thumbs brushed over her nipples. Ella arched her back, pushing into his touch. She loved the way he could pull her out of the mental and into the physical, how he managed to stop time in its tracks.

Micah pulled her hair to the side and ran his tongue up her neck, then back down again and across her shoulder, gently nipping it. His erection pushed against her bottom and lower back, hard and insistent, but Micah didn't turn her around, instead choosing to slide his hand over her ribs and down her stomach, flirting with the small triangle down below. Placing her hand on top of his, she guided his fingers between her folds, releasing a gasp when he hit her sweet spot.

He knew exactly how to touch her, when to slow down, when to speed up. When to retreat, when to push her harder. Tears forgotten, Ella arched into his hand, needing the amazing orgasm only he could give her.

She reached back and hooked her arm around his neck, turning her head to find his warm lips, his seeking tongue. They kissed like that for minutes, years, millennia, wanting to spin out this moment. But, when Ella pushed her hips back and stood on her tiptoes so that Micah could slide his finger inside her, he spun her round and captured her mouth in a kiss designed to shatter stars. Without releasing her mouth, he boosted her up his body, resting her back against the wall.

'Wrap your legs around me and hold on,' Micah told her, his voice guttural with need.

Ella did as he commanded and he positioned himself to enter her but pulled back at the last second, cursing. 'Condom,' he muttered, pulling a foil packet off the shelf to his right.

With her feet back on the floor, she watched him open the packet, jumpy with impatience.

"Hurry up, Micah, I'm dying here…"

She'd barely finished her sentence when Micah pushed inside her, filling her completely. The shower wall was cool against her back, and water droplets from the shower peppered her head, but all she cared about was that Micah was kissing her, rocking her to new heights.

Ella felt herself skimming along the face of a huge wave, wondering when she'd crash. Whenever she thought she would, Micah would slow down, pull back, and the wave would die just a little. But he'd build her up again to the point she was screaming, begging for him to let her tumble.

He surged once, then again, and he hit a spot deep inside her. Ella screamed in pleasure and she was hit from all sides by sensation…

She heard Micah's shout and felt as he tightened his grip on her hips, his release pulsing deep inside her. It was enough to make her come again. Smaller this time, but no less intense.

As their heart rates slowed down, Micah stepped back and held her steady as her feet hit the floor. He pulled her into his arms and held her close, his face buried in her neck. After a while, Micah turned the shower off, tossed his condom and led her, naked and soaking, to his bed.

CHAPTER TEN

THE NEXT MORNING Ella and Micah came downstairs to find Jabu laying two places at the end of the sixteen-seater wooden dining table on the veranda. It was another stunning day, hot and sunny, and the sky was a deep blue.

She was going to miss days like this when she left South Africa, she thought, wincing at the sharp pang somewhere around her heart. She greeted Jabu and, when he handed her a mug of coffee, she gave him her biggest smile. 'You're an angel, thank you.'

Jabu had no idea how much she needed caffeine after she'd spent most of the night being expertly loved by Micah. Or, judging by the twinkle in his eyes, maybe he did. Ella blushed. God, it was like trying to sneak out of your boyfriend's house after staying the night and finding his father standing at the front door.

'Morning, Mkulu,' Micah said, squeezing Jabu's shoulder. Micah, she noticed with amusement, had to pour his own coffee from the carafe on the tray.

'What would you like for breakfast?' Jabu asked her as he gently eased two gorgeous white roses into a slender vase.

Ella didn't feel comfortable asking the elderly man to cook for her, especially on a Sunday. But she was starving, so what would be easy to prepare and would require no effort? 'Cereal would be great, thanks.'

She saw disappointment flash across Jabu's face. He *wanted* to cook, she realised. He wanted to do something for them. Not because he had to, not because it was his job, but because he adored Micah and seemed to take pleasure in looking after him. Ella held up her hand. 'Actually, I'm really hungry and cereal isn't going to make a dent. What do you suggest, Mr Mkhize?'

Her use of his surname, the respect she showed, pleased him. 'Please call me Jabu. I have some smoked salmon in the fridge, some organic duck eggs, home-churned butter. What about smoked salmon, a poached egg and hollandaise sauce on a bagel?'

Her mouth started to water and her taste buds tingled. 'That would be amazing, thank you.'

Jabu nodded regally and walked into the house with a spring in his step. As soon as he was out of sight, Micah swiped his mouth over hers. 'Thank you for that. If I was here on my own, he probably would've tossed a piece of stale bread at me.'

'Nonsense,' Ella briskly told him. 'He adores you and just wants to look after you.'

'You're a wise woman,' Micah told her, kissing the tip of her nose before stepping away to look at the Sunday newspapers that Jabu had placed on the coffee table behind her. Micah's voice had held more depth of feeling than a comment about breakfast required, and Ella knew he wasn't talking about her observations about Jabu but referring to what she'd said last night. She looked at him, sitting on the couch and reading the headlines, and her heart triple-thumped in her chest. He wore a red T-shirt, plain black board shorts, his feet were bare and he looked younger than he had yesterday. Lighter.

After making love this morning, she'd touched his cheek and asked him how he was feeling. He'd smiled, low and slow, and gently asked if they could take the day for themselves, if they could lock out the past and the future and just enjoy being together. Thinking they both could do with an easy, stress-free day, she nodded. His gentle 'thank you kiss' had led to her straddling him and rocking them to another orgasm.

It was a miracle that she could still walk and talk.

Taking her coffee, Ella walked to the steps that led down to the pool and looked over the garden. She still thought Hadleigh House would be the perfect place for a wedding—rich and sumptuous, completely lovely.

A country house wedding… That sparked a memory.

Spinning round, she walked back over to where Micah was sitting and saw a black tablet, one of many she'd seen scattered throughout the house. The tablets, Micah had told her, ran a programme that controlled the alarm, lights, temperature and everything else in the house.

She picked it up and waved it under Micah's nose. 'Can I use this to access the Internet?' she asked.

Micah nodded. 'Sure.'

She switched it on, did a general search, didn't find anything and tried another route. After ten minutes she found the article she'd remembered.

The Grand Old Lady is Getting a Makeover...

The owner of one of Johannesburg's oldest mansions has caused controversy by gutting the inside of his newly inherited mansion and knocking down the non-load-bearing walls of the historic home without consulting the authorities trusted with preserving old buildings. The walls of the once-famous Cathcart House ballroom, its three reception rooms and dining room have been knocked down to form an extensive open-plan living space, much to the horror of architectural historians.

The owner of the property, Mr Samuel Dobson, has agreed to suspend the renovation of the historical home, but sources close to Mr Dobson tell us that the lack of progress is due to Dobson's financial issues and not because he has any interest in maintaining the historic importance of Cathcart House...

Ella did a picture search for Cathcart House and scrolled through the many photographs of the property. The gardens, she established, had been a showpiece even back in the late eighteen-eighties, a few years after the house had been built. As per an arrangement made by a previous Cathcart in the nineteen-nineties, the gardens were maintained by the local gardening club, and the club was host to a rather important flower show in the spring.

Beautiful gardens, a vast space indoor space that could be used as a wedding reception venue, close to the church… Cathcart House could possibly, with a little imagination and some cash, be the perfect venue for Thadie's wedding.

'Micah?'

Micah lifted his head and sent her that warm, soft smile that liquefied her organs. It was a 'I'm happy you're here' smile…a 'I like seeing you in my home' smile.

'Another pretty dress, sweetheart.'

Ella looked down at her cheap-as-chips dress, a Boho-inspired loose cotton shift that ended above her knees. It wasn't designer, or anywhere close, but he didn't seem to care. 'Thanks.'

He stood up to pour more coffee into his mug. He looked down at her screen and lifted his eyebrows. 'Why are you looking at pictures of Cathcart House?' he asked. 'Do you want more coffee, by the way?'

Ella shook her head, glancing at the tablet screen. 'Do you know it?'

'I know of it. A friend of mine...well, someone I went to school with...owns it.'

'Really?'

Micah sat down again and leaned back, looking relaxed. 'He's the last in a very long line of Dobsons to live in the house. They are a very old, very well-known Johannesburg family. There was a dust-up a couple of months ago because he did some insensitive renovations to the place, if I remember correctly. I know a property consortium showed some interest in acquiring it.'

'Were you part of that consortium?' Ella asked. Le Roux International had interests in the property sector so it was a fair question.

'No, we don't buy properties with partners, El. Or, if we do, it's multi-billion-dollar projects, like malls or hotel chains.'

Right, a Victorian mansion in Johannesburg was small fish for him. The mind boggled.

'Why are you asking about Dobson's house?' Micah asked.

Ella took a deep breath and tossed the suggestion out there, hoping Micah was open-minded enough to consider the idea. 'Thadie said that she'd love to have a garden wedding, that she wanted to be married at home. She can't, but I'm thinking that many another Victorian mansion would work just as well?' She gestured to the tablet she'd placed on the table. 'The photos online show that it has potential to host a large wedding, it has an award-winning garden and, because of those renovations, it now has a huge space on the ground floor. The guests wouldn't have to change any of their accommodation arrangements, and it's actually closer to the church than this house is.'

Micah looked thoughtful. 'I'm not sure, sweetheart. It sounds like a hell of a stretch.'

She felt deep down in her gut that Cathcart House was

the answer to all of their prayers. It was time to use Micah's contacts and his status as one of the city's best-known businesspeople.

'Would you be able to get hold of him, ask him if he'd be interested in hiring out the mansion? Maybe see if we could take a peek to see if it's suitable?'

Micah rubbed the back of his neck, his expression pensive. Then he picked up his phone, made a few calls and within ten minutes secured them a late-afternoon viewing of Cathcart House for the following Sunday.

There were huge benefits to being a powerful billionaire, Ella decided as Jabu walked into the entertainment area carrying a silver tray loaded with food.

A week later, Ella instantly fell in love with Cathcart House. She loved its gardens, bigger even than those at Hadleigh House and, although she'd never admit this to Micah, prettier too. The house looked as if it belonged in the Cape, a frothy behemoth of Cape Dutch gables, tall brick chimneys and a wide, wraparound veranda. Inside she was grateful to see that Samuel Dobson had left the entrance hall alone, which had a grand Burmese teak staircase running up the middle of the vast space before wrapping round to a gallery.

The downstairs area was a massive, cavernous and echoing interior space. Dobson had replaced the centuries-old wooden doors and windows with handcrafted, wooden bifold doors that opened to the veranda which overlooked the two-acre garden.

Upstairs, the magnificent bedrooms—still furnished—had been left untouched, with every room boasting a fireplace and some sporting Victorian tiles and fine, beautifully carved wooden mantelpieces. All the floors upstairs were Oregon pine, badly in need of waxing and treating. The door handles and light switches were brass and, she was sure, made for the house.

It would be, with some money thrown at it, a perfect wedding venue, Ella thought, wandering through the downstairs area on her own. Micah and Samuel were in conversation, no doubt reminiscing about their school days, Samuel having been a year or two ahead of Micah at an elite boarding school somewhere in the KwaZulu Natal Midlands.

Ella was glad to have Samuel's eyes off her for a while; she'd felt as if he was undressing her every time he looked at her, and when she asked him a question he'd replied to her breasts. He made her skin crawl.

Overreacting, Yeung? Maybe. She had a habit of doing that… But she just didn't like Samuel. At all.

Ella turned her attention back to the building. The gardens were spectacular and, were she planning Thadie's wedding, she wouldn't change much. She'd give the veranda a quick lick of paint and wrap the columns with fairy lights. There would be a string quartet in the hall to welcome the guests, and she'd cover the ripped-out ceiling with swathes of white cloth, behind which would be more fairy lights. She paced the area out and established that there would be enough room for all the tables plus a band and a big dance floor. Dobson had done the house no favours by ripping out the walls of the ground floor, but it was big enough to stage a huge wedding. The catering staff would have to work out of tents hidden at the back of the property, and they'd have to hire luxurious mobile bathrooms.

It was going to require a lot of additional cash. Good thing that Micah and Jago, who were paying for Thadie's wedding, had lots of that particular commodity.

Ella walked over to where Micah and Samuel stood. Micah pulled her to his side and dropped a kiss on her temple. Ella loved his easy affection and she responded by winding her arm around his waist.

Samuel noticed their connection as his eyes went to where Micah's hand rested on her hip. Ella waited for him to wind down—he was saying something about some cricket tour—but, when it looked as if he had no intention of shutting up, Ella interrupted him.

'It has possibilities,' she told Micah. 'I'd need to come back, measure up properly and gather some more information before I can present it as a decent option to our interested party.'

'Who needs a venue? And for what?' Samuel asked, his eyes glinting with waspish curiosity.

Ella jumped in before Micah could answer. 'We're keeping the identity of my client a secret, Mr Dobson.'

If Dobson knew the wedding was for Thadie, he'd either use the information to cop an invitation or leak it to the press.

'Would you consider hiring out the house and the grounds for a weekend?' Ella asked him.

'For the right price. Obviously, it'll be an enormous upheaval, so I'd have to be adequately compensated.'

You mean you need the cash, Ella thought, mentally rolling her eyes.

If he'd had funds, he would've finished the renovation. How stupid did he think they were? But, okay, she'd play his game. 'Would you object to some minor touch-ups?'

'Like what?' Samuel demanded.

'Painting the veranda, some of the inside walls. Neutral colours, of course. If I can, I'll try to match the original colour as closely as possible.' *The way it was before your insensitive, cloddish renovations.* Ella managed a small smile. 'Will you think about it and, if you agree, let me know?'

He shrugged, looking sulky. 'As I said, it will be a massive inconvenience,' Samuel whined. Ella knew that as soon as they left, he'd research rental charges for weddings and would at least quadruple the the going rate.

Micah placed a hand on her back and steered her towards the front door. On the front steps, he shook Dobson's hand, told him to call as soon as possible, walked her to his Bentayga and opened the passenger door for her.

They were halfway down the driveway when Micah turned to her. 'Are you okay? You seemed a bit off in there.'

She debated whether to tell him, then decided that she would. She trusted Micah not to dismiss her feelings. 'Your friend gives me the creeps. He spent more time talking to my breasts than my face.'

God, she was so sick of shutting down, retreating when she felt uncomfortable. She was tired of pulling into herself, mentally rolling into a tight ball and hiding in the corner when she felt even a little hot male interest. Yet Micah, whose eyes frequently blazed with desire, never once made her feel that way.

Micah hit the brake and the car came to an immediate stop. 'Did he say something to you when I stepped out to take that call? Did he try to grope you?'

Micah looked furious and she rushed to reassure him. 'No, nothing like that,' she answered him, lifting one shoulder. 'He was just creepy, that's all.'

Micah lifted her chin so that she had to look into his eyes. 'If you feel that way about anybody, ever, walk away. You don't have to experience that again, El.'

She appreciated the sentiment, but it wasn't a practical solution. As an event planner, she met all sorts of men all the time. Many—most—were decent, but there would always be one or two who'd try their luck, ask her out or try to cop a feel and laugh it off, claiming it was just a joke. She couldn't keep running away; she had to learn to live in the world as it was and not how she wanted it to be.

'Don't see him alone, okay?' After dropping an open-mouthed kiss on her lips, Micah pulled away. At the stop sign at the end of the road, he looked at her. 'I need to tell you something.'

The serious note in his voice caused every muscle in

her body to contract. It was late Sunday afternoon, and the end of the weekend, and he was calling it quits. She felt as if she was standing on the edge of a chasm, about to fall.

'I received an email from my PI regarding his investigation into Neville Pillay.'

If he was about to break up with her, why was Micah mentioning him? And what did his PI have to do with it?

'I don't understand.' Ella managed to push her words up her throat and over her tongue.

'He's tracked down a significant number of women Pillay has harassed over the years, most of whom are prepared to make an official statement accusing him of sexual harassment and, in one case, attempted rape.'

Ella gripped the bridge of her nose. Okay, so he wasn't breaking up with her. Good news. Right, now she could concentrate on what he was telling her about Pillay.

'I'm sad to hear about all of those women but happy your PI has made so much progress.' She sent Micah a quick look. 'So what's next?'

Micah's smile was cold and hard. 'I'm going to leak the story to a journalist I trust. It'll be headline news in a few days. After doing her research, Kendall, the journalist, will, officially, call me for a comment. Jago and I will then release a statement saying that, on investigation, one of our employees was sexually accosted by Pillay and that we are terminating our association with him and his entertainment company.'

Ella was thankful that he would be exposed but she still had a question. 'Why couldn't you release a statement like that when I first told you about what he did?'

Micah didn't hesitate to answer her question. 'Because—sadly and wrongly—one woman's accusations, even with our support, don't have the same impact of a dozen or more accusations. He could've said that you led him on and that we were overreacting by firing him. This way, he has many,

many questions to answer and there's a damn good chance he'll lose his career—definitely his reputation,' Micah explained. 'Naturally, we'll keep your name out of the papers.'

Ella nodded, glad that Pillay would never be in a position of power again. Strong men, as Micah had taught her, didn't need to wield their power like a burning sword. It was over and she could move on.

But to what? And where? Was emigrating still a reasonable option? How on earth was she going to live anywhere in the world without being able to see him, touch him, talk to him and love him? Because, judging by her reaction when she'd thought Micah was breaking up with her, she couldn't.

I'm prepared to let you hire my house for your client's wedding, I've emailed you a quote. We'll need to have a very boring discussion about the finer details—parking and bridal suites and space for the caterers and bar staff—and I'm sure Micah's time is too valuable to waste on things we can decide between us. I can see you at six this evening.

Ella, working from Hadleigh House, scowled down at the screen of her phone and tasted the sour panic at the back of her throat. Cathcart House was beautiful, historic and, after Anna de Palmer-Whyte and her team got hold of it, would be the perfect backdrop for Thadie's romantic wedding.

It was a flawless solution and she was the person who'd found it. The only problem—a huge one, in her view—was that Samuel Dobson wanted her to meet him alone at the huge, isolated house set in two acres of private grounds.

The price to rent the house as a wedding venue was steep but it was clear that Dobson wanted something a great deal more personal. Her.

Ella picked up her phone and sent a return message.

I am unavailable tonight. Could we meet in the morning?

Tonight suits me better. Or we could forget the idea.

Dammit, dammit, dammit, Ella thought as she typed a reply, telling him that she'd get back to him soon.

She didn't like Dobson. She really didn't want to meet him alone but she didn't know whether she was overreacting or not. She didn't know what to do.

She desperately wanted to talk to Micah about this, to get his down to earth, pragmatic point of view. He had a way of cutting through her emotion to reveal the heart of the problem, what was truth and what was perception. She knew she could show him her biggest fear, knowing he wouldn't mock or dismiss her.

She trusted him.

Ella placed her chin in her hand. She trusted him and she loved him. She loved that under the charming facade was a dented and damaged man, someone who had his own scars and issues; that he was imperfect but he kept showing up, trying to win at life. He was honourable and honest and, once he pulled you under his protection, you stayed there. He could've forgotten about Brianna, accepted that bad things happened and carried on with his life. But instead of doing that he'd carried her with him and had tried to make the lives of the people he loved better, easier. Micah took complete responsibility for his actions, determined not to repeat past mistakes.

Taking on the responsibility of finding Thadie a wedding venue was a perfect illustration of his sense of responsibility. He didn't need to—he could've handed the problem back to Thadie, Clyde and their wedding planner—but, because in his mind it was his job to smooth their paths, he'd taken on the work. Did the rest of his family take advantage of that? Maybe. But she also accepted that, once Micah decided to do something, wild horses couldn't stop him.

He was a strong, stubborn, sexy man, someone she'd told herself she could not fall for, but she had. She was so in love with him, and these were sensations she'd never experienced before. Her feelings weren't tempered by frustration and neither was she wearing rose-coloured glasses. She knew Micah, she loved him…

But Ella couldn't shake the feeling that the scales of whatever they had were uneven, definitely tipped in Micah's favour. And, no, she wasn't talking about wealth or business influence—she couldn't compete with him there. No, this was far more subtle than that.

Micah was completely self-confident, at ease with himself and his place in the world. He didn't second-guess himself or struggle with decision making and wasn't scared of people or situations. He knew exactly what he could offer the world…

Whereas she was still trying to figure out how to navigate her life.

She wanted to be his equal, to be strong, to claim her power and her confidence. And to do that she *had* to move past what had happened in the past.

Her mum had died because her dad hadn't believed her, but then why should he have automatically believed the word of a teenager? He was the one with the life experience and it had been a reasonable assumption that her mother would be fine after she slept off her midday drinking. He couldn't have been expected to believe in a teenager's gut instinct, a young woman with absolutely no medical experience. It was time to let her anger, hurt, and resentment go.

And she had to stop worrying so much about whether she was believed or not. Micah believed in her and, more importantly, she believed in herself. She could not carry on letting what had happened affect her self-worth. Micah had said to her, quite a few times now, that she was incredibly strong to have handled what she'd experienced on her own—both as a teenager and recently—and maybe it was time she believed that. It was definitely time to take back her power. She knew the truth, Micah knew the truth and that was all that mattered.

But...making a mental shift was one thing. How was she going to translate that into her daily life? If she stayed in South Africa, opened up her own business—and that scenario was looking more and more likely—and continued to see Micah, she couldn't expect him to be there every time she needed to meet a man for business. This meeting with Dobson was a good example of her dilemma. How would she be effective at her job if she didn't overcome her fear? How could she organise events if she couldn't meet with chefs, lighting guys, stage builders and two dozen other types of supplier without wanting to hide in a corner?

Pillay had taken that away from her. He'd made her scared to do her job but she was damned if she'd let him do that to her any more.

Micah had helped her come into her power and, for the first time in a long time, she felt confident in her ability to stand up for herself. Meeting Dobson alone would be the first test, the first steps on this new journey.

She knew she could handle herself, and him if necessary. The stakes were too great for her to fail.

But, because she wasn't one hundred per cent comfortable with Dobson, she'd ask Janie to come with her. She didn't need a bodyguard, but she wasn't foolish enough to go with no back-up at all.

She could do this; she *would* do this. Securing Dobson's agreement to stage Thadie's wedding at Cathcart House would be her present to Micah.

And, possibly more importantly, it would be a massive gift to herself.

Ella picked up her phone and made a call. 'Janie, what are you doing tonight around six? I need your help.'

CHAPTER ELEVEN

MICAH RUSHED INTO his office, uncharacteristically late. He dumped his leather briefcase on his desk, pulled out a couple of folders and grimaced. He had just a few hours to prep for an important meeting with a Swedish businesswoman who wanted to offload her small chain of English malls. Le Roux International owned a few properties in the UK, but this was a mega-money deal, and Erna Morganssen was reputed to be as quick as a whip and not above trying to take more than her piece of flesh.

But he'd caught Ella admiring his body in the mirror in the bathroom and that had led to some very creative fun on the bathroom floor. Thanks to indulging, he was now more than an hour behind schedule.

Worth it, though.

Micah heard the brief rap on his door and looked up to see his twin standing in his doorway, his face thunder-cloud dark. Oh, God, what now?

'I know you have bad news, Jay, I can see it on your face. But if no one has died, can it wait? I have an online meeting with Erna—'

'Have you seen the papers this morning?' Jago demanded, stepping into the office and shutting his office door behind him.

Micah sent him an irritated look. 'No. As I said, can this wait—?'

'Look online, twin,' Jago told him, nodding to his massive screen.

Right, Jago wasn't backing down. Micah sighed, sat down in his leather chair and booted up his computer. Jago loomed over his desk. Micah wished he could have one day without drama.

He pulled up his Internet browser and raised one eyebrow at his brother, silently asking where to go.

Jago walked to stand beside him, pulled Micah's wireless keyboard to him and rapidly typed. Micah caught the search results—something to do with Thadie—before Jago clicked on one of the more reputable entertainment sites, where the headline flashed…

Trouble in Paradise?

Yesterday we learned that Thadie Le Roux, South Africa's favourite heiress, asked her future in-law to step down as one of her bridesmaids. It's often been noted that Thadie and her fiancé's stepsister aren't close, but it seems like their relationship is a lot more fraught than any of us suspected.

We've also noticed that it's been a while since we've seen Thadie and Clyde out socialising together, as they used to do. Thadie attended two charity events solo recently, and did not accompany Clyde to the prestigious Protea & Passion Sports Awards, a glittering event to honour our country's best sportsmen and women.

Have they drifted apart?

Micah leaned back in his chair and rubbed his thumb and fingers along his forehead before looking at his twin. He gestured to the screen. 'Do they know about the wedding venue snafu?'

Jago leaned against his desk, his eyes steel-hard. 'No. And I don't understand why not. I mean, I would've thought that news would've made it to the press before Thadie firing Alta as a bridesmaid. Far more people knew about the wedding venue being cancelled than Thadie's unhappiness with Alta.' He pushed his hand through his hair. 'As a result of this, there's been a spike in people trolling Thadie on social media.'

Micah cursed. He loved his sister, but he couldn't deny that he'd be happy when this wedding was behind them. But then that would mean Ella would be gone, living ten thousand miles away. The thought was incomprehensible.

'I'll call Thadie when I have a moment,' Micah told Jago, frowning when he heard the discreet buzz of his intercom system: his PA needed to talk to him. On arriving at his office, he'd told her he didn't want to be disturbed. Jago was the one person exempt from that directive.

'Am I ever going to get to work today?' he grumbled, before issuing a voice instruction to turn the intercom system on.

'There's a Mrs Pearson to see you, sir. She doesn't have an appointment.'

Micah closed his eyes, irritated. He'd specifically told her that he wasn't to be disturbed, that he needed a solid block of four hours to concentrate. She could only interrupt him if the building was on fire or if there was an arterial blood spray…

Hold on—had she said Mrs Pearson? As in, Brianna's mother? Micah looked at Jago and frowned. 'Sorry, *who*?'

'Mrs Pearson. She says she knew you as a boy.'

Micah looked at Jago and, when he saw the astonishment on his twin's face, he knew he wasn't hallucinating. *Okay, well...* Micah ran his suddenly damp hands down his thighs and rubbed his face, the side of his jaw. What did she want? Why was she here? Was Brianna dead? No, if that had happened she wouldn't have come to his offices or he would've heard the news via Liyana.

The only way to know what she wanted was to let her in but Micah didn't want to. He'd only seen Kate Pearson twice since the accident, and both of those meetings had happened shortly before Bri had been moved from the local hospital into a long-term care facility. Kate and Phil had refused to see him after that, wouldn't take his calls or respond to his emails. They had severed their relationship with his father and stepmother as well.

'Micah?'

'Yes, I'm coming,' he replied.

'Do you want me to stay?' Jago asked him, looking concerned.

Micah sent his brother a grateful look. 'No, I'll be fine.'

Jago left the room and closed the door behind him. Micah cleared his throat, took a sip from the water bottle on his desk and hauled in a deep breath. Heart thumping, he walked to the door, wishing he didn't feel as if he was eighteen again, wretched, remorseful and so damn guilty.

He wrenched his door open and there she stood, an aged version of Brianna, the young girl he'd once laughed with and loved in his way, as much as a wild, rebellious teenage boy could.

Micah didn't bother trying to shake her hand or even offer a smile. He knew that neither would be welcome. He simply inclined his head and waited until she had stepped into the office before hauling in more air—why was it suddenly so thin?—and following her inside.

He closed the door and gestured her to the couch where the seating was more comfortable. Kate sat down and linked her hands together. 'I suppose you want to know why I'm here…'

Well, yes. Obviously.

'I heard that Bri has a respiratory infection, that she's very ill. How is she?'

Kate released a long breath. 'She's struggling. She hasn't responded to the antibiotics.'

'I'm sorry to hear that, Kate.' He was so sorry about so much, had been for so long.

Kate's eyes—so blue, just like Brianna's—collided with his. 'Should I remove her feeding tube?'

What? Where had that come from?

Kate placed her elbows on her knees and clasped her head in her hands. 'I'm so tired, Micah. So tired of seeing her like that.'

Of course she was, that was understandable. What mother wanted to watch her child—a daughter who should've had a career, been a wife, a mum—lie in a bed, unresponsive? He couldn't, genuinely, think of anything worse.

But…

'I'm not sure what you want from me, Kate,' Micah said, trying to be as gentle as possible. Yes, this woman had caused him grief, but his was nothing to what she'd been through.

Kate sprang to her feet, walked over to his massive window and placed her hands on the glass. 'I need you to help me make a decision, Micah.'

Man, the blows didn't stop coming. Micah followed her over to the window and stood next to her, watching the matchbook-sized cars far below him. He knew what she meant, but selfishly he didn't want to be a part of this conversation. It was too hard, too monumental…

They were talking about someone's life, Bri's life, for God's sake!

'Phil refused to even consider the idea of letting her go and I've resisted thinking about it. But seeing her struggling to breathe is too much. And if she recovers, it'll just be another few months, maybe a year or two, before it happens again.'

'But why ask me, Kate? You hate me.'

Kate turned sad, empty eyes on him. 'I did, for a long time. But Bri adored you. From the time you met as toddlers, she only had eyes for you. She once told me that you knew her better than anyone, and vice versa.'

That had been true, up until Ella had arrived in his life. But, unlike Brianna, Ella didn't see him through rose-tinted glasses, she saw his flaws and contradictions, but seemed to like him anyway.

He didn't *like* her…he was crazily, stunningly, top-to-toe in love with her. He couldn't imagine his life without her in it and didn't know how he was going to cope if she left the country. He had four days until she officially left his employ. He hoped to have things sorted by then—her sharing his bed, permanently in his life.

But that was for later. He needed to concentrate on Kate right now.

'What would she want me to do, Micah?' Kate whispered.

Oh, God, he knew the answer to that, could hear Bri's lilting voice in his ear. *Tell her to let me go, Micah.'*

'I don't want her to die, Kate,' he said, his voice croaky with emotion. 'But I hate the idea of her being kept alive, her condition never changing.'

'But what if she's in there somewhere?' Kate laid a hand on her heart. 'What if she comes back? People have, you know.'

Yes, he did, but Bri wouldn't.

He'd had a very detailed, scientific talk with one of the world's best neurologists and he'd been told that, the longer she remained unresponsive, the less likely she'd ever recover.

Tell her to let me go, Micah. Set us all free.

He'd need the courage to say what he knew he ought to, what he knew Brianna would want, more courage than he'd ever needed before. Because, at the end of the day, there was a bit of a 'playing God' element to this. But hadn't they been playing God by keeping her alive with the feeding tube? He clenched his fist, not knowing what to say, how to frame his words.

Knowing that if he thought about this any more, if he allowed himself any more time, he'd lose his courage, so he gently placed his hands on Kate's shoulders. 'I'm not telling you what to do, Kate. I can't. But I know that Brianna would not like to live like this; in fact, she'd hate it. But the decision will always be yours. You've got to do what you can live with and, no matter what your decision is, I will always support you.'

Kate rested her forehead on his chest, breathing heavily. 'I've hated you for so long, Micah.'

'I know,' he whispered. He'd hated himself as well, but he was done with that now. He wasn't solely to blame for the tragedy that had beset Bri. She'd chosen to follow him, to get behind the wheel of her car.

It was Ella who'd made him believe in himself and in his life. Somehow, that gorgeous, straight-talking, completely wonderful woman had cracked the door on his dark inner world and let in some light. Then more. Solidly black things were now grey, rising to opaque. Yes, he'd made mistakes—he shouldn't have stormed out and gone down to that bar in the first place—but Bri had made mistakes too. She'd also acted impulsively, stupidly.

So had Kate, Phil, Theo and Liyana. And, like him, they all had to live with the consequences of their actions.

Kate pulled back from him and pulled her fingertips under her eyes, collecting the few tears that had gathered there. She touched her neck, her eyes wary. 'I'm tired of fighting, hating, feeling sad and resentful.'

He understood that more than she knew. 'So am I, Kate.'

She swallowed and nodded. 'I'm not sure what I'm going to do. I'm not making any promises but…do you want me to let you know if I decide to…?'

He understood her reluctance to spell it out. It was too big for words. 'Yes, please.'

Kate nodded once, abruptly, and swiftly walked over to the couch, where she picked up her bag and pulled it over her shoulder. She gestured to the door. 'I'm going to go now.'

Staying where he was, Micah nodded. She had his entire sympathy—he couldn't imagine having to make such a hard decision on his own, and his heart bled for her. He felt exhausted and emotional but also relieved; progress had been made today.

He jammed his hands into the pockets of his suit. 'Kate?'

She turned to look at him. 'If you ever need to talk again, to talk to someone who loved her and knew her, you can always talk to me. I was young and stupid, but I loved her.'

Her smile was small but there. 'Thank you, Micah.'

She walked out of his office and closed the door behind her. Micah, feeling battered, slid down the glass wall to sit on the carpet, his back to the window. He dropped his head and closed his eyes, fighting tears. Losing Brianna had hurt—it still hurt—but he didn't love her a fraction as much as he loved Ella.

How would he cope if he lost her? He wouldn't. He'd crawl into himself, shrivel up and die. Not to be dramatic, but he didn't want to live in a world that didn't have Ella in it.

What if something happened to her? What if he lost her, what if she left him? What if he was reading their relationship wrong and she still intended to get onto that London-bound plane next week?

What the hell had he been thinking, allowing her to get so close, to slide into his heart?

And why did he think that things were different with her, that he could have a normal life, that he even deserved to be happy? Kate was thinking about letting her child die and he'd been consumed by thoughts of Ella—occasionally even allowing himself to think about having her as his wife, living with her at Hadleigh House, being a husband and a father.

What the hell was wrong with him?

Micah didn't make his meeting with the Swedish businesswoman. Or any other meeting that day.

It was much later that evening when Ella stepped out of the lift on the top floor of Le Roux International and looked around the empty reception area, wondering where the twins' second-shift PA was—they worked insane hours and needed after-hours help. She looked at the opaque glass walls of Micah's office, frustrated that she couldn't see inside. She didn't want to barge in on Micah if he was in a meeting, but she'd just come from seeing Dobson and she wanted to share her news.

Pulling her phone out of her bag, she banged out a quick message to Micah, asking what he was doing. His reply was brief.

At my desk, working.

Great, it sounded as if he was alone. Walking across the spacious area, she knocked on his office door and pushed her way in. Micah sat behind his desk, his head in his hands and his shoulders hunched. He jerked up abruptly but his face was sheet-white and his eyes red with fatigue…

It had to be fatigue because he couldn't possibly have

been crying, could he? 'What are you doing here?' he demanded. His happy-to-see-you smile was absent.

She dropped her bag onto the seat of the closest chair. 'I need to run something by you. Are you okay?'

Every hint of emotion drained from his eyes and face as he sat back and, very deliberately, placed his ankle on his knee. He looked past her to his door. 'Since when do you barge into my private office without my permission?'

Ella glanced back at the door, winced and shrugged. 'Your PA wasn't at her desk.' She pushed away her embarrassment at being scolded like a junior employee. She had more important things to discuss right now.

'Sorry, I know you have a lot on your plate, but I need to talk to you.'

'Could it not wait until I had time to talk to *you*?'

Wow, he was in a snit. She'd never seen him so cold, so irritated. Well, he'd soon get over it when she told him her news.

She'd start with the good news first. 'I think it's a go for Cathcart House.'

His expression didn't change. 'What are you talking about, Ella?'

'I went to see Samuel Dobson, and he and I hammered out an agreement in principle. I've arranged for Thadie and Anna to meet me there tomorrow morning and, if you can make it, I'd love you to be there too.'

Micah stood up slowly and placed his hands on his desk, his expression thunderous. 'You went to see him? On your own?'

Ella's temper started to heat. 'I was doing my job, Micah. The job you hired me to do.'

'I ordered you not to go there!' Micah shouted.

He'd ordered her? *What?* When they'd discussed Samuel, he'd been talking as her lover, not her boss.

'I cannot believe that you would be so stupid, after everything you've been through, to meet him on your own. What if he did something to you, what if he tried something?' Micah yelled, every syllable rising in volume. He caught something on her face and his expression—summer-thunderstorm-intense—darkened. 'What did he do? He did something, didn't he?'

'He asked me out,' Ella reluctantly admitted. 'I said no.'

'What else?'

Samuel had been pretty persistent, telling her that she needn't be loyal to Micah, because he'd never been loyal to a woman in his life. Micah didn't make commitments, he said, and didn't believe in monogamy. After steering the conversation back to business three times after the fourth time Dobson had raised the subject, she lost it and told him to shut the hell up. She'd then gone on to give him a loud and exhaustive lecture on consent and persistence. She'd also made it clear that she wasn't a toy to be fought over.

Janie, who had waited in the car and listened in via the call Ella had started before going inside, had told her that it was a masterful put-down. And, kudos to her, Janie continued, that she'd still managed to seal the deal to hire Cathcart House. Ella was convinced it was mainly down to the fact that Dobson was hurting for money and not because he was contrite.

She didn't want to fight with Micah so she pulled the conversation back to business. 'So, do you think you can meet us tomorrow?'

'I'm not done talking about the fact that you went there alone!' Micah snapped. Right, he was determined to pick a fight with her. Why?

'Well, I am!'

'After what you went through, why would you take that chance?' He walked around the desk and cupped her face in his hands, looking at her intently. His face softened and his thumbs skated over her cheekbones. 'Are you okay?

You know, mentally? Did it bring up any bad memories? Do you want to talk about it?'

'Micah, I'm *fine*.'

They turned at a sharp rap on the door and Ella spun round to see Jago standing in the doorway. He sent Ella a distracted smile and focused on his twin. 'Sorry, I only just managed to wrap up my meetings now. Micah, are you okay? What did Kate Pearson want? Is Brianna…?'

Micah shook his head. 'No, she's alive.' Micah kept his eyes on Jago, waves of emotion rolling through his eyes. 'I was coming to see you, to talk it out with you, but then Ella arrived unexpectedly. I'll be with you in five, ten minutes.'

So, she wasn't welcome to stay. And it was obvious he had no intention of telling her about his out-of-the-blue conversation with Brianna's mother. It was also obvious that Kate's visit had blown up Micah's day, but he wanted to talk to his twin, not to her.

When his world fell apart, she wasn't the person to whom he could turn.

Jago left and Ella gripped the back of the nearest chair, using it to help support her wobbly legs and keep her body upright. Micah wanted her physically, and might even enjoy her company, but she wasn't good enough or important enough to help him deal with the big things, the important things.

Micah looked back at her. 'Sorry about that. Are you sure you're okay? What can I do for you, El? What do you need? And, sorry, I still don't understand why you went over there without me!'

Why was he trying to fix something that wasn't broken? Ella stepped away from the chair, frowning. What was going on here? Ella touched her top lip with the tip of her tongue. Was he angry at her for going to Dobson alone, or mad because she hadn't allowed him the chance to play the Great Protector? Because that was what Micah did, he protected and fixed, rearranged his world to patch people and situations back together. Making things right was what he did, who he was…

He couldn't fix Brianna but he could fix her. Was she just another one of his projects?

She thought that she just might be. And when he deemed her to be fixed, having knocked out her dings and dents, he'd send her back out into the world.

But that wasn't what she wanted. She wanted him to love her with her dings and dents, scratches and knocks. She wanted to be able to be exactly who she was at every minute of the day. She might feel confident, then scared, unsure and then powerful, and she wanted him to ride those waves with her, let her fly down them when she was feeling assured and to catch her when the wave swept her off her feet.

But Micah only wanted smooth waters or to control the tides.

And it was obvious to Ella that when the storms built up in his life he wasn't going to turn to her for help, comfort or advice.

Ella felt tears burning the back of her eyes. 'I can't be who you need me to be, Micah.'

'What the hell do you mean by that?'

'Because of what happened to Brianna, you need to be the one in control of the situation, looking around to see who you can help, who you can fix. Because you can't fix her.' Ella bit down hard on her bottom lip, tasting blood.

'I am not talking about Brianna. I am talking about the fact that you went to see Dobson on your own,' Micah said, biting out the words.

'I'm not a child, Micah! And, for your information, Janie sat in the car while I met with him and my phone was connected to hers the whole time. I made a mistake with Pillay, but I am not stupid!'

'I never said that you were!'

'No, but you think I'm weak, and that's part of your attraction to me.' She saw something flash in his eyes, an acknowledgement that her words had hit the target. Oh, God, it hurt. It hurt knowing that his attraction was wrapped up in him perceiving her to be weaker than him, with his need to protect and fix. Ella knew that she had a choice to make, and she had to do it right now.

She could either let Micah guard her mentally and physically, allow him the opportunity to feed his need to keep protecting her. She'd have to keep swallowing down her frustration, but she'd be with him. But in time he'd get bored of doing that and, in a week, month or year, he'd break up with her.

Her other option was for her to claim her power, insist that he treat her as an emotional and mental equal, that he see her as a strong and competent woman. If she did that, she knew he'd break up with her straight away. She could either be a half-version of herself with Micah or a full version of herself without him.

It was a hell of a choice.

But, in the end, she needed to live in truth, her truth. She needed to look after herself first because nobody else would. Ella straightened and pushed her hands into her hair.

'I can't remain broken so that you can feel better, Micah. I can't make myself less because you need a problem to fix, someone to protect. I can only be me, and I want to be fully me—strong, confident, powerful. I want to be in a healthy relationship, a place where I can be strong for you, where you can be the same for me. I want to feel free to make mistakes, to do my own thing, for you to be proud of me when I succeed, to be my soft place to fall when I mess up. I want to do the same thing for you but, judging by the fact that you will talk to your brother but not to me, I know that's never going to happen. I don't want you to try and fix me, Micah, because I am *not* broken!'

Ella bent down, picked up her bag and slung it over her shoulder. She needed to leave, to walk out of his building and his life before she fell apart. 'I really think Cathcart House is perfect for Thadie; I suggest you give it serious attention. And just pay me the quarter-million pounds, the original amount we decided on. I don't want any more.'

Micah looked both shocked and confused. 'Ella, what the hell? Where are you going?'

She looked around. 'Right now, I am going home to my empty flat. And then I'm booking a flight to London. Then I'm going to start a new life…*again*. I thought I wanted to start one with you, but you want me to be someone I'm not prepared to be any more, Micah.'

She reached the door, placed her hand on the frame and turned round to look at him. Six-foot-three of pure frustration, anger and confusion. 'Oh, and I'm also going to contact that reporter, Kendall, and tell her that I was accosted by Neville Pillay. I refuse to hide any more, and I want to control the narrative of *my* story. And, maybe if I come forward, it'll give other women the courage to step out of the darkness and tell their stories.'

She loved him and she was walking away from him. But she had to; this was the right thing to do. For her. 'Bye, Micah.'

Refusing to cry, Ella pushed her shoulders back and left. In the empty lift, she rested her forehead against the mirrored panel and closed her eyes, feeling her heart starting to rip and then crumble.

CHAPTER TWELVE

MICAH STILL COULDN'T get Ella's stricken face out of his mind.

Leaning back in his chair, he threw down his expensive ballpoint pen—a gift from Thadie two Christmases ago—and scowled at the contract he'd been making notes on. Or not making notes on, since he was still on page two, which comprised nothing more than definitions.

There was no point in trying to work. His brain—and his heart—simply wouldn't cooperate. All they wanted to do was replay yesterday's catastrophic events.

Micah freely admitted that Kate's visit earlier in the day had rocked him. He couldn't stop thinking about their discussion, and the knowledge that he'd encouraged her to end Brianna's suffering ate at him. Had he said the right thing? Did he even have any right to an opinion? They were talking about ending someone's *life*! Had he been too glib, too quick to rush to judgement? Should he have given it some more thought?

But he knew, with every part of him, that Brianna would have hated living in a hospital bed.

On arriving at work after a sleepless night—he'd missed having Ella in his house and his bed—he'd told his PA he'd fire her if she put a call through or let anyone into his office, and he'd tried to focus on work. But he'd made little progress as his thoughts kept bouncing between his conversations with Kate and Ella.

He remembered Ella's initial reaction to hearing about Bri. Her take on the situation had been considered and wise and had left him feeling that he could have a full life, allow himself to be happy, fall in love…

Fall in love? He'd done that already. Somewhere, some time in the past two and a half weeks, he'd fallen in love with Ella and wanted her in his life on a permanent basis. He wanted her living with him in Hadleigh House, waking up with him, being beside him when he reached for her in the night. He wanted to have children with her, cousins for Thadie's twins.

Because he'd really opened up to her, more than he ever had to anyone—even Jago—she was now his closest confidante. She knew his quirks and his flaws, his secrets and his ambitions, who he was at the core of his soul. But he'd spectacularly sabotaged his life yesterday.

Ella had accused him of wanting to fix the world because he couldn't fix Bri—true enough—but he only wanted to fix *his* section of it. He'd spent twenty years trying to make up for what had happened to Bri and, because he couldn't fix her, he did everything he could to help out his siblings, working hard so as not to disappoint them. Or Jabu.

But Jago and Thadie were smart, healthy and wealthy individuals and they didn't need his input or his help. They were fully able to make their own decisions and live with the consequences.

As Ella had said, he was the family fixer, but he was done with that.

But what she'd got very wrong was this idea that he thought she was broken.

God, how could she think that? Ella was the most together, the strongest, woman he'd ever met. She'd stated that she wanted to be powerful and confident but she didn't realise that she already was. She'd been emotionally knocked around—more than once—but she'd got up, dusted herself down and kept fighting. When her life had flipped upside down, she'd wrestled with the world until she'd been able to make a plan, start again. She'd never stopped fighting and she'd done it alone.

That was what amazed him the most: Ella had gone through so much and she'd done it without parents, siblings or a support structure. He was in awe of her strength and capability. The last thing she was broken.

And, yes, he was over-protective of her—admittedly, he'd overreacted about her going to Cathcart House alone. But it was because he wanted her to know that she had someone on her side, someone who was prepared to go to war for her. He'd been trying to show her that she didn't have to be alone, that he'd always protect and cherish her, that he wanted to be the one she turned to when her life felt off-kilter.

Micah saw Jago walk past his open office door and frowned, recalling that Ella had said something about Jago last night. Amid everything else she'd lobbed at his head, he'd forgotten that detail. What had she said?

Something about Brianna…that when his life fell apart, he turned to Jago and not to her.

He did, that was true. He and Jago had shared a womb, and had been each other's comfort and strength during their volatile childhood. His brother was his best friend and Jago had known Brianna—she'd been a part of both their childhoods—so it was natural for Micah to want to talk to Jago about Kate's visit, about Brianna…

Confiding in Jago was also a habit.

The woman he loved and trusted, whose opinion he respected, had stood in front of him and, instead of talking to her about his awful day, he'd gone into 'fix it' mode to make him feel that he had control of something. Nothing could ever happen to Ella, so his protective instinct had risen and taken over.

And, when he'd seen Jago, he said that he'd explain Kate's visit to him. He'd made it sound as if he'd had no intention of talking to Ella. But he had—he'd wanted to tell her everything.

Still did.

Micah recalled the pain in her eyes and gripped the bridge of his nose. He'd hurt her, something he'd promised himself he'd never do—not her or any other woman. God, he… *He'd messed up.*

His private mobile phone rang and he snatched it up. 'Ella? Where are you?'

'Sorry, it's just me,' Thadie replied. 'You know, your sister? The one who's entertaining the country with her wedding disaster woes?'

Look, he loved Thadie, but on this occasion he needed to put Ella first. 'Sorry, Thads, I know you're going through hell, but I need to find Ella…'

Thadie was silent for a couple of beats. 'I was phoning *you* to find her. We were supposed to meet her at Cathcart House this morning—she sent me a message last night—but she's not here. She did email us a detailed proposal of why she thinks the house will work for the wedding, though—and, Micah, it's fabulous. It's everything I want! Anna is so impressed with Ella, she wants to know if she'll consult on other weddings, but I can't reach her.'

Ella had done as he'd asked—found him a venue and made his sister incredibly happy. God, he loved her.

'Why can't *you* get hold of Ella, Micah?' Thadie demanded. 'What did you do?'

'I messed up,' Micah confessed, a cold hand squeezing his heart.

'Well, Anna and I need her help with this wedding and you, brother, need her in your life. She makes you happy, Micah—and, God, you need some happy!'

He'd already come to that conclusion. 'I do,' he agreed.

'Then why the hell aren't you trying to get her back?'

Good question, Micah thought. Sitting behind his desk doing nothing wouldn't make her stroll back into his life. She was the air he breathed, the reason his sun rose, the beat of his heart...all those clichés that were clichés because they were so damned powerful and true.

She was what he needed. Now, later, tomorrow, sixty years from now.

His world would, if she left him, stop turning. It was that simple and that dramatic.

He was good at fixing things but this would be the biggest repair job of his life. He hoped he was up to it.

Ella sat cross-legged on her couch, her laptop resting on her thighs, listlessly searching for a flight to London. She'd been crying off and on for nearly twenty-four hours and didn't think she'd stop any time soon. She'd run out of tissues and had moved on to toilet paper to mop her eyes and blow her nose, and she was down to her last roll.

But the thought of leaving her flat was too much to contemplate, so when she ran out of loo roll she'd move onto kitchen towel. Anything was better than leaving her flat...

Another thing she couldn't do was to make a booking for her flight. Her credit card sat on the cushion next to her, but she couldn't choose a date or a time...she wasn't able to punch in the numbers, make the commitment.

She didn't want to go. She didn't want to leave Johannesburg...she didn't want to leave Micah. She wanted a life with him, to be his lover and his partner, to navigate life with him. But she needed to be an equal partner, able to give as well as receive. And, while she didn't want to come between him and his twin, she wanted to be the person he turned to first, his best friend and confidante. She also wanted them to be a team, facing the world together, a couple with equal stakes in the relationship.

Micah could pretend that they were not in a relationship, but from the moment they admitted their attraction they'd started the slide down that particular hill. They were not having a fling, an affair, or a three-week stand. He might not be in love with her but she did mean something—possibly quite a lot—to him. But, judging by his silence—she hadn't heard from him since she'd left his office yesterday—she didn't mean enough.

And, if she couldn't have everything, she'd rather walk away. She couldn't force him to be with her. Love that was coerced was just another strategy in the game of power and control. She was done with that nonsense.

Gathering her courage, Ella chose a flight for early the next week and punched in her credit card details. A confirmation number flashed up on her screen and she closed her eyes, tears coursing down her cheeks.

It was done. She was going to the UK where, yet again, she'd have to start over. Alone.

She should be used to it by now.

Ella closed her laptop, looked at the scads of crumpled tissue on her couch and floor and told herself to clean up, to pick herself up. But she didn't have the energy to do anything right now. She just wanted to sit here and mourn what could've been.

Grieve for the life she could envision but couldn't have.

Micah sat on the bench under his favourite oak tree, his head tipped back to look at the moonlight filtering through the leaves of the trees. It was a perfectly still night, hot and warm, and he couldn't hear a frog or a cricket. It was as if the world was holding its breath…

He certainly was.

He glanced at his watch and saw that it was nearly midnight. His shoulders slumped, and he checked his phone again, but it remained stubbornly silent. After running around all day, making offers and signing documents, he'd texted Ella around ten, asking if she could do him one last thing and meet him at Hadleigh House.

She'd oh-so-formally replied that she'd be there in an hour. He had Jabu waiting to meet her and bring her to him, but so far he'd heard nothing from either his butler or the love of his life. She wasn't coming; he'd lost her. His gamble hadn't paid off.

Micah cursed and bent over, holding his head in his hand. What the hell was he supposed to do now?

'It's late, Micah. I can't think why you've asked me to come here at this time of night.'

His head shot up. He looked down the path and there she was, moonlight touching her dark hair. He took in the details, drinking her in. She wore another of her simple sundresses and beaded flip-flops. Her hair was pulled back in a low ponytail but her face was still shadowed.

He needed to see her eyes, to look into her beautiful face. He needed to do that now and...when he was eighty, ninety...hers was the first and last face he'd want to see.

Micah picked up the tablet that lay on the bench next to him, hit a tab and the garden lit up, transforming into a wonderland of light and shadow that was fantastically romantic. Ella looked around and nodded. 'Your house is even prettier at night than it is in the day. But I still don't know why I'm here.'

How to tell her? Micah picked an opening line, considered it and discarded it. Frankly, words were currently impossible, so he patted the bench beside him. She reached him, sat down and crossed one luscious leg over the other, tipping her head back to look up into the branches of the tree. 'Switch off the lights, Micah.'

He killed the lights and immediately heard the sound of a bullfrog croaking, the buzz of a mosquito, the call of a nightjar. Ella's perfume, the aroma light and fresh, hit his nose and his soul settled. She was here, where she was meant to be.

He had to say something so he settled on the easy stuff. 'I transferred the money to your account today.'

'Thank you.' Judging by her still cool tone, he knew that she'd assumed he'd paid her just two hundred and fifty thousand. She'd get a shock when she saw that her account had been credited with an additional five hundred thousand. The amount didn't matter, though; he'd give her *everything* if he could.

'And Thadie and Anna love your ideas for the wedding.'

'So Thadie is going to have her wedding at Cathcart House?' Ella asked him, but her voice still didn't hold much excitement.

'She is. She's been trying to call you.'

Ella shrugged. 'I turned my mobile off. I didn't want to talk to anybody.'

'I think you should talk to her because Thadie wants to know whether she can give your number to Anna; apparently she's looking for a consultant, someone with flair and innovation. Someone who could, possibly, take over her business some day.'

He was gratified by the shock on her face, the hint of delight he saw in her eyes. But it quickly faded and he cursed himself for hurting her so badly that she couldn't take pleasure in a well-deserved opportunity.

'I'm going to the UK, Micah, I booked my ticket.'

He couldn't bear it. 'Don't go.' He choked out the words.

'Why should I stay?'

He hauled in a deep breath. 'Don't go because I messed up, El.'

'I'm going because you can't give me what I need.' Ella leaned forward, her forearms resting on her thighs.

'I don't think you are broken, Ella, and I don't consider you someone who needs to be fixed. I'm in awe of who you are, what you've achieved, how you've handled being battered by life. Life might've put you through the wringer lately, but you are far stronger than you give yourself credit for. Far braver, too.'

'I'm not brave,' Ella scoffed.

How could she believe that? 'Seeing Dobson on your own was brave. Agreeing to talk to that reporter about what Pillay did to you is incredibly courageous, Ella. So many women are going to take inspiration from your story and find their courage to come forward about him and other men. I am in awe of you,' Micah told her, his emotions evident in his voice.

'Yesterday was a very bad day, Ella, but you're right. I should've spoken to you as soon as you walked in the door instead of doing what I normally do—going into fix-and-control-the-world mode. I hurt you by telling Jago that I'd talk to him about what had happened, and made you feel like I wouldn't come to you with the important things… I'm sorry about that.'

She turned her head to look at him, concern in her eyes. 'Can you tell me now?'

He nodded. 'I'd like to.' He placed a hand on her back, needing to touch her. She didn't pull away and that tiny gesture gave him hope. 'Kate came to see me.'

'Brianna's mum?'

He nodded. 'She's thinking about letting Bri go, and she wanted my opinion on what Bri would want.'

Ella laid her hand on her heart. 'Oh, Micah, that must've been such a hard conversation.'

He nodded. 'It rocked me—totally derailed me, in fact—and I spent the rest of the day second-guessing myself because I told her that Brianna would hate her situation. When you walked in, I was feeling sad and miserable and lousy. I redirected my anger at not being able to do anything onto you. Also, I just felt this overwhelming urge to protect you, to not have anything happen to you, and the thought of you being alone in a situation that could've gone wrong overwhelmed me. I'm sorry I overreacted.'

She nodded. 'Going to see Dobson alone wasn't easy for me to do, I admit that. I did take precautions, but I think I'd like to get a taser, learn some self-defence. If I know I can defend myself, that would make me feel less stressed about being on my own with strange men.'

And he would feel better about it too. He'd offer to teach her Krav Maga but he knew that they'd be distracted as soon as they put their hands on each other. 'I know an instructor who could teach you enough to feel confident about your ability to handle yourself. That's if you stay here…with me.'

He gestured to his house, the one he knew and loved, but not as much as he loved her. 'Stay with me, El—here at Hadleigh House. Or, if you didn't see yourself sharing the grounds with Jago and Dodi—'

'Jago and Dodi? Thadie's best friend and the owner of the bridal salon?'

Yeah, that isn't important right now! 'We can talk about my brother and his love life later.' Micah growled, frustrated. 'Can I buy you a house?' he asked suddenly.

She looked confused. 'A house? What house? What are you talking about?'

'The why is easy, because I'm comprehensively in love

with you. For ever. I'm talking about Cathcart House. And, in the interest of full disclosure, I've already bought it.'

Ella looked as if she was battling to keep up. 'You bought it from Dobson?'

He shook his head. 'He's not the owner, he just manages it for them. He doesn't even live on the property any more. The consortium I mentioned the first day we spoke about the house? They own it and are happy to offload it.'

She rubbed the back of her neck, confusion on her face. 'You are ten steps ahead of me, Micah. Why would I want it?'

'You think I don't notice how you react to things but I do. I notice everything about you.' And he always would. 'I saw your face as you walked around that house the first time you saw it; you fell in love with it. I could see your wheels churning, thinking about how you would fix this, do that. I thought you might want to run your business from there, use it to stage events, weddings and parties and ladies' lunches…'

Since she wasn't jumping up and down with joy, he shrugged. 'Or, if you want to, we can convert it back to a home and live there.'

She placed her hands on her cheeks, her eyes wide. 'Micah, God, *stop*! Give me a chance to catch up, my mind is spinning!'

Taking a deep breath, she held up her hand, which he took, kissing her palm. Desire flashed in her eyes and her hand trembled. He loved the way he affected her, but it was a fraction of how much she affected him.

'We'll come back to houses and my career in a minute. Let's go back a couple of steps. Did you mean it? What you said about loving me?'

Why did she look so shocked? Wasn't it written all over his face? 'El, sweetheart, you…you are the switch that flipped light onto my life again. Up until I looked up and saw you standing there, my life was muted. The only way I can describe it is that it was like one of those old-fashioned sepia photographs, the ones that only show shades of brown.'

He gently dragged his thumb along her jaw. 'You injected colour, conversation, life and laughter and great, emotional sex into my world, and I can't live without you. I don't *want* to live without you.'

Yes, it had happened quickly, but it wasn't any less powerful, as he told her. 'You might need some time to catch up but the fact that you are here with me gives me hope that you might, some time soon, feel the same way.'

She moved closer, close enough to slide her lips across his in a heart-resuscitating kiss. 'I don't need time. I love you too, Micah. So much.'

'Does that mean you will stay?'

Ella's fingertips drifted over his jaw. 'I'll stay because you are my person, Micah. Because you make me feel strong and capable and powerful—but, best of all, loved.'

He'd heard the expression about having a heart so full it felt as if it would burst, but Micah had never once thought he'd experience it himself until now, when his heart was so very close to doing exactly that. Micah swallowed, then swallowed again, unable to believe his luck. Or pull his eyes off her lovely face. The face he was going to be looking at for the rest of his life.

Then Ella scrunched up her face, her nose wrinkling. 'I need to call Anna, think about your crazy house offer, move the rest of my stuff into your place and cancel my ticket. Damn, I'm going to lose so much money when I do that.'

Micah laughed, enchanted by her making a list in the middle of the declarations of love. And he loved the fact that, despite offering to buy her a house that cost upwards of twenty million, she still cared about saving money. 'You can sell your bed and your couch. Maybe you'll get enough to cover your loss,' he teased, thinking of her fat-with-cash bank account which she'd obviously forgotten about.

'I mean, it's not like your future husband is rich and can afford to spoil you or anything like that,' he added, his voice cracking with emotion.

She laid her open palm on the side of his face and raised her eyebrows. 'My future husband?' she asked, her mouth dropping open. 'Are you proposing, Micah?'

'I am.' He turned his face to kiss her palm. 'I want to be your husband, lover, house mate, the father of the kids we're going to have…'

She mocked-glared at him. 'Only one at a time, Le Roux! I couldn't cope with twins.'

He pulled her onto his lap and kissed her laughing mouth. 'Yeah, you can. We can do anything and everything, as long as we are in it together, Ella. Are you saying yes, darling?'

'Absolutely.'

Ella kissed him, long and slow. Heat started to build between them and it was enhanced by love, by trust, by the knowledge that he was home, in the place he belonged, with the woman he loved.

His world, finally, made sense.

Ella slipped off his lap and held out her hand to him. He stood up, took it and they walked back to Hadleigh House, where Jabu had champagne waiting. She rested her temple against his upper arm and sighed. 'I can't believe that we've known each other less than three weeks. Technically, I just got engaged to my boss.'

Micah dropped a kiss on her head.

'Technically, I don't give a damn. You are here, we are

together and that's all that matters,' he told her as he opened the door to his home.

Their home.

And the rest of their lives.

* * * * *

MILLS & BOON®

Coming next month

THE KING'S CHRISTMAS HEIR
Lynne Graham

Her cheeks were pink, her striking eyes downcast as she disconcerted him by reaching for the pen and scrawling her signature on the document that Dario had given him.

"You shouldn't sign a legal document without your own lawyer at hand to represent your interests," Gaetano remarked tautly.

"That's your world, not mine," Lara parried in a tone of scorn. "I don't require a lawyer to tell me I want to be free of you. You have disappointed me in every conceivable way, Gaetano –"

"I regret that you feel that way," he breathed curtly.

"No, your only goal is that I sign this form so that you can shed any responsibility you might have for me as discreetly as possible. That doesn't surprise me but I'm angry on my son's behalf!" Lara countered, throwing her head back. "He is an innocent party here and you didn't even look at him at the park!"

"You're trying to say that your son is also… my son?" Gaetano framed in open disbelief.

"He's sixteen months old, Gaetano. Who else could be his father?"

Continue reading
THE KING'S CHRISTMAS HEIR
Lynne Graham

Available next month
www.millsandboon.co.uk